FLOWERS FROM IRAQ

THE STORYTELLER AND THE HEALER

SUNNY ALEXANDER

Flowers from Iraq: The Storyteller and the Healer

Published by The Storyteller and the Healer

ISBN: 978-0-9846899-1-0

Book design by Maureen Cutajar
www.gopublished.com

Thanks to the human heart by which we live,
Thanks to its tenderness, its joys, and fears,
To me the meanest flower that blows can give
Thoughts that do often lie too deep for tears.

William Wordsworth, 1807

CONTENTS

PART ONE

The Memory Jar

CHAPTER 1

Kathleen took a deep breath, filling her lungs with smoggy Los Angeles air. She stood up straight, pulled her shoulders back, smiled, and began the four-mile trek from the Sunlight Motel to the University of California at Los Angeles—known as UCLA by the locals.

Boston and everything that was painful in her life faded behind her. Today was a new beginning in a place where no one knew anything about her. She was Alice from *Alice in Wonderland*, entering a new world where exciting things waited around every corner.

Her backpack held her acceptance letter from UCLA, her checkbook with the first installment from her scholarship safely deposited in the bank, and a map to the homes of movie stars. She had bought the map from a man on Sunset Boulevard and had circled ten homes that were within walking distance. She planned to keep her green eyes open in hopes of seeing a star sauntering along Westwood Boulevard, or patronizing one of the shops in Westwood Village.

She stopped at a hair salon on her way to student registration and got her hair trimmed. The beautician wanted to cut her dark brown hair in a more fashionable style and recommended a perm, but Kathleen insisted, "Just a trim," and declined a mani-pedi. She didn't know how much to tip but thought a dollar was about right. As she bounded along the sidewalk, her heart felt free, but occasionally a familiar looming fear would creep in when she thought about being alone and so far from Boston.

Kathleen continued through The Village, past the Fox Theater with its one-hundred-and-seventy-foot tower, and detoured at Stan's Donuts for breakfast. Munching on her pretzel-shaped chocolate donut and juggling her cup of coffee, she fell into step with other students ambling past the Mediterranean-style buildings of the neighborhood. Small restaurants overflowing with customers cluttered the busy sidewalks with cheap plastic tables and chairs. UCLA Bruin banners in blue and gold hung from the lampposts while windows displaying UCLA clothing beckoned to passersby.

Kathleen halted to gaze at one of the shop windows displaying Bruin sweatshirts and took the twenty-dollar bill out of her pants pocket.

Mrs. Roth had hugged Kathleen goodbye at Boston's Logan International Airport and slipped the money in her hand. "For you," she said. "I want you to spend it on something for yourself."

The twenty-dollar bill dampened in her clammy hand as Kathleen looked longingly at the sweatshirt. *Maybe another time,* she thought.

She walked through the UCLA labyrinth, past the quads, and followed signs directing her to the 1989 freshman class registration. She glanced at her leather banded Timex watch—it was nine o'clock, precisely matching the time on the registration form. She looked for the line matching the initials of her last name and stood under the MA–MU sign with a flock of freshmen as the row moved in spasms, a burst of movement followed by a grinding halt. Grumbles and groans from the waiting students filled the hall.

A young man about her age, standing in front of her, turned to say hello and extended his hand. "Gary Morales, premed."

Kathleen thought he was rather formal but appreciated his wide grin and dark brown eyes that sparkled as if he was holding onto an amusing story. She shook his hand, smiled, and said, "Kathleen Moore, premed also."

The line began to shift again, and they saw the cause of the delay. A student was arguing with the registrar over a class. With her mobile phone planted to her ear, she refused to move. Kathleen couldn't hear her conversation, but a look of triumph crossed the girl's face as she waved her class enrollment slip in the air. She turned to the registrar. "Next time, remember my name and your life will be easier." Kathleen heard her first name, Natasha, but her last name floated away. Kathleen and Gary giggled as they decided to call her Natasha Something.

They picked up their packets and discovered they shared two classes.

"I guess we'll be seeing a lot of each other; well, at least twice a week," Gary said. He glanced at his watch. "I'm starving. Let's walk over to the Village Deli and get some lunch."

With a nod Kathleen followed.

As they dodged fellow students, Kathleen said, "I really like your watch, Gary."

Gary held out his hand. "It was my graduation gift from my dad. It's his 1960s Mickey Mouse watch. I'm the first one in our family to go to college. My dad said if he couldn't go, at least his watch could."

Kathleen laughed, and then said, "Your dad sounds like a great person."

"I'm lucky, I guess. My parents are really good people and excited about having a doctor in the family, but everyone is in everyone's business. What about your family?"

"My parents both died when I was nine. I was raised in foster care."

"I'm really sorry to hear that. Do you have sibs?"

Kathleen hesitated. "There were seven of us...but we lost contact."

"That must have been hard. Maybe someday you'll find each other."

She shrugged. "Maybe... I was lucky to have one foster mother, Mrs. Adams, for nine years. I had a really good friend, Mrs. Roth, too. She was like a grandmother."

Gary's eyes softened. "I'm glad you had someone. I guess I need to be grateful for my buttinsky family."

Chattering about their lives, they continued their stroll to the Village Deli and stood in the serpentine line that went from the front of the restaurant to the end of the block. Gary smiled. "From one line to another. I guess that's what we can expect from now on."

The hot August day was a reminder of the semi-arid climate in Los Angeles. Occasionally, an ocean breeze found its way around the Wilshire Boulevard high-rise buildings, providing a welcome relief from the intense heat.

As the afternoon wore on, the sidewalks bulged with students looking for a last-minute reprieve before serious studying began. Groups of girls and boys flirted playfully as they exchanged names and phone numbers. Couples held hands or kissed, not wanting to lose contact for even a moment. A homeless man sat in front of a newspaper stand holding out an empty paper cup. A man and a woman, dressed in business suits, walked by ignoring his plea, "Can you spare some change?"

Kathleen and Gary sat at an outdoor table surrounded by the chatter of people still waiting to be seated. Kathleen studied the menu, looking for the least expensive items. She ordered a small bowl of soup knowing she would fill her remaining hunger with crackers.

Gary asked for a pastrami sandwich with fries and extra pickles. The waitress returned, deftly served their order, slapped down the check, and quickly moved on. "She must know we're broke college students," Gary joked as he picked up the check and insisted on sharing his meal with Kathleen. "No one person should eat a pound of meat. There is more than enough for both of us."

Gary leaned over to pile fries on her plate. "You have to try the kosher pickles. They're the best in town."

"Thanks for lunch, Gary." She took a tentative bite of the sandwich. "This is delicious. I've never eaten pastrami before."

"Are you enjoying living in Los Angeles?"

She nodded vigorously with her mouth full, swallowed and said, "It's different from Boston, the weather of course, but especially the people. It's less formal and I like the casual dress. I haven't had a chance to see much of Los Angeles, except for Westwood. I went to the *Star Wars* film festival. I've never seen all three flicks in one showing."

"Me neither. I'm a big *Star Wars* fan, too, but I missed the festival. Guess the Force wasn't with me, huh?" He smiled a little self-consciously. "Maybe next time we could go together. Are you living in one of the dorms? Most freshmen do."

"I decided not to live in a dorm. I'm on a scholarship and I was afraid the noise would interrupt my studying." Kathleen reached over for another pickle. She grinned between bites. "These are the best. I'm staying at a motel right now, but I'm looking for a room to rent, something reasonable."

Gary looked surprised. "That is our fourth coincidence. My mother says after two it is fate."

"Fate?"

"Yeah." Gary put down his sandwich. "Okay, here's how it works. A thousand freshmen in line, but we're next to each other. That's one. Two, we're both premed students. Three, we're sharing two classes. Now, the fourth, my parents have a room to rent in our home. My mother will say it was our destiny to meet. Of course, I have to admit she reads tons of romance novels.

"Seriously, our home is a bit of a distance from UCLA, but I've been taking the bus and a student pass is inexpensive. Our schedules are similar and we could ride together, at least some of the time. I'm not sure about the rent, but I'd be happy to put in a good word for you. Whaddaya say?" His friendly face beamed.

Kathleen returned his smile. "I'm free this weekend," she said.

On Sunday, Kathleen rode the Wilshire Boulevard bus to La Brea Avenue and walked two short blocks to a small Spanish-style house situated on a quiet, well-kept street lined with liquidambar trees. Planted in the 1930s, when the houses were new, their roots now reached out to fight the confinement of aging concrete. Small twisted branches and twigs dangled close to the ground giving the appearance of small reptiles ready to spring to life.

Gary opened the door, gave Kathleen a friendly hug, and asked her about the walk from the bus.

"I really enjoyed the walk. And the houses… really pretty with the tile roofs and walled patios! Something you don't see in Boston."

"Mexican influence," said Gary's father, flashing a proud grin.

Gary said, "Kathleen, I'd like you to meet my parents, Mr. and Mrs. Morales."

His mother gave Gary a gentle shove on his shoulder. "Oh Gary, don't be so formal. Kathleen, welcome to our home and please call me Isabel."

His father said, "Call me Jorge. Tell me, Kathleen, what did you think of the trees? They're over fifty years old."

"They're quite," Kathleen struggled for the right word, "fanciful. Their small branches reminded me of baby alligators."

"It's not the branches you have to worry about." Gary laughed. "During winter when the winds are blowing, the spiked fruit fall and so will you. We call them 'ankle biters.'"

Jorge said, "Don't scare the girl, Gary." He clucked his tongue and shook his head. "Always a story, always a story. Don't know who he gets it from. Come, Kathleen, let me show you the room. It's right off the kitchen, convenient for a late night snack." He smiled and rubbed his ample stomach.

The twin bed was neatly made up with a beige corduroy bedspread and pillows in bright primary colors. Across from the bed were a five-drawer dresser, a bookcase, and a desk, complete with a lamp and chair. Kathleen thought it was perfect.

Kathleen looked at Isabel and smiled, "The room is lovely. The colors are so cheerful and it's so immaculate."

Isabel smoothed her long black hair and brushed away the invisible wrinkles from her starched, flowered apron. Her face lit up at the compliment. "Why, thank you, dear."

Jorge, leaning against the doorjamb, snorted good-naturedly. "Rents two hundred a month. If you like it it's yours." He held out his wide, calloused hand. "Deal?"

Kathleen shook his hand. "Deal!"

Later, after Isabel treated them to the traditional Morales household snack of flan and coffee, Gary walked Kathleen to the bus stop and explained the family rules. "My father won't allow you to walk home alone at night. You have to give my parents your schedule and someone will meet you at the bus stop. "And—" he wagged his finger, "no boys in your room, ever." He chuckled. "The rules are the same for all us kids; you're no different."

Gary impulsively took Kathleen's hand, and she hoped he was not going to spoil their burgeoning friendship by asking her out. She wasn't sure why, but she didn't feel quite ready for dating.

"I'm happy you'll be living with us," he said. "I'd like to show you Los Angeles on the weekends. After all, we can't be studying all the time. I like you, and I think we can be good friends. Plus, you laugh at my goofy jokes, so that gives you bonus points."

He laughed at his own goofy joke, but became serious. "We may discover that we have other things in common. I want you to know, if you ever struggle with any feelings you can share them with me. Anything you tell me will be locked away and kept safe."

Kathleen didn't understand what Gary was trying to tell her. It would be months before she realized they had something else in common. That would be number five.

CHAPTER 2

Kathleen spent her time between morning and afternoon classes studying in a secluded corner at UCLA's Powell Library, surrounded by the smell of musty, aging books. Afterward, she would take the steps to the walled-in patio and sit on one of the gray, aggregate benches encircled by graceful Jacaranda trees. She zipped up her light-blue windbreaker and gazed at the leaves as they floated in the January breeze before falling to the ground. She opened her brown lunch bag and found a burrito next to her sandwich. She murmured softly, "Bless you, Mrs. Morales." She could have the burrito for lunch and eat her sandwich for dinner. She would not be hungry today.

Kathleen read her physiology textbook while she munched on the savory meat-filled burrito. It was an easy class, but she took it seriously and checked off each completed assignment in a small black notebook.

She had been living with Gary and his parents for five months. Twice a week, Kathleen and Gary rode the nearly empty, early morning bus to UCLA. They sat at the back of the bus, in the furthest corner that gave them the illusion of privacy. The smell of perfume, cologne, and stale cigarette smoke mingled as people filed in and scrambled for seats. It was obvious from their loud, gaping yawns that many of the riders had just tumbled out of the sack, while others, headphones over their ears moved in rhythm to the music playing on their Walkmans.

Kathleen was used to riding buses, but this was the first time she rode with a friend. As the rickety bus swayed and passengers got on and off, she and Gary would speak quietly, heads almost touching, sharing stories about their lives. Gary's stories always made her laugh; not because they were always especially funny, but he had a winning way of telling them that conjured up wholesome aspects of hearth and home.

"Christmas in our family is a major doing," he told her one morning in October, as the bus jounced along. "In a couple of months you'll find out for yourself. First, all the women will start making tamales. That will go on for at least three days. Then, on Christmas Eve, we all go to Midnight Mass. Are you Catholic?"

"Baptized Catholic, but it's been years since I've gone to church."

"But you'll still come with us to Midnight Mass?"

She nodded.

"Then, everyone sleeps over, but no one really sleeps. It's a real family gathering. There'll be bodies all over the place. Are you okay with sharing your room with some of my cousins? Girls, of course. You'll be packed in like sardines but—"

"It sounds like fun," she interrupted him, and meant it.

Christmas had come and gone, but the memory of this loving, somewhat rambunctious family warmed her on this chilly January day.

Kathleen thought about how safe she felt with Gary on those early morning bus rides. It was a new experience for her to have a friend, to share some part, any part, of herself.

Gary was always curious, always interested in Kathleen's stories. Gradually, over the months, she told him about becoming a foster child when she was almost nine and living with her foster mother, Mrs. Adams.

"My father died in an automobile accident and my mother died a few months later in childbirth. There were seven of us and we were all placed in foster care. I was closest to my brother Devon, but he got moved around a lot. We were all scattered. It's easy to get lost when you're in the system."

She found it hard to speak and whispered, "Gary, I never had new clothes—always just hand-me-downs from the church ladies. My fifth grade teacher, Mrs. Roth, became my friend and she started sewing my clothes. When I graduated high school, she took me shopping at a department store in Boston and bought me everything I needed, including the suitcases. She said I should start my new life at UCLA with new clothing."

Gary held her hand in a gentle, soothing way. "You're the most courageous person I've ever met. I'm so glad we've become friends. Thank you for trusting me with your stories."

What she didn't tell Gary was the truth, that was buried beneath layers of make-believe, distortions, and fantasies.

CHAPTER 3

Kathleen sat in her freshman English class, absentmindedly doodling on a blank sheet of notebook paper.

She sighed as her eyes drifted to the girl with long blonde hair sitting two rows in front of her. She tried to pay attention to the lecture, but her eyes kept roving back to the girl wearing a baggy UCLA sweatshirt, acid-washed Guess jeans, and Doc Martens shoes. Kathleen watched as she leaned closer to the gum-smacking Valley Girl sitting next to her. The Valley Girl took out a mirror from her purse, put on a fresh layer of frosty pink lipstick, and smiled lovingly at her reflection. She tossed her head, apparently satisfied at the way her side ponytail bounced, and returned the mirror to her purse. She whispered something to the girl with long blond hair and they laughed as if they were sharing the best secret in the world.

Kathleen's gaze moved to her standard wardrobe of inexpensive jeans, T-shirts, and sneakers, bought from an outlet store, and felt a sudden rush of jealousy. She thought about the single braid that lay halfway down her back. She sighed. *Like a horse's braided tail*, she thought.

When the lecture was over, Kathleen looked distastefully at her doodling of small hearts and cupid's arrows. She ripped the page out, crumpled it, and stuffed it in her backpack.

Kathleen walked across the campus, trying to avoid looking at the group of girls hanging out at the quad. They dressed in what appeared to be the uniform of the day, leg warmers, flannel shirts, and well-worn hiking boots. They talked and laughed, coffee cups in hand. Two girls, smiling, stood with their arms coiled around each other's waists, trading long looks that spoke of their attraction. Kathleen felt an immediate rush of desire, followed by an equally strong repulsion, and began to recite the periodic table silently to herself. She got halfway through before she passed the quad and her feelings began to dissipate.

She thought, *Is it possible? Could I be like them?* Just as quickly, another thought appeared. *Of course not.* She really enjoyed Gary's company, so how could she be...? She didn't like to think of the word, much less say it. She remembered the conversation she had with Gary several months before. She didn't think she could share her most recent feelings with anyone, not even on the long bus rides in the morning when the monotonous locomotion of the bus created a lulling, trusting feeling.

The struggle continued every day and followed her into the nights. She tried to suppress the nighttime images, but there were new sensations running throughout her body, and she began to touch herself in places she had never touched before. Desire and guilt were now fighting for dominance. She was certain hell was right around the corner, waiting for her.

Kathleen turned on the lamp and picked up one of the textbooks for her English class, *The Elements of Style*. She tried to read, but the words wouldn't stay still and kept dancing across the page. She put the book down and picked up the UCLA student newspaper, *The Daily Bruin.* She flipped through the pages and focused on a small advertisement placed by a therapist, Gayle Sutherland, announcing the opening of her psychotherapy office located near UCLA.

❀ ❀ ❀

Gayle Sutherland, LCSW, Ph.D., glanced around her new office, pleased at the way it was furnished. The light brown leather analytic couch rested against one wall. Two leather chairs faced each other, ready for the patient who might find lying down too awkward. Boxes of tissues were placed strategically around the room. Gayle had provided the neutral atmosphere for the patient to freely express their thoughts and feelings.

Walls, painted in Navaho white, held her certificates and licenses, a testimony to her years of education and experience. *Impressive,* she thought as she chuckled sarcastically and shook her head. A double major in Social Work and Educational Psychology, with more than fifteen years of experience as a social worker.

Her most recent certificate, beautifully rendered in Euphemia UCAS and Lucida Calligraphy fonts, and signed by three well-known psychoanalysts, confirmed her course completion at a prestigious analytic institute in Los Angeles. Years and years of education and training, a near empty appointment book, and a uterus that couldn't bear children—at age forty-one, was that all she had to show for her life?

Gayle sat at her desk wondering if her new profession as a psychoanalyst was only an attempt at escaping from the sadness that plagued her. She and Robert thought they had time: time to develop their careers, time to buy the home of their dreams, and time to start a family. Had she not paid attention to the years that disappeared from her grasp? Had she failed to notice a body that was slowly changing, hair that began to show signs of premature graying, and extra pounds that seemed to magically appear? The years of trying to get pregnant were followed by years of doctor's appointments and tests. The news they had dreaded was a force that drove to the center of their hearts and souls; Gayle could never have a child of her own.

The phone rang, jolting Gayle into the present. Dreading another crank response to her advertisement, she decided to let it roll over to voice mail. Without thinking she answered on the last ring.

"Dr. Sutherland, my name is Kathleen Moore. I'm a premed student and saw your ad in *The Daily Bruin*. I'd like to make an appointment, if you have time. Umm, your announcement said no fee for initial consultation. Is that correct?"

"Yes, I think it's important for us to meet before you begin therapy. I want to make certain that you'll be comfortable working with me. Would tomorrow at noon work for you?"

"Yes, Dr. Sutherland. Thank you, I'll be there at noon."

Gayle put down the phone and began to rock back and forth in her office chair. There was something intriguing about the way Kathleen spoke, as if every word had been carefully planned and rehearsed. Gayle felt a tug at her heartstrings; usually, this was a warning that she was about to get too involved with a patient. She knew her own feelings, her countertransference, would have to be discussed with her supervisors and analyzed by her therapist, Dr. Bernstein. After all, the institute's mantra was, "Don't be afraid of any feelings you have toward the patient. It's all grist for the mill."

Gayle tried to put any troubling thoughts aside and mumbled out loud, "Oh, for God's sake, Gayle. Stop your worrying. What could possibly go wrong?"

❀ ❀ ❀

The call light blinked; Kathleen was early.

Gayle waited until Kathleen's appointment time, noon, walked to the waiting room and, for a moment, was caught off balance. A pale, thin girl, with dark shadows under her eyes, was staring off into space. Gayle had fallen into her own stereotype of a UCLA premed student and had expected someone more robust and outgoing.

Gayle introduced herself and showed Kathleen to her office. Kathleen sat on the edge of the chair. *Perhaps ready to flee*, Gayle thought.

"Thank you for seeing me," said Kathleen. "I've been under some stress lately..."

As Kathleen began to speak, Gayle became distracted by her emaciated appearance. *My God*, she mused, *it looks like this child hasn't eaten in a week*. She had seen the same hollow look with some of the children in foster care. She knew this was a young woman who had grown up in the system. She sensed it. She smelled it.

"What kind of stress, Kathleen?" Gayle prompted her gently.

"Umm, classes during the day, working nights, and commuting." Kathleen looked down, mumbled, and turned red. "Some other things, too."

Gayle sensed the "other things" was the issue and knew if she probed, she wouldn't see Kathleen again. "I'm glad you're thinking about talking to someone. School can be very stressful—I should know, I've been in school most of my life." She smiled at her waifish patient and continued. "I was thinking twice a week might work well for you. I do have some time during the lunch hour. Could you manage that with your schedule?"

Kathleen nodded. "The thing is, I don't know if I can afford to see you. Your announcement said something about a 'sliding scale.' I'm on a scholarship and I work three nights a week cleaning offices. I don't have much extra money."

Gayle thought for a short minute. *Oh, what the hell.* "Would two dollars a session work with your budget?"

Kathleen reached up and wiped a tear from her cheek. "Thank you, Dr. Sutherland."

Gayle picked up her 1990 leather appointment book and wrote in the Monday and Thursday columns, in ink, *Kathleen Moore, Noon.*

Four days a week, Gayle left her office promptly at 3:30 pm and drove to nearby Brentwood for her analytic appointment with Joseph Bernstein, MD, PhD. It was a short distance, less than ten miles away, but she allowed one-half hour for the heavy traffic along the busy Wilshire Blvd. corridor. She reached the area in Brentwood that was fondly known as *analytic circle*. Within a mile radius, there was a cluster of the most influential psychoanalysts in the country. Many of them, now in their eighties, had fled Europe to escape the onslaught of World War II. Dr. Bernstein had left with only the clothes on his back and a single suitcase holding his most precious possessions, copies of Freud's published books.

Gayle lay down unceremoniously on Dr. Bernstein's couch resting her head lightly on a pillow and folding her hands, as she usually did, over her uterus. Sometimes, during her sessions, she would unconsciously begin to rub her belly with her hand, softly, as if trying to sooth the emptiness that never went away.

Gayle started to talk about something unimportant, sat up suddenly, and turned to face Dr. Bernstein. "Joseph, I need your help. I think I'm about to get into trouble. I saw this new patient and I'm feeling this incredible pull on my heartstrings. More than I should."

Dr. Bernstein put down the pad of paper on which he took notes of the session, and listened as Gayle described the time she spent with Kathleen.

The analyst, who spoke infrequently, said in a near-whisper with a touch of a lisp, "Occasionally, we find a patient who needs something more than either therapy or analysis can offer. Who can say what really helps? Is it our theories, or is it the kindness and understanding we can offer? You are telling me this child is hungry. I believe her hunger exists on two levels. One is concrete and deals with actual sustenance. Without adequate food we cannot go to the next level of finding security in our lives." Dr. Bernstein paused to let his words sink in. "The other is food for the soul, the nurturing she may not have received as a young child. I believe you tapped into her depravation and you feel that as a pull on your heartstrings. My advice to you," he paused as he picked up his pad of paper, "is feed her."

Gayle sat bolt upright on the couch and said dubiously, "Do you mean physically feed her?"

Joseph Bernstein, MD, Ph.D., had said all he was going to say. Now, it was up to Gayle to make her own interpretations and decisions.

On the drive home, Gayle thought about what Dr. Bernstein had said—and what he had not said. She had scheduled Kathleen for lunch hour appointments. Was that just a coincidence or was it a Divine Intervention? Robert always fixed her lunches, and if truth were told, they were feasts, which was why she couldn't lose those damn twenty pounds. She wondered what it would be like to share her lunches with Kathleen. After all, how can you either provide or receive therapy on an empty stomach?

Gayle saw the call light go on and reached for the wicker basket so lovingly packed by Robert. Turkey breast sandwiches on rye bread (Kathleen liked mayonnaise on hers), with homemade potato salad and fresh fruit on the side; milk for Kathleen and water for Gayle. They had been sharing lunches and talking for three months. Kathleen said very little. Gayle was beginning to know her not from her words, but from the way the color of her green eyes seemed to change with her feelings, growing darker or lighter according to her mood, or the way a single tear would roll down her cheek. A slight smile meant she was happy, and her hands trembled when she was overtired or anxious.

Kathleen sat in her chair and said, "I can't eat today." Her lips were quivering.

Gayle put down their lunch and sat silently.

Kathleen glanced at the couch. "I'm taking a psych class. Today, we talked about Freud. The instructor showed us a photo of Freud's office." She gestured toward the couch. "I know about the couch."

"Dr. Sutherland, something really bad happened in my anatomy class. I want to tell you." Two tears were weaving their way down her cheeks. "Could I lie on the couch and close my eyes?"

Gayle nodded and watched as Kathleen took off her shoes and lay on the couch. Gayle was barely breathing.

"Dr. Sutherland, do you think I have a soul?"

Gayle was stunned. She glanced at the clock. She hated the space when she had to wait for the patient's associations. How long should she—how long *could* she—wait? "What happened in class?"

"I heard some students talking about me. We were dissecting cats and I heard them say, 'She knows more than the instructor, but she's weird, like a robot.' Then Natasha Something said, 'I don't think she has a soul, maybe she's a vampire.' Then they laughed."

Kathleen began to whimper. "It hurts too much. It's the same, always the same. I thought when I grew up and moved here, it would be different. Do you think they're right? Do I have a soul?"

Gayle had never heard her cry before and she felt Kathleen's pain reach in and twist around her heart, as if it were her own.

"Of course, you have a soul. That's why it hurts so much."

Kathleen sobbed, and Gayle had to strain to hear the words that came between gasps. "Gayle, there's something really wrong with me. I'm attracted to women, not men."

Gayle's mind was racing. Where to begin, to interpret, to soothe a bereft child. She spoke carefully, quietly. "I'm so glad you called me Gayle. I've always thought Dr. Sutherland sounds so stuffy."

Kathleen's sobs were beginning to dwindle. "You're not mad at me?"

"Oh no, not at all. I'm so glad you called me Gayle and I'm glad that you trusted me and could tell me about liking girls."

"It's not normal for a girl to like girls."

"What is normal?"

"Umm, liking guys and wanting to date them and wanting to, you know, have sex."

"With guys?"

Kathleen nodded.

"Do you think about having sex with girls?"

Kathleen kept her eyes shut and turned her head away as she nodded.

"All the time?"

Kathleen began to cry again, softer tears running down her face. "At night or when I see a pretty girl in class."

"Kathleen, would you like to know the true definition of normal?"

She continued to cry, "Yes, please."

"Being normal is about being able to love and relate to another person; it's not about gender. It's about wanting someone to put their arms around you and tell you they love you, and for you to be able to do the same. It's about wanting to have a life together, to share good times and bad times. Is that something you want?"

"Dr. Suth… Gayle, more than anything. But I thought it could only be with a guy."

"Some people think it, believe it, but I want you to really hear what I'm saying. They're wrong."

CHAPTER 4

Kathleen entered Gayle's office, said hello, placed two crisp one-dollar bills on Gayle's desk, sat silently on the couch while she took her shoes off, and laid down with a relaxed sigh.

Kathleen liked lying on the couch even if it meant she couldn't eat lunch with Gayle. Now, when she left, Gayle handed her a paper bag filled with food, more than enough for lunch and dinner. She wondered rather sillily if Freud had fed his patients.

"Guess what, Gayle."

"What, Kathleen?"

"I'm officially a sophomore. One down, three to go."

"Congratulations. How's that feeling?"

"Really good. The classes are getting harder but more interesting. Gayle, I have a silly question."

"Ask away."

"Is there something, umm, magical about your couch?"

Gayle never knew what to expect from Kathleen, but this was off the charts. She had to suppress her amusement at the question. "Tell me what you're thinking."

"Well, when I lay down on your couch, I start to feel really little, like maybe I'm ten or twelve."

"Maybe even younger?"

"Yeah, well I don't want to admit to being younger than ten. It's really strange. When I walk in I'm nineteen. Then I lay down and I start to feel younger. Then when I leave, I walk a block or two and I'm nineteen again."

"Well, it's not magic like a genie in a bottle. But there is something that happens. Would you like to know what analysts call it?"

"Yes, please."

"It's called regression. Kathleen, do you read any science fiction?"

"Yes, they're one of my favorites."

"It's a form of time-travel. When you lie on the couch you may feel as if you're moving backward in time and you may begin to feel very, very little."

"So, it's normal?"

"Yes, Kathleen, it is, and you are normal."

Kathleen, relieved, sank into the couch's luxurious texture and commented, "Gayle, your couch is more comfortable than the bed I had at Mrs. Adams."

Gayle smiled. "What was it like?"

"Lumpy. Like lots of foster kids must have slept on it. I got used to it, though. I got used to almost everything. Except the kids."

"What about the kids?"

"I was scared to play outside. I got picked on—a lot. I was tall and skinny and wore hand-me-downs. My teeth were too big for the rest of me, and I had freckles. Everyone made fun of me.

"During the summer, before fifth-grade, I played in Mrs. Adams' basement. Well, twice a week, Mrs. Adams went to church meetings. I think they played bingo and gossiped. She left me alone, and that's when I snuck into the basement. The basement stayed cool and there were lots of boxes and newspapers stacked against one wall. The newspapers were really old, and I used to switch on the light and read the comics. Gayle, do you know what I wanted to be?"

"No, but I bet you're getting ready to tell me."

Kathleen laughed. No one had ever paid this much attention to what she was thinking and feeling. "I wanted to be invisible. I found this comic strip called *Invisible Scarlet O'Neil.* I just loved it! Scarlet could become invisible by pressing her wrist with her fingers. I tried pressing my wrists the whole summer, first one way, then another. If I could become invisible, I could walk outside and spy on the kids, but no one could see me or tease me, or I could walk into the room when Mrs. Adams spoke to the social worker and hear everything they were saying about me."

Gayle spoke thoughtfully. "Kathleen, what's the opposite of being invisible?"

Kathleen knew that when Gayle became serious, she was going to ask a question that had an easy answer, but would be followed by a deep thought. "Why, being seen, of course."

"Do you think I see you?"

Kathleen thought for a moment. *Was this a trick question?* "I'm here, so I know you're seeing me, unless you're closing your eyes the way I do." Gayle was quiet so maybe there was another answer. Kathleen sighed.

Gayle said, "What happens if someone can't see you?"

"They can't tease me."

"And?"

"What's for lunch, Gayle?"

Gayle laughed. "You're trying to get out of the question. You're quite a wiggle worm. Do you want the answer?"

"About lunch?"

Gayle laughed again. "No. About the benefits of being seen."

"Yes, please."

"If you're invisible, no one can see you, and it's true they won't tease you. But, they also won't get to know you. Now, do you want me to answer your other question?"

"Yes, please."

"Tuna with celery, no egg. Fruit salad, milk—and Robert baked a special apple pie last night."

CHAPTER 5

Kathleen was beginning to change.

At times she smiled, and her face lit up.

At times she shared something silly, and she and Gayle would laugh.

At times she cried, not only from pain, but from gratitude, as well.

Now, they were sharing more than a sandwich. They were sharing a relationship.

"Gayle, the tuna was really good. Would you thank Robert for the apple pie? It was extra delicious."

"He'll be happy to hear it."

It had been six months since Kathleen had shared her "shame-filled secret" with Gayle. Now, she seemed to focus on revealing painful parts of her childhood. She didn't talk about being lesbian again and Gayle, no matter how much she wanted to barge in with unanswered questions, was going to follow her lead. Becoming an analyst, Gayle was discovering, was similar to being a detective; you had to wait for the clues to appear through the patient's conversations and associations.

Kathleen was quiet. Sometimes, Gayle said, it was okay to be still and let her thoughts pop up when they were ready. Once, she fell asleep and missed most of her session. Gayle said that was okay, too, and maybe next time she'd have a dream they could talk about.

"I've been thinking about books, especially *Alice in Wonderland*," Kathleen said at length. "I still carry her in my backpack. Mrs. Adams gave her to me for my ninth birthday. She was a discard from the library and cost twenty-five cents."

Gayle found it whimsical and endearing the way Kathleen referred to the book as "her," but she winced at the word "discard." The interpretation could wait for a future day. "Tell me more," she urged.

"Okay. You know how much I love books. They were my best friends. Well, the social worker, Mrs. Martin, took me to the library one day, and helped me get a library card. Then, she took me out for ice cream, and we each had a three-scoop chocolate sundae. It was my first. The most I ever got before was a cone, single scoop. That was one of the happiest days of my life. I remember the feeling because it felt like a rainbow showing up after a rainstorm, and you get to see all the colors and think about the pot of gold at the end of the rainbow. I colored that memory gold and put it in my memory jar."

"Hmm, I don't think you've talked about your memory jar."

"Well, when I was little I used to try to remember the good memories. So, I thought, maybe I could have a jar inside me, like the kind of jar my mother used to can peaches. If I filled it with good memories I could open it when I was sad, and feel happy. Then I thought, maybe if I colored the special memories gold, they would be easy to find because they're so bright. Now, Gayle, I'm sort of crying a little bit—it was really hard to find good memories. Most of my jar is filled with black, not gold."

"What about now? Are you finding gold memories to put in your jar?"

Kathleen thought a moment. "Here, and with Gary, and sometimes in class." Kathleen was quiet. "Gayle, do you think if I start to put more gold memories in my jar, the black ones will disappear?"

"That's quite a question. What do you think?"

"Let's see. A jar can only hold so much. So, if I put in a lot of gold memories, maybe the black ones will get pushed out. I think I'll count today as a gold memory."

Gayle remained silent, a difficult thing for her to do, but she was learning to give Kathleen space for her thoughts and associations.

"Are we almost out of time, Gayle? I'm thinking of telling you about my first job. Do you know what I did?"

"We have time, and I think you're about to tell me a wonderful story."

"I earned a nickel. Do you want to hear the rest of the story?"

"I am sitting in absolute suspense."

"I like being here, Gayle. I don't feel hardly shy with you at all, but I keep thinking about lunch. Any hints?"

"It's a surprise, but I think you'll be happy."

"I like surprises. Okay, so here's the story about how I earned the nickel. Hmm, I'll do this one like a once-upon-a-time story. Just like a fairy tale."

"Once upon a time a little girl named Kathleen walked to the library with her eyes staring at the sidewalk," Kathleen began. Gayle was entranced by the regressive, singsong-ish, little girl tone of her patient's voice and listened raptly. "Usually, when she walked from Mrs. Adams' house to the library, she only saw sticky wads of gum and dog poop. But this time, she glanced down and saw a shiny dime with sunlight bouncing off its silvery face. She looked to see if anyone was watching and quickly put the dime in her pocket.

"She tried to decide how she would spend her treasure. She could buy two pieces of chocolate or three pieces of bubble gum at the neighborhood grocery store. The chocolate would be sweet in her mouth and trickle down her throat. If she put the bubble gum in a glass of water at night, it would keep for days.

"She was trying to decide between chocolate and bubble gum when she saw the big sign on the library window: *Book Sale, Ten Cents to One Dollar.* She stopped thinking about chocolate and bubble gum and looked at the books. She opened each one and checked the prices. The ten-cent books were all gone but she found one for fifteen cents, *The Swiss Family Robinson.*

"She walked over to the checkout counter with her dime held tightly in her fist. She handed the book to the librarian, who said, 'That will be fifteen cents.'

"Kathleen whispered, 'I only have a dime. Can I dust the books for you and earn a nickel?'

The librarian was a stuffy old lady with a long, grim face and her gray hair gathered in a tight bun. Kathleen was afraid she was going to say something cross, but instead she smiled, reached under the counter, and handed her a rag made from an old T-shirt. 'Do you see the books on that table?' The librarian pointed to a table near her counter. 'You can dust the books and arrange them so the table looks pretty. That's worth a nickel.'

"Kathleen dusted the books and arranged them by size. The librarian leaned over the counter and said, 'Thank you for helping. You did a very good job. I wasn't sure I would have the time to dust those books.' She handed Kathleen the precious copy of *The Swiss Family Robinson.* 'This must be your lucky day. This book was put on sale just before you walked in.'

"Kathleen skipped all the way back to Mrs. Adams'. 'This is my lucky day.' Skip, skip, skip. 'This is my lucky day.' Skip, skip, skip. She put her new book on the shelf next to *Alice*. Now she had two friends.

"The next day she read *The Swiss Family Robinson*. The book was about surviving on an island. But they were a family with a Mom and Da to take care of the kids. Something started to hurt inside Kathleen's chest. It felt as if her heart was cracking into little pieces."

Kathleen found it hard to speak, "Gayle, that's the story of how Kathleen earned her first nickel and found out her heart could break."

CHAPTER 6

Gayle turned the pages of the Sunday newspaper, trying to ignore the department store ads for spring clothing that catered to slender women and not the "full-figured woman" she had become. She finished her coffee, laden with heavy cream and sugar, cleared the breakfast dishes, and loaded them into the dishwasher.

She poured a fresh cup of coffee, sat down at the kitchen table, and opened the paper to the health section. She read the headline, "Broccoli holds promise for cancer fight" and made a face. *Eat broccoli, never!* But, she thought optimistically, *Maybe I can cut out the cream and sugar in my coffee. That should count for something.* She took a sip of the black coffee and reached for the bright red Fiesta cream and sugar set.

Six months had passed since Kathleen's last therapy appointment. The demands of upper-division classes were increasing and Kathleen needed to focus on preparing for medical school. She ended therapy more confident and able to handle the stress of school but had skirted the issues around her sexuality.

Gayle was reminded of Kathleen every day when she opened Robert's over-packed lunches. When her eyes fell across an anorexic-looking model in a J.C. Penney ad, she couldn't help but worry about Kathleen. *Was she eating? Was she eating enough?* "God, I sound exactly like a mother," she said aloud. "No, on second thought, I sound just like *my* mother."

Gayle sighed. *She will be a senior this fall.* She wanted to call, to have some contact, but they had left it open for Kathleen to call Gayle when she was ready.

Gayle opened the kitchen window welcoming the fresh spring air. She looked at Robert working in the garden, his face hidden beneath a floppy straw hat. She enjoyed watching the way he moved in a fluid, constant rhythm, planting row after row of flowers and bulbs. In a month, the garden would be in full bloom and they would begin to have friends and colleagues over for barbecues.

A small smile crossed her face when she remembered the night they met during a party at Gayle's sorority house. The summer heat had revisited Los Angeles and the windows were opened with hopes of capturing the evening breeze. The fragrance from the night-blooming jasmines filled the room as a 45-RPM record of Mama Cass singing "Dream A Little Dream of Me" played softly in the background. Gayle caught a whiff of sandalwood incense too, as the amorphous shapes in a lava lamp seemed to keep time with the music. She was glancing casually at a black light poster of Peter Fonda on his Harley from *Easy Rider* when Robert caught her eye.

Gayle and Robert were overcome by their instant attraction. Robert held out his arms and Gayle moved into them. They danced, looked into each other's eyes, smiled, but didn't speak a word. Words weren't needed for them to know they were in love.

They always agreed on the depth of their love, but disagreed on what brought them together. Gayle, a dyed-in-the-wool pragmatist, was certain it was a chance meeting; they just happened to be in the same place at the same time. Robert, a romantic at heart, was equally certain it was kismet.

Gayle felt her throat tighten as memories of the sad, childless years crept in. She dreaded walking into the near empty rooms that should have been filled with echoes of children's laughter. The space in her heart was never quite filled. She felt incomplete.

❀ ❀ ❀

In his own way, Robert grieved for the children that never were. When he worked in the yard, he would allow his fantasies to come to life. He imagined a little boy or girl following him as he gardened. He thought about how he would explain life through nature. The way time could be told from the sun casting a shadow over the face of a sundial. The cycle of life, from birth to death as seen by birds laying eggs in the nests of trees. The way the baby birds got fed until they were able to fly on their own, or how sometimes, unable to fly, they would fall to the ground. He wanted to show how a seed planted in the rich soil struggled to reach the top to blossom, only to wither and drop their seeds into the earth, slumbering, waiting for the next year, when the cycle would be repeated.

Robert carried his pain silently, but always missed the sound of a child calling him Dad.

Robert came in from the garden with the loamy smell of garden soil and peat moss clinging to his lean but well-muscled body. He wrapped his arms around Gayle. "What's wrong, sweetheart? You seem sad."

Gayle sighed as she rested her head against his chest and let his arms support her. "I miss Kathleen, and I worry about her. Is she getting enough to eat? Is she happy? I wonder if she's found someone to love." She snuggled closer, taking in his scent, feeling his beard rubbing gently against her face. "You know, I've broken confidentiality by talking to you about her."

He became thoughtful. "As your attorney, I would say I'm more of a consultant."

Gayle laughed and shook her head. "Ah, the power of interpretation."

Robert held her close. "Why don't you invite her over for next Sunday? I'll bet she misses you and doesn't know what to do. Sometimes these doctor-patient rules are just plain silly. Besides, I'd like to meet her."

He held Gayle even closer. "I'm finished in the garden, and we're going to have an exceptionally colorful summer, if Mother Nature cooperates." He added suggestively, "Do you know what I'd like?"

"I can't imagine."

"We can begin with a glass of your ice tea and a long shower." He kissed her with the same longing and passion as when they first met.

Kathleen grasped Gayle's directions tightly in her hand as she took the early morning Sunday bus from Los Angeles to Westwood. Gayle had offered to pick her up at the bus stop, but Kathleen said she enjoyed walking and would like to see the houses and gardens in the neighborhood. She moved at a fast clip and the two miles from Wilshire Blvd. to Gayle and Robert's home melted away. As she climbed the hilly streets, the houses changed from tract homes built in the 1950s to custom-built homes on sprawling lots. Evergreen magnolia trees lined both sides of the street creating a sense of unity to the otherwise eclectic neighborhood. One stately colonial house with columns reminded her of Tara and she wondered if Rhett and Scarlett were at home.

Kathleen didn't have to look at the address to know she was at Gayle and Robert's home. It stood out from all the others. She gazed at the sprawling ranch-style house with the beckoning red door. She thought she had fallen into Oz, where the lawns were painted an emerald green and flowers, in bright primary colors, sprawled across planter boxes and circled the birch trees carefully planted in groups of three.

A sudden feeling of shyness swept over her and she hesitated before knocking softly on the door. It felt natural for Gayle to open her arms and for Kathleen to rest her head against her chest. "I've missed you, Gayle."

Gayle whispered, "Baby, I'm so glad to see you. I've missed you too."

She shook Robert's hand. "And I've missed your lunches, Robert. You are the best cook."

Robert grinned. "Gayle, I like this girl already."

Sundays with Kathleen became their weekly ritual. Sometimes she would bring a book, and sit quietly in the den, studying. After a while, Gayle made one of their guest rooms into a bedroom for Kathleen. It didn't make sense for her to go home on a Sunday evening, only to take the long bus trip to Westwood the next morning.

Gayle looked forward to waking early on Mondays and making the waffles and eggs that Kathleen enjoyed so much. The emptiness that plagued her, for so many years, disappeared and, after a while, she forgot that Kathleen had been her patient and began to think of her as the child she never had.

Gayle opened the kitchen curtains and watched Robert and Kathleen with their heads together, analyzing a chair with a broken leg that Gayle had bought at a garage sale. She chuckled softly; they were both so serious, looking at what needed to be repaired and deciding how they would bring something damaged back to life.

They showed Gayle the finished product. "Better than new," Robert said. Kathleen grinned a lopsided grin that matched the tool belt hanging from her waist.

Gayle said, "You two inspire me. Wait until you see what's in the trunk of the car."

Gayle saw Kathleen growing stronger, coming alive.

Gayle saw Robert becoming happy in a way that had been lost, long ago.

From time to time, Gayle thought of the rules she had broken: feeding Kathleen during treatment, contacting her after she left, having her stay at her home.

Was it wrong, when growth and healing occurred?

Was it wrong if the healer also got healed?

What if there was a predetermined course of events that brought people together?

What if there was a way people healed each other?

What if kismet did exist?

CHAPTER 7

Gary knocked on Kathleen's door. "Come on, enough studying." He playfully shook her foot. "Off the bed and into your bathing suit. It's summer vacation, we're officially seniors, and we're going to the beach."

Kathleen put the book down, raised her head, and rubbed her eyes.

"Are you studying for classes that haven't even started?"

"Not exactly. Just reading a couple of textbooks." She yawned, opened her eyes wider and stared. "What are you wearing?"

"They're my official *Baywatch* trunks." Gary did a quick pirouette, showing off his bright red lifeguard trunks. "How do I look?"

"Fab. You may be ready for the chorus of *Swan Lake*, but I don't think you'll be mistaken for a lifeguard."

"Hmm... is it my early middle-aged paunch?" He patted his stomach and made a sad face before grabbing her hand. "Even a genius has to take a day off, and I can tell your eyes are ready to fall out. I'm giving you five minutes to get your bathing suit on. Mom's packing a lunch and I'm going to get my buckets and shovels."

"Are you serious? Buckets and shovels?"

"Kathleen, you can't go to the beach and not make sand castles."

Isabel lent them her car and filled a cooler—enough for a family of six—with food and drinks. Jorge gave Gary sixty dollars with the advice to "Take her someplace special for dinner."

They drove to Santa Monica and parked at the pier. They strolled down the walkway and stood in front of the fully restored 1922 carousel as calliope music, the most cheerful music on earth, made Kathleen feel like a kid again. Children climbed on their favorite steed and rode around and around, big smiles blooming on their faces as they reached for the brass ring.

Gary looked at Kathleen and smiled slyly. "Let's ride. We're only going to be young once."

They jumped onto the carousel as it began to move, looking for their perfect mount. Gary picked a tiger and growled mock-menacingly at Kathleen, pawing at her playfully. Kathleen picked one of the most ferocious looking horses, with wild eyes and its mouth opened wide, as if it were screaming into battle. She undid her braid and let her hair fly free. Kathleen leaned back, feeling the breeze on her face, and became an Irish warrior from one of her father's long ago stories.

They took the steps from the pier down to the beach. The day was overcast, but Gary insisted on putting sunscreen on her back every hour. "I've never seen anyone with such fair skin," he observed admiringly. "How do I love thee, let me count the ways, one two, three..."

"Gary, what the hell are you doing?"

"Counting the freckles on your back."

Kathleen leaned over and kissed Gary on the cheek. "No one else would put up with you."

They spent the day wading and splashing in the chilly water, building sand castles, and sitting on beach chairs, reading, and talking about their future. Occasionally they would glance at each other and smile.

Gary wanted to be a neurosurgeon and Kathleen hoped to complete a dual residency in Emergency and Family Medicine. They were both facing a financial crisis. Kathleen's scholarship was for four years and Gary's family would try to help, but it would have to be student loans and large debts for both of them.

They had attended a recruiting seminar, at UCLA, for the Army's Health Professions Scholarship Program. They went out of curiosity and because they were offered a free lunch, but left thinking; *This is not a bad deal.*

Gary said, "I don't know if I can learn to salute, but the package sounds awfully good. They'll pay for our education and we'll pay it back by serving. I wouldn't mind the traveling. France, Germany, who knows. How do you think I'll look in my uniform?"

"Stunning, I'm sure." Kathleen became pensive. "I think Gayle will positively kill me for joining."

"Roger that. My mom will have a heart attack and a stroke, both at the same time. You know, I think it's a good program. I want to be the best neurosurgeon and the Army can give me the training. My folks have offered to help, but they both work so hard now ...I really don't want to take anything more from them. I'll end up owing at least a million dollars and twenty cents."

Kathleen laughed at his corny joke but spoke longingly. "Actually, I kinda like the idea of serving and there's a lot of camaraderie in the military. In some ways, it can be like a family."

Gary became serious. "Yeah, but in one way a dysfunctional family. You can't always be who you really are."

Kathleen looked at Gary, but quickly averted her eyes.

Gary became serious. "Kathleen, are you dating at all?"

She shook her head. "I don't have the time."

"I think my parents wish we were a couple."

Kathleen looked directly at Gary. "Your parents are sweet and I love your family. I love you too; you're my best friend."

Gary leaned over and patted her hand. "I think people see us as a couple—maybe a bit of an odd couple." He couldn't resist cracking a joke. "I'm Felix. You're Oscar."

"Thanks a lot!" said Kathleen, laughing.

"I've never dated. That's why my parents are worried, but it isn't because of time."

"What do you think it is?"

"Sometimes, I think I am... you know..."

"You mean...?" She said meaningly and raised her eyebrows.

"Yes. Do you ever think about having sex?"

"Uh, I guess."

"With guys?"

"Sometimes."

"With girls?"

Kathleen blushed. "Sometimes," she admitted.

"You know, we'd have to really hide that part of ourselves if we joined the Army. I mean, if it's true, that we, I might be. Maybe we're just really inexperienced, though I've read all the sex manuals and lots of sexy magazines and I don't seem to get turned on."

"Not at all?"

Gary sighed. "Well, yes, but not by the girls."

Kathleen reached over and held Gary's hand. "I'm sorry."

They became quiet, lost in their thoughts, trying to digest the conversation.

Kathleen broke the silence. "How can you find out?"

"I guess the only way would be to try it with a girl and see if everything works."

"I could try the same thing with a guy." She shook her head. "But I couldn't, you know, do it with just *any* guy."

Gary asked, "Are you thinking what I'm thinking?"

"I can't think of anyone I would rather lose my virginity to, than you."

"So, what do we do?"

"Well, there are tons of hotels around here. Do you have any money?"

"My dad gave me sixty dollars."

"I've got twenty."

"Shall we?"

"Let's."

The first two hotels were too expensive, but one of the desk clerks gave them the address of a motel in nearby Venice. They took showers. Kathleen took hers first and Gary closed his eyes while she got into bed. She kept the blanket tucked under her chin until Gary joined her under the covers.

Gary rested on one elbow and stared into her eyes. "You're beautiful," he said, as he leaned over to kiss her.

❀ ❀ ❀

Gary was worried he might have hurt her. After all, he had read all the books. They stayed in bed; one more silent than the other until waves of giggles began to form.

Gary said, "Oh, Kathleen, I know I am, I know I am."

"Me, too. It was," she searched for a word that wouldn't hurt his feelings, "pleasant, but I did feel like something was missing."

"Me, too! Oh, shit, what am I going to do? I kept thinking about guys the whole time. Were you thinking about girls?"

"Oh, God, this is really embarrassing. Gary, I've never liked all the hair guys have on their bodies and, well, you..."

"It's okay. I know I don't have a lot of body hair. It's all on top of my head."

Kathleen leaned over and rubbed her hand through his black, straight hair. "Girls would die for your hair."

"That would be great, except it's not girls I'm interested in. So, when you touched me..."

"I thought about, you know, I kept pretending... Oh, Gary, I need to bury this. If I don't focus, I won't finish school."

"Ditto. What I said before about guys, I can't put it aside. I do love you, and I always want to be there for you. You're my best friend, and you're like a sister to me."

"I'm awfully glad my first time was with you, but I don't think we should be talking about being brother and sister, considering what we've done. Gary, do we have any money left?"

"About thirty dollars."

"Let's get something to eat before we go home."

They drove to the Third Street Mall, near the beach, and sat at an outdoor restaurant. People walking down the street would see a sweet young couple, perhaps in love. They were a couple that loved each other, but could never be in love.

CHAPTER 8

Wearing the "Real Men Cook" apron his colleagues had given him as a gag gift, Robert barbecued steaks to celebrate Kathleen's graduation and acceptance to the David Geffen School of Medicine at UCLA.

Robert hummed as he turned the steaks over. "Medium for you, Kathleen?"

She smiled, "Yes."

"Big doings, huh, Kathleen? Class of '93. Way to go! Not to mention getting accepted to UCLA's med school."

"Yeah, I have to admit, I'm pretty proud."

They dined on the patio, where a folding table groaned underneath the weight of bowl upon bowl of Robert's handiwork.

Gayle complained, "Too much food, Robert. How will I ever lose this weight?"

"I know, I know, I way overcook—it's my one flaw."

"Oh, I might be able to think of one or two more," she replied with a sparkle in her eyes.

Robert reared back in his wrought-iron chair, savoring his last bite of rib eye smothered in A.1. sauce. He turned to Kathleen and said, "Gayle and I have been talking about something and we'd like your opinion."

Kathleen became serious, put her fork down, and sat up straight.

"Once you start med school your bus commute is going to be impossible," Robert continued, "and once you start working at the hospital you'll have all kinds of crazy hours."

"UCLA has student apartments in West Los Angeles and I'm on the waiting list."

"Still a big distance. What would you think about moving in with us? We're only a couple of miles from UCLA. We'll give you a deal on the rent, and I'm already cooking for three..."

Gayle interjected, "or four..."

"I don't know what to say." Tears formed and rolled down Kathleen's cheeks. She wiped them away with the back of her hands. She began to cry, her head in her hands, her shoulders shaking softly. "I'm sorry, I'm just so grateful to have you both in my life."

Gayle placed her hand on Kathleen's shoulder. "It would mean the world to us. We're so proud of everything you've achieved. Your room is ready; it even has the pink floral wallpaper you wanted, and you'll be helping me by eating that extra food before I do! Why, it's a win-win situation!"

Gayle and Robert had a second gift in mind, one that Kathleen and Gary could share. The couple rented a bright red 1965 Mustang convertible for two weeks and gave them money for their vacation to San Francisco. Gary was accepted to the University of California at San Francisco and he and Kathleen planned to drive the coast highway, get Gary settled in his new apartment, and go sightseeing. They had other secret plans in mind, as well.

There were countless announcements during the graduation ceremony, but Gayle only heard two. Kathleen had finished second in her class. The other announcement came as a bigger surprise, one that put a rope around Gayle's heart and pulled it tight. Kathleen and Gary had joined the Army.

❀ ❀ ❀

It was 1993, they were official med students and they were on their way to San Francisco. The Mustang's V-8 engine hummed along the coastal highway and the car fetched admiring stares from passing motorists. The top was down, the ocean breeze caressed their faces, and they felt carefree.

They stopped at Monterey and stayed at a small hotel where the sound of the surf met the smell of the sea. The clerk asked, "One or two beds?" Gary and Kathleen smiled and said in unison, "Two!"

Gary grinned as he bounced on his bed. "Are you still a virgin?"

Kathleen laughed. "Yes, in the way it counts."

"Me too. I'm hoping that changes this week. I booked two rooms in the Castro District and we've got a list of gay friendly restaurants and bars. Do you think Gayle and Robert would take back their gift, if they knew?"

"Robert might be hurt, but Gayle's more savvy. What if one of us..."

"Scores?"

"Don't be crude! Let's say, gets a date, and the other one doesn't?"

"You can worry about that," said Gary teasingly. "I'm confident I'll get my dance card punched."

"Mr. Lucky," Kathleen teased back. "Remember, we need to be discreet. I don't want to get discharged before we've even started. First names only. No personal details and nothing about being a soldier."

They were giddy. Giddy with their newfound freedom, giddy with the thought of an MD after their names, and giddy with the possibility of discovering their sexuality.

They spent their first day in San Francisco cleaning Gary's apartment. They stood in the middle of a small, dismal single, watching a cockroach scurry across the kitchen counter.

"Gary, this place needs to be scrubbed and fumigated."

"Yeah, my mom would die if she saw this."

Kathleen touched his smooth, beard-free face. "Don't be sad. We can buy cleaning supplies and snacks at the market. We'll make it sparkle."

By the time they finished cleaning they were tired, dirty, and the last thing on their minds was meeting a stranger, in a strange city. They returned to their hotel, showered, ordered pizza, and fell asleep.

❀ ❀ ❀

Roman's was a well-known gay-friendly restaurant within the Castro District. Tucked away on a dark, side street and barely visible from the road, its black door opened to shiny black Formica tabletops glistening with the reflection from art deco chandeliers. The lights were kept purposely low and music from the 1970s and '80s *loud* created the atmosphere. Same gender couples sat at small tables, while others, sat alone at the bar waiting and hoping.

Gary and Kathleen studied the menu, ordered salads, pasta, and a bottle of the house red wine. Kathleen nibbled at her food. Her stomach was turning somersaults and her hands were shaking. After dinner, they sat at the bar and showed the bartender proof that they were over twenty-one. Kathleen was certain everyone in the restaurant was staring at them.

Gary disappeared first. Kathleen waited, alone. She sipped her glass of white wine until her liquid courage edged toward empty.

"Hi."

Kathleen turned to see a pleasant looking woman in her mid-thirties sitting next to her.

"Here by yourself?"

Kathleen nodded.

"I watched you come in with your friend. A lot of us do it that way. You're not Marines and you're not Navy; must be Army."

Kathleen froze. "I don't know what you're talking about."

"I'm sorry, I didn't mean to frighten you. I'm Roseanne." She held out a hand with a small tattoo—*Navy*—on her wrist. "There's a quiet table in the corner. Do you want to have a drink and talk?"

Kathleen sat for a moment, unsure and frightened. *Oh, what the hell, she doesn't even know my name.* She followed Roseanne to the table and ordered ice tea.

"You don't have to give me your real name, but I should call you something."

Kathleen looked down.

"Okay. I know you're scared, so I'll do the talking. Navy nurse, twelve years, hoping for twenty. Twelve years ago, I sat where you are. You and your friend—med students, is my guess. You can survive, but you have to be careful. Most in the medical field won't care. There are a few assholes, but that's true in every walk of life.

Kathleen, mesmerized by Roseanne's story, began to relax.

"I used to come in with my gay buddy for dinner, just like the two of you. This is about as safe as it gets. What you don't want to do is walk outside and hold hands or put your arm around someone. I always keep a picture of my gay friend in my locker and on my desk. I let everyone think he's my boyfriend. When you're in training or on base, be asexual. That's how you'll stay safe."

Roseanne twirled the stem of her wine glass between her long fingers and went on her practiced philosophical manner. "You will be giving up an important part of your life. You will fight for freedom, but not be free. As long as you're in the military you won't be able to live in the open with someone you love and who loves you. The hardest part is finding a partner who will hide in the closet with you. As for me—so far, no luck."

Roseanne lifted her glass and drained it in one swallow. "It's still a damn good career."

A small smiled played across Kathleen's face. "Hello Roseanne, my name is Kathleen."

CHAPTER 9

Captain Kathleen Moore rode the elevator from the ground floor at Madigan Army Medical Center in Tacoma, Washington, to the Administrative Offices on the seventh floor. She rested her head against the wall of the empty elevator and closed her eyes for a fifteen-second nap. Her shift at the Family Medicine twenty-four-hour walk-in clinic had been non-stop from the moment she walked in until she left for the day. Worried parents brought in fussy babies with earaches and sore throats. Overweight patients with uncontrolled diabetes needed their glucose monitored and medication adjusted. Soldiers returning from being deployed didn't want to deal with their nightmares or angry outbursts, and requested medication to make it go away. She referred three to the psych clinic.

Tomorrow was her day off and she began to fantasize about ordering a pizza and staying in bed all day, sleeping and watching TV, when her "things to do" list suddenly materialized. Her refrigerator was empty and so was her gas tank. The list grew: pick up uniforms at the dry cleaners, clean the apartment, pay bills. Her day in bed began to fade.

She was poised to knock on Colonel White's office door for her 2:00 pm appointment when the door opened, a quick salute, a gesture to sit, and an offer of coffee.

"Still taking it black, Kathleen?"

"Yes, sir."

"Never could understand drinking it neat," he said as he handed her a Styrofoam cup filled with a thick, murky liquid.

She held the cup close to her mouth and smelled the strong, stale coffee. Now she could understand his need to drink it mixed.

Colonel White sat behind a desk covered with random papers and thick personnel files. "Your review is in here somewhere." He spoke casually as he continued his search. "Got your results from the board exams?"

"Any day now, sir."

He nodded as he shuffled files. "Any concerns about getting your certification?"

"No sir," she lied.

"Good, we want our docs to get board certified. Here it is," he said, picking up a thick, gray-green pressboard file. "This'll all be computerized in a few years, or so they say."

Colonel White, a round-faced man who recently celebrated his fiftieth birthday, sat back in his office chair, tipping back and forth, his eyes half-closed. His broad hand moved over his bald head, stopping abruptly as if it was still expecting to find the thick black hair of his youth.

"You've seen your evaluation and signed off on it. It's excellent, Kathleen. Your clinical skills as a Family Physician are outstanding. Are you thinking of making the Army your career?"

"Thank you, sir. And, yes sir, I want this for my career."

"Don't thank me so quickly." He smiled. "There's a note in here, *not* part of your evaluation or file, something about interpersonal skills." He handed the note to Kathleen.

Dr. Moore is highly skilled in almost every clinical area. However, a concern has been raised about her interpersonal skills. For the most part, her interactions with patients and staff are thoughtful and appropriate. However, from time to time, she seems to change abruptly and becomes standoffish.

Kathleen could feel a blush starting and spoke hesitantly. "I'm aware of the problem, sir. It doesn't happen often and I'm trying to stay alert to the situation."

She returned the note to Colonel White. He nodded. "Get a handle on it. You'll be up for a promotion soon and you don't want anything negative in your file." He took the note, tore it into small pieces, and threw them ceremoniously in the green metal trashcan next to his desk.

He held his coffee mug in his hand and relaxed back into his chair. "I've been in the service for twenty years, enlisted in 1982." He blinked, trying to clear his eyes from the irritating paper dust and long hours of reading files. "Seen it all in those twenty. Assignments to Europe and Asia, deployed to Iraq during the Gulf War, then Bosnia and now a desk job." He sighed. "This," he pointed to the mess on his desk, "is critical, but after 9/11... I sure do miss the action."

He looked directly at Kathleen. "I've learned a lot over these years. Lots of posturing about strike first, hit 'um hard, get in and get out."

He shook his head. "Then there's the silent talk, the chatter between the lines that tells me, when we do invade Iraq, we'll be there for quite a while. Right now, there's a big push to get more physicians trained in emergency medicine." He paused to take a long-drawn-out swig of his coffee. "Interested in a second residency?"

Kathleen sat up straight, her mood shifting from one of embarrassment to excitement. "Yes, sir. I've always been interested in an emergency residency program."

"There's a spot at a civilian hospital. You know about Shock Trauma Center in Baltimore?"

"Yes, sir. It's where Dr. Cowley developed the concept of the 'Golden Hour.'"

Colonel White nodded. "Speed and skill of treatment in the first hour after injury. It's what our wounded deserve and what we're aiming for. This is a plum opportunity; best place for you to get trained."

"I would be honored, sir, but doesn't that mean I won't be eligible for deployment until I complete my residency? I've been ready since 9/11 and I'm eager to serve."

"If I'm reading this correctly you'll get your chance to deploy. I don't think this war is going away."

❀ ❀ ❀

She had two weeks leave before reporting to Shock Trauma Center. She would spend a few days in Los Angeles before flying to Baltimore to find an apartment and settle into what she knew would be a stressful but exciting three years.

The note had bothered her more than she had revealed to Colonel White. She desperately needed to talk to Gayle.

She wanted Gayle to see her as she was today, a thirty-one-year-old captain in the United States Army, and changed into her Green Service Uniform at LAX before catching a cab to Gayle's office.

Gayle's outstretched arms greeted Kathleen. A long hug and an even longer appraising look. "Baby, you're beautiful. I always was a sucker for a uniform."

Kathleen smiled, reached in her pocket, took out two crisp one-dollar bills, and placed them on Gayle's desk. She glanced at the couch, remembering the times she lay crying, telling Gayle her troubles and being fed in so many ways.

Gayle looked at her "fee." "Baby, what is this about?"

"Gayle, I need to talk."

"You know I can't be your therapist; that role changed years ago."

"Understood, but I need advice and you know me better than anyone."

"What's going on, Kathleen?"

"I'm getting called on my interpersonal skills and I've got to get a handle on it. Sometimes it happens when I'm examining a patient. I'll be talking with them and if I discover something during my examination I'll move completely into my head. It's hard for me to explain, but it's as if I've lost the human connection."

Kathleen reached for a tissue and wiped her eyes. "Lately, it's gotten worse. There are times when I'll be talking with someone... anyone actually... and suddenly, my body stiffens and I start to withdraw."

"When did you notice the change?"

Kathleen closed her eyes for a minute. "It was during my third year residency. I was doing a four-week rotation in the Psych Department; that was a hard one for me. I don't know why but I think that's when it started to get worse."

Gayle sighed and sat back in her chair. Her mind went back to those days when she had to comfort a frightened, confused child. Now, she was sitting across from an accomplished physician who only wanted practical advice. "Kathleen, do you remember, years ago, when I defined the word normal for you?"

"It changed my life."

"That was straight from my heart; no analysis, no bullshit. Would you like another straight from the heart?"

"It's what I'm hoping for."

Gayle handed Kathleen the two dollars. "I think you'd better keep these. There's no charge for what I'm about to tell you. You have two different situations and I don't think they're related." Gayle shook her head. "Not at all. The first one deals with being a physician. I know your heart. You're kind and compassionate and your patients feel it. When you discover a problem you move into your head; they sense the disconnection and feel dropped. I think the answer to that behavior is a matter of staying aware and racking up more years of experience."

"Okay, I'll buy that one, but what about the other situation? When I'm talking with someone in a friendly way and then *bang*, I become downright cold? Remember when I was called a robot? That's what it feels like."

Gayle sat back in her chair thinking. "You said you had a rough time during your rotation in the Psych Ward. I don't want you to answer, but I want you to think about it. What happened that upset you so? It sounds like whatever your experience was, it caused a reaction. *Something* pushed your buttons and they've stayed pushed."

Kathleen's hands began to tremble, a sign to Gayle that she had hit close to home.

"I can't talk about it and I can't go there. The next three years are going to be really intense and my mind has to be clear. Please don't tell me I need more therapy."

"Wouldn't dream of it. You've got enough on your plate right now."

Gayle stood up, opened the desk drawer intended to store her files, and returned with a black-and-white paisley gift bag. "I was saving this for tonight, but I think you should open it now."

Kathleen chuckled. "Therapy in a box, umm, I mean a bag." She reached inside and took out a black moleskin leather journal.

"Thank you, it's beautiful. I've never had a journal before. I'm used to e-mails and cell phones and post-it notes for quick reminders."

"Journaling is different. This is a place to hold your feelings and no one ever has to read it, unless you want them to. Write," she insisted. "Write about your feelings; it will help keep you in balance."

Kathleen settled into the aisle seat on the flight from Los Angeles to Baltimore. She purposely took the red-eye, knowing that most of the passengers would try to sleep and the plane would be quiet except for occasional snoring or a tired infant needing to be soothed. She wanted time to think about what Gayle had said and took the journal out of her backpack. She looked around the cabin. Most of the passengers were sleeping, some resting comfortably against the person next to them.

She wrote the date in the journal.

May 2, 2002 – *lonely.*

Her thoughts went to Gary. He was stationed in Germany at Landstuhl Regional Hospital. Goofy as ever, but earning the respect of his colleagues as a top-notch neurosurgeon. Gary was her best friend. He knew so much about her, but not everything. No one knew everything about her, not even Gayle.

She wrote another word in her journal, *sad.*

She usually didn't allow the sad feelings to surface. She wondered if Gayle's journal held the same magic as her couch. There were times when the pain from the loneliness would engulf her and she would long for someone to share her day, her thoughts, and her feelings. Someone she could love and who would love her. She wondered, *Would that ever happen?*

She sat back and closed her eyes. She would never forget that day in the Psych Ward. It was the woman sitting in a chair; long, matted red hair cascading down her back, faded eyes open and staring into nothingness. Even now, she could feel the visceral reaction racing through her body. She couldn't allow old memories to get in the way, not now, not ever. She had come too far, given up too much. She opened the journal and again wrote one word, *Never*.

She closed the pages, returned her journal to her backpack, and tried to sleep.

❀ ❀ ❀

The three years at Shock went quickly, oh so quickly. She felt time was out of control, spinning around like the *Mad Tea Cup* ride at Disneyland. She was grateful for the experience, she had learned so much, but was relieved when her residency ended.

She glanced around her Baltimore apartment. Packed suitcases and boxes covered the worn carpeting. Not much to say goodbye to; a place to rest her head between shifts at Shock. She opened her journal and glanced at her most recent entry.

March 20, 2005 – *Received my promotion to Major. Colonel White was right. The war didn't go away. I report to Fort Bragg then deploy to Iraq. Will get in a couple of weeks leave before reporting. Gayle and Robert want me to spend time with them but I'll spend a few days in San Francisco first. Hearing about horrible things happening in Iraq. Pray I'm up for the task.*

Kathleen didn't want to feel anything right now, but the word seemed to write itself: *Scared*.

❀ ❀ ❀

From time to time Kathleen thought wistfully about Roseanne. She would have her twenty years in and probably be retired by now.

Kathleen imagined her in a sweet house, somewhere in the country, with an even sweeter woman by her side. She saw them cooking dinner together, laughing, eyes sparkling, gently brushing against each other.

Roseanne was the first woman to kiss her tenderly, and bring her body to life. The only woman to massage her back, with lotion found in the hotel bathroom, until she began to cry, and the pain from all the years seeped out of every pore. When she began to fall asleep, Roseanne kissed her goodbye and whispered, "You're easy to love, Kathleen."

That night she had a dream. She was at the library she frequented as a child. She bought a book on sale and the librarian leaned over and whispered, "You're easy to love, Kathleen." She looked up and saw Roseanne. She held the book next to her heart and tried to skip home, only she didn't know where home was. A woman joined her and held her hand. "You're easy to love, Kathleen." Skip, skip, skip. "You're easy to love, Kathleen." Skip, skip, skip.

CHAPTER 10

Kathleen met Sam Hughes at Fort Bragg while they were preparing for deployment to Iraq. His deep blue eyes drew her to him; eyes that were like windows, and if she looked closely she could see what he had seen: not a photograph of a scene, but a photograph of pain.

They were assigned to the same Combat Support Hospital (CSH), and it was natural for their paths to cross repeatedly in classes and at the pistol range. Quite by chance, they picked the same time for the gym. In the beginning, they exchanged smiles and progressed to saying hello. Later, they began to sit together at the mess hall.

Kathleen was staring at her dinner: Salisbury steak, mashed potatoes, green salad, and broccoli, all about as appetizing as week-old road kill.

Sam watched her with amusement. "You'll be dreaming about this food when you're in Iraq."

She pouted. "I'm craving Chinese food. I'd rather dream about that than this." She put her fork in the mashed potatoes and watched as it stood at attention.

"Uh, Kathleen, I hate to tell you but you just pouted. I think that might fall under the category of behavior unbecoming an officer." He smiled. "Let's go. I know an absolutely authentic Chinese restaurant. It's the real deal."

They drove to a seedy part of town and walked into the dimly lit China Bistro. Black lacquered screens with faux-ivory inlays of flowers and horses were placed around small groups of tables, creating a private atmosphere for diners. There were some familiar faces, medical staff that would deploy with them, and they stopped to chat for a few minutes.

Kathleen thought, *Here goes the rumor mill. At least I'm with the right gender.*

At Kathleen's request, they were seated in a quiet booth at the back of the restaurant.

Sam said, "Let's start with the combination tray. We'll get an assortment of appetizers and after that, who knows?"

"I'm game, as long as it's fried and unhealthy."

The appetizers arrived, along with their drinks. They both ordered mai-tais, toasted to their health, and dove into the plate of assorted dumplings, spareribs, egg rolls, and fried wontons.

"Fried enough for you?" Sam said, between bites.

Kathleen dabbed her greasy fingers on her napkin and said, "Perfect, although I may end up in the ER tonight—as a patient, that is."

Sam wiped his hands, sat back and patted his stomach. "I've got to watch this paunch. No matter what, after twenty-years in the military, your corporation will start to grow, as my daddy always said." He smiled. "I saw your photo of Gary Morales. I took some training classes with Gary, back when he was a resident and I was getting certified as a Physician Assistant." He reached for another sparerib. "Holy flippin' Jesus, these are really good."

Kathleen felt her heart stop and her hands begin to tremble. She held on tightly to her glass, hoping the shaking wouldn't show.

"I've never heard anyone so in love. It was Kathleen this and Kathleen that." Sam smiled. "He wasn't exaggerating."

Shit, she thought, *Gary was probably terrified of being outed.* She smiled weakly.

"I hear Gary's stationed at Landstuhl."

She nodded.

"It must be hard for the two of you to be separated."

Sam was speaking casually. She thought she was safe.

"We try to coordinate our leaves and do the best we can. What about you, Sam?"

"I was married once, to Marie." He wiped his mouth. "A two-year disaster. The only good thing that came out of it was our son, Thomas. He's a teenager now and really doesn't want much to do with me." He shook his head, and Kathleen noticed the sad cloud in his eyes. "After our divorce, I decided the battlefield was much safer than love.

"The Army has been good to me. I came in, this skinny, blond, farm boy of eighteen." He raked his calloused hand, big as an oven mitt, through his thinning hair and smiled. "Not much of that blond hair left. Well, they trained me, taught me... educated me. It's my life now." He lifted his glass "To the Army." He set his glass down and looked at Kathleen. "You're easy to talk to, Kathleen. I've never shared this story with anyone."

They thought they had another month for training before deployment. A CSH in Tikrit, Iraq, was short-staffed and Kathleen and Sam were pulled from their unit and shipped out in three days. They would be deployed for a year.

Sam knew that no matter how much training Kathleen had, nothing could prepare her for the carnage. He couldn't help but think about his first deployment. A lieutenant, fresh out of West Point, lay in the ER with stumps for arms. He had to turn away to vomit. Sometimes, he would wake up from a dream and could feel the desert heat as it scorched his lungs, and hear the echoes of morphine muffled screams.

The flight to Kuwait took twenty-four hours. Kathleen stepped off the plane and felt the shock wave from the desert heat; 111 degrees and climbing. They boarded a bus to Camp Buehring where they would wait until they caught their flight to Tikrit. She and Sam found adjoining bunks in one of the massive tents shared by the men and women waiting to be transported to Iraq. They dumped their gear and Sam guided her to the chow hall. "The food's good here. We call it The Last Chance Cafe."

They boarded a C-130 Air force cargo plane at 5:00 the next morning dressed in full battle gear; Kevlar helmets, body armor, and M9 automatic handguns. Their four duffel bags, stuffed full of personal and Army issued gear, were thrown on board alongside them. Sam leaned over and whispered, "Try not to shoot yourself in the foot with that pistol."

Kathleen quipped back, "I'm an expert marksman, if you didn't notice on the pistol range. I'll challenge you any day to see who can clean their M-9 the fastest."

Sam laughed to himself. *I think I guessed her wrong. I thought she was all shy, and no pun intended, I can see she can be a pistol.* He settled back in his seat and exchanged smiles with Kathleen.

They were part of the plane's cargo to Contingency Operating Base (COB) Speicher, a massive military base in Tikrit, Iraq. The flight took one hour and was uneventful, but the drive to the CSH, within Speicher, felt like a rocky road to hell.

Their driver was a young blond kid, not more than twenty. "Corporal Benson," he said. "Recovering from an IED." He held up his bandaged arm. "Got lucky on that one."

He sped along the gravel-covered roads at ninety miles an hour. "Corporal," Sam said. "Slow down. I think they want us alive, not dead."

"Sorry, sir, bit of a problem, sir. You're needed in the ER, now, not later. Here's the deal—I'm dropping you off at the ER. I'll take your gear up to your barracks. You're lucky you're bunking in one of the *real* buildings." He pointed to a bullet-ridden concrete structure. "I'll be back to pick you up later," he said as he slammed on the brakes in front of the building labeled Emergency Room.

Kathleen and Sam staggered into the ER, looking more like the wounded than staff. A male voice boomed from one of the trauma bays, "Sorry to do this to you, but we need the extra hands, desperately. Lock box up front for weapons. Jesus, you brought in half of the damn desert with you.

"Clean scrubs on the shelves." He waved a bloody, gloved hand to the corner of the ER. "Real bathroom is through that door. Bet you have to pee. Do it; it's your last chance for the day. Oh, and by the way, the bathroom is unisex."

The adrenaline kicked in and the exhaustion they had felt before from the time change and heat was gone. Kathleen and Sam were ready.

A supply convoy had been attacked and the ER was overwhelmed. They were in the thick of the organized chaos known as the CSH.

The Medevac helicopters had picked up eleven wounded, and landed with nine wounded and two dead. Kathleen and Sam joined the staff in the ER. Sam became part of the team treating a soldier with two broken legs and a head wound.

Kathleen was waved over by a burly major in his forties, with thick hands and fingers that looked like rough tree branches. She recognized his voice. He spoke in a gruff, booming manner, and she couldn't decide if he was angry or had smoked too many cigarettes.

"Mike Turner," he said. "I don't have time to teach you; watch and assist when asked."

The patient was a twenty-three year old sergeant, one leg blown off by an Improvised Explosive Device (IED), the other leg badly damaged. Kathleen observed and lent a hand when asked. She took in everything.

The sergeant was mumbling through his drug-induced state. Kathleen leaned over to listen. "Ma'am, my junk?" She lifted the small towel covering his genitals. She whispered, hoping no one else could hear, "Sergeant, your right leg is gone. You're going into surgery and we're not sure if we can save your other leg. Your junk is perfect and it's the finest junk I've ever had the privilege of seeing." He smiled before he was taken to the operating room.

Now she understood what Sam had been trying to tell her. "No matter what you've trained for, nothing—and I mean nothing—prepares you for what you will see, hear, and feel. Until you're in it, you can't know it."

She called it the day that refused to end. The floors were littered with discarded sponges, gauze, tape, pads, and rubber gloves. Scrubs and boots were stained a ghastly yellowish red from squirting bodily fluids. The ER had treated a female, twenty-six: second-degree burns covering forty percent of her total body surface. Male, nineteen, brain injury: required an emergency craniotomy before being transferred to Germany. Four amputations.

The minor injuries were triaged and waited to be treated. Some held the hands of their buddies after they were stabilized. Others, traumatized, sat in chairs with their heads in their hands. The chaplain moved deftly from gurney to gurney, finally settled on one of the chairs next to the troops with minor injuries, and began speaking in a soft, soothing tone.

The ER became still as the injured were moved to the Surgical Wing.

One of the nurses held the hand of a dead soldier. Hard sobs racked his body. One by one, the staff surrounded the gurney. Some cried, some said a prayer. They knew that for every one they could not save, someone thousands of miles away would get the dreaded knock on the door.

They lost three that day.

❀ ❀ ❀

Mike Turner motioned to her. "Follow me to the Surgical Wing. Have you done any amputations?"

Kathleen had to walk quickly to keep up with Mike's long strides. "Yes, during my residency in Baltimore. Primarily vascular."

"This is a different world. You're not starting with a whole limb and conditions aren't pristine. We've got a bilateral above the knee getting prepped. We'll talk while we scrub. Let me change that, I'll talk and you'll listen.

"There's a reality to this goddamn war. The body armor can't protect limbs. It saves lives, but you'll be doing too many amputations. It's those damn IEDs. Young kids, mostly. You're going to feel shitty about taking someone's arms and legs, even if you've saved their lives. You want to give them something back, and that's the damn best surgery possible.

"They'll do better and you'll feel less guilty if you do it right. You'll be taking something away—hopefully not their junk."

Kathleen's face flushed guiltily.

His voice softened. "Yeah, I heard you speak to that poor grunt in there. That was an act of kindness straight out of Florence Nightingale—nothing to be ashamed of. Keep it up. We were able to save his other leg. He's in the Intensive Care Unit, but I'll bet he wakes up with a smile. He'll be transferred to Landstuhl tomorrow. Visit him when we're done. He'll tell all his buddies about the beautiful doc who admired his junk and held his hand in the ICU.

"By the way, I requested you and Sam. I've worked with Sam before and I know all about you. You've got quite a reputation. You did a residency at Shock, but spent your days off assisting in surgery. When you did your Family Medicine residency, you spent your off time in obstetrics and gynecology. Female troops will be happy knowing you're here. Do you ever rest?"

Mike didn't pause for an answer. He spoke with the jackhammer cadence of a seasoned veteran who didn't suffer fools gladly—or at all.

"I'm going to do the amputations and you'll assist. When I think you're ready, we'll switch roles. You'll be working with me in surgery, whenever possible. I'm the senior doc and you're the new doc, at least as far as this experience is concerned. I'll bet you thought your interning days were over. Welcome to a parallel universe, Kathleen."

❀ ❀ ❀

Kathleen reached under her mattress, pulled out her journal, and thumbed through the sporadic entries. It was hard for her to believe that her year of deployment was almost over. As always, Gayle was right. Writing had helped to keep her in balance.

June 20, 2005 – *Mortar rounds struck near living quarters. Scared. We ate MREs in the bunker. I realized how much I want to live.*

July 4, 2005 – *Hot dogs and potato salad for breakfast. Insurgents wanted to celebrate the fourth, their way. Mostly, civilians brought in. Children injured by IEDs. What will happen to these kids now?*

August 7, 2005 – *Blast walls and desert surround us. We have some amenities, PX, hot food, and I am so grateful for the showers. Sometimes my uniforms are soaked in blood, my boots are beginning to turn a bloody black. Heat everywhere. Tired of feeling.*

September 10, 2005 – *Today was from outer space. I was holding a civilian's intestines in my hands, hoping they wouldn't get infected, praying that surgery could give him a chance at life. Half an hour later, I'm walking out of the ER and I'm on the phone talking to Gayle and Robert. For a second I imagine I'm back in LA. They ask me, "How are you?" and I can hear their air conditioner running in the background. I pray to God I can catch a breeze from it. What can I tell them? My team saved a twenty-one-year-old's life but he's burned over thirty percent of his body, and I can't get the image or smell of his blackened flesh out of my mind. Instead, I try to act as if everything is okay and say, "I'm fine, tell me what you're doing," because anything that sounds normal gives me some peace, even if it's only for a second. What am I feeling? Sick, pissed out of my mind at the waste.*

December 25, 2005 – *Big Xmas dinner flown in. Ham, turkey, the whole nine yards. Sam played Santa to the staff. Lots of care packages from home. We share; we are a family. I feel like going to church. I want to get on my knees and ask God, why, just why.*

January 1, 2006 – *Happy New Year! One of the docs got a box of cigars for Xmas and we sat outside smoking. First and last time for me, I threw up. Good group here. Just when you think you can't bear to hear another scream, someone comes by and touches you on the shoulder or smiles or tells a stupid joke. It's how we survive.*

February 8, 2006 – *Treated two insurgents today. I was worried I wouldn't be able to stay professional. I could.*

March 19, 2006 – *Sometimes, late at night, I hear crying coming from our sleeping quarters. The tears of men and women merge. How I long for privacy, to curl up and cry where no one else can hear.*

April 1, 2006 – *April Fools' jokes mingle with the sadness. We're shorthanded and everyone is pulling extra shifts. I've been assisting in surgery. Have to remember, our goal is to save a life… no matter what. But sometimes… I know it crosses everyone's mind at least once. I'm glad at times I can be a robot.*

May 6, 2006 – *Three-minute showers are a blessing, but oh, how I long for a hot bath. Don't complain. Don't even think you deserve it. Some you treat will never have a shower again.*

She picked up her pen and wrote:

May 25, 2006 – *Our replacements have arrived. I have learned so much about life in this year. I'm in awe of the extraordinary care and compassion by the medical staff. I'm humbled by the bravery of those who serve. Feeling? Grateful I was here.*

She closed her journal and tucked it safely under her mattress. She rested her head against the pillow and fell into a deep, dreamless sleep. Her pager went off. She read the text:

Mass casualties inbound. All docs to ER.

She laced her boots, gulped some water, and walked the hundred yards to the ER.

CHAPTER 11

Sam and Kathleen sat on one of the clean emergency tables, eating a long delayed lunch of turkey sandwiches. Kathleen lifted up the bread, thought, *this doesn't look bad,* and dug in.

"Did you ever think you'd be eating surrounded by this?" Sam gestured toward the bloody gauze and empty IVs scattered around the room.

Kathleen had trained herself to be oblivious to the tools of her trade when she wasn't on duty. "Surrounded by what? I don't think I'll be able to eat at a regular table again. You know, Sam, I don't think I've tasted food since we got here."

"Roger that," Sam replied. "I barely chew, let alone taste. Are you going to eat the rest of your chips? I'll trade you my cookies for 'em. Trade?"

"Trade."

Without looking Kathleen lobbed her half-empty bag of chips in Sam's general direction. Sam thumped a pair of stale cookies across the table toward Kathleen's thigh.

"We'll have to relearn how to eat. No restaurant will let us in with these manners. What's number one on your list when we get stateside?"

Kathleen didn't have to think long. "A twenty-four hour bath with lots and lots of bubbles, a glass of wine, all the chocolate I can eat, and grapes. I've been jonesing for ice-cold grapes ever since I got here. What's yours?"

"I'm ordering a porterhouse steak, rare, baked potato smothered in butter with tons of salt, and absolutely no vegetables. Are you going to spend any time with Gary?"

Kathleen took a long swig from her water bottle and swallowed hard. "Undecided right now. Hopefully, we'll get a few days together."

Sam nodded as medics came in to remove the hazardous waste. Iraqi janitors followed with mops and pails and began to clean around them.

They were finishing the last few crumbs of their sandwiches when they heard the commotion coming from the ER waiting room. They both jumped off the table at the same time. They looked at each other as if to say, "What the hell?"

From the moment they opened the door to the waiting room, everything began to move in slow motion. A corporal stood in the middle of the room, surrounded by tipped-over chairs and tables. His eyes bulged, froth spewed from his mouth, a steel bladed knife waved wildly in the air.

Kathleen thought she recognized him. Hadn't she treated him for stress yesterday? She had suspected post-traumatic stress disorder and had taken him off duty for a week with a referral to a psychiatric nurse.

There was that crazy moment when Kathleen believed she was the superhero from one of her childhood fantasies. Had that ever left her? She thought she could stop the archenemy that came disguised as a soldier high on drugs, screaming and wielding a knife.

Kathleen approached him, holding out her arms as if welcoming a friend. "Corporal Billings. Hi, remember me? It's Kathleen. We spent time together yesterday."

Everyone else in the room stood frozen. She spoke in a whisper, and for a moment he stopped. She took a tentative step closer. "Let me help you. Put down the knife and take my hand. We'll go inside and talk, just you and me."

He began to lower the knife; his eyes narrowed and his raspy voice cut across the room. "There's evil inside you." He rushed forward, his knife pointed at her chest. Sam tackled him, throwing his weight against him and pushing him off balance, but not before the knife struck deep into Kathleen's shoulder.

The staff grabbed him, pulling him off of Kathleen. Surgical sponges were thrust into Sam's hands and he applied pressure to the wound. Sam barked to the staff: "Get that son of a bitch out of here!" He turned to Kathleen. "Kathleen, look at me. Come on, don't close your eyes, keep looking at me."

Kathleen's eyelids began to flutter, then her eyes opened wide. "Sam?"

"I'm here," he said. "I'm here."

Two trauma nurses lifted her onto a gurney. They moved into the ER and began to work quickly, one cutting off her clothing and inserting a Foley catheter. The other placed a large bore IV in her left arm and another in her right foot. They kept their eyes focused on their job, trying to forget their patient was a friend they had been joking with a short time ago.

Sam stood next to the table, continuing to apply pressure to her wound. His jaw clenched, thoughts raced through his mind. *I should have moved faster, I should have told her to wait in the ER. I should have taken that knife for her.*

The ER began to fill with staff. Mike ran in from the makeshift gym, still wearing his shorts and tee. "Okay, Sam. We've got her. You need to step aside."

The sharp rasp of Mike's questions came dully to Kathleen's ears as he hastily put on surgical scrubs. Kathleen was responding, her voice losing strength with every word. "Lungs okay... just ate... can't feel arm or hand."

The nurse anesthetist came in and began his assessment. He talked calmly to Kathleen as they began to move her toward the surgical wing. "We'll take good care of you. Don't worry about the food in your stomach. You're going to be fine."

Kathleen was beginning to fade, frightened words tumbling out. "Sam, call Gary... have to get to Gary."

❀ ❀ ❀

It was the longest four hours Sam had ever spent. They moved Kathleen from the recovery room into the ICU. *Jesus*, he thought, *she looks like any other wounded soldier.*

But she wasn't: She was his sister in arms. The realization hurt.

Mike motioned to Sam and they walked out of the ICU. "It's always hardest when it's someone you know and respect." Mike looked down at the floor, his lower lip quivering. "I need a minute, Sam." He turned away to hide his anguished face. When he turned back, Sam could see the dots of moisture in the corners of his eyes. "I'm out after this tour. It's my third. Gets worse every time."

Mike cleared his throat. "The surgery went as planned, and we did what we could at this level of care. You know the drill. We repaired some of the blood vessels. Some were too damaged and we tied those off. We stopped the bleeding, and she's not in any immediate danger." Mike shook his head. "She was damn lucky. The knife missed her brachial artery, but there's damage to nerves and tendons. It's hard to say if she'll ever regain the full use of her arm and hand."

Mike fixed his eyes on Sam's and said, "I heard you're taking your leave to go to Landstuhl?"

Sam nodded. Bitter words spilled out of his mouth. "Our replacements are here. Perfect timing, huh?"

"I'm glad you can go. She's going to need you. I've sent Gary my report. He'll be running further tests to determine the extent of the damage. I know he's assembled one hell of a team and if anyone can make Kathleen whole, it's Gary."

Sam knew that the surgery done in the CSH was only the beginning of a long, hard road. He sat next to Kathleen, looking at the chest tube coming out of her side and the nasogastric tube leading from her nose. He placed his hand gently over her left arm, avoiding the IV lines.

Kathleen struggled to open her eyes. "Sam?"

"Right here."

"Gary?"

"All set."

She moaned a soft sound filled with pain. "Journal... under mattress ..."

Sam leaned closer to Kathleen. "I'll get it before we leave for Germany."

"We?"

"I'll be going with you. From here on in, I'm your shadow."

She remembered her helplessness. She was heavily sedated with her shoulder and arm immobilized. She was strapped to a litter, carried onto a C-17 and connected to monitors. She couldn't move, but sometimes she heard an out of control moan coming from deep inside. People in Halloween costumes kept coming over to take care of her. She tried to tell them she was sorry, she must have left her costume at home, but they didn't seem to understand her. Sometimes they held her hand and spoke in murmured tones. Sometimes they were silent and gave her something that made her sleep.

She tried to force her eyes open, but they didn't seem to work. She wanted to fight the drugs, fearful of where she was being taken. Had she died and was this the flight to Hell?

They landed at Ramstein Air Base at night. She managed to open her eyes to see halos, cast by angels, floating in the sky. This must be Heaven. She never thought there would be so much activity in Heaven: buses and ambulances, and people in uniforms. They lifted her into an ambulance and someone held her hand and touched her forehead. She squinted and saw an angel. The angel leaned over and whispered, "Hello, my sister." She tried to say something, but nothing came out. The angel talked to her again. "Remember the carousel ride?" He touched his lips to her forehead, an angel's kiss as soft as a feather floating in air.

Gary stayed with her until she was moved to her room. He kissed her forehead again. "Sleep now. Sam will stay with you tonight. Tomorrow will be a busy day."

❀ ❀ ❀

She was moving through time and space. Sometimes, a group of people stood around her. She was presenting a paper on how to amputate a leg. She was describing the procedure in detail, but was suddenly moved into a spaceship before she finished. She heard buzzing, clicking, and whirring sounds. Someone said MRI and CT Scan, but she couldn't remember what the words meant.

They took her back to her room and moved her into bed. She kept hearing someone groaning as the nurses got her settled. They kept saying they were sorry and they were almost done, but she thought they were talking to another patient. She slept until her drug haze gradually cleared, and she began to feel in touch with reality. Gary was standing next to her bed; she managed a weak, "Hi."

"Welcome back. We had to keep you sedated for the tests. How's your pain level?"

She spoke hoarsely. "Okay. No more drugs, please."

"As few as necessary."

"Please. I was hallucinating."

"Have I ever told you you're a pain in the ass? Do you want your bed raised a little?"

"Yes, to both questions. Sam?"

"I sent him to get some air and food. He'll be back soon."

Gary held her hand. "We always promised to be honest with each other. Here's your situation. You have moderate to severe damage to tendons and nerves. Mike did a good job on your blood vessels, but we'll need to do some repair work. My team is scheduled to operate tomorrow morning, six o'clock. You're looking at eight to twelve hours of surgery. It's a slow, delicate procedure. I've spent the last couple of years gathering a team of the best specialists, anywhere.

"We can repair the damage, but you're looking at a long recovery. You'll need months of physical therapy and even then, we can't predict when or if you'll get the full use of your arm and hand. I've requested an extended stay for you at Landstuhl. The best physical therapist is right here; her name's Helen. You met her, but you kept talking about aliens and spaceships."

Kathleen wanted to be as brave as the troops she had treated. They carried their wounds, more severe than hers, with such dignity. She owed it to them. "Gary, I can take the pain. I don't want pain medication."

"Trust me on this. I can't have you thrashing around, undoing our fine work. You'll be in the ICU for three to four days, then we'll gradually wean you away from the meds."

Kathleen sighed. She knew Gary was right. "Gayle and Robert?"

"I spoke to them, and they'll be here by the time you're out of the ICU. Any other questions?"

"Yeah. Is there someone special in your life?"

"Are you sure you aren't hallucinating?" He smiled and spoke softly. "Yes, and don't ask me who. If he wants you to know, he'll stop by and wink."

The door opened and a round-faced woman in her forties, wearing scrubs decorated with teddy bears, stood in the doorway. She was wholesomely pretty, with dancing hazel eyes, shoulder-length auburn hair, and a pleasingly plump figure. Helen projected natural warmth that immediately made Kathleen feel better.

Gary said, "Hi, Helen. Look who's back from outer space. Kathleen, I'd like you to meet Helen. After me, she's your way back."

Helen walked over to Kathleen and held her hand. "Dr. Morales has you sitting up," she shot a mildly disapproving look at Gary, "and I'll bet you're starting to feel nauseous."

"I am, a little," Kathleen admitted.

"Well, then," said Helen. "I'm going to lay you down almost flat and get you some ginger ale." She turned to Gary. "Okay with you, Dr. M.?"

Gary grinned. "I'll fetch it myself."

CHAPTER 12

Helen expected to find Kathleen alone and was surprised to see three people standing around her bed. It was unusual for patients to have visitors so quickly, but there they were, a worried-looking couple and a man in fatigues.

The couple introduced themselves as Gayle and Robert Sutherland. The man in fatigues told Helen his name was Sam. They shook hands. Helen felt warmth and caring from Gayle and Robert, but felt something different when she touched Sam's hand. For a moment their eyes met, and Helen felt an instant attraction. Sam loved the woman in the hospital bed, but was not in love with her. Helen could tell.

Helen leaned over and stroked Kathleen's forehead, softly calling her name. Kathleen struggled to open her eyes. "Hi, Kathleen. You've been moved from the ICU, and you're in your room. You have visitors."

Kathleen's eyes moved toward Gayle, Robert, and Sam. She mouthed Gayle's name. Gayle walked over and used a tissue to wipe Kathleen's eyes. "What is it, Baby?"

Before her eyelids fluttered and closed, she said, "Next room, next room."

Gayle looked at Helen. "Do you know what she meant?"

"I don't know how she would know, but there's a young girl in the next room. Brought in late last night. Kathleen may have heard her crying when she was transferred from the ICU. I think she wants you to comfort her."

"I'll go in. How bad is she?"

"She may not walk again. It would be wonderful for you to spend time with her, but you all look exhausted, and you're not going to do anyone any good by being here."

Sam spoke as if there was cotton in his mouth. "We don't want to leave Kathleen alone."

"Why not take turns? Sam, how about if you take the first watch? Robert and Gayle, do you have a hotel room?"

They nodded.

"I think you should go to the hotel, get some rest, and come back in four or five hours," Helen suggested. "Kathleen is still sedated, and they'll be bringing her out of it gradually. My guess is she'll be sleeping for at least the next six hours. I want to remind you, this is not a five-k race. It's a marathon. The staff is awesome and nurses will be coming in frequently. I'll come back and check on her every couple of hours, as well.

"I'm going to spend some time with Stephanie in the next room. The word is she has no family. Gayle, I'll let the nurses know you'll be visiting later on."

Helen commandeered a recliner from the visitor's room. Sam could doze on his watch, and she felt she was beginning to take care of him.

❀ ❀ ❀

Helen returned to find Kathleen in a deep sleep, and Sam appearing more tired than ever. When Helen came into the room, Sam stood up chivalrously; and she liked that. To add to his cottonmouth, his eyes were now red and bloodshot.

Helen walked over to Kathleen's bed and held her hand. "Has she been awake?"

Sam shook his head. "Once in a while she opens her eyes, but it only lasts for a moment. I'm surprised we haven't met before, Helen. I've been in and out Kathleen's room in the ICU for days."

"I sneak in for a few minutes, usually in the early morning hours. The nurses let me roam the halls. I used to be one of them, before I fell in love with physical therapy. My kids need to know I'm around."

"Kids? Doesn't that baby them?"

"Sometimes I have to reach beneath the uniform and the bravado to get to their pain. To me, they are all boys and girls."

Sam hesitated. "Helen, would you have coffee with me?"

"Have you eaten today?"

"Someone brought coffee and doughnuts."

"I'm off in about an hour. My apartment's in town, and you look like you could use a real meal."

Helen fixed her "super salad." She was sure it could cure anything, including fatigue and love sickness. The salad, overflowing with vegetables, along with roasted chicken and fresh pumpernickel bread, became their dinner. They fell into a comfortable rhythm of conversation, as if they had known each other for years, not hours.

"Sam, you look as if you're ready to collapse. Where are you staying?"

"I've got a room at a hotel, but I need to find some other quarters. I've got a thirty-day leave and I just need a place to crash."

"I'm gone most of the time and this little beauty," she patted the couch they were sitting on, "opens into a bed. It's yours to use for as long as you want."

CHAPTER 13

She had lost weight since her injury and the confidence that had built up over the years evaporated. The outside began to match the inside and the muscles she had developed, atrophied. Now, she felt and looked like the lonely child who spent years in foster care.

~ Boston, 1980 ~

The social worker, Mrs. Martin, was taking twists and turns into unfamiliar parts of Boston. Kathleen tried to remember she was a big girl, almost nine years old and shouldn't cry. She sat in the front passenger seat with her hands covering her ears, hoping she would stop hearing her brother Devon begging her not to leave.

Mrs. Martin stopped at a drive-through and ordered hamburgers, fries, and Cokes. While they waited for their order, Mrs. Martin said, "I think you'll enjoy living with Mrs. Adams. She'll be your foster mother for a while."

Kathleen remained silent wondering how long is "for a while." She didn't want to know if it might mean forever.

They sat in the car, eating their lunch. In spite of how much she hurt, Kathleen had to admit it was the best lunch she had had in a long time.

❀ ❀ ❀

Mrs. Adams lived in a dingy frame house, in dire need of painting, on a squalid street, filled with vacant, dilapidated houses and overgrown, empty lots. Mrs. Adams opened the door and smiled, her lips held tightly together. "Whom do we have here?" she said, widening her grin as she looked at Kathleen. "What is your name, dear?" Kathleen had to fight her revulsion at the sight of the missing teeth in Mrs. Adams' now wide maw.

"Kathleen, ma'am."

"How old are you, Kathleen?"

"Almost nine, ma'am."

"Oh, my, what a polite child. Do you have a nickname, dear?"

"No ma'am, just Kathleen."

"Well, Kathleen, let me show you to your room."

Mrs. Adams held onto the shaky banister and climbed the squeaky stairs. Kathleen watched as Mrs. Adams lumbered up each step and thought, *if an elephant wore a muumuu with bright red flowers, it would look just like Mrs. Adams.*

Mrs. Adams turned the antique glass knob on the sickly green door, which opened with a spooky coffin-lid sound. A fusty smell assaulted Kathleen's nose. "This will be your bedroom," said Mrs. Martin, smiling. "What a lucky girl to have your own room. Why, it even has a desk for you to do your homework on."

Kathleen looked at the room, with cowboy wallpaper and a matching spread. *A boy's room*, she thought dejectedly. *Someday I'll have a really pretty room with pink flowers on the wall.*

❀ ❀ ❀

From physician to patient, it was so strange to be on the other side of the bed, looking up instead of down. When the nurses asked her to rate her pain on a scale from one to ten, she said two, and smiled. They gave her over-the-counter acetaminophen. She gritted her teeth, and suppressed her tears.

She couldn't chance any dependency on medication. *That's all I need,* she thought. *An ER physician with a record of prescription pain medications and limited use of my arm and hand.* She felt the mark of Cain branded across her forehead.

The psychologist from Gary's team came in to talk to her and do an assessment. Kathleen managed to chat casually while denying most of the symptoms listed on the military's post-traumatic stress disorder (PTSD) checklist.

Images of the CSH kept returning, and she began to shake when she heard the rattle-rattle of the meal cart coming down the corridor to her room. The sound reminded her of used instruments thrown into soiled instrument trays as the staff worked on the wounded and dying. She didn't want to be labeled with PTSD but she had all the symptoms and in her heart she knew.

The nightmares came every night: angry, black nightmares about her childhood. She couldn't stop them and she couldn't shake them.

"Kathleen, wake up, you're having a nightmare." Helen turned on the light to her room and Kathleen woke to see Helen holding a medication cup.

Kathleen gasped and grabbed Helen's arm. "Helen, what are you doing here?"

"I was called in earlier by the nursing staff. You've been having nightmares every night, and you're giving them a hard time about taking your sleep medication. I've seen lots of troops trying not to take their meds. Toughing it through won't bring anyone back. You need it now; don't force us to find another way to give it to you." Helen leaned toward Kathleen's ear and added in a curt whisper, "Do you know your screams are waking other patients?"

Kathleen collapsed against the pillow. "Oh God, Helen, don't be mad at me. I'm sorry; I thought I could fight them."

"You can't fight every battle at the same time. One battle at a time, and right now, I want to see you fighting to get the use of your arm and hand back. Promise me, you'll take the meds every night before you go to sleep. If you can't rest, you can't heal."

"I promise." Kathleen reached for the cup and swallowed the pills. "Helen, I'm scared. Will you stay with me for a few minutes until I get sleepy?"

Helen felt that old familiar tug at her heartstrings when one of her babies needed her. "Wild horses couldn't drag me away," she said, and taking Kathleen's hand, eased down beside her.

Tests and examinations showed Kathleen was healing. She was regaining some motion in her arm, but couldn't open or close her hand. Everyone applauded her progress and told her to be patient. Her depression wound its way throughout her body. She was tired of trying and longed to curl up in a ball and sleep the day away.

Sam came in, looking rested. "Wanna play hooky for the day?"

"You're kidding. Did you talk to God?"

"Almost. Talked to Gary and Helen. They both agreed. Helen told me about this great park next to a lake. We won't have another chance. I've got orders to report to Fort Bragg."

Kathleen knew that Sam could get his orders at any time, but this felt too soon.

"Sam, I'm going to miss you. I don't have the words..."

"We don't always need words. How about a hug?"

Kathleen was a child let out of the strictest parochial school. She sat in the back seat of the car and watched as Sam drove and Helen acted as co-pilot and tour guide. Today would be about the moment—no injury, no hand that wouldn't open or close, and no nightmares.

Tour guide Helen said, "We're taking a short detour. I want you to see Nanstein Castle. Sam, stop here," she ordered. "Let's get out of the car; this will give us a great view."

Kathleen was taken away with the beauty of the ancient castle looming high above Landstuhl. Once needed as a protector for the city, it now provided incredible views of the storybook town below. Helen and Sam seemed more interested in each other than the view; sly looks and engaging smiles told Kathleen of their attraction. Like a child, she crossed her fingers, closed her eyes, and spoke a silent wish for their dreams to come true.

Narrow winding streets led them out of Landstuhl, toward the Palatinate Forest. The road curled around white painted buildings with red and brown roofs. The sidewalks were busy with men and women shopping for groceries or dining at outdoor cafes. They drove past regal hotels with lush green lawns and gushing fountains, and businesses with brightly colored flowers planted in weathered boxes. A train whistle echoed through the Palatinate Forest and followed them to the lake.

Kathleen stepped out of the car and breathed in the fresh country air. She smiled at Helen, balancing blankets and cushions, while Sam carried thermoses and an over-packed lunch basket. They sat under the pine trees, eating slowly, taking in the scenery, and enjoying small talk.

Sam moved closer to Helen and put his arm around her. He cleared his throat. "Since I've been here I, um... Helen and I have discovered how much we mean to each other, and we don't want to waste another moment being apart." Sam looked at Helen. "We're in love, and we've decided to retire, so we can spend the rest of our lives together. We wanted you to be the first to know: We're getting married!"

Kathleen scribbled in her journal with her left hand.

January 2, 2007 – *Going to Walter Reed in four days. More tests scheduled for today. Why can't I bend my hand? Crying.*

Gary took her out to lunch. She felt as if she was twenty-one and she and Gary were on a pretend date. They sat at a quiet table toward the back of an Italian restaurant. I hope you don't mind eating Italian food in Germany. I know how much you like lasagna, and well, this is one of my favorite places.

"Let's start with some minestrone soup and, as your doctor, I'm ordering wine—for medicinal purposes only, of course."

"Thanks, Gary—not only for lunch, but for everything."

"Hey, you're the girl who cleaned my bug-infested apartment. The least I could do is give you an arm and hand that works—well, sort of works." Gary became serious and held her hand. "You have PTSD written all over you, and you haven't fooled anyone. We can't force you to confess, and I can understand why you don't want to be labeled. When you get home, talk to someone off the record. Wear a Groucho Marx disguise, give a phony name, but deal with it.

"I couldn't hope for better results from your tests, but you're still healing. Let's see, I've known you for what now? Eighteen years. You can't pull the wool over my eyes. I know you have more pain than you'll admit to. On a scale of one to ten, my guess is you're at a six or seven. It's from regenerating nerves and will probably last another six months, maybe longer. No medal for this kind of bravery. You know it can be treated. Think about it when you get to Walter Reed.

"The first six months after this type of injury are critical, and you've done better than I expected." Gary paused and kissed Kathleen's hand. "I wish I could give you a guarantee."

She smiled. "No guarantees in life, ever."

The waiter brought their soup and set a third place at the table. Kathleen looked puzzled.

Gary laughed. "Oh, honey, you've been out of circulation way too long. Look around."

She hadn't noticed. Same gender couples, talking quietly, some holding hands. She shook her head. "I wasn't aware; it's all so open and casual. So Gary, it isn't *just* the Italian food that makes this your favorite restaurant, is it? But why the third setting?"

"You'll see. Eat your soup before it gets cold."

They sat quietly, Kathleen eating with her left hand, Gary barely eating at all. Gary stood up, walked toward the door, and was joined by another man. They returned to the table. "Kathleen, this is David Clement."

"Hello, Kathleen, it's good to meet you." He smiled, sat down, looked at her and winked.

❀ ❀ ❀

She was disappointed, not in Gary or the staff, but in herself. She could lift her arm, but couldn't hold a fork. She could put her arm in a shirt, but not button it. See a therapist? She wasn't walking into that one. She wanted the past to be where it belonged, buried.

There was a knock on the door and Helen walked in, carrying a massage table. "Thought you might want an extra massage. Out on the floor, we only have about twenty minutes. That's barely a beginning for a real massage."

Before she had a chance to say no, Helen, humming softly, unfolded the table and covered it with a sheet. Helen helped her onto the table, undressing and covering her in the same brisk moment.

Thank you for pretending that modesty still exists, Kathleen thought.

"I'm using Rosemary oil. It's got a pungent scent, but it's good for blood circulation to your arms and legs." Helen drew the sheet down to Kathleen's waist and started to massage her neck, shoulders, and upper back.

Kathleen sighed as she began to relax. "It's quiet on the floor tonight."

"I'll bet you forgot. There's a magic show going on in the group room. We've got the floor to ourselves." Helen moved Kathleen's arms alongside her head. "You could have gone, you know."

Kathleen shook her head. She was drowsy and her words came out slower, thicker. "Is there still magic in the world?"

Helen didn't answer, but began to change the intensity of her massage. "Let me know if this is too much." Helen was going deeper, searching, finding muscles that felt like rocks. "You're carrying all your tension in your shoulders."

Kathleen gasped at the fierceness of the pain. It shot downward: from her shoulder, to her arm, to her hand. Her hand was on fire.

She gasped again, but Helen didn't release the pressure.

Kathleen moaned. The moan tore through her and echoed throughout the empty halls. She was a circus acrobat, dangling from a high wire without a net. She clutched the wire with her fists and squeezed, terrified she would fall to her death.

Helen opened Kathleen's fist and put her hand in Kathleen's. She urged, "Squeeze, Kathleen, squeeze." Kathleen was sobbing; she had no control of her hand, but she felt it squeezing as if Helen was the magician and her only connection to life.

❀ ❀ ❀

D-day finally arrived. Helen opened the door to her room, holding a large bag in her hands. "Supplements," she said. "I ordered these for you. Directions are inside, and make sure you take them. They'll be bringing a wheelchair for you in a few minutes."

Kathleen put her arms around Helen. "I don't know how to thank you for everything. You and Sam are perfect together, and I'm happy for both of you."

"You take care of yourself," Helen said with a catch in her voice.

When they broke the embrace, Kathleen's smiling lips trembled as she said, "Helen, I want you to see something." She held out her right hand and made a slight fist. "Look, it bends."

If Landstuhl was boot camp, Walter Reed was maneuvers. She was used to the different types of physical therapy, but the mandatory group therapy had her spinning. They sat in a circle, eight of them. Some brought their own chairs—wheelchairs that would be theirs, in some cases, for the rest of their lives. *They're so young*, Kathleen thought. She felt like a chaperone at the senior prom. They were boys and girls, proud of having served, but trying to make sense out of what happened. Struggling to find a new identity, knowing they would never be the same.

Kathleen was racked with self-doubt. *I've only seen them wounded, lying down, having to look at body parts, not always at the whole person, making quick decisions. Did I make the right ones?* She questioned the praise and respect her colleagues had heaped on her for her medical skills, now fallen into disuse, maybe never to be recovered. She felt guilty that perhaps she could have done more for those who died.

Sometimes the kids talked about their families, their sweethearts. What would it be like when they were no longer part of the military and had to face life as a civilian? Would they be stared at when they went to the grocery store? Would they have a flashback at a restaurant? Would anyone really understand?

It was her time to share. What could she possibly say? That her hand wasn't perfect? Oh shit, the Marine who sat next to her didn't have hands.

Should she tell them that she was tortured because she saved someone's life, but now he doesn't have a face? Had she done too much? She had taken an oath to preserve life and she had honored her oath. But what about the end results?

Anything she could offer would sound like a sob story, and these people had been through enough without listening to that kind of crap.

She sat quietly, tried to listen attentively, and when it was her turn to speak, she managed to mutter, "Everything's pretty good. I'm making progress."

The staff at her discharge planning meeting thought she was ready to continue treatment on an outpatient basis. She had regained some mobility in her hand, but the fine coordination that she needed as a physician was slow in returning. She knew and they knew, perhaps it never would. Her career in the Army was over and she would not be returning to duty.

Kathleen wanted to go home and be with Gayle and Robert. She needed to sleep in her own bed and try to sort things out. Her life would be as a civilian physician with undiagnosed PTSD and limited use of her hand. Her options appeared dismal.

❀ ❀ ❀

She had a break of two hours between lunch and occupational therapy. Kathleen thought of it as naptime. Her floor would be quiet except for the sounds of patients sleeping, exhausted after a morning of intense therapy. She was sitting on her bed reading when she felt her head begin to nod. She saw herself, as a young girl, working in the garden with Mrs. Roth.

~ Boston, 1984 ~

It promised to be a hot and humid summer day. Kathleen and Mrs. Roth began to weed the vegetable garden early in the day while the sun was still low in the sky. Kathleen wore a large floppy hat and a red bandana to shield her fair skin from the sun. She worked steadily, but every once in a while she glanced up at Mrs. Roth. Her gray hair and eyes that squinted in the sunlight reminded Kathleen of a small bird looking for a juicy worm for breakfast.

Mrs. Roth always wore long-sleeved blouses, but today, her sleeve inched its way up her arm. Kathleen saw something she had never seen before: blurry blue numbers on Mrs. Roth's arm. Kathleen tried not to stare but her eyes remained fixed.

Mrs. Roth stopped weeding and wiped her forehead with her bandana. "My goodness, it's getting hot. We should get out of the sun and have some lemonade."

Kathleen smiled and relaxed. Mrs. Roth made the best lemonade she had ever tasted.

They sat on the glider on the porch, sipping their tangy drinks. Kathleen had learned many things from Mrs. Roth. For instance, you don't need to gulp your drink because there will always be more. She also sensed from the way Mrs. Roth swung them in the glider, humming a bygone tune, that she was probably getting ready to tell a story, but she had to wait patiently until the story had "cooked" and Mrs. Roth was ready to serve it.

After a few minutes Mrs. Roth picked up her needlepoint and spoke gently. "I saw you looking at the numbers on my arm."

Kathleen blushed. "I'm sorry, I didn't mean to stare."

"You didn't do anything wrong. You were curious and that's a good thing. Now I am going to tell you a story of how I got those numbers. Do you remember in class when we talked about World War II and the Holocaust?"

Kathleen nodded.

"I was a child when World War II began. I lived in Athens, Greece, with my family. My father and grandfather were both doctors and I was to become a doctor, as well. From the time I was a little girl my father took me from village to village, and taught me all that he knew. I watched as he examined patients, using his skills and intuition. First, he would listen to their heart with a stethoscope or check their breathing by resting his ear against their back. Then he would close his eyes and touch their body. His touch told him what was wrong, and he healed many patients this way.

"My father taught me how to take perfect stitches, and by the time I was eleven, I could take the smallest stitches on wounds without leaving a scar. Even though I was a child, parents wanted me to sew up their children's wounds. After all, no parent wants their child to have scars.

"When I was thirteen..." She paused and looked at Kathleen. "I was your age when the Germans took control of Athens. All the Jews had to register their names and my family was sent to Auschwitz. Do you know about Auschwitz?"

"Yes, Mrs. Roth, it was a concentration camp. We saw a photo of it in our history book."

Mrs. Roth nodded. "When we arrived, we were separated and I was tattooed with the numbers you saw on my arm. But, that is only the beginning of my story.

"A German officer saw me and waved me over. I was so very frightened. He took me to his house where there were several other girls my age. He asked me if I knew how to sew. I understood German and told him I could sew and stitch wounds. That interested him. He said, 'You will stay here and help with the wounded soldiers. I have a daughter your age and I hope someone is looking after her.' That German officer saved my life. For the next nine months, I helped care for the wounded. Do you know what I discovered?"

Kathleen shook her head.

"They were the same as you and me. They cried from their pain and they asked for their mommies. Even though they were killers, I learned to forgive them and feel for their humanness." Mrs. Roth paused. "I believe there is a lesson to be learned from every experience, even the painful ones. You see, Kathleen, we can't always choose the things that happen to us. We can let them destroy us, or we can let them make us stronger."

Mrs. Roth picked up her glass of lemonade. "It's like this lemonade. It's sweet and a little tart at the same time. How do we make lemonade?"

"From lemons, then we add water and..." Kathleen paused, concerned about giving away Mrs. Roth's lemonade secret. She lowered her voice. "We use agave instead of sugar. That gives it the special taste."

Mrs. Roth sat back in the glider and smiled. "Yes, and agave comes from the cactus plant. From something sour, like the lemon, and something prickly, like the cactus, we make the most wonderful drink." Mrs. Roth picked up the glass of lemonade and drank. "So satisfying on a hot day. The numbers on my arm are a reminder of the cruelty that exists in the world. They are also a reminder of the kindness that lives alongside the cruelty."

The light in Kathleen's hospital room brightened until everything seemed clearer; more focused. Mrs. Roth stood in front of her and smiled. "Sewing saved my life. Perhaps it can save yours."

Kathleen came to herself with a start. Had she been dreaming?

She called Gayle and left a message on her phone: "Gayle, I'm going to start outpatient therapy in Los Angeles, probably in a couple of weeks. In my room, top shelf of the closet, is a sewing kit. Would you send it to me, overnight?"

She kept her embroidery and needlepoint with her, wherever she went. She thought of Mrs. Roth every time the needle missed the canvas and stuck her fingers.

She remembered the words she heard from Mrs. Roth on that hot summer day. “Sometimes, bad things happen. We don’t always understand why, but perhaps they are sent to us for a reason. It may be that we are meant to go in a different direction and find a new purpose in life.”

PART TWO

The Road to Canfield

CHAPTER 14

Kathleen settled into a new routine, living with Gayle and Robert in Los Angeles, and spending three days a week at the Veteran's Hospital.

She changed into her bathing suit when she arrived and joined the group for aquatic therapy. She used the resistance bells and gradually moved from 40 percent resistance to 80 percent. Her shoulder was gaining mobility and strength. After showering and changing back into her street clothes, she took the elevator to the third floor and stepped into the world of occupational therapy. There were aids for everything: a hook to help her button a shirt, shoes without laces, and even a zipper pull.

She spent time in the practice kitchen learning to make her own lunches. She began by opening the cupboard and taking out a plastic plate. Beads of sweat covered her forehead as she learned to use a set of curved-handle utensils, designed for her limited hand movement. Her sandwiches were a disaster; the bread tore, peanut butter was lumped in the center, and jelly oozed out from every corner. She wanted to throw her lunch across the room, scream, "Fuck this," and walk out. Instead she sat at one of the tables next to a veteran with traumatic brain injury. He stared at the utensils, trying to remember which was a knife, which was a fork. Despite her handicap, she managed to cut her sandwich, mangling it in the process, and shared it with him. He brought a smushed piece to his mouth and smiled vacantly at her compassion.

Kathleen progressed to loading and unloading the dishwasher. She removed the dishes one at a time, telling her brain to send messages to her hands: *Flex your wrist and bend your fingers to lift a plate. Curve your fingers to remove a glass. Grasp tightly around the silverware and lift.* She dropped the dishes, silverware scattered across the room, and glasses hit the floor. She picked each piece up, reloaded the dishwasher, and started over. Now she knew why plastic was invented.

Everyone applauded when she unloaded the dishwasher without dropping anything. She became aware of a new sensation running through her body. She called it hope.

❀ ❀ ❀

Kathleen and Robert passed the Chinese food take-out cartons between them. She focused on her dinner plate, then raised her eyes to meet Robert's. She wanted to show him; she wanted Robert to be proud of her. A shy smile played across her face. "I can empty the dishwasher."

"Great! You empty, I'll sit back and watch."

Okay, hand, she commanded mentally, *flex your wrist and bend your fingers.*

Plastic dishes would scoot across the floor, sometimes bouncing. Gayle's dishes shattered, a collage of scattered pieces spilling across the kitchen floor.

She stood shaking and crying, a little girl terrified of being punished. She couldn't stop. Something warm and wet trickled between her legs.

She sobbed, "I wet myself."

"That's okay, honey. You just got scared."

"I'm sorry, I'm sorry!" She was fairly bawling now. "Don't be mad at me."

Robert put his arms around her and held her. "I'm not mad at you."

"I broke Gayle's dishes."

He spoke softly as if talking to a young child. "Gayle won't care. She has more dishes than we can ever use." As if to demonstrate, Robert picked up one of the unbroken dishes and dropped it. Their eyes stood fixed as the plate made contact with the hard floor and shattered into small pieces.

Kathleen stopped crying and looked at Robert. "We're both in trouble now."

"Partners in crime, that's who we are. Say, I have an idea. I think we should fill the tub with warm water and scented oils. You can soak until you're sleepy. Do you like that idea?"

She did.

Gayle bought puzzles, large wooden pieces with handles, made for a young child's hands. Kathleen marked her progress by the number of pieces in the puzzle. As the number of pieces increased, their size decreased, and she knew her dexterity was improving.

Robert bought her a suturing kit. "When you're ready."

She stared at the kit. It was the same one she had used as a premed student. She couldn't open the box. How could she take stitches? She screamed and threw the kit across the floor. Robert picked it up and put it back on the table. "Next time I want you to count to ten. If you still want to throw it, use your right hand."

She stopped taking her sleep medication and joined "the association of nightmares."

Her nightmare was always the same. It claimed victory by possessing her dreamscape, until she woke up screaming.

She stood in the middle of a smoldering burn pit in Iraq. Trucks filled with surgical and hospital waste formed a long line outside the pit. The trucks moved, one by one, forming a circle around the crater. They began to drop amputated limbs and blood-soaked linens around her. No one saw her. She choked on the caustic smoke. She couldn't breathe. She tried to scream. Nothing came out. She wanted to run, but her feet were stuck. The ground began to sink beneath her. She was swallowed up. She was buried alive.

Gayle heard Kathleen's screams and flew to her bedroom. She sat on the edge of the bed and began to bring Kathleen out of her night terror. She spoke soothingly, as a mother speaks to a frightened child, aware that her tone was more important than her words. Murmured phrases, spoken late at night, meant to erase a horror that could only be imagined.

"Kathleen, it's okay, you're safe. Nothing can hurt you. I'm right here." Gayle repeated the words and prayed they would cross the barrier into Kathleen's nightmare world.

Kathleen opened her eyes. Gayle saw the vacant stare that told her Kathleen was still in her night terror. Gayle lifted her into a sitting position and propped her up with pillows.

Kathleen fought for air, gasping at every breath. She leaned against Gayle, whimpering and finally sobbing.

Gayle rubbed her back. "Good girl, let it all out."

Kathleen spoke huskily, "Gayle?"

"I'm here. More of the same?"

Kathleen nodded.

Gayle's hands became damp from Kathleen's sweat soaked T-shirt. Gayle whispered, "I'm going to get you a dry shirt."

Still groggy from being awakened, Gayle shuffled to the chest of drawers, prepared to carry out the nightly ritual. She steadied herself against the furniture and wiped her tears with the sleeve of her gown. The ticking of the grandfather clock floated from the living room to the bedroom. The striking chimes became a reminder of the late hour. She focused for a moment before returning to Kathleen and handing her a T-shirt, emblazoned—incongruously for the situation—with a yellow happy face.

"I'm going to make some chamomile tea and get the heat pack for your shoulder," said Gayle as cheerily as she could manage.

Kathleen hugged her knees and buried her face. Her hair fell over the blanket, giving the appearance of a turtle hiding from danger. Her head felt fuzzy and her thoughts were like pieces to an unfinished puzzle, without organization.

As Kathleen began to move away from the night terror place, other fears invaded the empty space. She could manage the days, but when the light faded and darkness crept in, the feeling of living in a horror movie began to surface. She was held prisoner in a crumbling, many-gabled old manse, surrounded by monsters. She heard eerie, discordant music playing in the background, subtly warning her that death was around the corner. As she came closer, the music increased in intensity until it reached a horrific climax. It was too late. She was destroyed.

Gayle returned and put the tea on the table next to the bed. She placed the hot pack over Kathleen's shoulder and watched as she relaxed. "Ready for your tea?" she asked.

Kathleen shifted her weight and reached with both hands. "Thanks. Did I wake Robert?"

"No, that man could sleep through a seven-point earthquake."

"I woke you, again." Kathleen sighed. "I'm sorry. I've really messed up your life."

"You haven't messed up my life and don't you ever be sorry. Robert and I thank God every night that you're safe and at home with us. Now, we both need to get some sleep. Can I get you anything else before I go back to bed?"

"My needlepoint."

Gayle held the canvas with a little kitten stamped on the surface. It was a child's first attempt; crooked stitches, dropped stitches. She held Kathleen's hands and turned them over to see fingers riddled with needle pricks. "I'm so proud of you for not giving up. The next one will be better. Maybe you'd like to try one with flowers."

Kathleen handed Gayle the cup and settled into her pillows.

Gayle smoothed the blankets and tucked Kathleen in. "Do you want me to leave the lamp on?"

Kathleen spoke in a soft voice. "Yes, please. Gayle, I'm so scared of the dark. Do you think I'm being a baby?"

"We all have our fears. It's good when you know what they are and brave when you can admit to them."

❀ ❀ ❀

Gayle returned to the bedroom she shared with Robert. The clock told her most of the night had slipped away.

Robert was reading a book, as he often did during these sleepless nights. "How is she?"

"Concerned she disturbed your sleep."

"I hope you told her I can sleep through anything."

"I did." Gayle got back into bed and, seeking a sense of comfort, moved tightly against Robert. "I can't stand to watch her go through these nightmares, over and over. She's fragile, and I'm worried these night terrors will break her."

Robert wrapped his arms around Gayle and held her protectively. "Don't forget, the psychologist at Landstuhl predicted this. We have to hold onto our faith in her and in ourselves."

"I know you're right. I've seen this in patients, but this is our..."

"Daughter?" Robert massaged Gayle's back, applying pressure to a knot. "Do you remember the first time Kathleen came here? She was so shy; we could barely hear her knock on the door. Then you opened your arms and she leaned her head against you. She didn't just walk into our home; she walked into our hearts. I promise not to let anything bad happen to her. I know how much you love her."

"It isn't just me who loves her, is it?"

"No. She's my girl, too."

❀ ❀ ❀

Gayle opened the kitchen windows, feeling the morning breeze touch her face. She picked up the single rose and the love note from Robert. Gayle held the white rose close to her face, greeting the fragrance as it wafted to meet her. The scent reminded her of the face powder her mother used when she was a child. She treasured the memories of those sweet days, when resting against her mother's breast and being rocked could wash all her worries away. Gayle read Robert's love note, tucked it away in the pocket of her slacks, knowing she would glance at it throughout the day.

Gayle made waffles, heated the syrup and melted the butter. Kathleen walked into the kitchen with the morning newspaper and laid it on the table. Gayle served the waffles and poured two steaming mugs of strong coffee. It was a routine they shared every morning.

Kathleen sat down, looked at Gayle, and smiled shyly. Gayle pretended not to understand. "What?" she asked, feigning irritation.

Kathleen, still smiling, responded, "Nothing."

It was their secret code for, "Thanks" and "I love you."

Kathleen and Gayle sat at the kitchen table, eating breakfast and sharing bits and pieces of information from the newspaper with a rhythm that spoke of familiarity and ease. Their hands touched briefly as they shuffled the paper between them. Gayle's hands, the color of lightly toasted bread and no longer as plump and smooth as they once were, contrasted against Kathleen's, which bespoke an Irish heritage and a much younger woman. Every so often they would glance up and smile as their eyes met; two women, so different in appearance, yet tightly connected by an unbreakable thread woven through time.

Gayle stood up and collected her briefcase and purse. "Got to go, full schedule today. I won't be home until after dinner." Gayle kissed Kathleen on top of her head and left for her office.

Kathleen continued to drink her coffee and read the newspaper, wanting to delay the start of another empty day. At first she missed the small article in the local section, but was drawn back to it by the photo of a chubby man with curly hair and thick-framed glasses. She stared at the familiar face and read the caption:

"Mark Epson, MD, heads new health clinic for the homeless."

Kathleen hadn't seen Mark for years, but never forgot the day they met.

❀ ❀ ❀

It was 1993, the first day of med school and the someday-to-be-docs were encouraged to form study groups. The first-year students gathered in a large classroom, looking each other over, trying to decide where they belonged or if they belonged.

Kathleen stood by herself watching as people began to pair off. She didn't expect to be asked into a study group, and rather than risk being rejected she decided to be a study group of one. She saw one of the students from her first-year anatomy class sauntering toward her. She remembered her name, Natasha Something, and she remembered the comment Natasha made about her not having a soul and being a vampire.

Natasha smiled as if they were best friends. "Hi, Kathleen. We saw you standing by yourself and thought you might want to join our study group."

"Why would you want me to join your group?" she asked suspiciously.

"We want to have the best study group in the school. You would add balance."

Kathleen was feeling something new. Anger was rising from her chest, beginning to form into rage and getting ready to spew out of her mouth. She forced herself to be in control. "Balance?"

Natasha nodded. "We thought it would be a good idea to balance interests and capabilities; you know... strengths and perhaps shortcomings."

"So, Natasha, what is your strength?"

"Contacts... that's my strength. Frankly, my father is a big contributor to a number of major hospitals and anyone in *my* study group will be on the fast track for the best residencies."

"And my strength?"

"Don't you know? You're the smartest."

"So, I do all the work and you?"

"Get you positioned to make it big. You may be a little naïve, but medicine and the Army are like any other profession. It's all about who you know."

"Well, I'll tell you, Natasha, I always thought my strength was in being a vampire and not having a soul. Even here, this dim light pushes me toward needing someone's blood. So, before I demolish you, why don't you fuck off?"

Natasha looked at Kathleen, shock replacing self-assuredness. Her brow furrowed and her eyes turned to icy slits. "We were right about you in the first place. You are a loser, Kathleen Moore."

Kathleen heard applause from the far corner of the room. There were four standing together. Janet, who wanted to become a missionary physician; Dan, who was interested in cancer research; Mark, who planned on working with the homeless; and Thomas, who wanted a simple family practice somewhere in the country. They wouldn't be the doctors sitting in penthouse suites thinking more about their investments than patients. Kathleen found where she belonged.

They would study together for four years and during that time form a tight bond. After graduation they went their own ways but stayed in contact through e-mails. Gradually, the e-mails became fewer and fewer until they stopped.

Kathleen glanced again at the article and reached for the phone.

Mark's health clinic was located in a run-down part of downtown Los Angeles. A small group of single-story commercial stores, freshly painted a pale green, stood out from the rest of the decaying neighborhood. A large sign leaned against the front window announcing, *Neighborhood Health Care.*

Kathleen was pleasantly surprised to find a welcoming waiting area with burgundy chairs and brightly framed scenic posters. The receptionist smiled and showed her to Mark's office. They hugged and said it had been too long.

Kathleen sat in the brown leather chair across from Mark. "Thanks for seeing me, Mark. I read the article in the newspaper. This is what you always wanted to do."

"It took a while, but we have more homeless than ever. The economy sucks and we're flooded with homeless vets, and not just men; lots of women vets, too." He handed Kathleen a brown bag. "Reminds you of our student days? No time and no money for lunches. So tell me, how's the Army treating you? Are you running the joint yet?"

Mark didn't pause for a response. "We haven't seen each other since that conference in Hawaii. That's more than five years ago. So, what brings you here? A sudden interest in the homeless?"

Mark was blunt to the point of being rude and obnoxious. Kathleen was going to put her faith in the Mark who was also honest and caring.

"Show and tell, Mark. Right to the point." She put the brown bag down and opened her blouse, exposing her scar. "Enough to the point, Mark? I can manage to unbutton a blouse, but my hand doesn't always respond to my commands and my confidence is shattered."

"Christ, Kathleen, I'm sorry. What happened?"

"Iraq, a year ago, damage to nerves and tendons. My arm and hand are improving and the sensitivity is beginning to return. I'm still outpatient at Veterans Hospital, three days a week, but it's winding down. The vocational counselor wants to put me into research or working for an insurance company, overseeing claims. I'd rather die. I know I can't work in an ER, at least not full-time and maybe never. I need to start somewhere; I need to find my place."

"You want to...?"

"Volunteer. Your clinic is open on Saturdays. I can do Tuesdays, Thursdays, and Saturdays. I need help, Mark. I'm asking—no, I'm begging for your help."

She felt like a med student. One day, she sat at the kitchen table, giving injections to oranges until their juice stuck to her hands and dripped onto the floor. Sensations were gradually returning. Her skills were coming back, slowly and not perfectly. She apologized to Robert for throwing the suturing kit across the room. It was exactly what she needed.

She followed Mark from exam room to exam room and he introduced her as his assistant. He asked, "What's your opinion, doctor?" She began to diagnose. She realized how much she had missed that part of her life. The part of her that, as a child, sat in a damp cold basement looking for evidence to solve fantasy mysteries, now listened, sometimes with her eyes closed, for subtle clues provided by her patients.

Mark and Kathleen stood drinking the last dregs of lukewarm coffee from the clinic's coffee pot. Mark said, "I've got more grinds than coffee. So, what's the problem? You're as sharp as ever."

"I don't always have complete command over my hand. I've got a suturing kit and I'd like you to observe my technique." She looked down. "Mark, I'm having nightmares and sometimes, I have an exaggerated startle response. You know that medicine has been my life... I need my life back."

Mark became thoughtful. "PTSD. What meds are you taking?"

"Officially, undiagnosed. No prescriptions. I'm taking vitamins, B-12 and extra magnesium. I can't be labeled. If I can't work as a physician, who am I?"

He nodded. "Understood. Let's start with your stitch kit. You know, you were always the best at suturing. It's strange what fear can do." Mark leaned back in his chair, thinking. "Hmm... Do you remember what we did in medical school? We played doctor—you'd examine me, and I'd examine you."

Kathleen shook her head. "I'm not undressing in front of you."

"No. I'll be the one undressing and I want you to give me a complete workup, and I do mean complete. Blood work, urinalysis, EKG, treadmill test, and don't forget my prostate. Do *not* tell me to lose weight. I hear that from my wife. I want you to analyze your findings and come up with a complete diagnosis and recommendations. If that's a success, I'll observe while you treat patients. Then, we'll start to funnel some cases to you."

Kathleen's hands shook and the stethoscope dangling from her neck swayed.

Mark sat on the exam table wearing a short paper gown. "We can be here all night if we have to. Slow down, you're not being graded. Think about something else. Hey, remember Natasha Something? Wasn't she the biggest pain in the ass? Well, did you know she's the plastic surgeon to the stars these days?"

Kathleen laughed and her shaking slowed to a slight tremor. She used her skills and all the medical equipment in the exam room. She had Mark lie down to examine his abdomen.

"You're still doing that close your eyes business when you examine?"

"Mark, shut up and take a deep breath."

Afterward, Kathleen said, as she would to any patient, "You can get dressed now. I want to order a workup on your gallbladder."

"Thank you, Doctor." Mark paused. "And I do mean Doctor. Two comments. One, you have the shittiest bedside manner. Christ, it's worse than mine and that's saying something. Two, my gallbladder has to come out. You knew the diagnosis when you examined me, didn't you?"

"Y-yes," Kathleen said sheepishly. "I just thought—"

"I know what you thought!" Mark's tone softened. "You've been through crap and you're scared to take the leap from patient to physician. You're afraid to make a mistake. Jesus, you're like a first-year med student. You're not the only one trying to hide your PTSD. I see vets all the time struggling with it. They don't want it to affect their careers or be thought of as cowards.

"Did you notice when you thought about Natasha Something and laughed, your hand became steadier? Some of this is physical, nerve and tendon damage, but some is psychological. You need to work this from both ends." He laughed. "Just like a physical exam, get it?

"I want you to take the next couple of months and work here with me. This is a clinic, but we've got sophisticated equipment and at times we function as an ER. If you can work here, you can work anyplace. Don't think I'm doing you a favor; I can really use the free help."

The two months working with Mark was what Kathleen needed. She found her skills returning and her confidence building. Her hand wasn't always perfect but as Mark said, "Sometime we have to settle for 'good enough.' It's time, Kathleen, for you to get your ass in gear and get back to work."

The Army was processing her discharge papers and she was ready to put her life back together. Now it was time to check the physician recruiting websites and get her ass in gear.

She started early Sunday morning browsing through websites. Most of them required a registration before allowing her to surf their site. She didn't want a headhunter contacting her and moved on. The few that allowed a preview showed an abundance of openings with health maintenance organizations (HMO), emergency rooms, or practices in large metropolitan areas.

She had to think this out. What did she really want? She put in her search terms, "Family Medicine Physician, board certified, looking for position in California, small town preferred." There were over five million hits. Most of them were selling something, but she kept scrolling down until she was at the end of page ten. The day had moved on, it was late afternoon, and she was tired and discouraged. She thought, *it's enough for one day. One more page and that's it.* Near the middle of the last page, one listing got her attention.

"Canfield is seeking a Family Medicine Physician. Must be board certified. One hour from Santa Barbara, CA. Near recreational areas. Not quite like any other town. We will provide offices and living quarters plus a generous compensation package. Send CV and copies of credentials to: Christen Mitchell, PO Box 752, Canfield, CA or e-mail with attachments to: c_mitchell2134@canfieldtown.org."

Kathleen was intrigued. After she did her exercises she would answer the ad.

CHAPTER 15

The grandfather clock struck nine and except for the sound of the chimes, Kathleen woke to a silent house. She missed hearing Gayle and Robert moving about in the kitchen; she had slept through their morning ritual. Hushed voices and an occasional laugh would mingle with the sound of water as it began to bubble its way through the stovetop percolator. The smell of strong coffee would work its way to her room, signaling it was time to get up and join them.

She shuffled from the bedroom to the kitchen, her feet moving sluggishly against the carpet. Her body was dazed and her thoughts confused. She couldn't shake the feelings from last night's dream. It was the same recurring night terror, but with a twist.

The dream began as it did every night. She was trapped in the burn pit, surrounded by waste. This time, she was able to climb out of the pit before being swallowed by the sinking ground. She wandered, lost, through the desert landscape. She wasn't wearing any body armor and felt unprotected and vulnerable. As she walked through the desolate terrain, she mumbled in anguish, "Where's my body armor? Where's my body armor?" She walked for miles over dusty, rock-filled roads. Her feet burned. The sun became a merciless enemy. She was alone and exhausted. Her throat was parched and she couldn't swallow.

She spotted a small stream with its banks covered in red, blue, and yellow flowers. The water ran swiftly over large rocks and stones. A woman, lost in thought, sat on the edge of the stream, trailing her hand in the water.

Kathleen was drawn to the flowers; she was drawn to the woman. She began to move closer, until she was almost in reach of the stream, when she stepped on an IED. She woke with a gasp and in a half dream state checked to see if her limbs were still attached. She buried her face in her pillow and smothered her cries. She didn't want to wake Gayle and Robert.

She followed the dwindling fragrance of the coffee and read the note from Gayle, hanging on the refrigerator door:

Robert made baked apples. Bagels in the pantry. I'll be home around five. Glad you could sleep in. Love, Gayle.

She poured a cup of lukewarm coffee and heated it in the microwave. She anticipated that moment when she would hold the cup in her hand and breathe in the aroma, remembering the feeling that would follow when she took her first sip.

She heard the post office delivery truck stop in front of the house and walked to the curb, yawning. The oversized mailbox was filled to the brim and Kathleen tugged with both hands to release the mail. When she returned to the house, the bundle slipped out of her hands, spilling onto the entryway table. She sorted the mail into neat piles, hoping there was something for her.

Gayle and Robert got their usual cornucopia of catalogs, magazines, and letters. Kathleen, who rarely received any mail, got three letters. She carried them into the kitchen and decided to play the childhood game of eenie, meenie, miney, moe.

A letter from Helen and Sam won the first game, and Kathleen, with recently recovered dexterity, tore open the envelope impatiently. Invisible lines seemed to have guided Helen's crisp handwriting—no cross-outs, no whiteout, and straight as an arrow. Kathleen tried to get her to use e-mail, but Helen was adamant. "I want to feel the paper against my pen," she had said defiantly. "It makes me feel closer to you. I don't want to join a billion other people, writing quick, generic messages. Pony Express is fine with me."

Helen and Sam's letter was filled with chatty news about their recent retirement from the Army. They had traveled in their motor home for six months, stopping at national parks along the way. They wanted to settle down, but weren't quite sure of where. Helen wanted a house with room for a garden and Sam wanted to work part-time.

Helen thought Sam could do anything he set his mind to do. "I discovered a side to Sam," she shared. "He loves to kibitz. A five-minute errand takes us twenty. I suggested his new career might be as a big-box store greeter."

Kathleen laughed out loud, picturing Sam in his new profession. *God, I miss them.*

Kathleen decided not to do eenie, meenie, miney, moe with the rest of the mail, and picked up the large manila envelope with a government stamp and return address printed on the corner. She knew what was inside: her Honorable Discharge certificate. She slit open the envelope and looked coldly at the letter-sized document with the Army seal and the standard boilerplate language. Except for the personalization of her name, it was interchangeable with the millions of others the government had issued. She thought it should contain a disclaimer: *Your life has been turned upside down and if you're lucky, you'll get to be right side up... maybe.*

Kathleen shuddered and became overwhelmed by the terror that gnawed at her, like a starving rat chewing through a kitchen wall, looking for food. What if she couldn't find a suitable job? What if her early days of deprivation returned with a vengeance? What if she became, once again, the frightened, lonely child?

Kathleen focused on the discharge papers and became surrounded by a veil of sadness. The Army had been her life for fourteen years. She had made friends, primarily within the medical community, but never came out to anyone. During those years she lived a lie, making her closet deeper and deeper.

Sometimes, she couldn't deny the longings that could only be satisfied by women. A trip to a strange city hoping she would be safe, looking for a gay friendly bar, then meeting a woman who would linger in her hotel room for a while, but always leaves before dawn. She wondered how it would feel to reach over and touch someone she loved, instead of an empty space left by a stranger.

There was one last piece of mail to open. It could be the frosting on the cake and she had wanted to save it for last. Kathleen held the letter postmarked Canfield, CA, and felt her hands dampen with anticipation. She carefully ran her fingers under the seal, trying not to tear the envelope. She felt a surge of excitement when she read the response from Christen Mitchell inviting her to meet with Canfield's Mayor and Town Council. She would make an appointment with Christen and talk to Robert and Gayle during dinner.

Kathleen first saw the back garden when she was a third year student at UCLA, struggling to balance classes and work. Raised in South Boston's Irish Catholic neighborhood, she thought a backyard like Robert and Gayle's only existed in storybooks. The garden took her breath away, then and now.

Robert had designed every bit of the garden, from the black-bottom lagoon pool, to the organic vegetable garden. He told her gardening to him was like standing next to God. She had learned so much from Robert.

Kathleen stood on the flagstone patio and carefully placed the dishes and silverware on the glass-topped iron table. She remembered when Gayle had bought the table and chairs at an estate sale and Robert had carefully removed layer after layer of chipped paint until he exposed the metal surface. As Robert's sinewy hands sanded and cleaned the metal, he talked to Kathleen about how much he loved restoring old furniture.

"Gayle finds it and I bring it back to life." He laughed. "Now, I'm going to share a secret with you. I learned this from my father."

He put on thin plastic gloves and covered his right hand with an old tube sock, turned inside out. "This is the best paint brush you'll ever find for painting these delicate curves."

Robert continued to talk as he patiently rubbed his paint sock over the iron filigree. "Restoring old furniture is a lot like life. We begin life the way this table did, in pristine condition. Then, over the years, we're faced with difficult, painful situations, and we begin to hide ourselves beneath layers of paint. We think we're protecting everything, but after a while, just like this furniture, we end up with a rough, peeling exterior. We have to risk removing all those extra layers to expose the beauty that's underneath."

Kathleen finished folding the cloth napkins, placed them gently on the table, and thought about how she had spent most of her life hiding beneath layers of "paint." She rubbed her hand across the back of the chair, feeling the smooth, flawless finish. She saw the vivid colors of annuals and perennials, so lovingly planted by Robert. She breathed in the fragrance of the blue beard shrubs and felt grateful for the magnolia trees that shielded her from the setting sun.

Gayle set the platter of barbequed chicken on the table. "Robert's secret recipe. Do you know he keeps it locked in his safe?" She chuckled as she passed Kathleen the chicken. "How was your day?"

"Fine." The aroma from the chicken made her aware of a twinge in her stomach. "I got some mail. I'm discharged effective the end of the month."

Gayle put down her fork and looked at Kathleen with interest. "How's that feeling?"

"Sometimes, it's hard for me to accept what happened. Now, it's real." She looked down. "I'll miss my career and I'll miss my friends, but I know it's time for me to look ahead and get back to work. It's just difficult to find where I belong."

Robert walked over with a basket heaped high with roasted potatoes and corn. "Have you found anything interesting?"

"Do you remember when I told you about the opening in Canfield for a family physician? I got a letter from them today. I've made an appointment to interview for the position and tour the town."

Gayle looked concerned. "I'm glad you're thinking about work—although, small towns can be isolating."

"Isolating?"

"Yes, it can be hard to meet others."

"You mean because I'm..." Kathleen paused. The word stuck in her throat, "lesbian?"

"You're single and in your thirties," said Gayle matter-of-factly. "At some point you may want to date or perhaps even have children. Your chances of meeting someone in a small town are slim to none. Will you continue to hide such an important part of your identity as you did in the service? I only want you to weigh all your options and their consequences before making a decision."

Kathleen spoke slowly, struggling to find words to match her feelings. "I suppose the chance of meeting someone in a small town isn't so great. Sometimes, I think I'm meant to be single. I've always wanted that something special you and Robert have, but I've never had much luck at romance. Maybe I'm not relationship material.

"The job market for physicians..." She fought to stifle the quiver in her voice. "Well, it's not exactly robust. Most of the full-time positions are with HMOs and ERs. I don't want to be stuck in an HMO where the load is so heavy that there's barely time to remember my patients' names. I want to treat according to my conscience. I can't work full-time in an ER anymore. There's too much fast action and I can't chance a flashback —at least not right now." She paused. "I've got to feel productive again and I like the idea of a small town and a family practice. The trip is for three days and it'll be good for me. It's been a long time since I've been on my own."

Gayle looked thoughtfully at her. "When are you going?"

"In two days. Gayle, please don't worry. Since I've been working with Mark, I feel so much better. More like my old self every day. I'm excited, not frightened. It's time."

"You'll remember your exercises?"

"Every day, and the bed and breakfast I'm staying at has a large hot tub right outside my room."

"You won't forget to eat?"

"Three meals a day."

CHAPTER 16

Robert took care of Kathleen in his own way. He lent her his 2006 Acura with the Global Positioning System (GPS) and he had her promise not to sign any contracts without his reviewing them first.

Robert checked his car's tire pressure and fluid levels, showed Kathleen how to use the GPS, and checked the tires and fluid levels—again. He packed her lunch just as he had packed Gayle's, every workday, for more than twenty years.

"Summertown is about fifteen minutes south of Santa Barbara," said Robert. "It's a quaint village filled with all kinds of interesting shops. I think you'll enjoy it, and it'll be good for you to stretch your legs. I set the GPS, but keep your eyes open for the signs." Robert handed her an envelope. "This is for you. Treat yourself to something special."

Kathleen hugged Robert tightly and thanked him. He made sure Kathleen was settled in the car and holding back bittersweet tears watched her back out of the driveway before returning to his home office.

She followed the GPS directions to the 101 Freeway, north. Gradually, the landscape changed from a densely populated city to a sprawling suburbia. The once rich farmland was replaced by housing tracts, created to give families the illusion of a rural life.

Within an hour, Kathleen was at the coast highway where views of the Pacific Ocean peeked around every turn in the road. She opened the car windows and took a deep breath of the fresh ocean air. She passed the small beach town of Carpenteria where surfers were catching the last of the morning swells. Kathleen heard the disembodied female voice of the GPS telling her to take the exit to Summertown. Robert had thought of everything.

Summertown was a charming village with enough small shops to keep Kathleen busy for days. She opened the envelope and took out two crisp one hundred dollar bills. She shook her head at Robert's generosity, but knew she wouldn't spend that much on herself.

She strolled the six blocks of Summertown, stopping to look at the stores' window displays. She stared at the mannequins wearing summer dresses and shorts outfits, and wondered how she would look in them. She sighed. Mrs. Roth had sewed her school clothing, but she had never learned how to shop. The Army fed her and told her what to wear for different occasions. Sweats, jeans, and T-shirts hung on a dozen hangers and supplemented her Army uniforms and hospital scrubs. One below-the-knee print dress along with a black pantsuit and two white suit blouses completed her wardrobe.

Gayle had insisted on taking her shopping for her birthday. "You can't begin a new life with such a limited wardrobe. I know how you hate to shop, but it's time."

They were ushered into the dressing room of an upscale department store. Pre-selected outfits, ready for Kathleen to try on, hung on hangers outside the dressing area.

Gayle said, "I wanted to make this as painless as possible so I called ahead for a personal shopper."

Kathleen looked at one of the dresses, a simple black sheath. "I like this," she said longingly as she reached to look at the price tag. Gayle quickly covered her hand. "Uh-uh," she said. "No looking and the tags are going to be cut off before we go home."

Now, Kathleen had a basic wardrobe of blouses and blazers, vests and slacks—an abundance of coordinating outfits for casual and business wear and one black, wear it anywhere dress, but she still clung to her familiar jeans and sweats.

She stopped to stare at a doll in the window of an antique shop and felt her heart go pit-a-pat. Alice from *Alice in Wonderland* stood in all her glory with arms beckoning. She thought about the two hundred dollars and walked in.

The salesclerk handed the doll to Kathleen. "This is a cloth body doll from the 1930s," she said. "We bought her at an estate sale from the owner's son. She's rare, in almost new condition, and comes with the original box and doll stand."

Kathleen looked at the price tag: four hundred dollars. "She's beautiful," she said, wishing she could hold Alice close to her heart. "Too rich for my blood," she sighed, and reluctantly returned the doll to the salesclerk. Kathleen found a multicolored scarf that was perfect for Gayle and asked the salesclerk for a gift bag.

She continued to walk along the street toward a wine tasting room. She found the ideal gift for Robert, a small wooden crate with room for two bottles of wine. She filled the container with his favorites, a bottle of Pinot Noir and a bottle of Sauvignon Blanc.

Kathleen walked back to the car, caressing the business card from the antique shop, and felt heaviness in her heart. She longed for Alice.

❀ ❀ ❀

On either side of the road, a long, unbroken line of eucalyptus trees marched toward the town of Canfield nestled in the coastal foothills north of Santa Barbara. The pungent smell brought back a long, forgotten memory as Kathleen sped along.

She was little, perhaps three or four, and ill with a hacking cough that made her chest hurt. Probably bronchitis, the physician in her concluded. Her mother rubbed her chest with an ointment made from eucalyptus oil, and covered the area with a flannel cloth. Kathleen slept feverishly and began to see a ghost covered in a white sheet, floating above her bed. Throughout that hazy time, her mother gave her sips of water and changed the damp cloth on her forehead as it went from cool to warm.

She stopped the car under the shade of the eucalyptus trees. Long forgotten feelings of having been loved began to wash over her. "Focus," she thought. "You have to focus on the task ahead. You can't collapse, you have to stay strong." She sat up straight, took a long drink of water, and pulled back onto the road.

The eucalyptus trees faded from sight, and were replaced by mile after mile of avocado orchards. Small farms and ranches began to dot the countryside with horses grazing in bright green meadows and signs along the road announcing organic fruits and vegetables.

It was early afternoon when Kathleen arrived at Canfield. Welcome banners hanging from antique lampposts, announced the annual Labor Day festival, dubbed *A Weekend in Scotland.* Trees shaded the cobblestone sidewalks, and flower boxes filled with colorful annuals hung from the front of Victorian style buildings. Scattered along Main Street were antique stores and restaurants that spoke of a burgeoning tourist industry.

The one exception to the Victorian style architecture was a stagecoach stop that served as the Visitors Center. The building showed a part of history firmly grounded in the Wild West. Constructed of weathered, hand-hewed timbers that had withstood the test of time, it was a reminder of an era when people endured the discomforts and dangers of stagecoach travel in hopes of starting a new life. Kathleen parked in a shady spot across from the building. A handwritten note, hanging from the door, told her the tourist center was closed until two in the afternoon. She reached for her lunch and discovered Robert had packed her all-time favorite: peanut butter and grape jelly sandwiches. She opened the bag of chips and carefully laid them inside the sandwich. Now, it was truly the perfect lunch.

❀ ❀ ❀

Kathleen saw the sign, *Victorian Past Bed and Breakfast Inn,* hanging from the bright yellow clapboard house trimmed in green. The scent from the flower garden welcomed her as she walked up the five steps and knocked on the front door. Michelle Anderson was a tall, solidly built woman with a handshake to match. She took Kathleen's suitcase and showed her to the bedroom on the second floor.

The room was decorated in true Victorian style with a canopy bed, marble-topped tables, and a steamer trunk. A couch completed the room furnishings. Michelle opened the French doors to the deck.

"I do hope you'll enjoy your stay with us," she said pleasantly. "You asked for the room with the hot tub, and it's right here on the deck." Kathleen stepped outside and admired both the tub and the exquisite view of the town.

Michelle continued with her tour. "You'll find extra blankets and pillows in the trunk and the bathroom is through this door."

Kathleen was staring at the couch. Instead of being flat and designed for sitting, the couch had one end raised and looked as if it was meant for reclining.

Michelle placed her hand on the carved frame. "Ah, I see you're intrigued by the fainting couch. I found it in an antique shop and had it restored."

"Fainting couch?"

"Yes, upper class women in the Victorian era wore corsets, of course, and by the time they climbed the stairs to the second and sometimes third story of their homes, they would feel faint. This type of couch was placed on the landings so that women could get their breath back." Michelle shook her head and smiled at Kathleen. "It's hard for us to understand, but it was a different time."

Kathleen dined at a small restaurant within walking distance of The Victorian Past. The owner and host of The Town Hall Restaurant showed her to a patio table overlooking the flower and herb garden. He explained that most of their food was grown locally and the menu changed seasonally. Kathleen ordered the homemade vegetable soup and herbal bread. A glass of Chardonnay completed her dinner.

She sat at the table watching other couples and families talking, laughing, sometimes scowling at each other, but at least not alone. She wished she had brought a book to hide behind.

A family was seated at the next table and a boy, about five or six, with blond hair and wide blue eyes, smiled and waved. She smiled and waved back. The woman walked over to Kathleen's table. "Excuse me, but are you Dr. Moore?"

Kathleen was caught off guard. "Yes, I am."

"I'm Christen Mitchell. We weren't expecting you this early or we would have arranged dinner for you."

"Oh, that's okay. I got here earlier than expected."

"Please join us. That is, if you can stand the distraction of a very active five-year-old and a somewhat moody teenager."

Kathleen's dinner turned out to be anything but dull or lonely. Christen and her husband Jeffrey kept up an easy flow of conversation. Kathleen discovered they were transplants from northern California and were realtors, as well as town council members.

Jeffrey said, "We wanted to give our children a safer environment and the schools are wonderful."

Their daughter Victoria, dressed in all black, scowled. "It's the absolutely most boring place in the world." She flicked her long hair, as raven-black as her attire, with a pale hand with outsized rings on every finger. Kathleen noticed the long black nails with little white skull decals. *Oh great, a Goth*, she thought, but kept her composure.

Christen gave an embarrassed smile. "Victoria and Alex, Dr. Moore was in the Army and served in Iraq."

Victoria glared out of eyes darkened by makeup. "I am so against that stupid war."

Alex squeaked, "How many bad guys did you kill?"

Christen apologized, "I am so sorry. It seems their manners were left at home."

Kathleen shook her head. "It's okay. Victoria, I'm glad you can express your opinion. It's what we fight for. Alex, I'm a doctor and I've never killed anyone. But, do you know, I once delivered a baby goat?"

Alex's eyes grew wide. "Really?"

Victoria chimed in, "I think you're making it up."

Kathleen laughed. "No one could make up this story. A farmer drove to the front gate of the Army base in Iraq with his goat in the back of a truck. He was quite upset and told the guards that his goat was about to have a baby and needed help. Do you know what a baby goat is called?"

Alex raised his hand and bounced up and down. "I know, I know. A kid."

"That's right. After seeing that the farmer's goat was in great distress, the guard called the emergency room and asked if one of the docs could come out to the front gate and help deliver a kid. Well, the guard forgot to say it was a goat and we thought he was talking about delivering a baby. So, I packed everything I might need and one of the medics drove me to the front gate.

"You can imagine my surprise when I found out my patient was a goat. I thought, I'm really going to get teased about this one, but I helped my patient and she had the most beautiful kid. It was really sweet. The farmer was so grateful he said he would name the kid after me. He asked, 'What's your name?' And I said, 'Doc. Name the kid Doc.' And he did."

"Isn't that a great story?" said Christen.

"Yeah!" Alex shouted.

"What*ever*," said Victoria, making no effort to hide her rolling eyes.

She's going to be one tough nut to crack, Kathleen thought.

The next morning, Kathleen walked the short distance to Canfield's administrative offices. The building appeared to be more than a century old, and she imagined the inside filled with wooden desks and outdated equipment.

"Dr. Moore?" Kathleen looked up to see a man in his mid-fifties walking toward her. A welcoming smile and kind brown eyes greeted her as he extended his hand. "Bill Langdon," he said. "Mayor of Canfield. Before we go into the meeting, I'd like to show you our communication center. The center will show you how we are blending the old with the new."

Kathleen was pleasantly surprised to see a sleek interior with up-to-date computers and phone system in place.

Mayor Langdon said, "Sometimes, people think small towns mean small minds." He shook his head while clucking his tongue. "Big mistake. We have modern communication equipment and a first-rate emergency plan in place. Our staff consists of one paid employee and about twenty-five volunteers. We offer class credits to our high school seniors for volunteering. They like anything high-tech and it makes them feel connected to the community. We hope, soon, to be able to handle any emergency."

Mayor Langdon took Kathleen's arm and guided her toward the meeting room. She mingled with the town council and guests, drinking coffee and eating sweets from the snack table. Two men shook Kathleen's hand and patted her on the back as if welcoming a long lost relative. One wore a hat with the logo, *Korean War Veteran, Semper Fi.* The other had a large patch sewed on his windbreaker, *Vietnam War, In Memory of Those Who Never Returned.* She wondered if, someday, she would be wearing a patch on the outside while carrying the pain of her memories next to her heart.

Christen walked up to Kathleen and gave her a friendly hug. "You certainly won over my kids. Believe me, it's not easy to win over Victoria! Thank you for the lovely story and for being so gentle with her."

Won over her kids? She knew Christen was just being polite. She had definitely won over little Alex, but Victoria had looked like she wanted to stick a knife in her back the whole evening. Still, she wondered why Christen had made it a point to use the word gentle. Perhaps the girl was more vulnerable and fragile than her fearsome façade suggested.

But there was no time to wonder. Mayor Langdon stood behind a podium and called the meeting to order.

"Special thanks to Janice for providing her incredible desserts." He patted his stomach. "Janice, I couldn't resist your chocolate cake and I snuck in a couple of cookies, as well."

Mayor Langdon smiled at Kathleen. "Dr. Moore, on behalf of Canfield I'd like to officially welcome you, and thank you for submitting your application. We were impressed with your professional history and would like to express our gratitude for your service to our country."

The Mayor and town council applauded Kathleen. She nodded in appreciation, smiled, and hoped she was not turning beet red.

Mayor Langdon continued. "War is a nasty business, and while we wish there was no need for our young people to be in harm's way, Canfield is proud of its service to our country. We have fought in every war since the town's inception in 1885.

"Just to bring you up to speed, Dr. Moore, our physician, Dr. Kerr, passed away a few months ago, and Canfield finds itself in somewhat of a predicament. The physician in Hayward, that's twenty miles away, has been filling in. Additionally, we have a nurse practitioner using Dr. Kerr's office three days a week.

"We realize it may be a challenge for a physician with your background to change to an individual practice in a small town. Keeping that in mind, we have prepared a slide show about Canfield's history, as well as our plans and dreams for the future. Please, feel free to ask any questions along the way."

The first few slides were sketches and photos from the late 1800s and early 1900s, showing the development of Canfield from a tent city to a bustling town with stores, offices, and automobiles crowding the streets.

Mayor Langdon narrated: "Otis Canfield emigrated from Scotland to the United States in 1885. When he arrived here, he saw farms and ranches, but he didn't see a store. He started the Canfield Mercantile Store in a tent and the rest is history."

The next slides showed Canfield House in all her glory. Kathleen stared at the photo and began to fall under its spell.

Mayor Langdon continued his presentation. "Canfield House was built by Otis Canfield in 1895. It is a Victorian Queen Anne style home situated on ten acres of land. It had, for its time, the most modern features available, including a full indoor bathroom. Dr. Moore, are you at all familiar with Victorian architecture?"

"Only from the homes in San Francisco."

"Some very fine examples, indeed. We are very proud of Canfield House. Several architectural magazines have written articles about her, primarily because of the arched entryway and rounded solarium—very unique, almost one of a kind. We recently painted the shingles in a rainbow of colors to reflect the fashion of the time."

Murmurs and laughter went around the room.

Kathleen looked puzzled.

"Well, Dr. Moore, it was a group effort and almost everyone in this room helped, lots of hard work and lots of laughing. I'm not sure who got the most paint, the house or us. What do you think of the colors?"

"I really like them," Kathleen replied. "The base is earth-colored, and the colors on the shingles look like a rainbow. It's fanciful. All you need is the pot of gold."

"Exactly! And our pot of gold will be providing the best possible health care to the citizens of Canfield. When the house fell into foreclosure it was bought by the town with the idea of turning Canfield House into medical offices. We are very excited about the possibilities. We plan to have emergency equipment installed and, sometime in the future, a helipad for transporting patients to St. Mona's Hospital in Santa Barbara."

The next slide showed some preliminary sketches of the new floor plan. "The first floor will be turned into medical offices with the most modern equipment and supplies available," Mayor Langdon explained. "We are prepared to offer a generous guaranteed salary package along with living quarters in a wonderful Queen Anne home.

"Now, I saved the best part for last, and that's our recreational areas. I think of Canfield as the undiscovered paradise. We are blessed to have mild temperatures for most of the year. The beach is close by and there are hiking trails everywhere. We have a five-mile trail that leads directly to Christmas River. Throughout the year, you'll find folks fishing or rafting or simply enjoying a picnic on the banks of the river with friends and family. People bike around town, and if you enjoy wine tasting, the vineyards are within easy driving distance.

"Although we're a bit off the beaten path, that can be a favorable feature for those who are looking for quiet and safety. We do have summer residents and the population almost doubles during vacation months. In September we celebrate our Scottish heritage by holding a festival, *A Weekend in Scotland*. The festival brings in an influx of tourists—along with the usual minor injuries.

"I hope I haven't bored you. I do have a bit of a reputation for going on." Good-natured catcalls from the audience attested to this. The mayor laughed heartily and asked Kathleen, "Do you have any questions or comments?"

Kathleen said, "I want to thank you for your presentation and your generous hospitality. You mentioned medical offices, and I'm wondering if you are planning on more than one physician."

"One physician will be adequate for our present needs. However, if our population projections are correct, we may need to establish a group practice in the future." Mayor Langdon handed Kathleen a thick folder. "We have prepared a portfolio complete with statistics and photos. I understand that you have a tour tomorrow, and we hope to be in contact with you in a few weeks."

Kathleen stared at the clothes hanging in the closet of her room. Christen would be picking her up at 10:00 am, so she had an hour to shower and dress. She took out one of her pre-coordinated outfits. "Bullet proof," Gayle had said. Tan slacks, a chocolate brown sweater, and dark brown loafers completed her outfit. She decided to use some lipstick, put on her small gold hoop earrings, brushed her hair for the last time, and was good to go.

Christen was wearing jeans, a T-shirt, and sneakers along with a gray cable knit poncho, to keep out the morning chill. Christen greeted her with a friendly hug. "It's weekend casual dress for me. I hope you don't mind it'll just be us gals. Jeffrey's doing sports duty this morning."

She continued to chat in an easy, friendly way. "Both kids have soccer practice and it's one of the few things that Victoria seems to really love. Gets her out of her black outfits." She shook her head. "Teens, you know..."

Kathleen spoke empathically. "It's a difficult time for kids and parents alike. It's a wonder that anyone gets through it."

Christen flashed a grateful smile. "I'm going to start with the recreational areas and save the house for last."

They turned off Main Street and drove through some of the less traveled roads that led toward Christmas River.

Christen parked the car at the entrance to the trail. "Let's get out for a minute and stretch our legs," she suggested.

Kathleen stood at the open entrance gate and felt a sense of peace surrounding her. "It looks as if they've kept the trail as natural as possible," she commented.

"Yes, it's a wonderful trail, lots of shade and a feeling of being deep in the forest," Christen replied. "There are several picnic areas before you get to the river. It's only a ten-minute drive from Canfield House. Close enough to bring your lunch and sit on one of the benches in the picnic area."

Kathleen was drawn to Canfield. She liked the small town atmosphere and the trails that seemed to be around every corner.

Christen backtracked to the main highway and exited at Thornberry Drive. She made a right turn onto a gravel drive that meandered through a wooded area. Kathleen peeked through the stand of dogwood trees and saw the house at the crest of a gentle hill. It took her breath away.

Christen parked in the driveway. "This is it! A real jewel—a little in the rough around the edges, but with some TLC, it will really shine."

They walked along the brick path that led toward the front of the house. The path continued through a garden area filled with rose bushes, benches, and a birdbath. A pair of black-capped chickadees splashed merrily in the basin, but quickly fled as the visitors approached.

They climbed the steps to the covered porch and as Christen unlocked the front door she slipped into real estate agent mode.

"There are nine rooms on the first floor, plus the solarium," she began. "It's important to keep in mind that this house has been vacant for three years. The previous owners were planning on a full restoration and made some significant changes before the house fell into foreclosure. There is some cosmetic work that needs to be done and, of course, the first floor will have to be remodeled for offices. Come inside!"

Christen stopped as they entered the house. "We are standing in the reception hall. This is a large room, complete with a fireplace. Dr. Moore, look at the ceiling."

Kathleen looked up to see a high ceiling with carved, patterned beams. "It's exquisite."

Christen smiled. "It's called a coffered ceiling, and it's very unusual to find one in such fine condition. Immediately to the left is the entrance to the solarium. At the end of the hall is the reception room. This is the room where, in Victorian times, visitors that had come calling would wait for their hosts."

It was the first time Kathleen had ever been inside a Victorian house, and as they walked through each of the rooms, she was taken by the well-crafted workmanship and attention to detail. Kathleen tried to get her bearings and think about how she would plan the office space, but was distracted by the beauty of Canfield House.

Christen continued. "There are three rooms to the right of the reception hall. Look at this parlor. Isn't this perfect for a waiting room? It's a bit chilly in here today, but the fireplace works and will warm the room without having to heat the entire house. Just think of your patients coming in on a cold day and being welcomed by the warmth of a fire! It's a homelike setting and will sooth the most anxious patient. The other two rooms, off the parlor, should be fairly easy to remodel into exam rooms."

As they walked through the house, it became obvious that there was more than light cosmetic work to be done. The kitchen had been remodeled in the seventies when green and orange were the "in" colors. Kathleen felt it offensive to this grand lady and began to get remodeling fever.

They walked upstairs to the living quarters. There were five bedrooms on the second floor, but only one outdated bathroom. Two of the bedrooms faced the front of the house and had doors that led to balconies overlooking the valley. Kathleen opened the door and stood outside. The day was clear and she could see for miles past the green valley toward the Pacific Ocean. The view was startling.

Christen said, "Quite a view, isn't it?"

"It's amazing."

"Come, there is something else I want you to see."

They went downstairs and walked toward the back of the property and stood in front of the garage.

"This is a real bonus," said Christen in her professional voice. "At one time the garage was a barn. The previous owners remodeled it into a three-car garage and added a second story apartment. The apartment has two bedrooms, a full kitchen, and comes with a washer and dryer."

"Dr. Moore, is it all right if I call you Kathleen?"

"Please."

"I'm aware that, legally, I can't ask about your marital status or if you have children. If we should offer you this position, I hope you will honor us with your presence." Christen looked down at the ground and spoke hesitantly. "However, this may not be the best place for a single woman to settle down. There aren't many opportunities to meet someone, especially someone who perhaps shares your same interests. I'm telling you this because, should you move to Canfield, I want you to be happy and make it your home for a long time."

Kathleen noticed that Christen was not using a gender. Instead it was "someone." She knew Christen was trying to be politically correct, but perhaps she was echoing the same concerns that Gayle had expressed a few days ago. This wasn't the time or place, though, to get into the subject.

Kathleen held out her hand to Christen. "Thank you for the tour and for being so welcoming. I enjoyed meeting and spending time with your family. Both Victoria and Alex are wonderful children. You're blessed to have them."

Kathleen had made up her mind to accept the position if it was offered, but with two conditions. She could buy Canfield House, and the practice would be under her full control. For that to take place, she would need Robert's help.

CHAPTER 17

Robert heard the front door open. He knew it was Kathleen by the way she closed the door. He lovingly called it her "almost unidentifiable break-in." He never knew how or where she learned the technique, but she could enter and exit in almost total silence. There was only one small sound that gave her away and Robert picked up on it, every time.

Kathleen hugged Robert in a way that said, "I'm happy and I love you." She smiled and hugged him again, resting her head against his chest, sighing. "I found where I belong. Everything I've ever dreamed of—well, almost—is in Canfield. They're planning on using a Victorian house for medical offices. It has the most incredible views, and it would be so much fun to restore it. The town wants to lease the building to the physician they choose, but if I'm offered the position, I want to own the house and have full control of my practice. Can you help me?"

Kathleen handed Robert the Canfield portfolio. "Look at the photos of the house. Isn't it incredible?"

Robert studied the information, settled back in his chair and smiled. "I can understand why you've fallen in love with the house—it's a bona fide page out of time. I think you know I love you as much as if you were my own daughter, and I want nothing more than for you to be happy. If this is what you want, and you get the offer to lease, I want to be prepared with a counter offer. We need to have a game plan in place. This kind of project requires in-depth research. You really want to go ahead with this?"

Kathleen nodded. "I'm ready for anything."

"Okay. Here's your part. First, how do you want your offices designed? What kind of equipment will you need? What is the cost? If you buy the house, you may have to take on all these responsibilities. Have you thought about staffing? You can't operate a practice by yourself. You need to get the answers to these questions. My part will be to put together a research team to determine the value of the property, cost of maintenance, and potential growth in the area. If you receive the offer to relocate, I want to be ready to present Canfield with what I hope will be a win-win proposition."

❀ ❀ ❀

Three weeks later Kathleen received an overnight package from Canfield. Inside was a letter offering her the position, a contract written by the town's attorney, and a lease agreement.

Kathleen found Gayle in the kitchen and put her arms around her. "I've got the job!" she squealed. "I wouldn't have been able to do this without you."

"I'm so proud of you. You've worked hard to get to this place, and here you are. Now go find Robert and figure out how you can buy your home." Gayle wiped her eyes. "Go quickly, I'm about to start blubbering like an old fool."

Robert looked over the agreement. "Honey, in a few years, this area will be ripe for growth, and they know it. Your credentials and experience are more than they could ever hope to get. If you sign the contract, you'll make a substantial income and have few worries. It does give them most of the power, and that's not what you want. I can pay them a visit as your legal representative and see if buying the house is an option. Money is going to be a problem because you can't buy something without cash. Do you have anything saved?"

"I have saved everything." She handed him a ledger printed from her computer's Quicken program with names of banks and account balances.

Robert was amazed at how much she had accumulated. "How did you save so much?"

Kathleen smiled proudly. "Mrs. Roth told me that if I saved my pennies my dollars would take care of themselves."

"A wise woman. This is a great deal of money, but the house needs work and maintenance will be expensive. It won't be enough to buy the house outright. I have some ideas that might make your dream a possibility but I need to do some more thinking. Why don't we meet tomorrow evening... hmm, say around seven?"

Kathleen smiled. "You've got a date!"

Gayle eased into bed, letting the days pressure escape through a sigh as she snuggled up tightly against Robert. "This is my favorite time of day," she said.

Robert wrapped his arms around her, pulling her closer. "Mine, too."

"I can tell you have something on your mind."

"Yeah, I do. Sweetheart, how do you feel about Kathleen's moving?"

"We can't keep her here forever, and I would like to see her strike out on her own and have that feeling of success. The only thing I worry about is her loneliness. What if Kathleen can never lie next to someone and feel she is the most important person in her life? What if she never experiences the kind of love we have for each other?"

"I worry about that, too. God has been good to us in almost every area of our lives, but we can't second-guess His plans. Kathleen wants to buy the house in Canfield, and I'd like to make her dream come true. She's fallen in love; it's not a person, but perhaps it's a beginning." Robert chuckled softly. "Well, you should have heard her today. She was lively and animated and interested in the future. We haven't seen that for a long time."

"Are you thinking of buying the house for her?"

"No, no, I'm a businessman and that wouldn't be good for her. Besides, you baby her enough for both of us. I'm thinking of becoming a partner so that she can float and won't sink. Once her practice gets off the launching pad, we can dissolve the partnership. What do you think?"

"I'm a lucky woman to have found you."

❀ ❀ ❀

The next evening, promptly at 7:00 pm, Kathleen walked into Robert's office carrying a thick folder in her hands and hope in her heart.

Robert said, "I've given this situation a lot of thought. I've crunched the numbers every which way, and there's no way you'll be able to buy the house and stay afloat on your own. What would you think about the two of us becoming partners?"

"You would do that for me?"

"Let's say for all of us. Gayle and I want to see you succeed, but to tell you the truth, my law practice has been getting a little boring lately. I think we're both ready for an adventure. I'd like to suggest that we form a temporary partnership, then when you're financially sound, we'll dissolve the business and the house will be yours.

"If you decide to go this route, I'll make an appointment with Canfield and try to get as much as I can for us—for you. We're going to have to work hard for the next week or so. I need to go to the meeting fully prepared. Have you done your research?"

Kathleen handed Robert the folder. "I've sketched the office configuration and I've worked on equipment costs. My guess is it will take six months to get the first floor of the house designed and equipped for medical offices. I'd like to open my practice in early spring. That will give me time to continue working on my rehab. My hand is almost back to normal, sensations and all, but I need to work on building muscle strength." She flexed her biceps Popeye style and laughed.

It's good to hear you laughing again," Robert spoke thoughtfully. "It's been a long haul for you. You've come so far..." Robert cleared his throat and looked over the floor plans, nodding his approval. "I'm impressed."

Kathleen's voice softened. "How can I ever thank you and Gayle for everything you've done for me? You made me part of your lives and treated me like a daughter. I'm so grateful." She caught her breath. "I'd like to continue staying here with you and Gayle, if you don't mind. There'll be trips to Canfield to oversee the work and it would be fun for us to go together."

She looked at Robert, eyes wide and a plea in her voice. "I want you to teach me everything."

"Aren't I the guy that taught you how to drive?"

"Oh God, Robert, don't remind me."

Robert laughed. "It was only the front lawn. You missed the house."

"I'll never forget that moment. I thought I would die."

Robert sat back in his plush office chair. "Kathleen, my father taught me how to drive and the first time I took the car out, I crashed into a telephone pole. My father didn't get mad either, but I had to work the whole summer to pay the bill."

"Is that why you had me reseed and work on the lawn that summer?"

"Yep. Everything in life has its consequences."

Kathleen nodded. "I've contacted St. Mona's Hospital in Santa Barbara and I can get a weekend shift in the ER."

Robert inched forward in his chair, as if to talk her out of that part of the plan.

"Before you say anything, the practice won't be self-sustaining for at least a year, possibly two," Kathleen put in. "I'm going to need the extra money, and I think I can handle a weekend shift. My hand has improved, and I'll be up to speed by the time I begin. I'm used to working hard, and I'll feel better if I'm working toward something. Remember, Robert, everything in life has its consequences. If I don't take a risk I'll never grow."

Robert smiled. "I can't disagree with that one."

Kathleen continued. "In doing my research, I believe that Canfield may be designated as a rural area. There may be government grants or low interest loans for bringing medical services to Canfield. Could you have someone check into government funding?"

"Sure thing," said Robert.

"Great!" said Kathleen. "Also, I've got my staff in place. I've contacted Sam and Helen Hughes. They've agreed to work with me."

CHAPTER 18

Kathleen reread Helen and Sam's New Year's note.

Enjoying Baja, CA, Mexico. We are perched on a cliff overlooking the Pacific Ocean. Can't wait to see you. We'll be there on the tenth wearing our work clothes.

Happy New Year.

Love,

Helen and Sam

P.S. 2008 is going to be a humdinger!

The Four Musketeers, as she came to think of Robert, Gayle, Helen, and Sam, insisted on helping with the move to Canfield. Kathleen couldn't protest after they told her they didn't want to miss out on all the fun.

Helen and Sam pulled up to Gayle and Robert's house in their motorhome. It had been months since Kathleen had seen them and she ran outside with arms outstretched.

Sam picked her up, twirled her around, and gave her a big hug. "I guess once you're my boss, I won't be able to do that," he said, flashing a broad, youthful grin.

"No one is ever the boss of you, Sam."

"Only Helen. She is definitely the boss of me."

Helen laughed and reached for Kathleen. "Sam, let me have a

turn with this girl and would you please get the massage table out of the RV?"

Sam and Kathleen exchanged a quick glance and an even quicker wink before he turned around to follow Helen's orders.

Kathleen had never seen Sam looking so handsome. The worry lines that had mapped their way through his face had faded and the slight paunch from, as Helen would say, "Too much junk food and not enough fruits and vegetables," was gone. Helen and Sam seemed perfectly matched.

As Kathleen watched them, she felt the familiar longing to be in a relationship, to have what they had: someone to love, someone to love her. She wondered if there was anyone who could love her.

After the others went inside, Helen asked Kathleen about her arm and hand. Kathleen held her arm up high. She walked to a nearby plant and stooped to pick a bright yellow chrysanthemum. "For you," she said, handing the blossom to Helen.

Helen held the flower next to her cheek. "It's one of my favorites." She took Kathleen's hand and spoke softly. "How's the pain?"

Kathleen's expression changed as if caught unaware by Helen's question. She sighed. "Still there, some of the time."

"When you lifted you arm, it looked as if you were forcing it and I saw the pain in your eyes."

"I should know not to try to fool you."

"I promised Gayle a massage this evening. How about if I massage you afterward? Maybe that will tell us something."

That evening Helen moved the massage table into Kathleen's bedroom. Kathleen lay on her stomach, trembling and shivering.

Helen covered her with a light blanket. "What is it, honey?"

"I'm scared. I'm naked, I'm on a table, and it reminds me of Iraq and hospitals."

"Think about where you are. You're in Los Angeles, surrounded by people who love you and will keep you safe. You're not in Iraq or

Germany and no one is going to hurt you."

Kathleen began to relax and drift off to another place. "Helen?"

"Hmm?"

"I never saw flowers in Iraq. Sometimes, one of us would get packets of seeds and we'd try to find a protected corner, someplace where there might be some shade. The seeds would begin to grow and peek through the soil. We would get so excited. Then, the heat and the wind would come from nowhere and kill everything. There were no safe corners. I've had bad dreams about there being no flowers."

"It was a harsh place and you saw more than anyone should ever have to see," Helen reassured her. "When we get to your new home, we should plant flowers—maybe some bulbs, too. You'll get out in the fresh air and it's something we can do together. Would you like that?"

Kathleen nodded her head and closed her eyes as if she was about to fall asleep.

Helen poured oil on her hands. "I'm going to slather you with sweet almond oil, give you a massage and get some of the tightness out. You have to tell me if I go too deep and if it hurts. Tomorrow, I want to watch your exercise routine. Maybe I can change or add something that will help loosen your shoulder. Now, I want you to take a deep breath, fill your lungs, and let all the air out."

The moving crew got to work after a long and lively breakfast. Gayle was feeling mellow after yesterday's massage and decided it was time to clean out her kitchen cabinets and closets for duplicates and extras. Gayle knew she had a "minor," as she referred to it, shopping problem and simply couldn't resist buying an item if it was on sale. Helen and Gayle hunted through kitchen cabinets and closets, chatting and laughing as they reviewed everything and placed the spare items on the kitchen table.

Kathleen watched them with their heads together, giggling as if they were two twelve-year-old girls with a special secret. Kathleen worked steadily, wrapping all the extras and duplicates in old newspapers and filling box after box. She didn't want to admit it, but she felt jealous and left out of their fun.

Robert and Sam were assigned to the garage to sort out Robert's extra gardening tools and supplies. Everyone knew how hard that would be for Robert, but after a couple of hours, with a look of triumph on his face and sweat pouring down his brow, a respectable pile of rakes, hoes, and shovels sat on the driveway waiting for a new home. After lunch and several tall glasses of ice tea, Robert and Sam left to pick up the moving van, but not before Helen tucked a long list of cleaning supplies in Sam's pocket.

It was still dark outside when they began their caravan to Canfield: four vehicles all in a straight line as if they were floats in a parade. Robert drove the moving van and led the procession. Sam maneuvered the motor home. Gayle and Helen shared Gayle's car while Kathleen's car brought up the rear.

Kathleen relaxed and enjoyed the quiet. She was tired from working nonstop yesterday and perplexed at the amount of giggling that went on between Gayle and Helen. It reminded her of school when she was friendless and felt left out of everything.

It was early morning when they arrived at Canfield House. The chatting and giggling stopped as all five stood immobile, awed by the regal beauty of Kathleen's Queen Anne home. Helen broke the silence by saying, "Wow!" and everyone began to laugh.

Kathleen unlocked the front door and took them on a tour. Some interior walls had been changed to allow for exam rooms and bathrooms. The contractor had made casts of the original moldings and matched the stain on the paneled walls. When the remodeling was completed the new and the old would be indistinguishable.

They moved some of the work materials to make a clear path to the kitchen. Kathleen opened the kitchen door, stopped frozen in her tracks, and turned to look at the Four Musketeers. They stood there with wide grins.

Helen spoke first. "You can't live in your new home without a refrigerator."

Gayle followed. "Or without a washer and dryer."

"Is this what all the giggling was about? Oh, you guys, I felt so left out!"

Kathleen hugged them and wished she could say the words that couldn't be released. They were simple words, spoken every day: "I love you."

PART THREE

Spring

CHAPTER 19

It was the first day of spring and Kathleen's office was due to open in ten days. Before undertaking the remodeling project, Kathleen was unaware that her need for perfection extended beyond the field of medicine. She had enjoyed the small restoration projects with Robert, but her need to return Canfield House to its original state now consumed her. She was content to wear a pair of sweats that were years old and threadbare, but nothing was too good for her home.

She became familiar with the history of Queen Anne architecture and poured over restoration catalogs and websites. She discovered a small company on the east coast specializing in Queen Anne hardware. Switch plates, outlet covers, and doorknobs were all ordered, but until they arrived, inexpensive stand-ins would have to do.

A cleaning crew spent the day banishing the dirt and dust that had occupied Canfield House for more than three years. The windows sparkled. The house smiled.

Kathleen looked at her list of "Things To Do," crossing them off, one by one. *Put books on shelves* was the lone "Thing" left on her list. She picked up a red pen and circled the words. She glanced at the unopened boxes of books near her desk: ten boxes neatly stacked and labeled *Estate of Anna Roth*. She got a box cutter and touched the tape sealing the top box. Her chest tightened and she sat on the floor next to the box, rocking back and forth, a little girl grieving for the woman who had given her a second chance at life.

~ Boston, 1981 ~

Kathleen wore a faded hand-me-down dress that was too large for her lanky figure, and shoes that were snug for her growing feet. She took a deep breath and held *Alice in Wonderland* tightly in her hands before entering Mrs. Roth's fifth grade classroom.

Kathleen kept her eyes on the floor, occasionally peeking at the kids sitting at their desks. Girls in new outfits, flirting with boys, became silent as she walked by. Giggles followed her as she walked to the aisle next to the window and sat at the desk in the back of the room. Tears stung her eyes and she tried to be less visible by slumping in her chair.

She opened *Alice* to a random page and tried to focus on dissolving words. She stared out the window and watched the white clouds lazily change shape as they drifted across the September sky. She imagined a chariot swooping down to take her to a land with gumdrop flowers and rivers overflowing with lemonade. She saw a gingerbread house resting on a green meadow with her family waiting on the porch. They surrounded her and smothered her with hugs and kisses. They went inside and her da told stories about fairies and leprechauns and strong women warriors, and they made peanut butter sandwiches stacked as high as the sky.

Mrs. Roth rose from her chair and wrote her name on the blackboard, an unspoken action that called for complete silence. She talked about the classroom rules and then passed out a handout with their homework assignment.

"There will be no math or spelling homework for tonight," she announced.

A happy murmur spread from student to student.

"Your assignment is to write an essay about your family. The handout asks you to answer some specific questions. I will be checking for spelling and grammar. It's points off for errors, so use your dictionaries. Your report must be between two and three pages. I want to see neat cursive writing. Absolutely no printing," she admonished. "They are due tomorrow, and I will return them to you on Monday."

❀ ❀ ❀

Kathleen walked to Mrs. Adams' home, a small skip in her step. This was the most important assignment of her life. She said hello to Mrs. Adams, got a glass of milk, and climbed the stairs to her room. *First,* she thought, *I should make a cover.* Kathleen found scraps of cardboard and drew crayoned flowers in shades of gray and blue.

She sat at the plain brown desk, scuffed and scarred by years of use by foster children. The tip of her tongue stuck between her teeth, she began to write on a sheet of lined notebook paper:

"My Family, by Kathleen Moore.

"I was born on June thirteen, and I am ten years old. There are nine Moores, my father, my mother and seven children. I am the eldest. We live in a very happy home.

"My father works for a bank in Boston. His title is Vice-President. My mother doesn't work. She stays home and takes care of the children. A woman comes in every day to help Mother with the cleaning and cooking. Sometimes, when my father comes home from work, he and my mother dance before we eat dinner. I love to watch them. They are the most beautiful couple I know.

"I am lucky, because as the eldest child I have my own bedroom. Here is a photograph of my room."

Kathleen opened the desk drawer and carefully took out a page she had saved from an old magazine.

She looked at it, smiled, and thought *perfect*!

She used her school scissors to cut around the outline of a picture of a girl's bedroom and pasted it onto the first page of her report. The room was furnished with a canopy bed covered with a pink floral chintz spread. Shelves, filled with dolls, books, and games, lined the walls. Dresses, shoes, and play clothing hung in the closet.

"Mother and I went shopping and bought everything for my bedroom," she continued to write. "We had so much fun.

"My parents travel a lot, mostly on business, but sometimes they take a vacation to Europe. I suppose I will go with them soon. They think traveling will be good for my development.

"I'm not sure what I want to be when I grow up, but I love to read and my favorite subject is science. Right now, I am working on an invention so I can become invisible.

"Father told me I could attend the University of my choosing. He is happy to pay the tuition. Perhaps I will become a doctor so I can help the poor."

❀ ❀ ❀

Kathleen's eyes lit up when Mrs. Roth returned the essays on Monday and she saw an "A" written boldly on the cover, in bright red.

That afternoon, after the dismissal bell rang, Mrs. Roth asked Kathleen to stay for a few minutes. Kathleen was shaking inside. Did Mrs. Roth know? Was she in trouble?

When the last child left, Mrs. Roth said, "You're not in trouble, Kathleen. Come sit next to me."

She wondered, was *Mrs. Roth a mind reader?*

Mrs. Roth opened the desk drawer and took out a plate of homemade cookies. She placed one on a napkin and offered the plate to Kathleen. Kathleen hesitated before taking a single cookie and placing it carefully on a napkin. Kathleen followed Mrs. Roth's example by breaking off a small piece before putting the morsel in her mouth.

Mrs. Roth said, "Kathleen, you are a bright girl and I thoroughly enjoyed your essay. In your paper you wrote about your love of science. I believe you could become a doctor, perhaps even a surgeon if you wanted."

Mrs. Roth paused for a moment. "I was wondering if you would like to stay after school for some tutoring. I thought you might enjoy a special reading assignment, something we won't read in class. After you've read the book, we can discuss it. You would be surprised at the hidden meaning in books."

"I like to read," she whispered.

Mrs. Roth nodded. "I thought so. *Alice in Wonderland* was one of my special books when I was child. What is your favorite part?"

Kathleen's lips quivered when she spoke. "When Alice gets to go down the rabbit hole into a different world."

"Yes, that was an exciting time for Alice. Kathleen, who looks after you when your parents are traveling?"

Kathleen focused on her feet and spoke shamefully. "Mrs. Adams. I stay with Mrs. Adams when Mother and Father are gone."

"I want you to take this note to Mrs. Adams. It's asking permission for you to stay after school to get tutored." Kathleen clutched the permission slip as if it was a life preserver ring thrown to a drowning person.

"Before you leave, would you mind taking the rest of the cookies with you? I'm starting a new diet and I won't be able to eat them."

Kathleen munched on the cookies as she walked home, leaving nothing but an empty paper plate and a few crumbs to be thrown away in a nearby trashcan.

The next day, Kathleen returned to school with the signed permission slip in her hand. The relationship that began with a fragile piece of paper lasted throughout her school years and beyond, until one day, Kathleen's letter to Mrs. Roth was returned and she learned that the woman who had given her another chance at life had died.

The daylight began to fade and Kathleen stepped outside her office to watch the sun disappear behind the hills. She vowed never to take her home, the sunset, or anyone she loved for granted. As the darkness crept in, the night air began to feel more like winter than early spring. Seeking protection from the night chill, she went inside, put on a sweater, and started a fire in the fireplace.

It was difficult for Kathleen to believe that Canfield House was hers. She looked at the room that had been the library. Her desk was positioned in front of three large windows that faced the north side of the house. During the day, natural light streamed through, brightening what might otherwise be a dark room. A small conservatory led outside to the wraparound porch. A single wing chair, covered in light brown velvet, rested comfortably inside the conservatory. Ferns and palms, placed near the door, made the outside and inside seem as one. It was a perfect spot to read a favorite book.

A couch and two chairs were arranged in front of the tiled fireplace. It would be a pleasant sitting area to be used for intakes and consultations. Kathleen didn't like the idea of sitting behind her desk when she spoke with patients. If she was delivering good news, she wanted to share in the joy, and if the news was bad, she didn't want a barrier between her and the patient.

Hunger pains reminded her that she had waited too long before eating. Kathleen turned around, not wanting to separate from the room she loved. She scanned her office as if she was creating a photograph and securing it to her heart.

As Kathleen walked toward the kitchen she took in every detail: the oak paneling on the walls, the hardwood floors that creaked, even the drafts that came through the old windows and made her shiver. She tried to stay in her lucky feeling and quiet the small voice that told her she must have been insane to take on such a huge responsibility.

Kathleen opened the kitchen door and hesitated before walking in. She flinched at the sight of the green cabinets and the orange patterned linoleum. She vowed that, someday, she would return Canfield House to its former state of glory.

CHAPTER 20

Claire Hollander sat at the dining table in her grandmother's efficiency apartment, while Bubba, as she called her, fussed over dinner. "Eat, eat," Bubba commanded, handing Claire a plate piled high with brisket, mashed potatoes, and peas.

Claire stared at the plate and thought, *from my lips to my hips.* "Uh, Bubba, do we have any salad?"

"Do we have salad? I'm always forgetting something."

"Wow! *That's* a salad," said Claire, when Bubba returned carrying a bowl heaped high with spring lettuce and raw vegetables.

"Now, down to business," said Bubba.

Claire was planning on taking her grandmother's green, 1997 Saturn station wagon on her trip from New York to Los Angeles—a generous and unexpected parting gift.

"Before I give you my car, I want three promises from you," her elflike grandmother had said.

Claire looked at her beloved Bubba, with hazel eyes that couldn't hide a glint of humor. "What kind of promises?"

"I want you to promise you'll always keep the car doors locked and don't give anyone a ride, not even a sweet-looking young girl." The old woman's index finger kept time with her words like a conductor's baton. "Last week on TV, I saw a program and this driver stopped to pick up a girl who was hitchhiking, and once the door was opened two murderous thugs jumped from behind a bush and slit the driver's throat. I want you to stop at a motel before dark and I want you to call me every night."

Claire almost laughed at the murderous thug comment, but she knew if she made a promise she would have to keep it. "I promise, Bubba."

Bubba handed Claire the keys and a bulging manila envelope. "Registration, proof of insurance and owner's manual. Use it in good health, *tatala*," she said, using the affectionate Yiddish term for child. "You're starting a new life, and it's time I gave up driving. Ah, if I were ten years younger I'd be going with you."

Claire threw her arms around her grandmother. "Oh, Bubba, thank you, thank you, thank you. You're the best! I'm going to miss you so much. Please don't worry. I'll be staying with friends along the way and I promise to be really careful. I don't take as many risks as people think."

"No? Skydiving? Hiking through Ireland? Climbing mountains in Switzerland? It's time you settled down. Maybe this change will be good for you. You'll have a steady job and a chance to meet a nice boy. He doesn't even have to be a doctor."

Claire knew Bubba was right; it was time for her to settle down. At thirty-three, most of her friends had at least one child and some had had more than one marriage. Perhaps her luck would change in Los Angeles.

Claire was amazed at how much the station wagon held. While a sixties VW bus would have been much more to her liking, free was free and she was grateful for Bubba's generous gift. She felt a little bit like a nomad with all her possessions piled high in a wagon. During the times when she would get fidgety, and feel the need to travel or try a different profession, she would wonder about the part in her that couldn't put down roots or stick with any one thing for very long.

She put the last box in the car. *Last box in, first box out*: that was her motto. She would try to spend some time going through the faded box that held a lifetime of certificates, diplomas, and photographs that Bubba had carefully pasted in an album. She hoped the box might help to solve the mystery of why she couldn't be in a lasting relationship.

Claire looked at the map with small red stars identifying her stops. These were friends she had met during her travels and adventures. She held onto these friendships as if they were precious jewels, but couldn't hold onto boyfriends for more than a few months. She wondered why. Was it simply part of her personality, as Bubba believed? She suspected it was more than that and hoped that the time spent alone while driving would allow her to examine those places deep inside where the hollow place lived.

Nick was the latest in her quest for a long-term relationship. When Claire discovered that Nick was having an affair, she felt betrayed and lost control. At first, she spewed angry epithets. Then, she felt her face turn red and she did everything that defined a tantrum except to lie on the floor, kicking and screaming. She tried to justify her behavior. After all, he had crossed a line that could not be tolerated. Once she calmed down, she felt ashamed and had to admit that tantrums at her age might be part of the problem. She vowed to gain control of her lifelong habit.

Claire had spent a month on the road, stopping along the way to visit with old friends, and was surprised at how they had changed over the years. Martin and Nancy had camped with her in Ireland and were now settled in a home in the suburbs near Portland, Oregon. Nancy held her two-year-old twins, balancing one on each hip. She looked tired and Claire was disappointed that bedtime was no later than nine p.m. Martin had developed a paunch and complained about the confinement of his job. She felt depressed when she left. *Was that all there was?*

Claire was eager to finish the last leg of her trip. There was more traffic on the road than she expected, and she knew it would be dark before she got to Santa Barbara. She hated to break her promise, but thought it best to call Bubba before she stopped for the night. Claire was relieved when there was no answer; she could leave a chatty message about her day and report that she was fine.

Claire began to get drowsy and opened the windows to let the ocean air revive her. It was chilly and she zipped up Nick's motorcycle jacket. She knew Nick would be pissed at her for taking his jacket, but it seemed to be a fitting act of revenge.

Claire's cell phone rang.

"Hey, Claire."

"Hey, Nick." Her tone was frigid.

"I want my jacket."

"It was a gift you didn't deserve, and I took it back."

"What the fuck are you going to do with it?"

"Well, it's a bit chilly and I'm wearing it, but I might be passing it on to the first homeless person I see in Los Angeles, you prick!" It felt good to yell with the ocean breeze kissing her face.

"Jesus, stop having one of your goddamn tantrums. I said I was sorry, but you didn't give me a chance to explain. What do you want from me? Do you want me to get killed on my bike? Come on, I really need that jacket."

Claire's voice softened and sounded like honey drizzled on a warm biscuit. "Do I want you to get killed? Of course not, Nick." Her voice began to increase in volume and tempo, reaching a strident rage. "I want you to break every goddamn bone in your body. Shithead!" Claire stopped yelling and spoke in a calmer voice. "I'll mail it back when I get to Los Angeles."

Claire mumbled to herself, "That was a mature way to handle it! So much for tantrum control. I should take the jacket off and change the energy."

Claire pulled onto the shoulder of the highway and stood by the side of the road. The fog, which only a short while ago had looked like wisps of smoke, began to thicken and move in with a vengeance.

Taken back by the sudden change, Claire moved toward the protection of her car. She heard a loud reverberating sound before she was thrown over the side of the road, tumbling round and round, like stones in a rock tumbler.

CHAPTER 21

Kathleen returned to her office, trying to ignore the unopened boxes of books. The near empty bookcases had been freshly polished with linseed oil and buffed with soft cotton cloths until they shined.

She wandered over to the bookcases and held *Alice in Wonderland* in her hand. She opened the book and glanced at the well-worn, dog-eared pages and recalled the time when *Alice* went with her everywhere. Kathleen stroked the cover and whispered, "Thank you for being my friend."

Kathleen's cell phone brought her out of her reverie. It was Lincoln Hathaway, the local sheriff. During the remodeling of Canfield House, Kathleen and Robert became fast friends with Linc, whose passion was restoring houses and cars from bygone eras.

Linc's home was a log cabin built in 1940, when Canfield first became a summer haven for vacationers. Surrounding his cabin, in neat order, were cars that Linc was in the middle of restoring. He drove a 1949 Ford convertible and had his clothes custom made in 1950s style: rockabilly threads reminiscent of Elvis in his heyday. He was an invaluable resource for contractors who specialized in restoring and remodeling Victorian homes.

"Look, Doc, with this old house you are going to need a truck," he said to her one day. "I'm restoring this 1975 Dodge and it has your name on it."

Linc was right, as he so often was, and Kathleen became the proud owner of a 1975 Dodge D100, complete with the original tan interior... a little tattered in spots ... and a Chrysler slant 6 engine that kept it humming... once it started. When it didn't start, which was fairly often, Linc was quick to do the repairs.

Kathleen answered her phone, "Hi, Linc."

"Hi, Doc, got a few minutes?"

"For you, always."

"We've got a major accident on the coast highway. A tanker and at least a dozen cars are piled up. The helicopters are grounded because of weather, and we're having problems getting the injured out of here."

"Do you want me to come down to help?"

"No, no. The EMTs are triaging and we're getting the worst injuries to St. Mona's. Other patients are being redirected to hospitals in the area. Part of the highway is blocked and the alternate routes have become our worst nightmare. I've got the county Emergency Medical Services Coordinator, Cheryl Troop, on the phone. Hold on."

Kathleen heard static on the line followed by a clear, crisp voice. "Dr. Moore? Cheryl Troop. We've got quite a mess here. You know, no matter how well you plan, there's always the unexpected. We're still triaging, and we've got several life threatening injuries. Some victims are trapped in their cars, and we're using our resources to get them out and over to St. Mona's. We've also got frightened parents and kids with minor injuries. I understand that you're in the process of equipping a trauma room. Do you have that in place?"

"Enough in place to help. How many patients and what kind of injuries are you talking about?"

"Up to twenty. The EMTs are telling me cuts and bruises. It'll be mostly stitching, tetanus shots, and TLC."

"I may be short on tetanus vaccine."

"I'll see what we can spare and get it to you ASAP."

Kathleen knew that she and Sam could easily take care of the suturing and tetanus shots, and no one was as good as Helen in handing out Tender Loving Care.

Together, they could take care of anything.

Helen made coffee and hot chocolate and took homemade muffins out of the freezer. The patients arrived in small groups, some transported by the highway patrol and some by volunteers from Canfield. Helen asked the patients, who were only frightened and not injured, to help serve coffee and muffins. Helen knew that when people helped someone else, they helped themselves as well.

It was past midnight before the last patient left for the temporary shelter at Canfield Middle School. Kathleen, Sam and Helen sat around the kitchen table drinking coffee.

Sam said, "Reminds you of old times, Doc?"

"It does when you call me Doc. It feels special to be a Doc again. I thought we'd have more of a problem with the kids, and now I'm not sure who was more frightened, the kids or their parents."

Helen said, "I had to drag a couple of parents away from their kids. The kids were fine and the parents were causing major hysteria."

Sam chuckled. "I saw the way you handled it during triage. It was perfect. You asked, 'Who knows how to bake?' Then you practically shoved them into the kitchen, showed them where the ingredients were, and got them making cookies. If you weren't a married woman, I'd ask you to be my wife." Sam leaned over and kissed her.

Kathleen's phone rang. She looked at the number. "It's Linc, now what?"

"Hi, Doc. I wanted to thank you for your help. The three of you are the toast of the town. Half the women have a crush on Sam, and the kids didn't even mind the shots. They said you have a magic touch. Let Helen know her muffins got rave reviews. You didn't have to feed everyone, as well as take care of them."

"That was Helen's doing. If someone walks in, they get fed."

"Well, you gave the town some great publicity. Some reporters have been hanging around and want to interview you."

Kathleen shuddered at the prospect and hoped it didn't come true.

Linc didn't pause or give her time for reflection. "Hey, Doc, we have a delicate situation here, and we have to ask you for another favor. When the tow trucks were moving cars, they found a car over the embankment."

"Was anyone in the car?"

"No, but someone was found on the ground nearby. Hold on, Cheryl is sitting right here at the Command Post."

Cheryl's voice was as fresh and crisp as it had been earlier that evening. "Hi, Kathleen. Thanks for your help. You're a godsend. We've got another situation. A woman was found at the bottom of the embankment. Apparently she's been on the ground for several hours. The EMTs have her on a backboard with her C-spine immobilized. The patient is alert and oriented to time, place, and person."

"Oriented times three," Kathleen interjected, instinctively quoting the medical shorthand.

"Check. The EMTs told me she made quite a fuss when they cut off her motorcycle jacket and jeans. She's in the Emergency Medical Services truck getting ready for transport. All her vitals are within normal range. The ER at St. Mona's is still jammed and we're concerned about transporting her through these clogged roads only to have her wait to be examined. The highway to Canfield is open and they can be at your office in about twenty minutes. Are you equipped to assess, and are you willing to accept this patient?"

"I have everything I need to assess. The EMTs can wait here until I've completed my examination."

"Done. I can't thank you enough. When this is all straightened out, I'd like to meet you and see how you've equipped your trauma room."

"Sounds good. I'd like to put a face to the voice."

Kathleen put the phone down and thought, *after all, what's one more patient?*

❀ ❀ ❀

The room that was once used to receive visitors to Canfield House now held medical monitors and equipment, including a hospital bed, crash cart, and a compact lab.

Sam and Kathleen laid out supplies and instruments, and Helen moved quickly to put blankets and towels in the warming cabinet.

They heard the vibrating sound of the EMS truck as it jostled to a halt on the pea gravel driveway. Kathleen saw a look of exhaustion on the EMTs' faces and a glazed look in their eyes that spoke of the horrors from the night. She remembered that feeling from Iraq, when the thought of a night's sleep became a vague memory and new memories were being formed that would steal any possibility of sleep away.

Kathleen looked briefly at their written report. "Okay, let's get her off the gurney and onto the exam table. We'll take it from here."

Helen showed the EMTs to the kitchen. "I made roast beef sandwiches and fresh coffee, and there's fresh fruit in the bowl on the sink. Better than the chips and Cokes dangling out of your pockets. Relax if you can. I'll come get you if you're needed."

Kathleen leaned over the exam table. "Hi, Claire, I'm Dr. Moore. Can you open your eyes for me?" Kathleen saw Claire struggling to open her eyes. Kathleen used a silver and black otoscope and shined its finely focused ring of light into Claire's eyes. "Keep your head still and follow the light with your eyes... Excellent."

Kathleen put her hands in Claire's. "Can you squeeze my hands?" She felt Claire squeeze as if holding onto a lifeline. "That was a really strong squeeze! Now I want you to push your feet down like you're stepping on a gas pedal. Good. Now lift your toes up toward your head." Claire was following directions and was able to move her hands and feet: two good signs.

"Can you tell me where you hurt?"

Claire groaned, "All over. My back."

"Okay. We're going to take some x-rays, and make sure nothing is broken. It'll just take a few minutes and if they look okay, we'll get you off the backboard. I'll let you know what we're doing every step of the way."

Kathleen reviewed the digital x-rays and stood by Claire's side. "You're a lucky woman—no broken bones. Claire, can you look at me, because this is really important. We have to roll you on your side so we can remove the backboard. When we start to roll you, I want you to lie still and let us do the work. Don't try to help."

When they log-rolled Claire and she was on her side, Sam removed the backboard and Kathleen examined her back. Claire cried out. "I'm sorry, I know that hurt. I'm only seeing soft tissue injury. Sam, I want an ultrasound of her belly. Follow with a Foley and draw me some blood."

"CBC and chemistries?" Sam asked.

"No, draw a rainbow; we don't want to stick her a second time if we need to run additional tests."

Claire was mumbling and Kathleen leaned over to hear her. She smiled briefly and said to Helen, "She wants to know where the EMTs put her jeans. They're original 501 Levi's."

Helen bent over and whispered, "Don't worry, honey. They're safe with me."

Kathleen watched Sam as he operated the ultrasound. Sam and Kathleen looked at each other and nodded—their tacit shorthand for pronouncing the test normal.

Claire groaned and her eyelids fluttered open.

Kathleen stood over her so that their eyes met. "I know you're in pain, but I need you to tell me where it hurts when I touch you. Do you think you can help me?"

Claire managed a weak "yes."

Kathleen started at the top of Claire's head. At first she looked at her scalp, trying to see if there were any cuts or abrasions. She examined her scalp again, but this time she closed her eyes and allowed her fingers to see for her. She did this with every part of Claire's body, looking, examining, as if she had never seen that part of a body before, closing her eyes and examining again. Claire cried out when Kathleen probed her left thigh.

Kathleen checked the information on the paramedics' report. "Are you allergic to anything?"

Claire shook her head.

Kathleen patted her arm. "Good. I'm going to give you an injection for the pain. You did really well and when you wake up, one of us will be here with you. This will sting for just a second, then you'll have a nice sleep." Kathleen watched as Claire closed her eyes and drifted off.

Kathleen said, "She's a lucky woman. That motorcycle jacket did its job. Abrasions on face and hands. Muscle strains to shoulders, back, and left thigh. Multiple contusions on her back. No breaks. Let's run a CBC and test her urine for blood."

While Sam and Helen treated Claire's abrasions and contusions, Kathleen went into the kitchen to get a cup of coffee and release the EMTs. She would stay in the trauma room until Sam relieved her in the morning. Kathleen looked out the kitchen window. The fog was lifting and she could see a glimmer of light in the valley below.

Kathleen wondered about the woman in the trauma room. It was curious she was wearing a man's motorcycle jacket that was easily two sizes too big for her, but the young woman could be a bohemian type—that wouldn't be unusual for California. When she had examined Claire, she saw a tattoo on her arm, not of a flower or some other feminine graphic, but numbers. It was the kind of tattoo that was given to the Jews who were sent to concentration camps during WWII.

Kathleen brushed the tears from her eyes as she remembered that day at Walter Reed, when Mrs. Roth appeared to her. She moved her right hand and felt the sensations in her fingertips. She hoped that Mrs. Roth could hear her: "Thank you, Mrs. Roth, for staying in my life."

CHAPTER 22

Kathleen was awakened by Claire's groans. She could feel the stiffness in her body as she stood to move closer to the bed. "Hi, Claire."

"Is this a hospital?"

"No. I'm Dr. Moore and you were brought to my office after the accident."

"I really hurt."

Kathleen saw tears making their way down Claire's cheeks. "You took a bad fall and you've got bruises and abrasions over most of your body. I'm going to make you more comfortable. I need you to turn a little bit on your side so I can change the cold packs. Then I'll give you something for the pain."

"Is Oscar okay?"

"Oscar?"

"He was in the car with me."

"There was no one in your car."

Claire became agitated. "No, Oscar was in the front seat. I left him there when I stepped outside. Please, you have to find Oscar."

"Just hang in there for a minute. I'm going to call over to the sheriff's office and we'll get this straightened out."

Kathleen called from the kitchen. "Linc, it's Kathleen."

"Hi, Doc. Busy night, eh? How's that patient doing?"

"She's doing fine, but she keeps talking about another passenger in the car, someone named Oscar."

"No other passenger. Hold on, let me check the report on that car." Linc returned to the phone. "Doc, there was no person, but a cat was pulled out of the car and is at the vet's. Ask your patient if Oscar has four legs and tell her he's going to be okay."

Kathleen returned to Claire. "I think we've solved the mystery. Is Oscar your cat?"

Claire nodded and whispered, "Yes."

"He's at the vet's and he's going to be fine. So, his name is Oscar?"

"Oscar Tilquist, the Third," Claire replied, wincing as she pronounced the regal name.

Kathleen was surprised at the name. Oscar she could understand, but Oscar Tilquist, the Third? Some pet owners really went overboard she supposed, with their "children." "Well, you'll both be okay. Someone will call the vet's office later today and see how Oscar is doing. Would you like that?"

Kathleen heard the softest "yes" and noticed that Claire seemed to have relaxed.

Kathleen put the side of the bed down and undid the tie on Claire's hospital gown. She put her stethoscope to Claire's back, checked the bruises, and replaced the cold packs. She walked over to the medicine cabinet, prepared and gave Claire an injection, and watched as she relaxed and fell into a deep sleep.

Kathleen wrote in Claire's patient chart and settled back into her chair. For a moment, before falling asleep, she wondered about the woman who wore a motorcycle jacket, had a tattoo on her arm, and a cat named Oscar Tilquist, the Third.

Sam walked into the trauma room a little before seven in the morning. Doc and their patient were sleeping. He looked at Claire's chart

and saw that she had been examined and medicated two hours earlier. He left, got a cup of coffee, and settled into the chair opposite Doc. It didn't make any sense to wake either of them.

Sam remembered when he thought he was in love with Kathleen. It began when they had dinner at the China Bistro. There was something about her, an interest in him, without judgment, that allowed him to talk about his failed marriage with Marie. After his divorce, he swore he would keep his heart shut tightly. He never wanted to chance the pain and anger that seemed to follow love.

Kathleen had opened his heart and touched him in places he thought were dead. Gradually, the feelings he had interpreted as love changed, and she began to feel like a best friend or the sister he never had. Without Kathleen, he wouldn't have been able to fall in love and marry Helen. He owed her so much, more than she would ever know.

Kathleen woke and blinked her eyes in an attempt to focus. As the space around her sharpened, she saw Claire in the hospital bed and Sam sitting across from her. She smiled when she saw Sam; it felt good to have a friend close by. "How's Claire?"

"She's been stirring and groaning for the past few minutes. How are you doing?"

"A little groggy and a crick in my neck. Nothing that coffee and a hot bath won't fix."

"I checked her vitals. They're excellent. I think we can remove her from the monitors."

Kathleen agreed. "Except for contusions and abrasions, she's okay. I want to make sure she can empty her bladder on her own."

Claire stirred and Kathleen leaned over the hospital bed. "Hi, Claire. You're doing really well, and you don't need to be connected to these monitors."

Sam and Kathleen worked together to remove Claire from the monitors and settled her into a more comfortable position.

"Better?"

Claire nodded. "Yes, thank you. I didn't break anything?"

"No, but it may feel like it. Let Sam know if you're having much pain. No more injections, though. I want you to start taking sips of water and clear broth. I'll be back in a couple of hours to check on you."

❀ ❀ ❀

Kathleen opened the door to her bathroom and sighed with relief, knowing that in a few minutes she would feel the curative powers of hot water.

When Kathleen first saw Canfield House, she was disappointed that the five bedrooms on the top floor shared one outdated bathroom. She claimed one of the bedrooms that faced the valley as hers, and had an adjoining room remodeled into a closet and bathroom. It was the one personal luxury she allowed.

The oversized stall shower was lined with tiles from a less fortunate Queen Anne home that had been razed to make room for a development. A rain dome showerhead hung from the ceiling and multiple height showerheads were placed on two of the tiled walls.

The tub looked like the original claw tub, but was deeper and meant for soaking. Kathleen filled the tub and slowly lowered her body into the water. With a sigh, she allowed the hot water to sink into every pore and surrendered to the feeling of floating. Kathleen kept refilling the tub and soaked for more than an hour, knowing that the tankless "forever hot water heater" would guarantee hot water, always.

Kathleen wrapped herself in an oversized beige bath towel. She glanced in the bathroom mirror, defocusing her eyes so that her reflection was blurred. She saw, but didn't see. It was a trick she had learned many years ago when, as a teenager, she watched as her body changed and developed. She saw her chest begin to swell and hair pop up in new and strange places. She was embarrassed. She was ashamed. She had no friends her age to share the angst or excitement over her metamorphosis.

Kathleen traced the scar that ran from her shoulder to her chest with her fingertips. The prominent scar only served to make her feel less attractive. The women she had been with had told her how bright or talented she was, but no one had told her she was pretty, and no one had stayed the night, ever.

There were times when no matter how long she soaked or scrubbed, she couldn't feel clean.

There were times when no matter what she did, she couldn't stop the bad feelings from creeping in.

There were times when she was thrown into a place where emotional darkness reigned, and she was lost to the fear that seemed to be waiting around every corner.

Kathleen crawled into bed, looked at the bottle of pain medication on the nightstand, and knew it would stay untouched. She needed to be self-reliant and in control of her physical and psychological pain. Kathleen lay on her left side and got into a fetal position with her knees bent tightly against her chest. The pressure on her scar was relieved; the pain began to evaporate and she fell into a sound sleep.

She was startled to discover it was almost one in the afternoon. She felt a sense of panic. How did she sleep so long? She got dressed quickly and went downstairs. Sam had finished organizing one of the exam rooms and was busy on the second. A quick "hello" and an equally quick bite of breakfast and she was ready to see her patient.

Kathleen opened the door to the trauma room and saw that the bed had been raised.

Helen smiled. "Good afternoon, Dr. Moore. I didn't think you would mind if I let Claire sit up for a few minutes."

Kathleen trusted Helen's judgment, always. "I'm glad you did."

Kathleen took Claire's pulse. "Your hands feel warm." She took Claire's temperature. "Your temperature is normal. Are your hands always this warm?"

"Just sometimes, Dr. Moore."

"Why don't you call me Kathleen?" She looked at Claire's chart and saw that her vitals had remained within a normal range. "Have you had anything to eat or drink?"

"Some clear broth, ice chips, and water."

"When I'm done examining you, Helen will make you some lunch. I want you on a soft diet for a day or two. Liquids are important, preferably water. I'm going to remove the cath and see if you can pee on your own. Are you having any headaches?"

"Yes, it feels like caffeine withdrawal."

"I can understand that. Helen makes the best coffee. I want you to limit it to one cup, at least for now. Let me know if your headache doesn't go away. Can you turn on your side for me?"

Kathleen examined Claire's back and reviewed the x-rays from the previous night.

"Do you remember the accident?"

"Only that I got out of the car to take my boyfriend's—" Claire faltered. "My *ex*-boyfriend's jacket off. We had been on the phone, and he was really pissed that I had taken it, and I was pissed that he had an affair. I was going to mail it back to him. The last thing I remember was a really loud sound and then I woke up here."

"There's not much left of the jacket. The paramedics had to cut if off. It's here, but in pieces." Kathleen started to smile and quickly changed back to a serious expression. She had an angry impulse to tell Claire to return the shredded jacket with a nasty note. "You can tell your boyfriend, your ex-boyfriend, that his jacket may have saved your life. You have some abrasions on the side of your face." Kathleen touched her face, "right here, and on your hands, but they should heal without a problem. Your back took most of the impact, and that's why you've got all these bruises. You're going to be sore for a few days, but nothing was broken."

"Do you think I can get out of bed to use the bathroom?"

"One thing at a time. Let's see how you feel dangling your feet over the side of the bed. You can tackle the walking a little later. I'm going to leave the IV in for now. It will help keep you hydrated. You're looking at a week to ten days for healing and another week to get your energy level back."

Kathleen decided to practice her bedside manner, brought to her attention by Colonel White during her evaluation and then by

Mark, who had once memorably described it as "shitty." "Tell me, Claire, where were you going when the accident happened?"

"I was headed for Los Angeles. I have a job offer at a museum, creating exhibit displays."

"That sounds like a fun job. Where were you driving from?"

"New York."

"That's quite a drive."

Claire winced as Kathleen removed the cath. "I took a month off to visit friends. Santa Barbara was my last stop before LA. I'm supposed to start my job on Tuesday."

Kathleen shook her head and spoke in a clipped voice. "I'm afraid that's not going to happen. You can call them on Monday and explain your situation. I would be looking at delaying your job by two, maybe, three weeks. Is there anyone we can call for you?"

Claire shook her head. "I only have my grandma and I don't want to scare her. I'll have to call her tonight, though. I promised I would call every night while I'm on this trip."

"There's a phone on the table next to your bed. You can use that to make your calls. Do you have any other questions?" Kathleen's voice still sounded like someone had put starch in it. She had lapsed into her frosty clinician mode and didn't even realize it.

"My things? My cat?"

"I'll ask the sheriff to bring everything over, and we'll call the vet's office to see how Oscar is feeling. In the meantime, Helen will take good care of you, and I'll check back in a couple of hours."

Claire's shoulders slumped and tears formed as she reacted to Kathleen's sudden change in demeanor. She reached for a tissue to wipe her eyes. "I guess this is a stressful time for Dr. Moore, trying to get her offices opened and having to take care of me."

Helen smoothed the bedding. "Are you referring to her bedside manner? I'll admit it could use a little spit and polish sometimes. But you could look a long way and not find a finer doctor. If you're looking for warm and fuzzy, that *was* her warm and fuzzy."

CHAPTER 23

Helen was born into an ordinary family, was raised in an ordinary, mid-sized city, and thought of herself as ordinary. She did admit to having one unusual talent. She was a born matchmaker. Helen considered her matchmaking skills to be a gift from God and could, therefore, remain comfortable in her perception of being ordinary.

It had been years since Helen had felt the allure that told her a match was in the making. One day the gift was there, and the next morning it was gone. She felt different, as if some deity had reached inside her and blew out a spark.

But over the past few days, since the accident happened and Claire arrived, she began to suspect that her matchmaking instincts had only been dormant and were, once again, on the rise. She watched Kathleen and Claire talking and interacting and thought she saw that certain spark developing in their eyes. She wondered if that something special might be there for them. Helen felt that "love was in the air," and she was ready to put her talent to the test.

Kathleen had put her hair in a ponytail and was wearing a pair of faded jeans and a red and white checkered shirt. Not-so-white sneakers completed her "I have to get something done" outfit.

Helen fixed a breakfast tray for Claire. "Kathleen, are you on your way to see Claire?"

Kathleen spoke absentmindedly as she reached for a slice of toast. "Mm-hmm, it's time to discharge her."

"Poor girl. I don't think she has any place to go, and here you are with all those spare rooms upstairs. Maybe she could stay here for a couple of weeks and recuperate."

Kathleen thought for a moment. *Well, why not? What's the harm in extending help to someone without a car or a place to go?* She smiled at Helen. "Thanks for thinking of it. I'll talk to her."

Helen returned the smile. "Oh, you're welcome. I'm really bogged down with phone calls. Would you mind bringing Claire her breakfast? I've got a mug of coffee for you, too."

Kathleen carried the tray with two mugs of coffee and breakfast for Claire. Helen knew how much both girls enjoyed their coffee and had added homemade banana bread and fresh fruit to the tray.

Claire was sitting on the bed with the phone in her hand. "They can't hold my job," she announced dismally.

Kathleen put the tray on the table next to the bed and sat down. "I'm really sorry."

Claire wiped her eyes. "I want to thank you for everything. You really did save my life. Is there a hotel in town? I need a place to stay until I can travel to Los Angeles."

"There's no hotel but there is a bed and breakfast that's quite charming. I stayed there for a few days." Kathleen was quiet and sipped her coffee. "I don't know if they take cats, though."

Claire nodded. "I can call them later. Maybe they'll be okay with Oscar. I don't have an address to give you, and I'd like to pay your bill before I leave, if that's possible."

"There won't be a bill from me."

Claire looked surprised. "I really can't accept that, it doesn't feel right to me."

"Okay." Kathleen took a prescription pad and wrote, "For Medical Services provided to Claire Hollander, two dollars."

Kathleen handed her bill to Claire.

"I don't understand."

"Let's just say that someone helped me when times were tough and I'm paying it back," said Kathleen. "We do need this room but I've got three spare bedrooms upstairs. You might feel fine now, but you've gone through a trauma and I don't want it to bite you later on. Helen and I were talking and we both agree it would be a good idea for you to stay here to recuperate. It'll give you a chance to decide on your next step."

As she rose to leave, Kathleen said over her shoulder, "Why don't you have your breakfast and I'll come back in a couple of hours to give you a final exam and discharge you."

Claire smiled. "From patient to guest?"

"From patient to guest."

❀ ❀ ❀

There was a flurry of activity in the guest room with Helen acting as director. Linc brought all of Claire's belongings and gave her the sad news that her car was totaled. Linc looked at her carefully. "I have just the right car for you. I can tell you're a VW girl." Claire looked surprised, and by that look, Linc knew he was right.

Helen called the vet, and assigned Kathleen to pick up Oscar that afternoon. She gave Kathleen a list of cat supplies and sent her on her way. Kathleen wondered if there was anything that Helen didn't know how to handle.

Kathleen got in her truck, said a little prayer that it would start, and left to rescue Oscar from the vet's. Everywhere she stopped, people were waving to her and saying, "Good job, Doc," or "Thanks a lot, Doc." Kathleen was beginning to feel part of the town and guessed her nickname was going to stick wherever she went.

By the time Kathleen returned to Canfield House, Sam and Helen had left for the day. She found a note from Helen:

I've made barley soup and baked fresh bread. The salad is in the fridge. Would you bring Claire her dinner? It might be easier for her.

P.S. Why don't you eat with Claire? I think she may be lonely.

Kathleen carried Oscar upstairs in his carrier. She knocked on the door and was taken aback when she saw Claire sitting on the floor. She was wearing a pink floral tank top and black leggings and had painted her toenails a bright pink. Her caramel-colored hair fell into ringlets above her shoulders. Gold hoop earrings danced as she turned toward Kathleen.

Kathleen put the carrier on the floor and the bottle of antibiotics for Oscar on the nightstand, next to the book *The Annotated Version of Sherlock Holmes*. Kathleen thought, *Aha, a clue! She's a Sherlock Holmes fan.*

Quickly regaining her composure she said, "Here's Oscar, a few cuts and bruises, but he'll be as good as new in a day or two." She watched as Claire opened the carrier and Oscar crawled onto her lap. He was a large gray tabby with four white paws and a grating meow. Oscar had a round head—slightly too big for his well-fed body—and huge, luminous green eyes. His wide mouth seemed to curl in an impish grin. Kathleen thought he looked exactly like Sir John Tenniel's illustrations of the Cheshire cat in *Alice in Wonderland*.

Oscar, with a piercing tone, began mewing and mewing as if he was telling Claire about his adventure. Claire leaned over, kissed Oscar on his head, and spoke to him in mommy talk. She looked up and smiled. "Kathleen, I'd like you to meet Oscar Tilquist, the Third."

Kathleen sat on the floor next to Claire and rubbed Oscar's head. "Hello, Oscar." Oscar purred and arched his back. Kathleen looked at Claire and hinted, "I'd like to hear more about his name sometime."

But Claire was engrossed in petting and kissing Oscar. "He needs to be loved up right now, but a little later I'll tell you how Oscar got his name." Oscar walked over to Kathleen and crawled on her lap as Claire continued to pet him like there was no tomorrow. "I can tell he likes you. He usually doesn't go near people he doesn't know."

They sat next to each other, "loving up" the cat named Oscar Tilquist, the Third that had just used up one of his nine lives and seemed none the worse for wear. After a while Oscar left them to explore his surroundings and found the perfect hiding place under the bed. Kathleen and Claire continued to sit on the floor, talking.

Kathleen felt warmed by Claire's affable nature and began to feel more at ease.

"I'd love to know about this house," Claire said, smiling. "I saw several Victorian homes in San Francisco and of course, on the East Coast. Have you ever been to San Francisco?"

Kathleen could feel a blush beginning and hoped it wasn't showing. "A few times, years ago. You're thinking of the houses on Steiner Street?"

Claire nodded. "Right, the Painted Ladies! Oh, they're so gorgeous. And so is your home. Do you think I could have a tour? I've never been in a Queen Anne home."

"In a couple of days, when you're stronger. Although, I should warn you that the kitchen has been mucked up from a really bad 1970s remodel."

"I'll look past it, I promise."

Kathleen looked at Claire with the eyes of a physician. "You're not looking well." She placed her hand on Claire's forehead. "You're warm and you shouldn't be on the floor."

"I was feeling fine."

Kathleen's curt, no-nonsense tone returned. "But now not so fine? I want you to get back into bed. Did you take your meds?"

Claire looked down as she shook her head. Kathleen reached over to the nightstand and handed Claire her medication. "This one is to help with pain and fever, and this one is an antibiotic. You have to take them both. Okay?"

Claire nodded; her face flushed and her lips trembled.

Kathleen sat on the edge of the bed. "Everyone does this, including me. You start feeling better, then you figure you don't need the meds. Except it's the meds that are helping you to feel better."

Claire's voice was shaky. "I'm sorry, I don't like taking anything that isn't natural."

Kathleen looked around the room and saw Claire's possessions stacked against one wall. No car, only a grandmother to call, and in a strange place, alone. She had to be feeling frightened.

When Kathleen had nightmares, Gayle had held her and comforted her. Would that be appropriate to do with Claire? She wasn't sure and began to feel confused.

Kathleen stood up abruptly. "I have some phone calls to make. Why don't you try to sleep? I'll come back in a couple of hours with dinner."

When she stood on the other side of the door, she heard Claire crying. She had her hand of the doorknob, but turned away and walked downstairs.

❀ ❀ ❀

Kathleen placed the dinner tray on a small round table next to the balcony. Claire was sitting on the bed with Oscar on her lap.

Kathleen sat on the bed, petted Oscar and looked at Claire. "Feeling better?"

Claire nodded. "I slept."

"I'm sorry if I was abrupt before. This whole experience can't be easy for you."

Claire gestured toward the boxes and suitcases stacked neatly in a corner. "Everything I own is in this room and I'm worried about my computer."

Kathleen spotted a red computer case. She moved some bags and small suitcases and brought the computer to Claire.

Claire tentatively unzipped the case. "It looks okay, but I'll know more after I charge the battery."

Kathleen motioned to Claire to give her the computer. "I'm going to charge it and you can test it in the morning. I don't want you working on it tonight. You need time to rest and regain your strength. Doctor's orders."

❀ ❀ ❀

The barley soup was rich with meat and vegetables. Freshly baked sourdough bread and a salad with organic lettuce, herbs, and vegetables rounded out their meal. The aromas were tantalizing, and both women's appetites were aroused.

Claire took up a spoonful, blew on it, and put it in her mouth. "Mmm, this is outstanding. Does Helen do all your cooking?"

Kathleen nodded and smiled. "She doesn't trust my cooking or my eating habits and rightfully so." She put her spoon down and wiped her mouth. "Okay, so the name Oscar I can understand, but Oscar Tilquist, the Third? That's quite a mouthful for a cat."

Claire, seemingly in a better mood, leaned back in her chair. "Well, to get to Oscar's name, I'll have to tell you a little bit about me. I was raised in New York City in a small, rent-controlled apartment. My parents were lucky to have it. They were both teachers but my dad was sick a lot, really couldn't work much, and with medical expenses, well, things were tight. When I was born, my grandma, my dad's mother, came to live with us and take care of me. I call her Bubba, which is Yiddish for Grandma. My mother worked a lot and when she was home she wasn't emotionally available. Bubba was more like a mother to me than a grandma."

Engrossed by Claire's story, Kathleen sat back in her chair, listening attentively.

"My bubba was a teenager, back in the 50s, when television was just starting. There was this entertainer who she especially loved to watch on Saturday nights. She told me there were only three TV stations in New York and the whole family would hover around this tiny black-and-white set with indoor antennas, waiting for Oscar Tilquist, the Third, to appear. He was famous for making witty, sometimes sarcastic comments. He would play the accordion and say something outrageous, especially for those times."

Claire looked up at Kathleen and smiled. "One day, as I was leaving for work, I heard this rattling noise and mewing coming from a garbage can. I picked up the lid and I saw this little kitten. Someone had thrown him away. He was so vocal that I named him Oscar Tilquist, the Third. It made my bubba happy, and that's how Oscar got his name."

"You saved his life."

Claire spoke slowly and a sad look crossed her face. "He's saved mine more than once."

Kathleen stayed for a while until she thought Claire was looking tired. She began to clear the table. "Do you need help with anything?"

Claire turned red.

Kathleen guessed. "Do you need help getting to the bathroom?"

"No, I'm just embarrassed. I was going to look for something but I realized how sore I am."

"I'll look, but you'll need to tell me what the something is."

"Can I whisper it?"

"Whisper it so..."

"So I can't hear what I'm saying."

Kathleen felt a giggle starting somewhere in her belly. She nodded.

Claire leaned over and whispered, "Could you see if Mr. Fluffy is with my things?"

Kathleen was holding in her laughter. "Um, Mr. Fluffy?"

"He's a rabbit."

"Alive like Oscar?"

"No, stuffed as in a bunny rabbit. Okay, you can laugh. I can see you're trying to hold it in."

Kathleen burst out laughing. "You're kidding."

Claire's eyes twinkled and a small dimple appeared on her cheek. "No, Mr. Fluffy sleeps with me."

"Always?"

"Well, not always, but if I'm alone and scared."

Kathleen walked over to Claire's pile of stuff. She tried to be serious, but every time she thought of this grown woman with a stuffed bunny, she burst out laughing. She found Mr. Fluffy—a pot-bellied white rabbit with pink ears, button eyes, and a cottony tail—inside one of the shopping bags and held him up triumphantly. It looked altogether silly—nothing, she decided, like Alice's tardy, waistcoat-wearing rabbit—she couldn't control her hilarity.

"I'm sorry," she said, trying to catch her breath. She handed Mr. Fluffy to Claire and became serious. "Is he injured? Because, you know, I am a doctor."

Claire turned him over, one way then another. "He looks okay, maybe a slight fever. Could you give him a quick check?"

Kathleen cradled Mr. Fluffy as if she were examining a newborn baby. "He's in amazing condition, considering his trauma. I do see a small injury near his head that will require some stitches. He'll be fine tonight and I'll take the stitches tomorrow."

"I'll share him with you, if you want. You can have him tomorrow night."

"Oh, I wouldn't want to deprive you. My room is across the hall. Why don't you leave your door open? I'll hear you if you need me."

Kathleen got into bed and instead of muffling sobs from a nightmare, she buried uncontrolled laughter into her pillow. She moved around fitfully, trying to find a comfortable place. She couldn't imagine how in God's name, Claire got dropped on her doorstep. An obviously straight woman with a cat called Oscar Tilquist, the Third, and a stuffed rabbit called Mr. Fluffy. *Shit*, she thought, *and I'm attracted to her!*

She punched her pillow, put her legs under and over the blankets, and then punched her pillow again. She knew that tonight, sleep would be hard to come by.

During her sleepless hours Kathleen kept mouthing the word lesbian. Then she thought, maybe it would be easier to say gay. She couldn't get past the "g." Why was it so difficult for her to say it? If she couldn't say the word, how could she begin to think about having a relationship? It was obvious that Claire was straight. Was she attracted to her, or was she simply longing for a friend? She didn't trust herself to know the difference.

Sam, lost in a John le Carré spy novel, and Helen, lost in her own thoughts, were lying in bed. Helen was having some doubts about her latest matchmaking foray. She suspected Kathleen was gay and, in spite of the "don't ask, don't tell," policy, there was the usual hospital gossip, but how could she be certain? Questions kept rising within Helen: *Can I be wrong in my thinking? Am I reading signs that aren't really there? Is my gaydar that far off?*

Helen turned to Sam. "Sam?"

"Hmm."

Helen snuggled closer. "Has Kathleen ever had a boyfriend?"

"You're not thinking of making a match, are you?" He chuckled and began to stroke Helen's back. He drew Helen closer and gave her a long lingering kiss.

Helen knew where that kiss was going to lead, but before that happened she continued, "Do you think, maybe... do you think that perhaps... she's attracted to girls?"

Sam laughed at that one. "Oh God, Helen. She's had a boyfriend for years. I thought everyone in the hospital knew that Gary and Kathleen are together." Sam propped himself up on his elbow and yawned. "Sweetheart, where are you going with this?"

"Nowhere, Sam." She stroked his rugged cheek with one hand and tossed John le Carré unceremoniously on the nightstand with the other, and took up where his earlier kiss had left off.

CHAPTER 24

Canfield House, once vacant and subject to decay, was now filled with life, activity, and laughter. The silence, like tombs from time out of mind, had disappeared.

Claire woke up first and as the sun was rising, walked to a small clearing near the house to practice tai chi and meditate. She noticed a change in Oscar. She wasn't sure if it was the unfamiliar scenery or the trauma from the accident, but he seemed to have lost the bravado of a city cat. He followed her to the clearing, waited patiently as he cleaned his paws, and then trailed behind her, meekly, to the house.

Afterward, Claire would hum show tunes as she showered and dressed. She could hear Kathleen stirring in her bedroom and Helen puttering about in the kitchen. Claire and Helen would drink coffee and chat until Kathleen joined them for breakfast. Claire thought it was easy to be with Helen, and she seemed interested in hearing about her adventures and struggles with boyfriends. It wasn't that Claire flitted from guy to guy; they just never seemed to fit.

The three women would sit around the kitchen table, talking, laughing, and enjoying Helen's wholesome, stick-to-your-ribs breakfast. It reminded Claire of the sleepovers when she was in high school—giggling with girlfriends, gossiping about boys, and sharing secrets until the night faded. She would miss these mornings, but she was beginning to feel restless and thought it was time to complete her trip to Los Angeles.

Claire was alone in the house. She sat on her bed listening to a Michael Feinstein album of Gershwin. She loved the romance that came from that era, when songs reflected love and most of the movies had a happy ending.

Claire visualized Fred Astaire and Ginger Rogers dancing off into the clouds, to live happily ever after. She longed for that feeling. Friends and family told her it didn't exist, and she wondered why. She thought about the phrase happily ever after, and thought that the word "happily" didn't necessarily mean there wouldn't be sad times. She knew there would be bumps in life, but if the love remained, wouldn't happily ever after still be true?

Sometimes, at the mall or in a park, Claire would see an older couple walking hand in hand, still in love, still supporting each other both physically and emotionally after a lifetime together. Perhaps, the phrase should be changed to love ever after. After all, wasn't it the love that would keep the happiness in a relationship?

Kathleen knocked on Claire's door and peaked in. Claire thought about how tired and pale Kathleen looked and wondered about this woman who seemed so professionally driven but personally bereft.

Claire looked up at Kathleen. "Rough day?"

"More long than rough."

"Have you eaten dinner?"

Kathleen shook her head.

"Helen left a note. She made one of your favorites, Irish stew."

"I'm too tired to eat."

"Have you eaten *at all* today?" That comment was right out of Helen's mouth and while she had not written it down, she had instructed Claire to ask.

Kathleen looked dazed. "I can't remember."

"Why don't you get cleaned up and I'll fix dinner? You won't have to walk downstairs, we can eat here."

"Oh, I don't know. I'm really exhausted. Lots of minor emergencies and no time for a nap."

Claire said entreatingly, "I would really like the company."

Kathleen paused. "In an hour, okay?"

Claire went downstairs to the kitchen, moving at a leisurely pace. She was used to Kathleen's lengthy showers and baths; she couldn't help but hear the water run for what seemed like forever.

❀ ❀ ❀

It was only yesterday, while Kathleen had been at St. Mona's, that Claire and Helen discovered the dumbwaiter that went from the kitchen to the upstairs hall. They pulled an unwilling Sam into their newest adventure. Sam stood in the upstairs hallway while Helen and Claire pulled on the rope. He could hear their laughter and was sure he heard them singing the Merchant Marine anthem "Heave Ho! My Lads! Heave Ho!"

The rope seemed strong but the connected pulley made all kinds of squeaks and squawks. Sam got his trusty cure-all, a can WD-40, and generously sprayed the pulleys and wiped the rope. Helen and Claire tested the dumbwaiter with a tray loaded down with canned vegetables and were surprised and excited that it worked.

Helen said, "Claire, I have an idea. Why don't you make dinner for Kathleen and surprise her by bringing it upstairs in the dumbwaiter?"

❀ ❀ ❀

Claire set the table in her room, and waited. When she heard the water stop, she went downstairs, gave the stew a final heating, and put it in the dumbwaiter. She took the rope and pulled and pulled until she heard the lock click into place.

Claire ran upstairs to find Kathleen opening her door. Kathleen had thrown on an old T-shirt and shabby sweat pants that clung to her damp body. Claire stopped and stared for a moment at Kathleen. Claire had seen young women in Ireland with the same flawless complexion and olive green eyes. Claire remembered how their quick smiles lit up their faces. She rarely saw Kathleen light up and wondered what could have happened to make her so serious.

Claire motioned to the dumbwaiter door. "Could you open that door for me?" Kathleen looked surprised, but did as she was asked. She smiled broadly. "This is great! You got it working."

Claire took the tray. "It took three of us and one can of good ol' WD."

Kathleen chuckled. "Sam's fix-it-all."

They ate slowly. Claire thought if she kept eating Helen's cooking she would become positively Rubenesque. Kathleen on the other hand, seemed to stay thin—almost too thin.

They finished dinner and were sitting quietly, when Claire told Kathleen it was time for her to complete her trip to Los Angeles. "I'll never be able to thank you enough for everything you've done for me and Oscar, but I can't keep leeching off of you."

Oscar heard his name and decided to come out from his hiding place under the bed. He walked to Kathleen, purring as he rubbed his body against her leg.

Claire continued. "I spoke to Linc today and he said he has the perfect car for me. If it's okay with you, I'd like to stay for a few more days and get everything organized."

Kathleen's voice caught in her throat. "Do you have a job lined up?"

Claire shook her head. "No, but I have a couple of contacts and leads."

Kathleen wanted to say, "Please don't go. Please." Instead, she spoke slowly, trying to keep her voice steady. "I've never considered you leeching and you're welcome to stay for as long as you want. We'll miss you," she leaned over to rub Oscar's pumpkin head, "and Oscar, too."

❀ ❀ ❀

Kathleen looked out the kitchen window and watched Helen working in the vegetable garden. Starter flats of beets, broccoli, and tomatoes joined the sweet corn, parsley, and spinach as Helen gently lifted each plant and tucked it into the carefully prepared soil.

Kathleen hesitated before pouring two cups of coffee and joining Helen in the backyard.

"Hi, Helen. I'm sorry to be bothering you. I know Sunday is your day off." Kathleen looked down, her eyes filled with pain and her lips trembling. "Can we talk?"

Helen motioned her over to the nearby bench. "I'm ready for a cup of coffee. Let's sit here for a while." Helen spoke softly. "What's wrong?"

"I'm really sad and I don't know what to do. Claire is leaving."

"What happened?"

Kathleen swallowed hard. "She told me it's time for her to find a job. I don't think she feels useful."

"It's odd that this is coming up right now. Canfield has so many summer homes and cabins, and in a few weeks, they'll start to fill up with families. They're going to be thrilled to have a physician in the area. Since your practice seems to be growing rather quickly, it's getting difficult for me to manage the front office by myself and still help in the lab.

"Have you seen Claire when she comes downstairs when there are patients? She's a natural—a friendly, likable chatterbox—and the folks really take to her. Why don't you offer her a summer job? That would be a big help to me and it will help Claire to feel more useful. Also, I noticed that your books are still in boxes. Why not let Claire organize them and get them on the shelves? You'll feel better just having things put away."

Kathleen sighed and gave Helen a hug, thanked her, and went inside to find Claire.

Helen sat for a few minutes, sipping her coffee and feeling satisfied that her matchmaking plans had not been thwarted. Merrily humming "Hello, Dolly!" she returned to her gardening.

PART FOUR

Summer

CHAPTER 25

Spring turned into early summer. As Helen predicted, the small town of Canfield began to swell with tourists and summer residents. Narrow lanes, identified only by homemade road signs, led to small summer cottages built in the 1940s and'50s. SUVs and vans, loaded with children, toys, and provisions dotted the twists and turns of the hillside roads as families began to settle in for the summer.

❀ ❀ ❀

Claire was perfect for the front office, and not just for entertaining the parents and children. Kathleen began to see the many sides to Claire Hollander.

Kathleen had a break between patients and the waiting room was empty. She saw Claire pulling and filing patient records.

"Is this boring for you?"

"No, but I've been thinking."

"Dare I ask?"

Claire stopped filing. "I think you're missing an opportunity."

"What do you mean?"

"What happens to Canfield from mid to late August?"

Kathleen was reminded of Gayle's trick questions: an obvious answer, followed by a mysterious interpretation. "The summer residents go home."

"Right. And guess what all the moms will be planning?"

Kathleen had to think a moment. Her mom didn't do much of anything to get ready for school. Then she remembered, Mrs. Adams would go to the thrift shop and buy her clothing. "School clothes, I guess."

"Yep, and doctor's exams for their kids as well. Vaccinations, permission slips for school sports, et cetera, et cetera, et cetera."

Kathleen knew where the "et cetera, et cetera, et cetera" came from. They had watched the movie *The King and I* three times in the past month.

Claire shut the file drawer and leaned against the cabinet. "What if you made August the back to school examination month? I could make posters and flyers, and I'll bet the moms would be thrilled."

Kathleen grinned mischievously. "Know what?"

"What?"

"'Tis a puzzlement I didn't think of this myself!"

Claire carried the large carton, marked *Next-day Air, Perishable,* into the kitchen. "I'm going to share this with you," she said to Helen, Sam, and Kathleen, laughing as she opened the box and began to unpack layers upon layers of frozen gel packs. Claire couldn't stop laughing. "We'll get to the bottom of this; it's just that my bubba overdoes everything, including the packing."

Kathleen and Helen shared a look and rolled their eyes as Claire pulled out the last of the gel packs and began to lay containers and butcher paper-wrapped packages on the table.

"Corned beef, pastrami, potato salad, coleslaw, and my bubba's homemade kosher pickles," said Claire, her mouth watering. "Oops, and don't forget the rye bread and hot mustard, too."

They sat on the porch, munching on their corned beef sandwiches. Kathleen said with her mouth full, "This is good… I'll have to send your bubba a thank you note. Helen's already got appointments for mid-August. How did you learn to do so many different things? Posters drawn, computer programs uploaded, stories for the kids?"

Claire shrugged. "Don't shortchange your own talents. You're like the Super Doc. All you need is a cape."

"And all you need is a Sherlock Holmes cap."

They laughed.

"I have to admit, I am a mystery addict." Claire was thinking and Kathleen could almost see steam coming out of her ears.

"Okay, Dr. Watson," said Claire coquettishly, "if you are really curious about me, come to my room tonight at eight."

Kathleen took a quick shower, changed into her jeans, changed back into sweats, put her jeans back on, tried them on with a belt, then without a belt. "Oh God, I have no clothes. A top, a top, I need a top!" She riffled through her closet and found an aqua sweater. She remembered her Christmas gift from Gayle and Robert— a turquoise necklace and earrings—and thought they matched her sweater. "Shoes, shoes!" Gayle had taken her shopping for her birthday and bought black loafers to go with her new clothes.

It was ten minutes to eight. She thought, *what's wrong with me, I feel like a teenager on her first date! This is not a date. Oh, God, I've never even* had *a date!* She watched the clock, as the second hand seemed to barely move.

She walked across the hall, smoothed her hair, and knocked on Claire's door. "Hi."

"Hi. That's a beautiful necklace."

"Thanks, it was a Christmas gift from my friends, Robert and Gayle."

"Well, they have very good taste."

"You look sad, is everything all right?"

"I wanted to tell you not to come over."

"Why?"

"We were having fun today, kind of bantering back and forth, and I thought I would show you my keepsake box. When I opened it and took a good look at the contents, I realized I'm really a jack of all trades, and I'm feeling, well, not exactly proud of who I am."

"Have you done something illegal—uh, robbed a bank, murdered one of your boyfriends?"

Claire shook her head. "No, but it's a thought. What I've done is completely legal. Well, I guess I should show you." Claire sat on the bed and handed Kathleen a stack of certificates. "Come see. I move from thing to thing, don't put down roots and have no purpose."

Kathleen looked through the certificates. She smiled secretly at one of them, Certified Dog Groomer. For a minute, Kathleen had a picture of Claire grooming a large dog and being full of soapsuds. "These are amazing. I'm very impressed. Brooklyn College and Parsons School of Design."

"Yeah, I was going to be a teacher, but realized I couldn't sit in a class, year after year. Then I thought about writing and sketching, so I hitched a ride to Parsons. In between was Massage Therapy School and Dog Groomer. Afterward, I traveled throughout Europe."

Kathleen peeked inside the box. "You've got a photo album. Show me?"

"Sure," said Claire. She patted the bed, indicating Kathleen should sit down next to her. With a shy smile, she did.

Claire opened the photo album to the first page. A chubby, curly haired infant sat in an old-fashioned metal washtub with a big grin across her face. "That's me, eight months old."

"It looks like you. Well, at least the smile does."

Claire flipped the pages, one by one. "This picture is when I learned to ride a bike. Skinned knees and all. And this is when I got a black belt in karate."

"Who's this?" said Kathleen when they came to the photo of a puffy looking, overweight preteen.

"I should throw that one away."

"That's you?"

"The summer I went to fat camp."

"What happened?"

"My dad had died and I couldn't stop eating. It started right after my dad's funeral. In the Jewish tradition everyone who visits the family brings cakes and sweets."

Claire looked down. "This is a little embarrassing. I began to sneak cookies and candy into my room and lie in bed, eating and eating until I fell into a drugged sleep. I did it every night. Bubba would come in the next morning and tell me to change my sheets; they were so full of crumbs. Then I began to blimp out, my clothes were getting tighter and I had these unsightly bulges. I don't know why they call them love handles. There's nothing to love about them. So, this one night I'm in bed eating the last of a Boston cream pie..."

Kathleen looked at Claire in amazement. "A whole pie?"

"I told you this was embarrassing. Well, I could hear my bubba and mother arguing about my weight gain and it got pretty hot and heavy. My mother's screaming, 'It's a phase, it's a phase,' and my bubba's saying, 'Adele, she's grieving and it's becoming an addiction.'

"Finally, I hear this glass shattering against the wall and my mother walks out, slamming the front door. I'm not sure we had much to do with each other after that.

"So, off I went to fat camp. You know, my bubba was right and I learned some really important things. One, I will lose weight if I move a lot. Two, I will lose weight if I eat more vegetables and fruit and less fries. Three, there's a boys' camp on the other side of the lake and kissing can be lots of fun."

Claire smiled briefly and picked up her certificates. Thumbing through them, her face grew sad and pensive. "Bottom line, they're just pieces of paper that don't amount to much of anything."

"You have so much talent," Kathleen tried to reassure her. "Maybe you just haven't found the right thing."

"Did you always want to be a doctor?"

"I never thought of being anything else. Hmm, come to think of it, when I was much younger, I thought how much fun it would be to solve mysteries. I still like to do that, only they're medical mysteries."

"So, we have that in common. I'm a major Sherlock Holmes fan and a snoop extraordinaire. Kathleen, I've been thinking. I'd really like to explore this area. The hiking trails look like fun and maybe try river rafting. Would you want to hang out with me?"

Claire became the "event planner," with unusual and exciting adventures waiting around every corner.

Wednesday became movie night. After the last patient was seen, Kathleen and Claire would drive into town, stop at the video store for a movie, and make a final stop for take-out food.

"What's your favorite movie, Kathleen?" Claire had asked that first Wednesday night.

"I guess the original *Star Wars*."

"Okay, let's do a double feature, *Star Wars* and a musical. We'll need extra popcorn if we're doing a double."

Claire had a passion for the old romantic musicals from the 1930s and '40s. At first, Kathleen rolled her eyes, but finally gave in to watching Fred and Ginger dance and sing their hearts out for the twelfth time. Claire was a sucker for dapper Fred in his tuxedo, top hat and snazzy boutonniere, and elegant Ginger in her long, flowing gown.

"Have you ever seen anything as romantic as that?" Claire would habitually sigh, sometimes turning a sofa pillow into a makeshift dance partner.

As Kathleen watched Claire, and saw her so in love with love, she began to think that perhaps that wasn't such a bad thing to be.

For Kathleen, the happiness she felt from her friendship with Claire was accompanied by confusion. A nonsexual relationship with another woman was something new to her, and she wasn't sure of where the boundaries were. If Claire cried during a romantic but sad movie, was it appropriate for Kathleen to comfort her by touching her hand? Or would Kathleen's longings get out of control and spoil the friendship that was becoming so important? She handled it the only way she could. She kept her distance.

❀ ❀ ❀

One Saturday evening after Kathleen returned from the ER, Claire suggested that they spend Sunday in Santa Barbara. Kathleen moaned a little to herself, thinking Sunday was her only catch-up day, but she couldn't resist Claire's excitement.

"I'll drive," said Claire. "All you have to do is relax."

True to his word, Linc had found the ideal car for Claire. While it wasn't a VW bus, it was a 1960s VW Beetle convertible, and it fit Claire's free spirit style perfectly.

They drove to Santa Barbara in the mellow-yellow Bug with the top down and, appropriately enough, Beatles music—Claire's idea—blaring from the CD player Linc had graciously installed. Kathleen wasn't sure if relax was the right word to use with devil-may-care Claire driving, but she could see that Claire was as happy as happy could be.

By the time they got to Santa Barbara the morning gloom had lifted and the sun was beginning to warm the beach air. The tide lapped at their feet as they walked along the shore. They watched children playing in the water and digging holes in the sand. Kathleen had a moment of sadness when she remembered the before time, at the beach with her brother Devon, when they almost reached the other side of the world by trying to dig their way to China, as all kids will do. She wondered if Devon was all right and if he ever thought about her.

Claire dug into her beach bag, laid towels on the sand, and took out the sunscreen. "Let me get your back."

Kathleen sat quietly as Claire rubbed her back with the lotion. Claire's touch was an out of control electric current, rushing, finding its way throughout her body. Kathleen hugged her knees and thought about how much she wanted Claire. She didn't know how much longer she would be able to contain her stirrings.

Claire handed Kathleen the bottle. "After you get your arms and legs, would you get my back?"

Kathleen prayed, as she put the sunscreen on Claire's back, *please God, take these feelings away.* She could feel the velvety texture of Claire's skin as her hand moved slowly over her shoulders. She longed to lean over, put her face next to Claire's hair, and breathe in her fragrance. Instead, she put the top back on the tube of sunscreen and returned it to Claire.

Claire leaned back on her elbows. "This is where I was heading when the accident happened. I'm finally getting to see Santa Barbara. Life is strange, isn't it? We wouldn't have met if it wasn't for that accident." Claire looked at Kathleen. "I know so little about you. I don't even know what kind of music you like."

"Music? I haven't had much time for music or other things, I guess. I was studying all the time. I like opera, and there are a few pop songs I like."

Claire absentmindedly dug her toes in the sand. "Which opera?"

Kathleen had to think for a minute. "Probably *Madame Butterfly*."

"And what pop songs?"

"Hmm, let's see. Whitney Houston's 'I Will Always Love You.' And k.d. lang, I really like her version of 'Hallelujah,' and just about anything by Melissa Etheridge.

Claire thought, *k.d. lang and Melissa Etheridge? Two gay icons?* Regaining her composure she said, "Yeah, you like music that tears at your heartstrings. 'One Fine Day' from *Madame Butterfly* really does it for me, too. Have you ever been to the opera?"

Kathleen shook her head and smiled. "Studying and long hours in hospital settings and the Army, that's been my life. I must seem boring to you."

"Not boring at all. I'll bet you could tell all kinds of stories about your adventures. It's all in the way you see it." Claire stood up and offered her hand to Kathleen. "There's an art show at the park. Let's spend some time there and then have lunch."

Kathleen and Claire walked toward a large grassy area. The art show was in full swing and they strolled through aisle after aisle of crafts and paintings. Kathleen enjoyed watching Claire as she stopped to talk to the vendors and artists and seemed to know something about each craft or painting technique.

One of the artists recommended a secluded restaurant specializing in California cuisine. They strolled down the walkway to a small restaurant on one of the side streets. It was the down time between lunch and dinner and the restaurant was fairly deserted. The headwaiter suggested the outdoor dining area. They were escorted through a narrow, dimly lit passageway that opened to a patio reminiscent of those found in Spain. Moorish style tiles decorated the floor, while pots, filled with every variety of geraniums, hung from the white stucco walls. A fountain in the center of the patio danced rhythmically in the shade of the surrounding Indian Hawthorne trees. The tables, covered in cloths in bright primary covers, held various patterns of antique silverware, creating a cosmopolitan atmosphere.

Claire ordered a bottle of Merlot. "I can't thank you enough for everything you've done for me and Oscar. I was so worried about him. You not only took care of Oscar, but loved him as well. If you don't mind, I want this to be my treat, and will it be okay if I order for both of us?"

Kathleen wanted to say more than thank you, but her words and desires were twisted around each other and she couldn't trust herself to release one without the other. She wanted to say what she was feeling: "This is the best day I've ever had, and I want us to go home and make love." But all she could safely say was, "Thank you."

Claire told the server they preferred to graze rather than eat a large meal. He suggested they begin with the roasted pumpkin soup and follow with several items from the starter menu. It would give them the experience of the cuisine while not overwhelming them with large portions. It was perfect for both of them.

When they returned to the car, Claire dug into her box of CDs. "I don't have *Madame Butterfly* but I do have *La Bohème*. I should warn you that I always shed a few tears at, 'They Call Me Mimi.'"

It was the end to a wonderful day, and Kathleen thought about how her world had opened up since Claire came into her life.

CHAPTER 26

It was dusk when Kathleen returned from the ER. She had been treating a patient, for over a month now, whose symptoms varied from week to week and didn't seem to fit any disease. She had a "medical mystery" to solve and needed the solitude and privacy of her office. She was surprised to see Claire sitting cross-legged on the floor with her elbows resting comfortably on her thighs and a book held tightly in her hands. The natural light was dimming and as she scrunched closer to the page, her hair fell loosely around her face, obscuring all but the book from her view. She reminded Kathleen of a Princess who was held prisoner in a castle, waiting to be rescued by Prince Charming. For a moment, Kathleen wondered why it couldn't be Princess Charming who did the rescuing.

Claire looked up with a startled expression.

Kathleen smiled. "Sorry, didn't mean to scare you."

"Whoops, I meant to be out of your way before you came home. I was just sorting the books and I got caught up in *Doctor Hudson's Secret Journal*. It's about doing a good deed and keeping it a secret." Kathleen knew if a book had the word "secret" in the title, it would get Claire's attention.

Claire struggled to stand up. "Ugh, my legs have fallen asleep."

Kathleen offered to help and put her hand out. Claire took Kathleen's hand, her face flushed, and a strange expression crossed her face. Then, as if she was shaking off a new and indefinable feeling, Claire offered the book to Kathleen. "Someday, you'll have to read this one."

Kathleen held the book in her hand. "Claire, do you understand patient confidentiality?"

"Yes, Helen had me take an oath when I first started working here."

"An oath?"

"Well, the oath was my idea, but Helen explained how important it was not to talk about a patient except with the staff. I thought if I'm part of the staff, I should take some kind of an oath, like the Hippocratic Oath that physicians take."

Kathleen had to suppress her laughter, Claire looked so serious. "What was the oath?"

"Helen made it up." Claire raised her right hand and recited: "I, Claire Marie Hollander, do solemnly swear to uphold the laws of confidentiality by keeping my ears open, my mouth shut, and not discussing patients with anyone except Kathleen, Sam, and Helen—unless, it's an emergency and I have to call 911 or Linc. Above all, remember: Do no harm."

"That's a perfect oath," said Kathleen, clapping her hands lightly at the performance. "Since you've been sworn in, I feel I can ask for your help in my medical investigation. There's a patient who comes in almost every week with different symptoms that evade a clear diagnosis. I can use your computer skills to see if we can find some kind of a pattern. I'm going to check medical websites for information and perhaps together we can help this patient."

Claire's eyes lit up like the Empire State Building on New Year's Eve. "I know exactly what to do. I can see a spreadsheet in my mind. Can I bring my computer downstairs to your office? That way we can share the patient's file and information."

She hugged Kathleen impulsively and gushed, "Oh, Kathleen, this is the best job I've ever had."

Remembering the power of her physical therapy, Kathleen willed her hands to stay on Claire's back and not go exploring.

❀ ❀ ❀

All Kathleen could think about was Claire.

She watched Claire working in the front office and imagined brushing against her. Claire would look up and smile, a smile that said, *I love you and I can't wait to be alone with you.* At night, she fantasized about walking up the stairs with Claire to her bedroom; slowly undressing each other, soft kisses that lingered and explored, touches as velvety as butterflies, falling asleep nestled against each other.

She was tormented. Her desires were getting stronger and as hard as she tried, it was becoming increasingly difficult to deny their existence. She was in an unenviable conflict between passion and prudence. She thought she would go crazy.

Kathleen couldn't allow her confusion to reign. She needed to talk with someone, and she thought about Gayle. Perhaps this would be a good time for Gayle and Robert to visit. It had been a while, and they hadn't met Claire.

❀ ❀ ❀

The Four Musketeers were going to be reunited. Helen was busy preparing meals for the weekend and Sam was putting their guest room in order. The Four had plans for a late Friday night bridge game, and at some point Robert and Sam were going to tour the grounds for potential landscaping chores.

Kathleen knew that Helen would be cooking something special for the weekend and wasn't surprised when she gave her a long grocery list. Kathleen and Claire went shopping at Canfield Supermarket. Neither one could stick to Helen's list. They kept finding items that might be fun to nibble on or, as Claire would say, "To nosh on." They came home that evening loaded down with bags. They chuckled at some of the extras: exotic olives chosen by Claire, and fresh strawberries covered in chocolate, Kathleen's pick.

Kathleen couldn't resist the chocolate ice cream infused with peanut butter. They sat at the kitchen table with two spoons, passing the carton back and forth as they chatted and laughed. "Whoops," said Kathleen as she gazed at the empty carton. "I knew we should have bought two."

Kathleen saw her last patient at noon on Friday and a little while later a blue sedan pulled up to the driveway. She rushed down to the car. Gayle put her arms around her, called her Baby, and told her she had made Kathleen's favorite, lasagna with meat sauce.

Robert hugged her, looked at the house, and whispered, "Honey, we stole it from them." Kathleen put her head against his chest as he wrapped his arms around her and held her close. She loved the way he felt and looked. Although Robert had turned sixty, he had the tall, lean body of an athlete and when he hugged Kathleen she felt safe and protected.

Gayle called to Robert to get "the things" out of the trunk. When Kathleen saw "the things," she had to laugh. Gayle had gone shopping and the trunk was overflowing with grocery bags. Kathleen told Gayle and Robert not to move and ran up the stairs to get Claire. She introduced Claire to Gayle and Robert, and together they carried bag after bag into the house.

Sam and Helen were waiting in the kitchen. After hugs and kisses, the groceries were put away and they sat down to a sumptuous feast of lasagna, Claire's homemade chicken soup, and freshly baked Italian bread. Everyone complimented Claire on the soup. She explained it was her bubba's famous recipe and took three days to make.

"Could I have the recipe, honey?" asked Gayle.

"Over my dead body," said Claire without missing a beat. "And Bubba is the one who would kill me!"

Gayle leaned over to Kathleen and said, "I really like this girl."

Oscar came down from his second story lair to say hello and make his presence known. Claire told them how Oscar Tilquist, the Third got his name and Robert sat up straight and said, "I haven't heard that name for years. I remember him! My older cousin and I used to watch his TV show. I felt so privileged to be watching such a grown-up program. We thought it was racy back in the day, but looking back, I can see how innocent it really was."

They fell into an easy rhythm of storytelling and laughter. Claire looked at Kathleen. "Your turn to tell a story. Tell them about our adventure with river rafting."

Kathleen hesitated.

Claire said, "Come on, Kathleen. If you don't tell the story I will, and I have to warn you, if I tell it, I'll end up being the hero."

Kathleen smiled and began talking about their adventure. At first she spoke slowly, as if measuring every word. Then a veil lifted, her eyes brightened, her smile shined, and she became a storyteller.

"I think you all know about the rafting at Christmas River. Claire and I decided it could be fun. I made reservations for a Class Two trip, thinking this is a good way to start and gradually work our way up. Well, on this day someone overslept," Claire pointed to Kathleen and Kathleen pointed toward Claire, "and we missed our group. So there we are, standing on the bank of the river without a raft. After a while, a supply raft for one of the downriver campgrounds showed up. The guides saw us and said, 'Hey, climb aboard and join us.' Claire elbows me and says, 'Let's take this raft, how bad can it be?' Being a person of few words I said okay. I'm thinking Claire's the big adventurer. She must know what she's doing.

"We climbed onto the supply raft with these eight-foot tall dudes with muscles that would shame the Hulk. Our job was to sit down and try not to drown. The trip started out with some gentle rapids, almost like a Disneyland ride. Keep in mind that Claire and I are sitting next to each other and the guides are doing all the work. We're going through a gorge that was forested with all these beautiful trees, really beautiful, and I'm enjoying the scenery. All of a sudden we hit some rapids and the raft bounces way up and—" Kathleen demonstrated with her hands the up and down motion. "Smack! Smack! It hits down with incredible force.

"At this point, Claire gets really scared and starts to stand up. One of the guides grabs her and throws her down right on top of me.

For the rest of the trip Claire's clinging to me and crying like a baby. The funniest part was coming home. We're sitting in the bed of a truck soaked to the skin, and wrapped in blankets that stink from fish, and Claire's telling me how much fun she had and wants to know when we can do it again."

At this point everyone was laughing and clapping their hands.

Claire was beaming. "That was a great story. I had a feeling once you got started, you'd be a natural."

❀ ❀ ❀

After lunch Robert and Sam left "to look into some things that need to be done around the house." Helen and Claire volunteered to clean the kitchen and Kathleen and Gayle went for a walk.

They took the path that led through a stand of trees to a small clearing that was once used as a meditation retreat. A gazing ball graced the center of the clearing while three cast-iron benches formed a semicircle around the ball. Azaleas, hydrangea, and ferns were planted around the perimeter of the clearing, creating a natural enclosure. They sat quietly on one of the benches.

Gayle held Kathleen's hand. "You told a wonderful story."

"Thanks. I didn't think I could do it."

"It looked as if you and Claire were having so much fun together."

Kathleen put her head down.

"You have feelings for her?"

Kathleen nodded.

"You're in love?"

Kathleen nodded.

Gayle put her finger under Kathleen's chin and lifted her face. "Kathleen, look at me. You have to talk about it."

"It hurts too much. I didn't mean for this to happen. I let my guard down and opened my heart and she crept in. I have so much fun with her and I'm so much in love and I can feel my heart breaking, all at the same time."

"Love can be the best and the worst. I wish it wasn't so hard for you. Do you think you can talk to her?"

Kathleen shook her head. "I can't. She talks a lot about guys and dating. She's about as straight as anyone can be. What happens if I say something and she leaves? Then I've lost her friendship. I don't want that to happen. I feel so different when I'm with her. She makes me laugh and she makes me want to talk. When I'm near her, all I can think about is being able to reach out and hold her."

"Anyone who can make you talk and tell stories is worth keeping and fighting for. It seems to me that she was enjoying your company as much as you were enjoying hers. Kathleen, you can't keep running away from who you are."

"Gayle, are you mad at me?"

"No, why?"

"You've called me Kathleen twice."

Gayle laughed softly. "Oh, Baby, I'm not mad at you. My heart breaks for you and I want you to be happy, that's all. Have you thought that you may be making your life more complicated than it has to be? I was watching the two of you at lunch and, quite frankly, the way you were interacting… it was more like sweethearts than friends. Maybe it's her style, but the way she kept looking at you and reaching out to touch your hand while you were telling your story—"

Gayle shook her head. "Well, it makes me think that maybe she has feelings, too, and doesn't understand them. If this is all new to her she might be as afraid of them as you are. Sometimes, you have to take a risk. Look at how you wanted this house, and look at the risk you took to get it."

Kathleen sat quietly, trying to collect her thoughts. "Do you remember when I told you about Mrs. Roth?"

"Yes, she was a wonderful friend to you."

"When she died she left me her books. It was too hard for me to open the boxes and look at them. I asked Claire to help and she had the best time organizing and putting the books on the shelves. If she read a book, she would tell me all about it. It felt as if I was little and someone was telling me a bedtime story. She's so excited about life; I feel better just being around her. Everything is an adventure and every adventure is a story."

Gayle understood perfectly; she always did. "Those are some wonderful qualities, and you love her for having them. If you don't say something, she'll never know how you really feel, and that is more likely to break up your friendship than being honest with her. You don't have to tell her you're in love, but maybe you can talk to her about who you are. She's a New York City girl and I don't think there's any shortage of gays and lesbians in New York. I'm sure you're not the first lesbian that Claire has been friends with."

Kathleen shook her head. "I made a conscious decision to stay in the closet and now I'm stuck. I should be able to deal with this without having to call you."

"Everyone needs someone to go to, and I'm glad you came to me. I know how hard this is and I wish I had a way to take your pain away."

The sun was beginning to set and the early evening chill forced Gayle to button her sweater. "We should go back to the house. Let's see what everyone is up to, and I want to see your office with all those wonderful books."

When they walked back to the house, they heard music coming from the solarium. Sam and Helen were dancing to the romantic song "Someone to Watch Over Me." When the song ended, "Dream A Little Dream of Me" began to play.

Robert stood up and bowed in front of Gayle. "This, I believe, was playing the night we met. May I have this dance?" Everyone applauded as Robert and Gayle fell into a natural rhythm that belied the passage of time.

Sam sat with his arm around Helen. As the moments passed, Helen moved in closer and let her head rest on his chest.

Kathleen and Claire sat on the couch, inches apart. Kathleen felt they were separated by a deep crevice that couldn't be traversed. She was in love with someone whose life was built around dancing and romantic music from a bygone era. Kathleen had never learned to dance and didn't understand romance. She felt her heart aching and wondered if it was true that you could die from a broken heart.

CHAPTER 27

Kathleen and Claire woke early to hike the five-mile trail to Christmas River. The summer weather had been unpredictable: one day they were wearing T-shirts and the next day the air was chilly enough for sweaters. Today began as a T-shirt day.

They walked along the trail, listening to the rustling of the surrounding foliage as small woodland animals scurried about. The trail was wide enough for them to walk side by side, and they traded juicy town gossip, compared favorite foods, and chatted about the best movies they had ever seen. They laughed when they realized they had a common favorite in *Young Frankenstein*. They had watched it several times and could recite dialogue and act out scenes together.

"Remember this one?" said Kathleen, imitating Gene Wilder: "What knockers!" As soon as the words were out of her mouth, she wanted to push them back in.

Claire affected a German accent and replied, "Oh, zank you, Doctor!"

They laughed—Claire bawdily, Kathleen self-consciously—but then fell into a companionable silence, each left to her own thoughts and feelings, as they ambled along the trail.

During those quiet moments, Kathleen revisited some of her childhood memories— the pain of being bullied, the knowledge that friends were for others and not for her. Her memories felt like animal traps waiting to be sprung. The torment she felt now came from the longings that wanted to go beyond friendship with Claire. She knew, or at least tried to convince herself, that sometimes you have to settle.

Kathleen and Claire continued to walk until they came to a clearing next to the river. A summer storm had been predicted, but they had decided to ignore the weather report. Others had paid attention and the clearing, usually filled with families, was deserted. Claire spread a blanket on the ground, placing it where the sun was shining through the trees. They sat quietly eating their lunch. Claire lay down and motioned to Kathleen. "Come," she said, as she patted the blanket, "see how the trees look."

Not a good idea, thought Kathleen, but felt compelled to sit next to Claire. Danger signals were going off in her head as she found herself moving closer. She tried to keep as much physical distance as the blanket allowed.

"Lie down," beckoned Claire. "If you lie down and look up, you can see the fairy dust through the trees."

Kathleen wondered, was it possible that Claire was so naive that she didn't feel the growing sexual tension? But she complied, as if her better sense was no longer operating. She lay down, their legs barely touching. She should move, put more distance between them, but she wanted the contact and more. They stayed until the clouds began to hide the sun.

Claire sat up, shading Kathleen from the remaining light. She took one hand and brushed away the hair that had fallen over Kathleen's eye. She sat quietly, gazing at Kathleen, then in what appeared to be a startled move, stood up. "It's going to rain, we should go."

The warm summer day had suddenly turned cold and the sun, which had sparkled through the trees, was arguing with the dark clouds for dominance. Shadows descended, giving them an ominous warning. The rain that began as a drizzle quickly changed to a downpour. The trail that had been friendly and welcoming became slippery and unforgiving.

By the time they got to the truck, they were rain soaked and splattered with mud. Kathleen started the engine, put the heater on, and pulled old blankets from the storage area.

Kathleen said, "At least they don't smell like fish."

They laughed at how they looked, but the laughter soon faded and they became serious and stared at each other as if time and hearts had stopped.

Claire touched Kathleen's face and moved closer until their lips met, touching gently, exploring slowly. She put her hands on Kathleen's shoulders, drawing her closer, hungry for new feelings that were rushing through her body.

Kathleen got lost in the intensity of the kiss. Her hands drifted under Claire's shirt and rested on the curve of her back. She pulled Claire closer, then stopped suddenly and moved away.

"I'm sorry, I shouldn't have let this happen." She was shaking again, but this time it wasn't from the cold. She put the truck into gear and started to drive home.

Claire's hand reached out and covered Kathleen's. "Wait." When Kathleen continued to drive, Claire pleaded, "Please, wait."

Kathleen pulled onto the shoulder of the road, resting her head against the seat.

Claire's voice quivered. "Don't be sorry. I'm glad we kissed. I've wanted you to touch me and I don't want us to stop."

Kathleen spoke tersely. "This is new for you. You have no idea what this kind of relationship can be like... I don't get it. How can you be straight one minute and lesbian the next?"

"Do I have to put a label on it? Jesus, Kathleen, I've never felt this way before and I can't explain it." Claire spoke hesitantly. "I only know when I'm near you... I have all these feelings. When I'm near you, I want us to make love."

Kathleen reached over and drew Claire close. Kathleen stroked Claire's head and spoke softly. "I want to... believe me, I've wanted to for so long. I think about making love with you during the day and I dream about it at night. I have to tell you... there are things about me..." Kathleen stopped, looked at her and spoke abruptly. "I'm damaged goods, Claire."

She drove home and parked on the gravel driveway. The windows began to fog up until the only world that existed was inside the truck. The storm that had plagued them changed direction and weakened. The passion that had been denied replaced the weakening storm and intensified. Dormant feelings came to life as they kissed.

Kathleen leaned back. "I've kept this part of my life a secret. I've lived in the shadows ever since I knew I was lesbian. You may not be able to understand, but it's the only way I feel safe."

Claire reached over and touched Kathleen. "You said you're damaged. Help me to understand. I want to know you." Claire stopped and looked down. "I want to be alone with you... I want to feel you next to me."

Claire took the blanket, folded it neatly and put it back in the storage area. "We haven't done anything wrong." She opened the truck door and waited for Kathleen. They walked, in silence, side by side toward the house.

Helen was in the kitchen putting pots in the cupboard. "Hi," she called out enthusiastically. "Well, it looks as if you two got caught." Kathleen and Claire exchanged a quick glance and a knowing smile.

Helen was very proud of her culinary skills and informed them, "Shepherd's pie for dinner. One of my specialties and slap-your-mama delicious, if I do say so." She artfully opened the oven door and took out a casserole. "Salad's in a bowl in the fridge. Hope you've worked up an appetite."

She looked at them appraisingly. "You both need to get out of those wet clothes. I don't want to be taking care of two sick ones. I'll be leaving in a couple of minutes, so off you go, and make sure you leave those muddy shoes by the door."

Helen's concerns became an opportunity for them to leave together. As they began to go upstairs, they heard Helen say, "Kathleen, I started a fire in your room. Get warm."

Claire and Kathleen couldn't keep from tittering, but their laughter quickly faded when they reached the landing. They climbed the rest of the stairs slowly, silently. They stopped as they approached their bedrooms.

Kathleen held Claire. "I want you to listen to me carefully. Before you enter my world, you have to understand how I live. I'm only out to Gayle and Robert. A couple of other people too, whom you haven't met. I can't let this leak out. There are things about me, about my life, that I haven't shared with anyone. I repeat, *not anyone*, and I can't promise you that I ever will. Can you live with that?"

Claire could smell the scent of the woods on Kathleen and touched the smudges of mud on her arms. "I can't promise that I won't be curious and ask, and you know I'm a nag. I promise, if I ask and you say no, I'll drop it. Can you live with that?"

Kathleen pulled Claire closer and, as they kissed, opened the door to her bedroom.

They stood near the fire, hands and mouths moving slowly, savoring every touch, letting time move at its own pace. Kathleen took off Claire's shirt, gazing, caressing newly exposed places.

Claire unbuttoned Kathleen's blouse and slipped it from her shoulders. She removed the band that held Kathleen's hair in a ponytail and stared as her hair fell loosely around her shoulders. Claire stepped back, keeping her eyes fixed on Kathleen.

Kathleen cast her eyes down. "I'm sorry about the scar. I don't want you to be disappointed."

"Disappointed? I don't think you realize how beautiful you are." Claire touched Kathleen's face, tracing her fingertips downward to her neck and shoulders, lightly following her scar, continuing until her hand rested on her breast.

They lay down, breast touching breast, bodies merging into one. The fire cast a glow as flames danced the dance of recently discovered love. Hands and mouths that had been strangers found their way to hidden places, searching and exploring, bringing new and forgotten feelings to life.

They lay in front of the fireplace until the fire began to die. Claire put another log on the embers. The flames leaped again as they continued to discover hidden sensations. They fit.

❀ ❀ ❀

Kathleen was lying on her back, her hand touching Claire's shoulder as she lay on her side. "You're staring."

"I love to look at you, you're so beautiful." Claire leaned over and brushed her lips against Kathleen's. "You're not nearly as shy as I imagined."

Kathleen blushed. "I've been thinking about you for a while."

"Me too." Claire ran her hand lightly over Kathleen's face and neck. "Your skin is like silk." Her fingers moved downwards until she touched Kathleen's scar.

Kathleen flinched and Claire moved her hand away. "Does it hurt?"

"Not always."

"Does it hurt right now?"

"No, I winced because your hands feel hot."

"It happens sometimes, but it's nothing to worry about. Kathleen, how did you get hurt?"

"I got injured in Iraq."

"But how?"

Kathleen shook her head. "I can't talk about it."

She shifted onto her side to face her lover. She relaxed and a heavy weariness crept over her. She took Claire's hand and placed it over her scar.

Claire kissed her eyelids. "You look like you're going to fall asleep. Why don't you close your eyes and later tonight, I'll tell you the story about why my hands get so warm."

"Promise?

"Uh-huh."

Kathleen curled up next to Claire with her head resting against Claire's breast. As she drifted off to sleep, she heard Claire's heartbeat and felt the comfort of her hand against her scar.

❀ ❀ ❀

The summer light was beginning to fade when Kathleen yawned and reached for the water on the nightstand. She turned toward Claire with eyes half-open and spoke sleepily. "What time is it?"

"Almost six."

"P.M.?"

"Yeah."

"I thought I slept the night away." Kathleen reached for Claire, lightly circling her breast with her hand. "God, you feel wonderful. I hate to get up, but I'm really hungry, are you?"

Claire nodded. "Starving. Let's go down to the kitchen and bring something up. The fire is still going."

"You owe me a story."

"I haven't forgotten. You know, all stories are supposed to be told at bedtime, preferably in bed. That's the story rule."

They went downstairs, brushing against each other as they bustled about in the kitchen, stopping for a minute to kiss, to reconnect, and feeling their bodies coming to life again.

Kathleen heated the pie while Claire got the salad out of the refrigerator. Claire chuckled and Kathleen looked at her curiously.

Claire said, "You may not want to hear this, but I think Helen has been acting as Cupid and plotting this all along."

Kathleen became alarmed. "How would Helen have a clue?"

"I don't think Gayle and Robert are the only ones who know your secret." She held up a plate of heart-shaped brownies.

Kathleen, who was usually so serious, walked over, took a bite and smiled. "Hmm, they're good. Taste?"

❀ ❀ ❀

They ate in front of the fire, sharing their meal, sharing their passion. They showered before getting into bed. Kathleen was finally making good use of her multi-head, extra large shower. Claire was certain it was the most interesting shower she had ever had.

It was still early when they got into bed. Kathleen snuggled next to Claire. "I like it when you hold me," she murmured.

"You feel soft, so soft."

"It comes with being a woman."

"I've just never felt it before."

"Is it okay?"

"It's wonderful."

Kathleen nestled in further. "I'm ready for story time. I didn't get bedtime stories when I was growing up. My foster mother wasn't the story-telling kind of person. What about you?"

"Oh, yes, my bubba always told me a bedtime story. Sadly, some were about concentration camps, so I would call them more nightmare stories."

"Is that why you have the numbers on your arm?"

Claire hesitated. "You want to know all about me, don't you?"

Kathleen nodded.

"Hmm… what a coincidence, because I want to know everything about you, too. You can hide from me for a while, Dr. Moore, but not forever. At some point, you're going to have to stop being a woman of mystery and trust me with your stories."

Kathleen sat up, hugging her knees against her chest. "I do trust you. If I talk about some things, I'm afraid I'll fall apart and…"

"And no one will be able to put you back together again." Claire became serious. "Relationships have a hard time surviving when they're built on secrets. I made a promise and I'll keep it. I'm curious as a cat and snoopy, and I'll probably ask too often. All you have to say is you don't want to talk about it, and I'll stop. I promise."

Claire was quiet for a moment. "I'll make a deal with you. How about for every story I tell you, you tell me one?"

"But I don't know any."

"Sure you do, because the stories I want are about you."

"What do you mean?"

"Let's say, I tell you a story and when I'm done, I get to ask you a question, something about yourself. Then, you answer by telling me a story with a beginning, a middle, and an end."

"I don't know if I can do that," Kathleen demurred.

"How would it be if you try to answer it in some way? If you feel uncomfortable we'll stop."

In spite of a mind that was churning with doubts, Kathleen whispered, "Okay."

"So, which story do you want tonight?"

"Can I have two?"

Claire chuckled. "You're already bargaining?"

"Just this once? I want to know about the tattoos on your arm, and I want to know why your hands are so warm."

"Okay, two stories for the price of one." Claire spoke tenderly. "You're a hard bargainer, Dr. Moore. So, how did I get this tattoo? I got these numbers after I visited the Holocaust Memorial Museum in Washington, D.C. Have you seen it?"

Kathleen shook her head.

"There's a holocaust museum in Los Angeles—I'd like us to go sometime."

Kathleen noticed that Claire spoke about them being a couple as if they were the same as any two people in love. She felt safe in Claire's arms, and the anxiety that was part of her fabric began to disappear.

"Anyway," Claire went on, "I was walking through the holocaust museum and when I got to the section about the concentration camps I sat for a long time, thinking about the people who died and wondering how I could honor them. There were lists of victims; names, ages, where they were from, and then the identification numbers that were tattooed on their left forearm. It was record keeping at its evilest. I looked down the list and saw a little girl's name, *Rachel Sarah Weiss, thirteen years old*."

Claire held out her arm and showed Kathleen the numbers. "These are Rachel's and for as long as I'm alive, she will be remembered every day."

Kathleen leaned over and kissed the numbers on Claire's arm.

They lay in bed, Claire holding Kathleen, feeling the silky softness of her skin, and the quiet rhythm of her breathing. Kathleen curled up closer and said, "I want to know why your hands are so warm."

"Time for story number two?"

Kathleen nodded.

"This is a true, once upon a time story.

❀ ❀ ❀

"Many years ago, my great-great-grandmother Deborah, and her family lived in a *shtetl*, somewhere in Russia."

Kathleen interrupted. "What's a shtetl?"

"Did you see *Fiddler on the Roof*?"

"Years ago with Mrs. Roth."

"Picture that; small dirt streets, tiny homes, and lots of poverty, but no singing. It doesn't mean they were sad or miserable, it just means life was hard.

"Deborah at sixteen was about to be married to an older man whom she didn't love. There was a part of Deborah that longed to be free and discover what life was like outside her shtetl.

"One day a traveling carnival came to the small town near Deborah's shtetl, sort of a bit of a circus with fortunetellers and fire-eaters and lots of storytelling. The allure of the carnival was too powerful for Deborah to resist and she snuck off to the carnival.

"A young girl, about Deborah's age, was on the stage dancing. She was wearing a long flowing dress and shaking a tambourine as she swayed to the hypnotic sounds of the violins and guitars. While Deborah was watching the dancer, she became spellbound by the sensuous sounds of the music and, at the same time, happened to notice a very handsome young man who smiled at her. He was tall and olive-skinned, with wavy black hair and eyes as black as onyx. He was buying a new horse and after he mounted, he rode over to Deborah tipped his hat, smiled, and said hello in a deep, mellifluous voice.

"Before he rode off he smiled again and after that second smile she was in love. A little later, he came over to Deborah, told her his name was Ferka, and asked her if she wanted her fortune told."

Kathleen said, "Ferka?"

"Yes, that was his name and it means free… Okay, back to the story.

"Deborah didn't have any money, but Ferka took her into the tent and spoke to the fortuneteller in a foreign language. Deborah sat down at a creaky, wobbly table and the fortuneteller took hold of her hands. As soon as she touched Deborah's hands, a strange expression fell over her face. She spoke to the young man, again in a different language, but from their expressions Deborah could tell it was an intense conversation.

"Now, the sun was beginning to set and soon it would be very dark because that night there would be no moon and Deborah would have to go home alone through the forest."

Kathleen's hand dampened and she moved tightly against Claire.

Claire said, "Are you getting scared?"

Kathleen whispered, "It's getting a little spooky."

"Snuggle up then; I won't let the boogeyman get you."

Claire continued. "So, Deborah left the carnival, but not before promising to meet Ferka the next day. She ran home through the darkening forest as fast as she could. She was very frightened. Frightened by the shadows that looked like wild animals waiting to gobble her up, and even more frightened about having to face her parents.

"When Deborah got home she lied to her mother and father. She told them she had fallen asleep under a tree and they believed her because Deborah was a good girl and had never lied before.

"The next morning she got up early and began her chores with a gusto her parents had not seen before. She finished early and told her mother that she wanted to pick some wild berries and left to meet Ferka. He helped fill her basket with the succulent berries and one thing led to another, and they made love. Now, even more terrified of what she might face at home, and under the spell of passion, she ran off with Ferka. It was just as well, because unknowingly she had become pregnant."

"What happened next?" Kathleen said in hushed tones.

Claire kissed Kathleen on the top of her head. "I can tell you're liking this story."

Kathleen, bewitched by Claire's tale, began to twirl a strand of her hair.

"Now, remember the fortuneteller who held Deborah's hands? Her name was Lala, and she was Ferka's mother. The night of the carnival, as soon as she touched Deborah's hands, she knew Deborah was a healer and needed to be taught how to use her gift, because a gift like that should *never, ever* be wasted. Lala treated Deborah as one of her own daughters and taught her everything she knew about healing. How to collect wild herbs and bark from trees to make medicine, and most of all how to take the energy from the earth and heavens and transfer it to help others.

"The months went by and Deborah had a beautiful baby girl. They named her Lyuba, which means love. As Lyuba grew into a toddler, something changed in Deborah and she began to long for her own home and family. Were they all right? Did they miss her? Would they forgive her?

"She loved Ferka, but the pull to return to her parents became stronger than her love. One night when Deborah's daughter was five, in the deepest dark of night, she snuck off and hid in the forest. Lala and Ferka were very worried when they couldn't find Deborah and Lyuba; had a wolf eaten them? Deborah could hear them searching for her, calling her name, but she stayed hidden until they left and traveled to another place.

"It took several months for Deborah to find her way home. When her parents saw their daughter and granddaughter, their love was stronger than their anger and they forgave Deborah.

"The gift of healing has been passed down through the generations, from female to female. When I am practicing tai chi or meditating, I am gathering the life force energy, and that is why my hands become warm. Today, I transferred the energy to you. This was the first time I tried to use this gift."

Kathleen snuggled closer. "Why was this the first time?"

"Because my bubba told me that it is love as much as the energy that heals."

"That's a wonderful story." Kathleen had never felt quite so relaxed. "I guess it's my turn to tell a story."

Claire snuggled up to Kathleen. "Are you getting shy?"

Kathleen nodded. "I don't know if I can do this."

"Let's try it. Remember, you can always stop. When I asked for your bill, you charged me two dollars, and said that a long time ago someone had helped you out. Tell me a story about how someone helped you, and don't forget, a story has to have a beginning, a middle, and an end."

Claire snuggled into Kathleen's arms, just as Kathleen had done with Claire.

Kathleen sighed with relief. She could tell that story. "Okay, beginning. I started UCLA when I was barely eighteen. It was the second quarter of my freshman year and I began to be flooded with new sexual feelings, anxious… tortured by them.

"Gayle had finished her course work to become a psychoanalyst and placed an announcement for new patients in the campus newspaper. Her office was close by and I could walk there on my lunch break. I liked Gayle right away. There was something about her that made me feel safe. The subject of fees came up. I think she knew how broke I was and only charged me two dollars a session. That's the beginning. Hmm, now for a middle." As she was thinking she pulled Claire tightly against her.

"I saw Gayle twice a week for almost two years. My appointments were during the lunch hour. Do you know what Gayle did?"

"No," Claire said softly.

"She fed me twice a week for almost two years. She started by telling me that Robert always over-packed her lunches. She was afraid she would gain another twenty pounds unless I helped her. If we didn't eat together, she would hand me a lunch bag as I left the office." Kathleen wiped the tears that were streaming down her face, hoping Claire wouldn't notice. "I didn't always have enough food and there were days when Gayle kept me from being hungry. I've had so many people help me."

Kathleen stopped abruptly and whispered, "I don't think I can go on. Have I let you down?"

Claire reached up and touched her face. "I couldn't be prouder. It was a wonderful story. Why don't we end it with to be continued?

Come, snuggle in my arms."

Kathleen rested her face next to Claire's heart. "I hate to have the day end. Could you… would you stay the night with me?"

Claire stroked Kathleen's back. "I can't think of a more wonderful way to end the evening." Claire felt her chest become damp. "Are you crying?"

Kathleen nodded. "It's just, no one has ever stayed…"

"No one?"

Kathleen nodded.

Claire held her tightly. "I'll be here all night, every night, if you want. I should warn you, I talk in my sleep."

"That's nothing. I have nightmares and cry in my sleep."

"If I'm sleep-talking, just tap me on the shoulder."

"If I'm crying, hold me."

"I knew we would be perfect for each other."

Kathleen woke up, startled. She was naked. She never slept naked. Where were her shorts? Where was her T-shirt? She felt confused and hung over. It was four in the morning. She had the oddest dream. She dreamed that she and Claire had made love in front of the fireplace, in the shower, and in bed. She heard soft breathing. She saw Claire sleeping next to her. It wasn't a dream. She sank back into her pillow. Before she fell asleep she thought, *oh, God. What have I done?*

When Kathleen woke again around six, Claire's arms and legs were wrapped around her. Claire was talking in her sleep, "Hello, Bubba. Guess, what? I'm gay. I'm gay." Kathleen thought, *oh, my God; she really does talk in her sleep. Should I tap her on the shoulder?* She stifled a giggle that wasn't quite stifled enough. Claire cuddled even closer and mumbled in a half-asleep voice, "Can we do this again soon?"

Kathleen held her close and wondered if soon would be soon enough.

CHAPTER 28

Kathleen couldn't wait to get home from St. Mona's. Claire had left a cryptic message on her cell phone, in a clipped, upper crust British accent that sounded exactly like her hero, Sherlock Holmes:

"Precisely at seventeen-hundred hours, Dr. Moore, a package will be delivered to you at the hospital. Secrecy is of the upmost importance. Do not open until you are in the car. Contents are to be eaten on your way home. Dinner will be late, very late. When you approach the turnoff to Canfield, call me with your location and expected time of arrival."

It was so Claire!

Kathleen's heart was light and she laughed all the way to her car. She opened the package to find a small wicker basket filled with finger foods—assorted cheeses, crackers, grapes, dark chocolates—and a bottle of nonalcoholic red wine.

The house was quiet when she arrived and there was no sign of Claire. Kathleen knocked on Claire's door, looked in the kitchen, and finally gave up. She had called Claire's cell phone as instructed and now felt disappointed. She sighed, thought she would take a shower, and hoped that Claire would show up, soon.

"I thought you'd never find me," said Claire, smiling as Kathleen opened the bathroom door.

Soothing music filled the air as candles, placed around the room, danced in concert and cast their shadows against the walls. The tub was filled with warm water and sprinkled with floating gardenias and herbs, tied in white cloth packages.

Kathleen stood immobile. Claire walked over and began to undress her. Kathleen moved closer, reaching for Claire.

Claire lightly brushed her hand away. "Uh-uh. This is a sensuous, healing bath, just for you. Let me do everything."

"Sensuous?" Kathleen could barely get the word out.

Claire took off her robe.

Kathleen couldn't hide her disappointment. "You're wearing your bathing suit."

"That's to make sure we keep this sensuous."

Claire slowly undressed Kathleen and helped her into the tub. She began to bathe her, using soft cloths filled with delicate oils. Claire lowered herself into the tub. "Rest your head against me and let your body go. I'll do everything." Claire washed Kathleen's hair with shampoo that smelled of flowers after a spring rain. Kathleen could feel every part of her relaxing, letting go, traveling to places she had never been before.

She must have fallen asleep. Claire was whispering, "It's time to get out."

How long had they been in the tub? She felt spacey and needed Claire's help to stand.

Claire wrapped her in a thick white towel and led her to the bed. "Lie on your tummy." Claire covered her with a light cotton blanket and warmed the cool body lotion between her hands. Kathleen tried to move; she wanted to reach for Claire, to make love to her, to have her enter the same space she was in.

Claire purred, "Not yet, not yet." She began to massage Kathleen with fingers as light as butterflies' wings, but strong as the roots of oaks, starting at her neck and shoulders, following the lines of her body, downward. Kathleen felt the warmth of Claire's hands transporting her to a new level of existence, one that made her forget every care. Kathleen was grabbing the sheet, making soft sounds, not from pain but from pleasure.

Claire leaned over and whispered, "Move on your back." Claire began to massage again, with the lightest of touches, tracing Kathleen's face, moving to her shoulders, then her waist and hips, and finally reaching her legs. She moved slowly, until she held Kathleen's delicate feet in her hands, applying lotion first to one, then the other, with extraordinary gentleness.

Kathleen opened her eyes; a small smile played across her face. "How did you learn to do this?"

"I'll save that story for another time." Claire took off her robe and, before seeking Kathleen's lips said, "I'm in love with you, Kathleen."

CHAPTER 29

Kathleen stretched her legs and felt Oscar lying on top of her feet, purring like a motorboat and twitching now and again from some secret feline dream. She thought about how the three of them had slept together for the past two months; Oscar sleeping contentedly on her feet and Claire cuddling next to her, sometimes reaching for her throughout the night or keeping her entertained with sleep talking. Kathleen had never slept so well.

Ever the romantic, Claire showered her with little surprises: sometimes a small box tucked under her pillow with a single piece of chocolate wrapped in gold foil, or a light caress before they went downstairs for breakfast. She wanted to give Claire something special—a way to say I love you, I'm thinking about you—without having to try to get the words out.

Kathleen remained amazed at the sound of Claire's breathing, so gentle and soft; she slept like an innocent child drifting in white clouds of dreams. Claire reached over, burrowing her body next to Kathleen's, while making small groaning sounds that told Kathleen she was waking up.

Kathleen held her and hoped she would never get used to Claire lying next to her; she wanted each morning to feel like the first time. "Are you awake?"

"Hmm-hmm... sort of."

"There's something I want to show you."

"Is it something I've never seen before?"

"Oh yes, but for this you have to put some clothes on."

Claire's curiosity was now aroused and she sat up, with eyes half-opened. "Such as?"

"Shorts, tee, and shoes will do."

"I have to go to the bathroom first." Claire got out of bed, stretched, yawned loudly, and shuffled half asleep into the bathroom, shutting the door tightly behind her.

Kathleen was learning about some of Claire's ways. She didn't understand why going to the bathroom was such a private ritual when sex was completely unrestrained. *Well, I guess I could ponder that mystery of life all day.* She grabbed her shorts and tee from yesterday and when Claire came out, ran in to brush her teeth.

Claire asked, "Where are we going?"

"Not far." Kathleen held Claire's hand and guided her into the hallway. She opened a narrow door with stairs leading upwards.

Kathleen turned on a light switch. "Watch your step, there's not much light."

As they climbed the stairs Claire said, "This is a real mystery. We could call it *The Mystery of the Secret Passage.* Did I ever tell you how much I love a mystery?"

Kathleen laughed. "Only a thousand and one times."

When they reached the top of the stairs, beams of sunlight floated through the bank of oriel windows, illuminating a sprawling room cluttered with boxes and intriguing shapes hidden underneath yellowed sheets. Dust motes danced in the sunshine, which cheered the dim space; the air was stale and fusty, but not unpleasantly so—it promised adventure.

Claire blinked at the change in lighting. "It's the attic! Wow, the natural lighting is incredible up here."

Kathleen said nothing. She wanted Claire to see and discover for herself. She watched Claire's eyes widen as she walked around the attic, removing old sheets that hid riches from a long ago era.

Claire gasped. "Oh, my God, it's antique heaven."

Kathleen laughed. "Not quite."

Claire moved from area to area, peering under sheets, looking inside boxes. She was a child at Christmas with too many presents. She discovered a fantastic rocking horse that must have given some Victorian-age boy or girl hours of pleasure, and she couldn't help being reminded of one of her favorite short stories, "The Rocking Horse Winner." A box contained crinoline skirts and that, looked positively barbaric to Claire.

"I wouldn't be caught dead in these," she said. Her eyes fell on an odd-looking couch. "What's this weird-looking thing?" she asked Kathleen.

"It's called a fainting couch, used by our Victorian sisters after they climbed the stairs and darn near fainted because of their corsets. It belongs on the landing, just in case one of us..."

Claire flopped down and reached out her arms for Kathleen. "Oh, dear, I feel a faint coming on," she said in a distressed maiden's voice, clapping the back of her hand to her forehead.

Chuckling, Kathleen sat next to Claire, lifting her up gently until their lips met. "Now I know why the Victorians invented these couches."

Claire relaxed against Kathleen. "Where did all of this cool swag come from?"

"We discovered it during the house inspection. Robert brought his home inspector from Los Angeles. He called us up to the attic and said he was having trouble checking everything because of all the junk up here. He thought we might want to have it carted off.

"Well, I thought Robert's eyes were going to explode when he saw the so-called junk. He was very nonchalant in front of the inspector, but later on he took me aside and said, 'Kathleen, someone has left you a real treasure. You'll know when it's the right time to use it.'"

"Is this the right time?"

"It's perfect. I must have been waiting for you."

Claire put her arms around Kathleen. "Thanks for waiting."

Kathleen held Claire close, wanting to stay in the moment. She could feel Claire pulling away, releasing her.

Claire said, "Can I stay here? I want to investigate everything."

"Of course, my darling Sherlock. You'll find a million mysteries to solve. I'll bring breakfast to you. I have a feeling I've lost you for the day."

Kathleen felt a newfound lightness in her heart as she went downstairs. She said a little prayer of thanks to the Someone who left the treasures and sent her Claire.

❀ ❀ ❀

Kathleen hired two odd jobbers to move the furniture from the attic to the empty garage for easier access. Claire brought Helen and Sam to see the furniture and while Helen was almost as excited as Claire, Sam was wondering how he was going to get drafted into this Mansion Makeover.

Kathleen never saw anyone work so hard or be so excited. Claire started with the wicker furniture. It would be perfect for the solarium. She discovered a roll of chintz fabric and had paint mixed to match one of the fabric's colors. Helen hand-washed and ironed the delicate material, and sewed new cushions. They were paying exquisite attention to every detail.

After work Claire would rush over to the garage. She worked steadily into the night, cleaning and repairing. By the time she came to bed she was exhausted and fell into a deep, dreamless sleep.

❀ ❀ ❀

The night began to fade, replaced by streaks of morning light, when Kathleen woke to find Claire's side of the bed empty. She glanced at the clock and became gripped with terror. She hurried toward the open garage door. Claire was on the fainting couch, snoring softly, a stiff, dry paintbrush gripped in her hand.

Kathleen flashed back to her first day at the CSH in Iraq. She and Sam arrived shortly after the wounded from a supply convoy were brought to the ER. Later that night, she stayed in the ICU, holding the hand of a dying soldier. She knew, as did the other physicians, that death had to be accepted on its own terms. After he took his last breath, she could think of nothing but that soldier's life, cut tragically short. Did he leave behind a spouse? Children? Parents? What had he hoped to do with his life, after the service? She had stroked his peach-fuzzed cheek for a moment, thinking what a waste, what a waste.

Kathleen covered Claire with her robe and returned to her empty bed. She rested her head on Claire's pillow and breathed deeply, wanting to absorb her essence. Kathleen thought about the complexity of love. The way Claire's love wrapped around her heart, warming her, and the fear that followed when she thought...

...that Claire might leave.

CHAPTER 30

Canfield's *Weekend in Scotland* was approaching and the town would be magically transformed into a Scottish village with Highland dancing contests, Scottish sports, and pipe and band competitions, and other frivolity.

Claire was excited about the festival and for movie night insisted that they rent the video of *Brigadoon* with Gene Kelly and Cyd Charisse, another old-time dance team Claire admired. "You'll really like this one," she told Kathleen. "It fits right in with the festival. It's about a Scottish village that's lost in time and can only appear for one day every hundred years. These two guys stumble into the village on that magical day, and guess what happens?"

Kathleen looked serious but was laughing on the inside: different movie, different music, same plot as the umpteen other romantic flicks that set Claire's heart aflutter. "Don't tell me. One of them falls in love, almost loses the girl, and finally gets the girl."

Claire looked surprised. "How did you know? Well, there's a real twist to this one. Do you think someone else will rent it before our movie night?"

"Don't worry. We'll drive over now and hang on to it. If you want to, we can watch it twice."

Claire wrapped her arms around Kathleen. "I'm so glad you're my girlfriend."

It was these kinds of memories that brought a smile to Kathleen's face when she least expected it. Sweet memories and painful memories were now in competition. People began to notice a welcome change in their beloved doctor, who could be downright off-puttingly sobersides at times. Laughter could be heard coming from the exam rooms, and in general there was a new lightness in the medical offices of Kathleen Moore, MD.

Hallelujah!

❀ ❀ ❀

Tourists came from all over Southern California to enjoy *A Weekend in Scotland*. Nearby hotels were booked a year in advance and the roads swelled with buses driving from park and ride lots in surrounding cities.

There were the usual festival injuries: sunburns, blisters (a bunch this time from the log toss that was one of the manly-man activities), and tummy aches. Helen volunteered for the first aid tent and Sam was on call at the office until Kathleen returned.

Kathleen and Claire rode their bikes for the short trip. They strolled around the festival as the omnipresent sound of bagpipes filled the air, stopped to watch the Scottish games, and listened to the pipe band made up of a piper and three drummers.

Claire said, "Doesn't this connect to your soul?"

Kathleen nodded and suggested they try some haggis from one of the food vendors.

"Mmm, this ain't bad," said Claire after she had taken a big bite. "What's in it?"

Kathleen grinned mischievously. "Sheep's entrails, oatmeal, and suet—boiled in a bag made out of the sheep's stomach."

Claire just about turned green.

"Am I going to have to carry you back to the office?" Kathleen laughed.

Claire tossed the rest of the Scottish delicacy into a trash bin. "I like natural food, but not *that* natural."

As they continued to walk, Claire brushed her hand against Kathleen's. She wanted to share her experience and hoped for a response, any response that would let her know that Kathleen was feeling the same way. Instead, she felt Kathleen abruptly move her hand away.

After that, a dark shroud seemed to settle over their fun, and Kathleen became self-conscious and withdrawn. They began to walk in different directions. Kathleen stopped to chat with neighbors and patients. Claire was drawn toward the dance stage. Where there was dancing, Claire would find her way. Some dancers, wearing the traditional Scottish dress of velvet jackets and kilts, were finishing up a rousing version of the Highland fling. After they ended their performance amidst loud applause, they asked the audience to join them in a Scottish folk dance. Some of the dancers knew Claire and waived her onto the stage. As the lilting music played, Claire began to follow the dancers. At first she was a step behind, but her natural ability took over and she began to dance to the rhythm of the music. A crowd began to gather around the stage, clapping and shouting, "Claire, Claire, Claire!"

Claire was out of breath and grinning when she caught up with Kathleen. "That was so much fun." She looked at Kathleen. "You look so serious. Is something wrong?"

Kathleen shook her head. "No, I just need to get back to the office and relieve Sam."

They returned to their bikes and rode home, side by side, in silence.

Claire was stinging from yesterday. She discovered it was one thing to try to understand Kathleen's need to be so entrenched in the closet; it was another to live it. For Claire, to be in love meant that you wanted to be visible to the world, and Claire was very much in love.

Why couldn't she and Kathleen have what others had? Claire had noticed gay and straight couples at the festival holding hands, speaking softly to each other and proud to be seen together. She didn't understand it. Did it really have to be so complicated? Were people really fixed in their contempt, or was this coming from a dark place within Kathleen?

Claire finished her office work for the day and went up to her room. She was feeling sad and the lump in her throat didn't want to move. She sat on the bed with Oscar, petting and kissing him while they listened to Ella Fitzgerald singing achingly romantic songs from the 1940s as only the first lady of song could. The sophisticated Cole Porter and Johnny Mercer lyrics harked back to a bygone era when love and romance seemed so real, so palpable; Claire thought they seemed to fit her.

Claire put her face next to Oscar and whispered, "Damn it, Oscar. Is it the same with a woman as it is with a man? Maybe I just don't know how to pick them. I seem to always go for the damaged ones. I love you, Oscar; you're the one constant in my life." Oscar purred, content to have Claire petting and whispering to him.

Kathleen went upstairs and stood in the hallway. Her first impulse was to go to her room, shut the door, and be miserable. Her insides were fused into a single, painful mass. She longed to hold Claire and tell her how much she loved her, but she knew the words wouldn't come out. Kathleen stood for a moment with one hand on her door. She wondered if there would ever be an end to her pain or if it would continue to flow through her life and follow her into death. She moved to Claire's door and rapped lightly.

Claire sat cross-legged on the bed. The romantic music that she loved so much filled the room. Kathleen looked at her and felt an overwhelming rush of love, overshadowed by fear.

Claire patted the bed and Kathleen sat next to her. Claire spoke quietly. "I've been sitting feeling really sad and kinda depressed. I think it bothered you when I danced at the festival. I thought maybe I was a bit outlandish, especially for a small town. But what can I say? I'm uninhibited, and when the spirit moves me, I'm not above making a fool of myself. Then, when I caught up with you, I thought you were angry. Were you ashamed of me?"

Kathleen shook her head, "No, no. I just wish I could be everything you want and need. When I saw you on the stage, I thought *Claire can do everything*." Unexpected tears filled her eyes. "I don't even know how to dance! What do you see in me? I'm shy and awkward and I usually don't know what to say or do. I don't even know what to do right now. I want to comfort you but I don't know how."

"You could start by putting your arm around me... if you want."

Kathleen put her arm around Claire, and spoke softly. "I can't take the chance of alienating the people in Canfield. I've put everything into these offices and I'll probably be in debt for the next twenty-five years. I can't... I'm not willing to move out of the closet I've built. I tried to tell you that when we first kissed, and I've been afraid of this ever since."

"So what the hell do we do?" said Claire frustratedly. "Live together as if we're two old maids? Pretend and look around corners when we're out? We can't even hold hands in public. Is it wrong to want it all? I want a family. I want you in my life, and someday I'd like to think about having children."

Claire took Kathleen's hand and held it up to her cheek. "You asked me what I see in you. You're such a special woman. I know how you struggle with your feelings, but you don't give up. That's why you're here right now. I'm in love with you, and it's sweet and painful at the same time. At least now, I know why it never quite worked out with men.

"Kathleen, I don't want to hide us, I'm proud of who we are and besides, we're really a cute couple." The music was still playing. "Dance with me?"

Kathleen whispered, "I don't know how to dance, and I don't know how to do a relationship. I'm sorry."

"I can teach you how to dance, but I think we both need lessons on how to be with another person."

Claire stood up and held her hand out. "For now, put your arms around my neck and hold me. You don't have to move your feet."

Kathleen stood and put her arms around Claire and drew her close until there was no space between them.

"Now, close your eyes and take in the music and lyrics."

Their bodies touched as Ella Fitzgerald sang, "I'm Old Fashioned."

Kathleen rested her face on Claire's shoulder. She knew all too well the cost of hidden relationships. Kathleen feared she would lose Claire, perhaps not this time, but some other time. Kathleen breathed deeply, wanting to take the moment inside and place it securely in her memory jar. She wanted to color it gold.

PART FIVE

Fall

CHAPTER 31

Kathleen drove to Santa Barbara every Friday for her double shift at St. Mona's. She kept her car windows down and let the ocean air refresh her. Inexorably, as they always did, her thoughts turned to Claire. For the first time in her life, she wanted to spend money, not save it. Robert tried to calm her fears by telling her they were ahead of his predictions and were moving out of the red. She dreamed about the day when she could afford to take Claire to San Francisco for a weekend. She fantasized about staying at a luxury hotel, The Ritz-Carlton, she thought, ordering breakfast in bed, and making love until it was time for the opera. A limo would drive them to the War Memorial Opera House where their box seats would be waiting. They would end the evening at a gay bar on karaoke night. She was certain it was something that would delight Claire.

Kathleen arrived at St. Mona's and pulled into the staff parking lot. She walked in juggling her coffee and bagel and was handed a chart by the unit secretary, Nancy Wright. "Got one for you, Doc. Exam Room Three."

Kathleen looked at the chart. "It's not like Keith to leave a case unfinished."

"We had a cardiac emergency and he knew you'd be here any minute. Besides, he thought they needed your magic touch."

Kathleen could hear scuffling and arguing as she approached Exam Room Three.

"I am so the bravest!"

"Nuh-uh, I am! En garde!"

A man, a defeated sound in his voice, said, "You've done enough damage for one day. I want you both to sit down and wait for the doctor, quietly."

Kathleen knocked on the door and smiled at the family of four.

"Mr. & Mrs. Kaplan? Hi, I'm Dr. Moore. Joshua and Marcie... hi. I understand we have a couple of dueling wounds that need to be looked after." She looked at the two six-year-olds, bandages on their arms and legs, who couldn't stay still.

Joshua said, "My wound is bigger."

Marcie replied, "No, mine is."

"Hmm, how about if I take off the bandages,and then if you're very quiet we can try to find out." Kathleen examined the twins' arms and looked at their charts. "I see they're up-to-date on their tetanus."

Mrs. Kaplan said, "Yes."

"How did this happen?"

Marcie said, "Mommy and Daddy needed to take a nap and we got bored."

Kathleen avoided looking up, but got a glimpse as the Kaplans' faces turned a bright red. "What did you use for swords? There's a lot of dirt in your wounds."

"Hot dog sticks."

"Hot dog sticks?"

Mr. Kaplan sighed. "Old barbeque cooking forks used for roasting hot dogs and marshmallows."

"Well, you can't say they aren't inventive. The good news is: no stitches for these wounds. When I'm done you're going to have some awesome looking bandages, but I need you to promise not to do this again. Okay?"

Kathleen kept up a light conversation with the family as she cleaned, irrigated the wounds with a sterile saline solution, applied an antibiotic ointment, and completed her treatment by bandaging the wounds of the two dueling warriors.

"Okay, all done. You were both very brave. Mom and Dad, can they have some juice and a cookie? I'd like to go over the discharge instructions and talk with you for a few minutes."

❀ ❀ ❀

She finished charting, chuckled as she thought about her conversation with the Kaplans suggesting tactfully that they might want to keep a keener eye on their boisterous twins, and letting them know that the local Y had fencing classes for children.

She looked at the file for the patient in Exam Room Two, female, Tiffany Scott, eleven years old, presenting with abdominal tenderness and pain during urination. Tiffany sat on the exam table, hunched over, her hands grasping at the corners of the gown. Her mother sat in the corner, aloof from Tiffany, on a small, brown, stackable chair. Their silence made Kathleen uneasy.

Kathleen smiled at Mrs. Scott. "Hi, I'm Dr. Moore."

Mrs. Scott nodded, her lips a tight band across a prematurely wrinkled face.

Kathleen stood next to Tiffany. "Hi, Tiffany. I understand it hurts when you pee."

Tiffany's mom answered, "She's been complaining about pain when she has to pee. And stomach aches."

"Is that right, Tiffany?"

Tiffany remained silent. Kathleen was focusing on her eyes: dark eyes filled with rage and pain. Kathleen knew something was wrong, horribly wrong. "Tiffany, do you go to a doctor, you know, for check-ups?"

Her mother said, "Regular check-ups are for the rich, not for us."

"What about vaccinations?"

"County clinic. We go before school starts, every year."

"Good. Tiffany, I'm going to give you a check-up and we'll try to figure out what's going on." Kathleen proceeded, chatting lightly as she began to examine her. "Your temp's a little high, almost one hundred degrees. What's your favorite subject in school?"

"Math. I like numbers."

"I'm impressed. Now, take a deep breath and hold it. Excellent, now let it out. Have you started your periods?"

Tiffany shook her head.

"I want you to follow my fingers with your eyes. Don't move your head. So, what do you want to be?"

"A space explorer."

"Science and math, a good combination for astronauts. Have you ever had a blood test?"

"No."

"How long ago did you pee?"

"Before we came here."

"Okay, we'll start by getting a urine sample then I'll check your tummy. When we're done I'll send you to the lab for a blood test."

Kathleen hit the intercom. "Nancy, Exam Room Two. I need a urine sample."

Nancy arrived in a trice with a specimen cup. "Tiffany, this is Nancy. She's going to take you to the bathroom and show you how to give us a urine sample."

Kathleen turned to Tiffany's mom. "There's coffee in the next room. You can get a cup, if you want."

"I'm not leaving."

Kathleen sat down with the chart. "How long has Tiffany been complaining about her symptoms?"

"She's had them on and off, maybe three months."

"Vaginal itching and discharge, as well?"

Her mother sat without movement, a tight-lipped statue. "I don't know."

Tiffany returned from the bathroom. Kathleen smiled at her and patted the exam table.

"Tiffany, I want you to lie down and bend your knees, so I can examine your private parts. Nancy is going to help me. This isn't something that will hurt, not at all."

Tiffany held her legs tightly together and started to scream.

Her mother walked over and handed Tiffany her clothes. "Sit up and get dressed. We're going home."

Kathleen pushed the emergency call button as she said sternly, "Ma'am, you're not going anywhere."

"Don't you tell me what I can and can't do with my daughter! I'll sue you and this damned hospital."

Kathleen held her arms out to Tiffany. "It's okay. No one is going to hurt you."

Tiffany continued to wail, leaning against Kathleen. "Daddy always gives me candy first, Daddy always gives me candy first," she chanted, like an obscene mantra.

Kathleen spoke softly, words she hoped would feel like a safety net. "No one will hurt you, you're safe here; you're safe here."

There was a lull. Kathleen went into the staff room and stretched out on the cot. She lay on her back, one foot touching the floor. She learned to sleep that way in Iraq, where sleep was always an uncertainty. She thought, *it doesn't matter where I am. It's a war zone, always a fuckin' war zone.* She thought about Tiffany. Cervical cultures would come back positive for gonorrhea, she was sure. Now what? Antibiotics would take care of the sexually transmitted disease and psychological counseling might help, but most likely she'd be thrown into the system. And she was only eleven. Not a promising future.

She dozed fitfully as Tiffany's cries combined with the screams of wounded troops and injured Iraqi civilians.

"Dr. Moore, wake up."

Kathleen sat up, putting her head in her hands. For a moment she thought she was in Iraq. She rubbed her eyes and glanced around the room expecting to see sand seeping through small cracks in the walls. She looked at what she was wearing. Civilian scrubs.

"What is it, Nancy?"

"There's been a residential fire. We just got the call, there are victims coming in."

Kathleen stood up. "Do we know how many? When can we expect them to arrive?"

"EMTs on their way. Reports are family of five. Mom and dad, first and second degree burns. Three kids, second and third degree burns, smoke inhalation. I've called pediatrics. They're sending a nurse practitioner with experience in burns."

"Where's Theo Chandler? Has he been contacted?"

"I called him and he's on his way." Nancy looked distressed. "He's more than an hour away."

"Shit! He's the Medical Director. Where's the rest of the staff?"

"Trying to get things ready. Doc, they need your help. Most of the team here, well, you know what we usually get, nothing like this."

"Get everyone assembled. I want security at the meeting. I'll be out in one minute."

She ran into the bathroom, peed, and splashed cold water on her face. She knew she had to stay alert and focused. If she lost contact with the present she would be hurled into the past. She silently recited her Rosary of Reality: *My name is Kathleen Moore. This is a hospital in California; it is not a CSH; I am not in Iraq. I am safe in Santa Barbara.*

She feared her worst nightmare was lurking around a dark corner.

She looked at the staff. Keith Omafu, emergency physician; Kim Larson, registered nurse; Glenn Marston, physician assistant; Mason Temple, emergency technician; and Nancy Wright, the LVN and ER clerk, who knew more about the hospital system than anyone. Looks of anxious anticipation crossed their faces.

"Security, I want the ER waiting room cleared right now!" Kathleen boomed. "Move everyone to the cafeteria until they can be triaged and sent to surrounding ERs. No one, and I mean no one, enters the ER except the police, medical staff, or EMTs bringing in burn patients. How many critical do we have on hand, and status?"

Keith Omafu answered. Kathleen knew he would be one she could depend on. "Two, one cardiac and one orthopedic, car accident, broken ribs and leg. Both stable."

"They need to be cleared out of the trauma rooms. Nancy, work your magic and get them moved upstairs, stat. Has anyone here had experience with burn patients?"

"I have."

Kathleen turned to see a small woman in her late forties, with graying hair pulled tightly in a bun. "Do you work here?"

"Yes, I'm Cheryl Troop. I'm a nurse practitioner and work part-time in pediatrics."

Kathleen immediately recognized the name. "Thank God! Cheryl, you're the County Emergency Medical Services Coordinator, too, right?"

"Yes, we spoke over the phone a few months ago. It's nice to put—"

"—a face to the name, I know. We can sure use somebody with your skill and pull. We're going to need to transport up to five."

"I can call the burn centers in Los Angeles and see if they can accept. It won't take me long; I know who to talk to and then I'll be ready to help with your patients."

Kathleen nodded and turned to the staff.

"We've got five burn patients arriving in about ten minutes. Two adults, first and second degree burns; three children, second and third degree burns. Our goal is to keep them alive and ready them for transport to burn centers in Los Angeles."

The staff exchanged uneasy glances.

"Keith and Kim, you're assigned to Trauma Room One. You'll be treating the two adults. As soon as your patients are stabilized I want Keith to join us in Trauma Room Two. Kim, you'll stay with your patients and continue to monitor.

"We're going to put the kids together in Trauma Room Two. Glenn, Mason, Cheryl, and I will be treating the children. Glenn, you're the guru with IVs, I've watched you. I want you to focus on that one task. Mason, Cheryl and I will concentrate on airways, intubating, and resuscitation."

Kathleen spoke softly to her staff. "I know you're scared and you've probably never had to handle anything like this. I have, and this approach will work. With any luck, we'll be transporting all five.

"We've got about ten minutes to assemble supplies and equipment. We may need ventilators for all five patients. Make sure we have pediatric equipment in room two. Nancy, I want you to move between the rooms and keep the supplies flowing.

"Reminder, intravenous access should be through unburned skin if at all possible. Stay steady and you'll all be fine. If you have trouble with intubating, or starting a line, call me."

Kathleen turned to Cheryl. "Where did you work with burn patients?"

"I did a stint at Children's in Los Angeles."

Kathleen nodded. "We'll work together. They'll be bringing the kids in. I don't think the others have seen..."

Cheryl nodded. "I know, I know."

Kathleen heard the sounds of helicopters overhead as they prepared to land. All five patients survived to be transported to Los Angeles.

An eerie silence filled the ER as orderlies and janitors began to ready the exam rooms for the next shift and the new wave of patients needing care. Kathleen saw her team standing dazed by their experience, looks of pain etched on their faces. She knew this would be a day they would never forget. She went over to each one, held them, and whispered words of comfort.

Cheryl came over. "You've done an incredible job, Kathleen, and it's been a real privilege to work with you."

"Thanks, Cheryl. You were a godsend."

"It's what we do." She looked at Kathleen. "Are you okay?"

"Yes, probably just tired."

Kathleen didn't wait to use the hospital showers or to change her clothes. She could feel the world closing in, and she knew she couldn't hold on to reality much longer. She covered her stained scrubs with a lab coat, taking the smells and sounds from the ER home with her.

She stayed focused, and walked erect toward her car. The smell of burnt flesh and hair from the fire victims had entered her nose and permeated her hair and clothing. The patients' screams became a collage of pain, joining and reverberating with cries from the past. No one who saw her would have known she was slipping into a time warp where the past and the present had merged and the future had dissolved.

Weekend visitors to Santa Barbara crowded the roads and the drive home took longer than usual. Kathleen tried to stay in reality by playing the loudest music she could find and opening the car windows. In spite of her efforts, she felt her hands shake and sweat ooze from every pore. She was falling into another dimension.

The stairs to the second floor were steeper than she remembered and she had to hold onto the railing, pulling herself up, one step at a time. She heard Claire on the phone talking with her bubba. Laughter, belonging to another world, floated from Claire's room and followed her down the hallway. Kathleen slipped into her bedroom, quietly shutting the door behind her.

Kathleen stripped off her clothes, found a plastic bag, and threw them in the trash. She turned on the shower, made the water as hot as she could tolerate, and watched as the bathroom filled with steam.

Kathleen scrubbed her body until her skin became red and irritated. She didn't feel clean. She had to find a way to feel clean, to erase the screams from the soldiers and noncombatants, which bullets and bombs devastated equally, without prejudice; her own silent screams, ghostly visitors from the past, erased from her consciousness.

She took the small scrubbing pad from under the sink and returned to the shower. She scrubbed her arms and legs until they began to bleed. Then she reached as far as she could onto her back. She turned off the water, dried her body, and brushed her hair.

She opened the cabinet under the sink and found the bottle of alcohol.

Kathleen pulled the sheets tightly around her neck and let her hair fall over her face. The only part that showed was her eyes that drifted between open and shut until nothing but darkness remained.

She dreamed, she dreamed. Dark dreams that made her shudder until she gasped and woke with a start. Her eyes were slow to focus. As the haze cleared she saw Claire sitting on the edge of the bed. Her face was a study in worry and concern.

"What happened?" she asked.

"We had a bad scene at the ER. I'm really tired and I can't talk about it. I have to sleep." Kathleen turned over. "This has been a really rough day. Would you feel bad if I asked you to sleep in the other room?"

"I'm okay with that, but let me get something to put on your skin."

"Why? My skin is fine."

Claire said plaintively, "No it's not… I saw your arms, Kathleen, I saw."

"Please, go away. Leave me alone."

"I'm worried about you and I'm not leaving you alone. If you want to be pissed at me, go for it."

"I can't, I can't fight anymore."

Claire leaned closer to Kathleen. "You don't have to fight. Please let me in. We can't go on pretending nothing's wrong."

Kathleen shook her head and sighed. "Do what you have to, then leave me alone."

Claire went downstairs to the medical supply cabinet, got several tubes of antibiotic ointment, and ran up the stairs to the bedroom.

Kathleen's back and arms looked as if she had fallen on a patch of hard pavement. Claire's voice quivered, "Is it like this on your legs, too?"

"I shouldn't have let you see. Why can't you go away? I don't want you here."

Claire clenched her jaw and planted her feet firmly on the floor. "I'm not leaving, and you have no idea of how stubborn I can be."

"You want to see?" She pulled off the sheet. "Happy now? Come see what I've done—more future scars for you to love."

Claire flinched. "Lie on your tummy first; I'll get your back."

"What are you using? Do you know what you're doing or are you playing doctor?"

"Definitely not playing doctor; I leave the doctoring to you. This is a special balm with magical properties. Would you like to know how I got it?"

"I'm too mad for storytelling." Kathleen sighed. "I don't have any tears left, and I don't want to have to tell a story."

"This one's on me." Claire put some ointment on her fingers. "Did I ever tell you about the time I went camping in Ireland?"

"No."

"About three years ago, I was camping with a group of friends near a lake. They decided to go fishing, and I was hanging out by myself. I was sitting quietly under a big tree, reading, when I heard this rustling sound. I didn't move and I wondered, *are there bears in Ireland?* I turned, trying not to make any noise, and saw these two tiny men wearing green suits, red caps, and buckled shoes. I thought, *if only my bubba was here to see this marvelous sight: two real leprechauns!* Well, they were having a terrible argument over a jar filled with some kind of lotion. The jar was almost as large as they were, and I watched as they had a fierce tug of war over it.

"I stood still so that I could overhear their conversation. Naturally, they had thick brogues and I couldn't understand every word, but they were saying if you touch someone with this balm they would forever, and for all eternity be your true love. I thought, *wow, if only I got my hands on that jar, all my relationship problems would evaporate.* I was trying to formulate a plan to catch a leprechaun and barter his freedom for the magic balm, when—" Claire stopped.

"What's wrong?" In spite of her pain, Kathleen had been hanging on every word.

"I need you to turn over."

Kathleen turned over, sighed, and looked at Claire. "I'm sorry, I've been horrible."

Claire sat on the bed. "I love you, Kathleen, but someday you are going to have to let someone in; if not me, someone. Shoot, I've forgotten where I was in the story."

"You were trying to formulate a plan."

"Oh, yeah. All of a sudden there was this snapping sound and the leprechaun who was holding the jar fell into a hole. The other leprechaun ran away so it was just the two of us, *mano a mano*. I thought, *this is my big chance*. I leaned over the hole and said would you like to get out? He replied, 'Aye, faith and begorra! And I will shall you one wish for getting me out of this blamed hole!'

"I reached in and picked him up. He looked me straight in the eye and said, 'What is your wish?'

"I want your magic balm!

"He chuckled and said, 'Ah, having love problems, eh? Well, use it wisely, because if you use it on the wrong person you are stuck!'"

"Are you stuck with me?"

Claire held Kathleen's hand. "Being stuck goes with being in love. I think we're stuck with each other, but perhaps it's not always a bad thing. Can I get you anything before I go to bed?"

Kathleen touched Claire lightly on her arm. "I'm afraid to be alone. Will you stay with me?"

"Tell me something, anything. Please, don't shut me out of your life."

Kathleen whispered. "It was a fire. Kids burnt."

"Are they okay?"

"It's bad. They'll have years of pain and a lifetime of being stared at. I couldn't put it aside, and I slipped into a place with dark memories. Claire, I'm sorry for the way I've treated you. I wouldn't blame you if you wanted to leave. I can't understand why you want to be with me."

"I'll tell you a little secret, but you have to promise not to tell anyone. Okay?"

Kathleen nodded. "Okay."

"I have to whisper it."

"So you won't hear it?"

"No, so you will." Claire leaned over and whispered. "You're easy to love, Kathleen, you're easy to love."

Kathleen stirred and turned on her back. God, she hurt. What day was it? Oh, please God, let it be Sunday, not Monday. Saturday seemed like a dim memory. Had it happened? She looked at her arms. She remembered. She put her fist in her mouth to muffle her sobs. She curled up in a ball and fell back to sleep.

She woke. She felt hung over. She looked at the bottle of pills. *Oh, Christ.* How many had she taken? She thought two. Two was okay. She was afraid she had taken more. She heard Claire making soft, dreamless sounds. She fell back to sleep.

She stirred, eyes trying to open. She saw Claire walk in, put a cup of coffee on the cup warmer, and get back into bed. Kathleen whispered Claire's name. Claire turned over and nuzzled gingerly against Kathleen.

Kathleen said, "I had the strangest dream. Can I tell you my dream?"

"Only if you hold me."

"It's hard for me to hold you. My arms hurt."

Claire sat up. "Rest your head on my lap. You need to know my heart is breaking right now. I can't stand that you hurt yourself."

"I'm sorry. It was so bad, I tried not to go there, but I slipped in and it was all black. I couldn't find my way out."

Claire touched Kathleen's face. "I never knew loving someone could hurt this much."

"Are you crying?"

"Yes, and I can feel your tears with my fingers."

"I didn't think I mattered this much, to anyone."

Claire leaned over and kissed Kathleen's face. "You matter to so many. I want you to know it, to believe it. Now tell me your dream."

"I was riding a large white carousel horse. Its mouth was open and its nostrils flared. He looked so angry and horror stricken. Suddenly the carousel stopped and the horse began to move. He jumped off and we began to ride through a battlefield. There were tanks, and artillery, and bodies strewn everywhere. It was as if I was seeing every battle through the ages. Some of the equipment was ancient and some was modern. Bodies were clothed in uniforms from the past and the present. Everywhere I went I could see rotting corpses and smell the stench of decaying flesh. There was no life anywhere. I felt lost. I didn't know where I was and I had no sense of direction.

"There were dark, angry clouds everywhere. It began to pour and at first, I felt grateful for the rain. Then I noticed it was blood, not water. No matter how hard I tried I couldn't wipe it away or avoid it. It was everywhere—in my hair, in my eyes. My horse kept moving forward although he, too, was covered in blood.

"Finally the rain stopped and we were at the bank of a river. My horse began to swim to the other side. The water came up to my neck and in some places, I was underwater, but I wasn't afraid. As we crossed the river, the blood washed away and by the time we reached the other side all the blood and filth were gone. My horse was transformed from a carousel horse into a live horse. His mouth was closed, and he had a calm, gentle look about him.

"This side was different. There was a flowing green meadow where wildflowers of every size and color grew. The flowers began to change into men and women. They lined up, forming two columns. As I rode between the columns, they saluted and threw flower petals in my path. It was odd, because some were in uniform, clean and crisp, while others had on casual beachwear or golfing togs. They were all smiling as they saluted. As we passed through the meadow I felt calmer and more at peace.

"I came to another area that was smaller and sheltered by trees. I saw two children, a boy and a girl. The girl was holding a butterfly net and the most beautiful butterflies, in an ever-changing kaleidoscope of colors and designs, surrounded her. After she caught them she would set them free. This game went on for quite a while. The boy was more serious. He was lying on his back, reading *The Wind in the Willows*. One leg was crossed over the other, and he seemed to doze from time to time.

"The girl had red hair and freckles and didn't seem to notice me; she was too busy running around, having a marvelous time. The boy stared at me and smiled. It was a small but sweet smile, as if he knew me. As I looked at him I saw that his skin was darker than the girl's, and his hair was black. His eyes were the deepest blue I had ever seen and because his hair was so black, they appeared purple.

"That's when I woke up."

Claire recited a prayer in Hebrew.

"What is that?"

"It's Kaddish, the prayer Jews recite for the dead. We say it every day for eleven months, and if the person was wicked, we say it for twelve. The extra month is to protect their soul from punishment in the afterlife."

Kathleen thought about Mrs. Roth, and all the troops who had died. "Teach it to me? I want to say it every morning, for eleven months."

CHAPTER 32

Fall was ending and winter was getting ready to take its place. The leaves on the deciduous trees, like the occupants of Canfield House, were in transition. At first the leaves fell in gentle numbers, then cascaded in spurts as if to say, "Come see me. I am as beautiful bare as when I am adorned in the protection of my leaves." From oval to tapered shapes they fell to the ground, creating a patterned quilt in colors of soft orange, yellow, and scarlet.

Sam started a men's health support group and used the solarium one evening a week.

Helen began to have doubts about her matchmaking skills. She saw Kathleen's need for secrecy struggling against Claire's need for intimacy. She wondered if she had done the right thing by interfering with Eros, the god of love.

Claire finished the furniture project and the rooms in Canfield House were filled to capacity. Kathleen and Claire's love ran deep, but unresolved conflicts moved quietly beneath the surface of normality.

Claire and Kathleen were sitting in front of the bedroom fireplace, wrapped in each other's arms.

Claire said, "I have an idea."

Kathleen pulled her closer. "Okay, let's have it." Life with Claire was never dull and surprises were always around the corner.

"Why don't we have a party? The house is furnished and it looks great. I thought you might want to invite the staff from the ER, the mayor, and town council. It would be good publicity for you, and they're going to be green with envy when they see what you've done with the house."

"What *I've* done? *You've* done most of the work. I don't know. I've never really had parties. What if it's a dud?"

"Didn't you have parties when you were a kid?"

Kathleen knew she had walked into that one. She turned the doorknob and now Claire wanted to force it open. "Once, only once."

~ Boston, 1979 ~

They were five: Kathleen, Devon, Evie, Frank, and Liam.

It was Kathleen's eighth birthday, and the house was filled with excitement. Mom got up early and baked a chocolate cake and Da taped a Pin the Tail on the Donkey game to the living room wall. Mom was singing and laughing, and Da kissed her neck and swung her around.

"Kat," her mother called out, "change your clothes, your friends will be here soon." Kat put on her best dress and wished she had better shoes to wear than her sneakers. She thought about decorating them with flower stickers, but there wasn't time. She couldn't be late to her own party!

The doorbell rang and she pushed Devon out of the way. "I'll get it, I'll get it! It's my party!" She expected to see all the kids, but only Susie Nelson stood at the door.

"Hi, Susie. Did you see the other girls?"

Susie shook her head and wiped her runny nose on the sleeve of her dress. She handed Kat her gift, wrapped in pink floral paper with a large red bow on top. Kat smiled and said, "Thank you." Mom handed Susie a tissue. "Here, dear, for your nose."

Kat watched the clock as the hand moved slowly, marking the time. Her invitations said two o'clock and it was now two-fifteen. Kat wanted to believe the other girls got lost, but after a while she knew they weren't coming. Her heart dropped, and she wished she had a magic wand that would make Susie disappear.

Only a few slices of her cake were eaten, and the pins, blindfold, and paper tails from Pin the Tail on the Donkey sat untouched. She opened her gift from Susie, and found a used doll with faded hair and bald spots. Disappointment rose from her toes, twirled its way around her stomach, and continued upwards until a lump formed in her throat; tears stung her eyes.

Mom said, "What a lovely gift, Susie."

"Thank you," said Kat, as a forced smile, like a plaster cast, crossed her face.

After Susie left, Kat walked to the back of the house, near the alleyway, and threw the doll in a dented trashcan. That night, she buried her face in her pillow and cried until the tears ran dry and she fell asleep.

The next morning she found the doll sitting on the kitchen table. Mom stood by the stove spooning lumpy oatmeal into bowls. Mom frowned. "You're being selfish not to appreciate a gift, even if it isn't what you wanted. Jesus would be disappointed in you."

Kat lowered her eyes and thought about how she would burn in hell, until nothing was left but her blackened bones.

CHAPTER 33

Helen was as excited as Claire and for the next month, The Party became the favorite topic of conversation.

Claire insisted on a clothes-shopping expedition. "We have to have something new to wear!" Convincing Kathleen was not easy but finally, after much moaning and grumbling, they drove to Santa Barbara with Claire's list of antique clothing stores. Claire was planning on going to the party in true Victorian style. She found an ankle-length, ivory lace under dress at the first store. "Perfect! Exactly what I'm looking for."

Kathleen was startled and thought, *don't tell me she is going to wear a slip to the party!* With Claire, anything was possible.

But Claire was just getting started. At the next two stores, nothing. Then, at the last store on the block, Claire found a beautiful mauve crushed velvet dress with mother-of-pearl buttons. Kathleen had to admit that Claire had created a lovely period outfit that was perfect for her and the party.

Claire was bubbling over with excitement. "Now, we have to shop for you."

"You're kidding, I hope. You know how I hate to shop."

"Come on, we're going to The Dungeon, and I'm going to find the perfect dress for you."

"The Dungeon? Is that some kind of torture shop?"

Claire laughed. "Torture for you, fun for me. We have to buy a dress for you and shoes for both of us."

Claire was on one of her adventures and Kathleen knew there was no stopping her.

When they drove into the parking lot of The Dungeon, Kathleen understood the origin of the name. The main building, called The Castle, was filled with small upscale clothing shops. Designed to resemble an English castle, the exterior walls were covered in a thick, rough gray stone. Towers and turrets rose from the roofline, creating square and round silhouettes against the darkening sky. A sign pointed to The Dungeon, and led Kathleen and Claire toward a narrow stairwell.

Claire laughed. "Let's take the stairs instead of the elevator. It's so much more authentic, just like being in a real castle. No hand rails and you never know what's around the corner."

The Dungeon, held the largest selection of discounted designer clothing in Southern California. The store swarmed with bargain-crazed shoppers, hunting through racks and tables filled with the latest markdowns. Kathleen couldn't think of a worse way to spend her day. She felt like an observer at the zoo on a crowded Sunday afternoon, except the animals were out of their cages and shopping at The Dungeon.

Claire guided Kathleen to a quiet corner. "It's a jungle out there. You'll be safe here. I'll be right back." With a gleam in her eyes that spoke of a hunter after prey, Claire was off on her expedition.

Less than ten minutes later, Claire was back with three dresses. She guided Kathleen to the large public dressing area.

Kathleen whispered, "Where are the private dressing rooms?"

Claire whispered back, "Be brave, this is it."

"You're kidding. One room? I can't undress in front of everyone and try on clothes; they'll see my scar."

"We'll tell them you got it in a fencing duel, rescuing me from an evil princess." Pouting, Claire held up a black, below the knee dress with an A-line skirt and cap sleeves. "Come on Kathleen, just this one."

"I'll try it on, but only if you promise not to throw a Claire tantrum." Looking shyly around, Kathleen put on the dress.

Claire was pleased. "I like it. It suits you. It's simple but elegant, and you've got the perfect figure for it."

The ever-frugal Kathleen asked, "How much is it?"

"Don't worry, it's on me. Now, let's hit the shoe department."

Claire found a perfect pair of Victorian style lace-up shoes for herself and simple black pumps with a low heel for Kathleen.

"You're going to look so elegant!" Claire declared, with a look of triumph on her face, as they carried their packages back to the car.

Claire sent out the invitations and was busy working on music and decorations. Sam was drafted to be the "light decorator." At first he grumbled, but finally succumbed to party fever and placed lanterns around the porch and solar lights down the driveway. Linc volunteered his sons for valet parking and insisted that they wear double-breasted jackets with gold buttons for the occasion.

The "party committee," consisting of Claire and Helen, decided to use the reception hall for a buffet supper. The reception hall was a spacious room with a large paneled fireplace that would chase away the fall chill. Low cabinets, perfect for the buffet supper, were placed along the staircase wall.

Helen created a spectacular menu. She insisted on "absolutely no turkey. By the time everyone's gone to holiday parties, Thanksgiving, and Christmas, they're sick of turkey. I have some *other* ideas that will positively knock their socks off." Helen's menu consisted of a prime rib roast, cold poached salmon, roasted rosemary potatoes, and a variety of salads. For the vegetarians, she added a dish of roasted vegetables, picked fresh from the garden, and baked sesame seed tofu.

Another setting was created in the solarium for coffee and Helen's special desserts.

Claire insisted on live music and *The Music Gal* was engaged to provide entertainment throughout the evening on her 61-key keyboard.

Kathleen hired a professional staff for food serving and cleanup. She wanted everyone she loved to be available for the fun.

❀ ❀ ❀

The night of the party, Kathleen's anxiety level, on a scale of one to ten, was pushing twenty. Why had she let Claire talk her into this? *Damn it,* she thought, in a moment of incredible uneasiness, *that woman is going to be the death of me.*

Kathleen heard Claire knock on her bedroom door. It was Claire's secret knock; three long raps followed by two short. She opened the door to see Claire, a vision of old-world loveliness in her Victorian outfit, and bubbling over with excitement.

Kathleen gathered Claire close and felt her anxiety melting. She playfully undid one of the buttons on Claire's dress. "Do we have time for you to faint?"

Claire laughed softly. "Oh, those Victorians knew exactly what they were doing with fainting couches and all these buttons. I may feel a faint coming on after the party, when the guests have left, of course." Claire handed Kathleen a small box wrapped in soft blue paper and trimmed in white antique lace. "This is for you."

Claire looked at Kathleen. "What is it? You look so sad."

Kathleen couldn't speak for a moment and just shook her head.

"Please, tell me, don't shut me out."

"I'm not used to getting gifts."

Claire held her closer. "I'm sorry, I know I can't make up for the past, but maybe we can think of this as a new start. I love buying you presents and I think you'll like this one. Won't you open it?"

Kathleen opened the box to find a necklace and matching earrings. "They're beautiful."

"Let me help you with the necklace."

Kathleen looked in the mirror. She saw Claire's reflection, beaming and filled with love. She turned to Claire and held her. "Thank you for being in my life."

"Me, too. I knew marcasite would be perfect with your dress. It has just a bit of Victorian flavor."

"I didn't get you anything."

Claire held Kathleen and whispered, "You have no idea of what you've given me."

They left Kathleen's bedroom holding hands.

Half way down, Kathleen let go.

Kathleen welcomed the guests as they arrived and eyes opened wide at the changes to the house. Gayle and Robert greeted the guests as they entered the solarium where wine, cheese, and fruit were being served. Claire moved from group to group, answering questions about the furniture, talking and laughing and putting everyone at ease. Sam and Linc were engaged in an intense conversation about antique cars. Kathleen was sure Linc had the ideal car for Sam. When the food was served everyone insisted on Helen sharing her recipes. Kathleen smelled a cookbook in the future.

Kathleen relaxed and discovered she could enjoy a party. She was talking to Mayor Bill Langdon when Claire walked over.

Bill gave Claire a hug. "It's always good to see you. Do you have any dancing planned for tonight? Maybe a Highland fling?"

Claire laughed and stood close to Kathleen. "I'll reserve the fling for the festival. We do have dance music planned and I'd love to cut a rug with you, Hizzoner."

"Great, I just hope I can keep up!"

Kathleen interrupted rather rudely, "Bill and I were discussing next year's festival. We were thinking of offering health screenings." She turned to Bill; Claire had to stifle a gasp when she found herself looking at Kathleen's back. "I'll come up with some suggestions. I'm thinking about something that will be family oriented. We'll make it fun for the kids and informative for the parents."

Bill laughed. "No shots at the festival."

"Definitely."

Claire stayed for a minute and moved away to speak with Theo Chandler.

The Music Gal began the evening by playing easy listening songs, setting the perfect mood for the dinner hour. After dinner she took requests and soon the floor of the solarium was filled with dancing couples. Claire found the mayor at the dessert table. "Okay, Bill, plenty of time for dessert, now it's time to show me your moves."

Claire nodded and the slow dance music changed abruptly into The Macarena. As Claire was known to do, she led the dancers in a ruckus rendition. Hizzoner did his best to imitate his uninhibited partner's moves, as did the rest of the pack. When the music stopped Claire leaned over planting a kiss on the cheek of the out-of-breath mayor. "You're awesome, Bill."

After the last guest left, the house took on an unearthly quiet. Kathleen walked over to Claire and started to put her arms around her. "Everyone had a good time and you did a sensational job."

Claire stepped back out of Kathleen's reach. "It's better if you don't touch me. I'm stinking mad."

"What's wrong, did something happen?"

"Did something happen? I hope you're kidding. Did you see other couples? They were, well, shit, *like couples*—sometimes touching, sometimes holding hands, kissing, for Chrissake. You couldn't even hold my hand all the way down the stairs."

Claire felt her face flush. She was Mount Vesuvius, ready to erupt. "When I came over to you and Bill, you turned your back on me. You rejected me in front of Bill. Do you have any idea of how that felt? Why didn't you include me in your conversation? We might as well have been strangers. No, let me rephrase that: You wouldn't treat a stranger the way you treated me.

"Do you want to know what Theo and I were talking about? He asked me out on a date. He thinks I'm available. Am I? Because I might take him up on the offer."

Claire saw an incredulous look on Kathleen's face and said sharply, "Oh my God, you really don't get it, do you? You don't know how to be with another person! What the fuck happened to you? It wasn't only the war, was it?"

"No, it's more than the war. I'm sorry, Claire. I don't want to make excuses for my behavior tonight. I just didn't want the guests to guess our secret. And you're right. I don't know how to be with another person."

Claire was still fuming. She knew she was crossing the line of sanity and moving into a full-blown tantrum. "Now it's *our* secret? It's always been *your* secret, not mine. Everything is in the dark. Everything is a goddamn secret. Well, I got news for you. This is a small town. The rumor mill's probably been working overtime. I'd be surprised if every man, woman, and child here didn't at least suspect that we're shacking up."

Kathleen stood feebly by, unable to get a word in edgewise.

"And by the way, is your loving me a secret, too? Do you know you've never told me that you love me? Do you love me? How can I know, when you've never said the words and you treat me as if I'm nothing to you? I'm not going to be someone hidden away in a fucking closet."

Claire could feel her heartbeat starting to slow and the volcano cooling. "I'm sorry, I lost it. Shit, I hate when I do this. You didn't deserve the things I said." Claire shook her head and looked at Kathleen. "Jesus, I've hurt you. I never meant for that to happen. Don't you see? I want to be proud of who I am, who we are. I want it all, and I want it with you. I love you, Kathleen, but to me, that means the whole package. I want to be surrounded by family, friends, and someday, children."

Claire took Kathleen's hand and led her over to the couch. "There's something I have to tell you. Remember the museum in LA I was supposed to go to work at? Well, I got a call from them. They're preparing an exhibit on the History of Storytelling and they've asked me to work with the designers in New York. It's a year-long contract, and I'll need to be based in Los Angeles for the first four months.

"Once the design phase is finished they want me to write and illustrate a companion book. It's a real opportunity, something that doesn't come along every day. They'll rent an apartment for me near the museum, and I'll fly to New York for design meetings.

"I didn't know how to tell you, but I need to take this offer, now more than ever. I have to see if I have what it takes to succeed on my own and, for once, finish something.

Kathleen felt her heart drop and her hands tremble. "Why didn't you tell me sooner?"

"I wanted to speak to you right away, but the party was coming up and I didn't want to ruin it. I'm sorry, I know this is really bad timing." Claire spoke slowly. "I'm no better at doing a relationship than you.

Claire looked soulfully at Kathleen. "This crap between us isn't going to change unless we both do something about it. Maybe it's just where we are: You can't step out, and I can't step in and lock the door... It's not who I am, I'll suffocate."

Kathleen's eyes glazed over; she was beginning to disappear. Claire's words were a boomerang, vanishing into space only to return with a vengeance. "When will you leave?"

"They want me in New York in a week. I'll spend a few days with Bubba, and then fly directly to Los Angeles."

Kathleen shook her head. She felt every part of her shaking. She wanted to curl up in bed and wake to find this was all a bad dream. "What about the holidays? This Christmas will be our first."

Claire covered Kathleen's hand with hers and spoke hesitantly. "I don't know about the holidays. We'll have to see where we are. Kathleen, I don't want to lose us, and I don't want this to be a breakup. This may buy us time so that we don't end up saying and doing things we regret. I'm afraid I may have already said too much. There's no way to take back something that hurts the person you love. I know you've begun to withdraw from me. I can see it in your eyes. I want you to look at me even if it hurts. I want to see your eyes alive, even if it's with anger."

Claire looked down. "I'm not happy about my tantrums, and I know I can be a brat. It's time for me to grow up. Maybe it's time for each of us to face our demons."

Kathleen looked at Claire. Her eyes were now focused and the pain that lived there shone. She wanted to cry and beg Claire not to leave. Instead she heard words escaping as if they belonged to someone else. "Maybe it's time."

Claire was silent for a long moment. "One other thing and, this is a big favor," she said at last. "Can I leave Oscar with you? I don't want him to have to adjust to another city or board him when I go to New York. Oscar will be happy here—he loves you every bit as much as me."

CHAPTER 34

Kevin Meath, Licensed Marriage and Family Therapist, waited in his office for his seven o'clock patient, Dr. Kathleen Moore. Kevin usually worked a half-day on Saturdays, but this was a referral from Helen Hughes, and any referral from Helen received Kevin's full attention.

Kevin rubbed his right leg. He felt fortunate to have a below the knee amputation, but he knew it was time to get his prosthesis adjusted. Operation Desert Sabre was the name of the massive ground attack launched in Iraq and Kuwait during the Gulf War. February 25, 1991, marked the second day of Desert Sabre and Kevin considered it his rebirth day. After being wounded on that fateful day and treated in a field hospital, he was flown to Germany, then to Walter Reed where the doctors determined that amputation was the only course of treatment.

Kevin's family had served in the Army for five generations. It was no surprise, and even expected, for Kevin to choose an Army career. His parents visited him at Walter Reed, beamed at his Purple Heart, and expected him to carry his wound without pity or tears.

Helen entered his life the day after his surgery. He looked at her through drug-glazed eyes and was sure he was seeing his favorite childhood character, Winnie the Pooh. But any drug-induced fantasy was where it ended. Helen was a taskmaster, but not a vicious one—although it sometimes seemed that way. There was always compassion behind her eyes, even when she coaxed her patients to undreamt of plateaus of pain—for their own good, as she not so subtly reminded him. Regaining the motion in his knee was the hardest work Kevin had ever done in his life, and Helen was his drill sergeant and his cheerleader.

Suddenly, one day, he was transferred from the ward to a private room. The door to his room opened and Helen walked in. "Hi, Kevin. Wondering why you're getting the VIP treatment?"

"Crossed my mind."

"You'll need some privacy for a couple of days; your physical therapy is going to get more strenuous—bet you didn't think that was possible, huh?—and you'll be more comfortable here."

Helen wasn't kidding. Kevin was being weaned off of pain medication, and she was pushing him until he broke down and the tears came. He expected her to be angry, the way his parents would have been. When Helen saw the tears start, she whisked him off to his private room and massaged his back as he cried for his loss.

Two days later, he returned to the ward. Other patients came over and patted him on the back. He knew then he was not the only one to receive Helen's VIP treatment.

It was Helen who directed Kevin toward his new calling. "You have a way with people, Kevin. You're bright and enthusiastic and you know what it's like to return from hell. Someone is going to have to counsel returning vets as they transition into civilian life, and I can't think of a better person for the job."

Kevin learned to walk without a limp, enrolled in school to become a therapist, married his childhood sweetheart, and had two children. He felt truly blessed.

Kevin saw the call light go on. He looked at the clock on his desk. It was exactly seven o'clock. He opened the door to see a woman, he guessed in her mid-thirties, wearing hospital scrubs and with a look of exhaustion written all over her. They settled in, Kathleen on the couch and Kevin in a chair opposite her.

"I'm here because..." Kathleen stopped and started again. "I'm here because..." She stopped again. "I don't know why I'm here. That's not true, either. I'm here for so many reasons, and I don't know where to start. I'm tired and I'm not sure if this will work for me. I've just finished a double shift at the ER, and I can't remember if I've eaten today."

Kevin walked over to a small refrigerator and handed her some yogurt and orange juice. "Let's start with this."

"Thank you, just the juice please. I was injured in Iraq, and I lied to the doctors about having PTSD. I function all right, most of the time, but I have nightmares— different ones, but they play over and over. I had one really major meltdown, so maybe I'm not functioning as well as I think.

"My girlfriend left me a couple of weeks ago. It feels as if she abandoned me. It was my fault though. I'm too far in the closet, and I can't tell her I love her. I can't say the words. Does it bother you that I'm ...?" Kathleen paused; a look of suffering distorted her face. "I can't stand the thought of losing Claire."

"Is it okay to call you Kathleen or do you have a nickname?"

"No nickname, Kathleen is fine. Well, I used to have a nickname, as a kid, but that was a lifetime ago." Kathleen started to stand up. "I should go; this isn't going to work for me."

"Kathleen, before you leave, let me tell you what I've noticed, and then you can decide if you want to stay."

Kathleen sighed and rested her head against the back of the couch.

"You're exhausted physically and are carrying a heavy emotional burden. It sounds to me as if you feel you have to carry it alone. I think you're afraid of making a mistake or telling what you perceive is a lie. It's as if God is waiting to strike you down. Changing your mind about something or being unsure isn't a lie. It's how we process things. Think of it as a road trip. We may have to go down many side streets and make lots of turns, until we finally get to the main road.

"You started to ask me something. You said, 'Does it bother you that I'm—' Would you like to finish that sentence?"

"Does it bother you that I'm—" she hesitated. "That I'm lesbian?"

"Would you believe me if I said no?"

"Probably not."

"Would you believe me if I said yes?"

"Probably. Why would you lie about the yes?"

"So, how can I answer the question? Kathleen, we have a half-hour left. Seems a shame to waste it. Why don't you tell me about your question."

When Kathleen left, she made two appointments for the following week.

PART SIX

Winter

CHAPTER 35

Kathleen and Claire spoke on the phone from time to time, but couldn't get past a casual conversation.

"How's Oscar?"

"He's up to his old tricks—or I should say a new one. He caught a mouse yesterday."

"Oh, no! Did he leave it as a present?"

"Right on the bed."

Claire laughed.

"How's work?"

"It's slow and sometimes tedious. I'm going to New York next week to meet with the designers. There are a couple of glitches that need to be worked out."

"I'd love to see it, when it's ready."

"The design phase should be done in early spring. I'm really excited. Maybe we can have dinner and you can see the models."

The bed felt so empty without Claire. During the night, while Kathleen was sleeping, she would reach over to Claire's side, expecting to feel the warmth of her body or the softness of her skin. Nothing but rumpled sheets greeted her, and she would awaken with a startled shiver, sit up, and begin to gasp.

Kathleen spent most of her evenings in the solarium. There were times when she could feel a large weight sitting on her chest, as if all of her unspoken feelings were rolled into a ball, waiting to be released. The solarium was the first room Claire had furnished, and it was the room they sat in when Claire told Kathleen she was leaving.

Kathleen could close her eyes and feel the sweetness and the pain of their love. She realized that she could not have one without the other.

Kathleen continued to see Kevin twice a week.

In one session, Kevin said, "I'd like to know something about your history—parents, brothers and sisters. Tell me about your upbringing."

"My parents both died when I was nine, and I was raised in foster care. I don't like to talk about my childhood. It wasn't pleasant; let's leave it at that.

"I'll cut to the chase, Kevin. I'm not interested in talking about the past. I want to focus on what I have to do to get Claire back. I have to be able to tell her I'm sorry, and I have to be able to tell her I love her. I have to get the words out. I don't know why it's so hard.

"You see, she's my first girlfriend, and I don't think I know enough about the structure of a relationship. Like, how often should I give her gifts? The holidays, of course, but what about other times? And, how do I know what to get her? Or, when I learn to tell her I love her, how often should I say it? Will I say it often enough or too often? I just don't know how this works!

"Claire always knew how to do it. One time, when I came home from the ER, she had candles lit all around the bathroom and flowers floating in the bathtub." Kathleen began to cry. "It shouldn't be this hard—other people know how to do it. I can take notes, if you'll just tell me."

"Does it feel as if I'm withholding something from you?"

"Isn't that what shrinks do? Withhold and let you dangle when they know the answers and could make it easy."

"Do you have any thoughts about why it's so hard for you to tell Claire how much she means to you and how much you love her?"

"It isn't about what happened when I was little, if that's what you're hinting at. That's another time, another world. Are you trying to trick me into telling you all my dark secrets? I just need Claire back. I want to make it up to her. I can learn how to do it: to buy her presents, maybe bring her breakfast in bed. Is there a book I can read?" She looked at him with pleading eyes.

"I don't know how to do any of it. A long time ago, someone said I was a robot. Maybe that's true. Maybe if I'm cut open they will find nuts and bolts and batteries."

"I don't think you're a robot, not at all. Somewhere inside, there's a frightened little girl and you're protecting her and taking care of her the only way you know. Making love with Claire is wonderful, but you may also be using it as a way to avoid dealing with your pain."

Kathleen stood up, her eyes narrowed and her brow furrowed. "You are so fucking wrong." She pointed her finger at him. "You goddamn therapists think everything is about some fucking childhood trauma. Don't you dare imply that I'm using Claire! You know, Kevin, you can go fuck yourself. See how that one feels."

She walked out, slammed the door, moved down the hallway, and punched the walls with her fists until the skin on her knuckles became raw. She got in her truck, heard the starter grinding until she flooded the engine. She got out swearing, slammed the door, and kicked the tires until she couldn't lift her foot.

She walked the floors all night, thought about quitting therapy, and finally left Kevin a nasty message on his phone about how he didn't understand her or have a clue about how to be a therapist.

The next session she was still furious and decided not to talk. She shot invisible daggers across the room. None of them seemed to hit Kevin. They sat in silence for fifty minutes.

The session after that, she began to sob and couldn't stop. Kevin let her cry. He didn't even offer her a tissue.

The next session Kathleen came in and, instead of sitting, lay down on the couch. She was too ashamed to look at Kevin. She closed her eyes tightly before she spoke. "I want to tell you about a little girl named Kat. I guess I should begin when she was eight and had a birthday party. No one liked her and only one girl came and brought her an ugly used doll.

"Now, this is a pretend story. You have to understand that it can't be real. Not yet and maybe never.

"Kat was eight and a half and was certain she had discovered the secret to being popular. The popular girls wore new dresses and shoes and ate bologna sandwiches for lunch. They sat together talking softly, their feet swinging back and forth in a rhythm that said, *Look at my beautiful shoes.*

"Kat didn't want to wear the clothes that Mom found at the Catholic Thrift Shop. She wanted a new dress, patent leather shoes, and bologna sandwiches for lunch. Then she could sit with the popular girls and swing her feet to the rhythm of the beautiful shoe dance.

"Kat had been praying for a new dress and shoes for weeks. Maybe she wasn't praying enough. She thought she could pray as she walked to and from school. That would be three times a day and would be sure to impress God. A new dress, shoes, and a bologna sandwich had to be the magic formula to popularity. Then, when she was nine, all the girls in her class would come to her party. She imagined wearing her new dress, velvet she thought, shiny shoes with fresh white socks, presents stacked high, and a big smile on her face.

"Mom's belly had never been so big and Da and Mom seemed angry all the time. Da didn't work anymore. Da looked funny and smelled funny, too. He smelled like the men who stood outside of Michael's bar, smoking.

"Kat stood in the kitchen watching Da making lunches. Did she dare? Should she risk it? She stood next to Da and said, 'Da, can we get some bologna for lunch?'

"Da just stared at her, a scowl on his face and deep lines across his forehead. His breath smelled the way water in a vase did, after flowers had been left in it to die.

"Once she watched a squirrel trying to cross the street. It ran one way, then the other. A car came and the squirrel froze. Kat closed her eyes, so tight, and held her breath. She heard a thud and when she opened her eyes, the squirrel was lying in the street, dead. Now, she froze like the squirrel.

"Da's hand thumped against her head, sending her falling into the kitchen chair. His face turned red until the muscles stiffened and his eyes bulged. With a rage, he took off his belt and began to use it like a whip.

"She scooted under the kitchen table and covered her face. The belt flew through the air, sometimes missing her, sometimes hitting her. Her leg burned as if it was on fire. Had she slipped into hell?

"The belt stopped and Kat saw Mom standing next to the table. Something wet was dripping between Mom's legs.

"'Frank, my water broke,' she said. 'I have to go to the hospital.'

"Mom bent over and glared at Kat. Her face was tight and her hair was matted from sweat. 'You have to stay home from school and take care of the kids. Make sure you clean the house and stop being a bad girl and making your da angry.'

"Kat cleaned the house, made scrambled eggs and toast for dinner, bathed Franky and Evie, and got everyone into bed. Maybe, Da would come home with a package of bologna as a reward for her being so good. Her leg burned, but she pretended she was Peter Pan and got hurt making a rocky landing on a pirate ship.

"Da came home late, smelling funny again. He glared at her. 'Why aren't you in bed?' he demanded crossly.

"Kat stayed quiet. Talking got her into trouble and made her bad.

"Da said, 'Two more mouths to feed.' He motioned to her. 'Come here.'

"She walked over silently. He turned her around and lifted her dress. Da said, 'Get the bottle of alcohol from the bathroom.' Her lips quivered. Mom used alcohol on scrapes and she remembered how much it hurt. If she said anything, would Da take off his belt? Like the squirrel, she stood trapped in her terror.

"Da spoke harshly. 'Didn't I tell you to get the alcohol?' She put her head down, got the alcohol and held the bottle in a trembling, outstretched hand. 'Turn around, and I don't want to hear you sniveling.' She turned and bit her lip. She made the tears stay inside and she didn't make a sound.

"Something bad happened to Mom. She sat on the floor, resting her head against the wall. Her long red hair was tangled and matted and her eyes open, staring into nothingness. The babies cried and Kat was scared, so scared. She tried to feed them and change their diapers. She stopped going to school. She prayed to Mary and Jesus and all the saints she had learned about in Sunday school. She stopped asking for a new dress and patent leather shoes. She prayed for Mom to come alive and for Da to stop hitting her with his belt.

"It was a winter night and the kids' room was cold and dark. Devon stood next to Kat's bed, shivering, making little sobbing noises. 'Kat, I can hear the aliens. They're coming to get us.' She moved over, creating a space as she did every night. She put her arms around him and they slept, curled up like two puppies trying to stay warm.

"The first streaks of the morning light came through the window and Kat could see fairy dust dancing around the room. She got up quietly and tucked the blankets under Devon to keep the cold from creeping in. She put on her wool cap, mittens, and heaviest coat. The house was quiet. No fighting kids, no smelly Mom and Da, and best of all, no belt.

"She shivered as she walked toward the living room, but kept thinking about the warmth that would come once she started a fire in the fireplace. She stopped. A scarecrow hung from the ceiling. Was it Halloween? She didn't have a costume. Had she forgotten? Would she get candy? Suddenly, terror ran through her veins like ice water on the coldest day of winter. It wasn't a scarecrow. It looked like a scarecrow dressed in a black suit. It wasn't a scarecrow. It was Da.

"Kat knelt on the hard wooden floor and began to pray: 'Forgive me Da, and God and Jesus and Mary for I have been a bad girl.' She kept praying, until the police took her from the room.

"An ambulance took Mom to the hospital and all the children went for a ride in the police cars. The policeman sang silly songs and put on the siren for them. When they got to the station they ate ice cream and cookies for breakfast. Later, the social ladies came and took away the kids, one at a time, except for the twins. They were so small that Kat was sure that two only counted as one. Kat wanted to cry when she found out she had to stay at Mrs. Adams without Devon. Devon kicked and screamed. 'Kat, don't leave me! Kat, come back!' She cried inside tears, so nobody would know, and she didn't look back."

"That's the end of the story and the end of Kat. She went to live with Mrs. Adams and became Kathleen. All she wanted was a new dress, shoes, and a lousy bologna sandwich."

Kathleen stood up, her gaze transfixed and vacant, and began to cross the room to leave.

Kevin did something he had never done before. He moved between a patient and the door. "You've spent your life carrying the guilt for everything that happened to your family. Kat, the little girl, doesn't have to feel guilty or be ashamed of who she is. That little girl has grown into a wonderful woman capable of loving and being loved. It's time to set her free."

CHAPTER 36

Kevin was a dream gatherer. As a small child brings home a school painting, Kevin's patients brought him their dreams. He couldn't hang the dreams on the refrigerator, but he could take each one inside, and think of it as a chapter in an unfinished autobiography, written in code. Kevin knew that it wouldn't be enough for him to see Kathleen's story in her dreams; it had to be validated and felt by her.

Kathleen brought in two "chapters" for Kevin's consideration. *Nightmares,* he thought, *that continue to haunt her.* The first dream was of her being in the burn pit and swallowed up by the ground. The second was of her climbing out, but getting dismembered by an IED. Kathleen recited the nightmares without emotion, as if she was presenting a dry paper at a lecture. Kevin didn't push for associations, and he didn't make any interpretations. For now, he was letting Kathleen lead. It was his job to sense when she might be open to having him join her on the journey. For that, she would have to trust him as they descended into her personal hell.

Kathleen settled into the couch, scrunching around until she found her comfort spot. She didn't mind if she could see Kevin, although at times, she kept her eyes shut tight so that he couldn't see her. She remembered, so many years ago now, when she would lie on Gayle's couch and become a little girl. She knew it was happening again.

Kathleen told Kevin about the dream she had the night of the fire. Kevin listened carefully as she described the three parts of the dream. The first was her journey through the desolate battlefield on a carousel horse. The second was her crossing the river to a side that was filled with flowers and contented people. Finally, she saw two children playing in a field of green. Kevin felt it was a transitional dream and it was time to push.

"You've had three dreams that are tied to Iraq and your injury. However, I believe there is more than one level to the dreams. On the surface they're about Iraq, but they may connect to your story about Kat. I'd like us to look at them as one continuous dream. Also, I'd like to focus on your feelings during the dreams. How does that sound? Shall we give it a go?"

Kathleen sighed. "I don't suppose there's another way around this. Can't we forget the dreams ever happened? Maybe they'll go away on their own. Maybe we're giving them too much power."

"The only way I know to defuse the power is to talk about the dreams and try to gain some understanding."

Kathleen rubbed her forehead. "I don't want to do this. Can I talk about something else?"

"Sure, it's your hour. I'm wondering, what are you avoiding?"

"I was relieved when I told you the story about Kat. I'm more relaxed and less troubled. I don't want to stir things up."

"That's not a bad reason. What would you say to a patient who didn't want treatment because it might be painful, but could be helpful?"

Kathleen continued to rub her forehead. "I'd tell them to try the treatment and if they wanted to, they could stop."

"Okay, shall we agree to that? If you want to stop, we'll stop. Let's go back to the first dream when you're in the pit and you can't get out and you're being swallowed up. Do you recall the feeling?"

Kathleen sighed. "All too well. I'm terrified. I can't lift my feet and I can't scream. I'm being suffocated. I feel alone and helpless."

"What about being in the pit? What comes to mind?"

Kathleen's hand left her forehead. She ran her hand through her hair and began to twirl a long strand. Her voice became softer, more childlike. "Discarded; I'm being discarded like useless pieces of flesh that are no longer valued."

Kevin was quiet for a moment. "I want you to take a moment and think of when you've had those feelings or experiences in other situations, perhaps earlier in your life."

"It wasn't always bad. There was a before time, when it was just Devon and me, and Da worked. He would come home and give Mom kisses, and they would dance until Mom got out of breath and dizzy. Then, at night, he would tuck me in and tell me stories about Ireland and call me his Little Warrior."

Kathleen began to shake and said abruptly, "I have to stop now. I don't want to do this. I can't do this. Please, don't make me do it. I don't want to go back."

"Where are you, Kathleen?"

Kathleen buried her face in her hands. "You know, don't you?"

"I can't know. I need you to tell me."

"I've never told anyone."

"Secrets are like vampires. They can only live in the dark. Once you let them out they begin to lose their power and die. Tell me about feeling discarded."

"I was thrown away. New babies came every year to take my place. Then my da began to beat me, his hand across my head or his belt across my back or leg. I tried so hard to be good. Mom told me I was a bad girl, that's why Da beat me.

"I had a dream after I was injured. I saw my da hanging. The rope was around his neck, but he wasn't dead. He kept struggling, trying to move the rope away from his neck. I stood and watched. I didn't save him… I didn't want to save him.

"Can't you see, I prayed for a new dress and shoes and I got them, an ugly black dress and shoes, but for his funeral, not for a party. I prayed for the beatings to stop and he died. That's how God answered my prayers."

Kathleen began to cry, guilt filled tears of a little girl. "I was glad he was dead. I wanted the pain to stop and I was glad... I was glad."

Kevin sat silently, letting Kathleen's sobs play themselves out. He spoke gently, "I know this is hard, but I want to see if we can push through this. Your da used alcohol on your leg after he beat you, and now you use alcohol after you hurt yourself."

Kathleen covered her face with her hands. When she spoke she sounded far off and little. "Isn't it time to stop?"

Kevin looked at the clock. The hour was up. "Let's keep going. What about the alcohol?"

"This hurts too much." She turned on her side and buried her face in the couch.

"I know this hurts, but you're almost there. Tell me about the alcohol," he insisted.

"Please, don't look at me," she begged. "I want you to close your eyes when I leave."

"I'm not going to close my eyes, and I don't want you to hide either. You've tried, for most of your life, to be invisible. Now, I want you to sit up. I'm asking you to look at me. No more hiding."

Kathleen sat up. She felt as if she was little and Kevin was her da. She couldn't say no. She covered her eyes. "I can't look at you. I'm too ashamed."

"I can wait," said Kevin. "We have all night."

Kathleen sighed. There was no way out of this one. They were off the clock. Time was on Kevin's side. She put her hands down and looked at him.

"It's my punishment for being so bad. I must be evil. Why else would Da have beaten me and used the alcohol?"

CHAPTER 37

Kathleen wandered through the empty house looking for Oscar and discovered him hiding under the Christmas tree. She lay on the floor and waited until he sprawled comfortably on her stomach. Oscar's purrs vibrated through her hands as she rubbed his head.

"Hi, Oscar. It's just the two of us for Christmas dinner. Santa, that's me, gave the Four a holiday cruise. Were they ever surprised!" She chuckled. "Wouldn't you like to be a fly on that wall? I would. There's some turkey in the fridge. Do you want the drumstick? Oh, Oscar, I miss your mommy so much. She's in New York visiting her bubba. I wonder if she's missing us."

Kathleen's personal phone was ringing. For a moment she wondered who might be calling. Everyone she knew was gone, and patients would call the office number. She hoped it wasn't an emergency.

A man's voice said tentatively: "Dr. Kathleen Moore?"

"This is she."

"Dr. Moore, were you born in Boston?"

Kathleen's heart began to pound and her hands sweat. "Who is calling?"

"My name is Devon Moore, and if I have the right Kathleen Moore, I am your brother."

"Devon?" She could barely speak his name; she had to lean on the kitchen counter for support. "Devon? Is it really you?" Her voice was a raw croak.

"It's me! Kathleen, are you okay?"

Kathleen whispered, "Yes," cleared her throat and said excitedly, "Yes, yes! Oh, Devon, I've thought of you so many times over the years. Dev, are you all right?"

"Yes, Kat, I'm more than all right."

Kathleen hadn't heard that nickname since they were children. It seemed as if there was a tape on fast rewind and she was instantly reviewing the early years with Devon.

"I know this is a shock, but I need to see you."

"I want to see you, too."

"Now, Kat."

"Now?"

"This might be a crappy time for you. I know it's Christmas, and you might be with friends or family."

"I'm alone. How did you find me?"

"It's a bit of a story, Kat. Can I come today, please?" There was a plaintive note in his voice.

"Where are you?"

"I live in San Diego but I had this feeling it was you, and drove to Santa Barbara this morning."

"You're only an hour away. Please come."

Kathleen never believed an hour could be so long and so short at the same time. She ran upstairs, made the bed, and took a quick shower. She went into the kitchen to start a fresh pot of coffee. She looked carefully at Helen's note hanging on the fridge. She found detailed instructions about meals, snacks, and desserts. Kathleen had ignored the note, preferring to graze as she so often did. Now, she sent a blessing to Helen: There would be food for her beloved brother.

Kathleen heard a car pulling up on the driveway. Suddenly, she felt as if she had to vomit. She had to think for a moment. How old was Devon? When she last saw him, he was a skinny kid with deep blue eyes, red hair, and a quick smile. She was pulled from the past to the present by a knock on the door.

There was a moment of surprise when Kathleen saw a man standing in the doorway instead of a boy. Was it Devon? His hair was copper-red, but thinner, and he was so tall. His eyes were the same color, but the pain that had hung in them all those years ago was gone. In an instant, his arms were around her and the years evaporated.

"Oh, Dev, you are so handsome."

All Devon could say was, "My beautiful, beautiful Kat."

Kathleen took his hand and led him into her home. They sat in the solarium crying, drinking coffee, eating Christmas cookies, and crying again. They talked about the early days when it was just Mom, Da, and the two of them. Then they spoke of the bad days.

Devon looked tormented. "I have always felt guilty because you got most of Da's anger. You took it for all of us, and I am so very sorry."

Kathleen had never thought of it that way, that somehow she had kept the rest of the kids safe. "Dev, it wasn't your fault. I thought you disappeared because you were mad at me. Then the social worker told me you ran away, and I never knew where the other kids were placed. Everyone was gone. Just gone."

"They put me in a group home, and it was really abusive," said Devon. "Running away seemed like the only solution. I bummed around the country, working at odd jobs, and ended up in San Diego. I was sleeping in the doorway of a bakery when the baker came to work. He stepped over me, looked down and said, 'Kid, do you want a job?' That was Paul. I worked for him, and he let me sleep in a storage room until I saved enough to rent a room. He got me on the right road. I went to night school and got my high school diploma. A few years ago, I bought the bakery from Paul. I'm a baker, Kat, and I make the best pies in California!"

"I bet you do!" Kathleen interjected. "I'd love to try one sometime."

"I'll make you one special," Devon replied. He smiled, studying his sister's face. "Did you ever marry, Kat?"

She hesitated, then said carefully, "No. Never got around to it."

"Well, I'm married to Amy, a wonderful woman, and we have three kids. After my kids were born, I started thinking about our family, but it was hard for me to make that move from thinking to doing. Three kids, a bakery to run, I had the best excuses for not searching. It was Amy who finally got me to see how scared I was. If I didn't look, I could always hope to find my family, but if I looked... what if they didn't want me? I didn't think I could take that rejection.

"Well, one evening, a few months ago, I came home from work and the house was really quiet. Amy's parents had taken the two older kids for the weekend and Amy ... first she fed me, then she kissed me and then she said, 'It's time,' and took me into the den where we keep the computer. She sat me down and said, 'Devon Matthew Moore, I love you more than life itself. But, it's time you face your devils.' I did all kinds of website searches and the rest is history. I've been able to trace all the kids except for Rose and Charlie. Haven't found them yet. I discovered they were adopted, and that's where the trail ends.

"What about you, Kat? Did you ever wonder?"

"Oh, Dev, all the time. Especially about you, we were so close. Remember when you would climb into bed with me?"

He laughed. "Every night during winter. Christ, it was cold. You took care of me, Kat, you kept me warm, you kept me alive." Devon put his head in his hands and sobbed the tears of a little boy. "Why did you leave me? Why didn't you come and get me? Didn't you want to find me?"

Kathleen knelt on the floor and put her arms around Devon as his shoulders shook. "Oh, Dev, I'm so sorry you had to suffer. I only seemed more grown-up to you. I wasn't even nine when we were put into the system. I coped by shutting down and running away from every feeling. I can't expect you to forgive me when I've never forgiven myself. I'm so sorry."

They sat for a while, brother and sister holding each other, trying to close a twenty-five-year chasm. Kathleen sat next to Devon, holding his hands, not the hands of a child but the hands of a man. "Do you know what happened to our mom? She stopped coming around, and I thought she didn't love me anymore."

Devon shook his head and wiped his eyes. "It wasn't about her not loving you. Our mother is schizophrenic, in and out of mental hospitals and on the streets for years. You know how it goes. She's fairly okay if she's on her meds, then she stops her meds and ends up back on the streets.

"I kept trying to find her and then about a month ago, I found this missing persons website and there was a posting placed by a hospice. There was a copy of an old photo and I remembered that picture. It was Mom and Da and the two of us at the beach. Man, I cried and I cried. Kathleen, I cried for her and I cried for us. God, I've missed you all these years."

Kathleen put her arm around Devon and leaned her head against his shoulder. She began to sob, more for his pain than hers.

Devon caught his breath. "I had her transferred to a hospice near me. Amy and I visit her almost every day." He looked up at his older sister. "She's end stage liver cancer, Kat."

"She asks for you. I think you're the only one she fully remembers. I'm asking you to come back with me to San Diego for the day. I know how hard it must be for you to get away, being a doctor and all, but maybe you can give her some peace before she dies."

"Peace?" Kathleen nearly choked on the word. "I've been angry with her for not keeping me safe. Part of me, and God forgive me for saying this, wants her to suffer."

"I've learned the hard way that the best revenge is to live well, not to let someone take you down with them."

Kathleen thought for a moment. "I need to make some phone calls. Are you hungry, Dev?"

"I'm a Moore, aren't we always hungry?"

❀ ❀ ❀

It was early evening when they finally arrived at the hospice. They went into the family waiting room and Devon walked over to a sweet looking woman holding a baby. There was something about her, a childlike innocence that reminded Kathleen of Claire. A boy and a girl were sitting close by, engrossed in playing with their Christmas toys.

"Kathleen, this is my wife, Amy."

Kathleen crossed the room. "Hello, Amy. I'm happy to meet you."

Amy smiled. "Me, too. Kathleen, this is your niece and her name is Kathleen, too."

Kathleen held her namesake in her arms, and felt her heart doing somersaults. She thought, *this is what it feels like to be in love with a little one.*

"We call her Kat," said Amy.

Kathleen chuckled at the weight of Baby Kat, and Amy told her they were a little worried about her being a butterball.

"Our other babies never got quite so... fat!" said Devon, and winced when Amy playfully socked his arm.

"Can I undo the blanket?" asked Kathleen.

"Sure," said Amy.

Kathleen opened the blanket to see fat little legs underneath a more than ample tummy. "She's what? About six months?"

Amy nodded.

"What is she eating?"

"She's only getting breast milk."

"Don't worry, she'll thin out when she starts to walk. I see it in my practice all the time. Just keep feeding her when she's hungry." Baby Kat gave Kathleen a big smile and began to fuss.

"Uh-oh, time to go back to Mommy."

Amy unbuttoned her blouse, took Baby Kat, and managed the blanket so that her breast was covered. "We haven't had her baptized yet. We were hoping we would find you, and that you would consider being her godmother."

Kathleen couldn't speak and became gripped with sadness. She couldn't be Baby Kat's godmother because of who she was and who she loved.

She smiled wanly, excused herself, and walked over to the two older children. She knelt down, played with them for a few minutes, and told them she was their aunt. They both gave her a big hug and smothered her in sugary kisses. Kathleen felt unexpected warmth kindling in her. *They are my family,* she thought. *Sweet, sweet gentle souls, loving me without knowing me. Loving me simply because I am.*

A nurse entered the room. "Mr. Moore, Dr. Moore, your mother is lucid right now, but that changes from moment to moment. I don't think she has more than a few hours before—" She left the statement unfinished.

Devon and Kathleen went into their mother's room. The room was painted a soothing green, and pastoral paintings hung on the wall. A small wooden cabinet with glass doors was next to the hospital bed and held a CD player along with an assortment of CDs. Kathleen looked through the CDs and played *Pachelbel's Canon in D.* She remembered listening to it when she was a child; it was one of her mother's favorites. She sat on the upholstered beige chair next to the bed and took her mother's hand in hers.

For a moment Kathleen wondered, who is this woman? Where is my mother? Her memories were of a woman whose hair shined with a copper glow and eyes that were as vibrantly green as Kathleen's. The stranger lying in the hospital bed had hair that was gray and wispy, with rheumy eyes that were like dusty marbles in a sallow face. Kathleen looked at the photo on the nightstand from the before time of Mom, Da, Kathleen, and Devon. It was the photo that led Devon to find their mom. Badly creased and faded, Kathleen thought how much it must have meant to her mother, to carry it with her for the lost and lonely years.

Devon leaned in close to their mother. "Hi, Mom. Kat's here."

"Hi, Mom," she said softly. When she uttered those words, the years vanished and she was little again and everything in the Moore house was sweet. For that moment, she felt the security and peace of a loving family.

Her mother struggled to speak. "Kat, you've come to take me home. I need your help with the children."

Kathleen had hoped to hear different words, words that spoke of regret and apology. Part of her wanted to get up and run away, but she knew she had been running for most of her life, and it no longer worked. She thought of everything and everyone she had in her life. *How different it feels,* she thought, *if you run toward someone instead of away.*

She kept her mother's hand in hers. "You'll go home soon, Mom."

Kathleen watched as her mother's breathing changed. She had seen it many times before. Her ragged, noisy breaths signaled that death was not far away. She remembered Iraq, and how she would go into the ICU to be with the men and women waiting to be transported to Landstuhl. She knew that some would never make it. She would hold their hands and sometimes watch them take their last breath. She thought, *no one should die alone.*

Devon and Kathleen sat quietly on either side of their mother, holding her hands. Her labored breathing grew shallow until, with a shudder that shook her frail body, she lay still.

Kathleen hoped and prayed that her mother had finally gone home.

CHAPTER 38

Kathleen put on the porch light and looked out the window of her office. The lawn had turned winter brown and a blanket of frost was providing a white coverlet. Soon, the bulbs that Sam, Helen, and she had planted in November would begin to work their way through the soil, heralding the birth of spring.

Helen had mail-ordered the bulbs of tulips, daffodils, crocus, and hyacinths. Kathleen and Helen stood on the lawn, next to each other, trowels in their hands, bags of planter mix resting near their feet. Helen held a large, bushel basket trimmed with green and red bands filled with the mixture of bulbs. "Come on, Kathleen. We'll do it the way nature does."

Together they began to randomly scatter the bulbs across the lawn. Where they landed was where they would be planted. Sam joined them—spade in hand. "How about an old farm boy helping out?" he said. Together, they began to plant bulb after bulb. When they finished, Helen stood up, rubbing her back. "Wait until spring. We're going to have quite a show."

Kathleen sat at her desk, sorting through the mail and thought about the months since Claire had left. Her life was busier than ever. Her practice was growing, she was still working weekends at St. Mona's, and she faithfully kept her twice a week appointments with Kevin.

She and Claire spoke a couple of weeks ago on New Year's Eve. Claire was at a museum party… "business," she had said. Kathleen had wondered, would Claire be kissing someone when the clock struck twelve?

She sorted the mail into piles: *Throw Away, Can Wait,* and *Get To It Now.* Most of the mail went into the Throw Away pile. Bills went into Can Wait pile, although she thought about renaming the stack *We're Still in the Red.*

One piece of mail went into the *Get To It Now* pile. Kathleen was scheduled to speak at a conference in Los Angeles in six weeks and had to prepare her presentation.

Kathleen heard the doorbell ring. It was her evening appointment with Christen Mitchell, the realtor who had shown her Canfield House. Christen wouldn't tell Helen the reason for the appointment, only that it was personal.

Kathleen and Christen sat in the chairs near the fireplace.

"It's pleasant in front of the fire, Dr. Moore," said Christen, a little nervously.

"I'm not even Dr. Moore to most of my patients. Please call me Kathleen."

"Kathleen, I wanted to speak to you about my daughter, Victoria. You met her at dinner and you've seen her twice, I believe. Once for her sports physical and then when she sprained her wrist playing volleyball. Victoria's a wonderful girl and I'm proud of her. She has the usual teenage issues. She thinks she knows more than her parents and chafes under our 'Gestapo tactics'—her term—and can't wait to get her driver's license."

"Sounds typical all right," said Kathleen. "So what can—"

The waterworks started to flow; Christen reached for a tissue. "I don't know what to do. I believe Victoria is gay."

Kathleen felt an arrow through her heart. She forced herself to keep still and hoped her expression hadn't changed.

Christen went on, "I'm worried that she may be confused—"

Kathleen was sure she had stopped breathing.

"—and not be able to accept herself. I've read about the higher rate of suicide among gay teens." Christen hesitated. "I was hoping you might meet with her. She won't talk to me, but I thought she might open up to you. I'm frightened she won't be able to accept who she is and end up being unhappy or hurting herself."

Kathleen was puzzled. "Perhaps a therapist might be a better choice. I can give you a referral if you like."

"Oh, I thought you were... oh, I'm so sorry. When we first met, I thought, oh my, I must have put things together that weren't there. I thought that if someone, who might have struggled with the same issues, could speak with Victoria... I'm really sorry, Kathleen."

"Christen, you weren't wrong, and it would be a privilege to speak with Victoria. I'm curious, what made you think—I mean, how did you know about me?"

"Why, I think everyone in town thinks you're gay. In a small town like Canfield, there are few secrets. We felt so bad when Claire left. You made such a sweet couple. We loved to see you on your bikes or taking hikes. It was all over town when you ran your errands and stopped at the ice cream parlor. Everyone could tell you were sweethearts. It was the way you looked at each other, you know, with that certain sparkle. You can't hide that.

"I may as well tell you, when you came to Canfield for the interview, it wasn't a consensus to offer you the position. Bill and I knew we'd be lucky to have you as our physician, but we had to convince the other council members. After you left, we had quite a lively discussion. Bill and I thought people would change their minds once they got to know you, and most of them have. There are some in Canfield who are not quite ready, but perhaps with time..."

Christen smiled warmly at Kathleen. "You are loved by the people in Canfield, and so is Claire. Most of us hope for a little happiness in our lives, and we wish the same for you."

Kathleen hurriedly wiped tears from her eyes. "Thank you, Christen," she said, sniffing a little. "What you said means so much to me. I'm curious, why do you think Victoria is gay?"

"A mother knows her child. She's different—not in a bad way, just different. I'm worried she may be confused and struggling with her identity. She has pinups in her room—you know the way the kids do, singers and movies stars. Except Victoria's are all of young women. She stays in her room and plays the same few songs all the time. One of them is 'I Kissed a Girl.' Should I keep going? It seems obvious to me, but when I've tried to talk to her, she shuts me out. If she's gay I want her to be proud, not ashamed. I love my daughter and I'm worried. I don't want her to become a statistic. All I want is for her to be happy in her life, not tormented."

Kathleen nodded. "Is Jeffrey on board as well?"

"Yes, one hundred percent."

"She's lucky to have you and your husband. Why don't you call Helen in the morning and have her make an appointment for Victoria?"

"She wants to be called Vic."

"Okay. I'll remember that. Tell Helen to make it on a Sunday, and I'll take Vic for a walk. I can't promise anything, but perhaps she'll open up to me. By the way, is it okay if I tell her I'm gay?"

Christen smiled. "Oh, I think she knew it the night we had dinner together. It was right in her face. That's why she was so nasty toward you."

That night, Kathleen got into bed and Oscar followed, lying on her stomach and purring. She rubbed his head and fantasized about buying a toy piano and teaching Oscar to bang on it. She envisioned Claire's laughter at such a sight.

Kathleen knew she should have been fighting for Claire, not pushing her away. She chuckled when she thought about Claire's mysterious ways. She missed so much about her: the outfits that bordered on costumes, the way every outing was a mysterious adventure, the way she pouted when she was upset. Most of all, she missed the way Claire loved her; the way Claire beamed when she put the necklace on Kathleen, and the way she wouldn't let Kathleen push her away on the night of the fire.

Kathleen thought of all the lost opportunities. The times when Claire wanted to hold her hand or to be seen as a couple; and Kathleen rejected her and their love.

She hoped it wasn't too late.

CHAPTER 39

The weeks were going by so quickly, it seemed. Kathleen thought about how time was measured in concrete terms, but there was nothing concrete about it.

Kevin was pushing her in every session, forcing her to take her armor off, little by little, exposing her most vulnerable hiding places. She felt exhausted. She missed Claire.

"Tell me," he said, when they were exploring the second nightmare about walking through the desolate landscape of Iraq.

"It was bleak; rocks and dirt and danger everywhere. I felt lost, disconnected. I wanted to walk to the stream where the flowers were growing. There was a woman sitting on the bank with her hand in the water. It looked so peaceful, like a painting from a different time. Then I stepped on the IED.

"I never saw flowers in Iraq. It was either hot and windy or cold. Robert sent me seeds, and I tried to grow them in pots. They would start to come up, struggle for a few days, and die. I couldn't get them to grow. I was surrounded by death; it was everywhere."

"I think this somehow connects to the dream you had the night of the fire."

Kathleen looked surprised. "How? I don't understand."

"Have you heard the adage, 'All roads lead to Rome?' The Romans had fifty-thousand miles of paved roads, and they all took you back to one central place. Let's try to follow the roads in your dreams and see if they take us back to Rome."

Kathleen was listening attentively. She was curious about the connections.

Kevin sensed Kathleen's interest. They were becoming a team. It was time to interpret.

"In your first dream, there is no hope," he began. "You're stuck in the pit, helpless, the way you were when you were a child, without the means to save yourself or to have anyone else save you.

"In the second dream, you are stronger. You're able to get out of the pit, and you see flowers by the stream and a woman who is enjoying the simple pleasure of a peaceful day. You're trying to find a soothing place filled with life, but a bomb explodes before you can reach it.

"The third dream starts out in bleakness. You are surrounded by death and destruction. It changes when you cross the river and get to the other side. What do you make of crossing the river?"

"I wasn't afraid of the water, even though it was deep in some places and I would be submerged. All the blood was washed away, and I felt renewed. It reminds me of a baptism. I finally felt clean. I've spent most of my life feeling dirty and terrified. The fear is always there, unless I'm working. I'm feeling afraid right now and I don't know why."

Kevin nodded. "We're going to come back to the fear in a minute. For now, let's concentrate on the dream and see where it leads us. There were flowers when you crossed the river. What can you tell me about them?"

Kathleen closed her eyes, bringing the dream back to life. "They were incredibly beautiful and so alive. The colors were bright and unusual. What stays in my mind is the way the flowers changed into people. I think about some of the men and women I saved. Sometimes, their wounds were so severe. I know it was my job to save them, not to play God, but did I do the right thing? What kind of life will they have?

"There were soldiers I couldn't save. Sometimes, I couldn't tell how severe their injuries were, and I would feel optimistic. Then, I would discover an internal injury and they would die. I couldn't stop death."

Kathleen wiped her eyes and looked at Kevin. "The flowers were the troops I couldn't save. They were in a better place. They were thanking me for trying. They were forgiving me."

"What thoughts do you have about the last part of the dream? The two children?"

"Kevin, they were so innocent. The little girl reminded me of my family. She had red hair and freckles, like my mother and Devon. She was so free, and she never hurt the butterflies.

"The little boy, I'm not sure—he didn't look like anyone I know. He was darker, and so calm, the way he was holding the book and looking at me. Such a sweet smile, as if he knew me." Kathleen held her head in her hands. "There were children we treated, innocents, horribly injured." Kathleen looked up. "In my dream, these children had nothing to worry about. They were safe and secure. I think they represented hope and peace."

Kevin nodded. "What about the terror that's always inside you?"

Kathleen's voice changed and became soft and childlike. "I want to talk about the night my da died, when I was eight and a half and I lost my family. I want to make it real, not a fairy tale. I want to be free."

Kevin sat quietly and nodded. "Tell me."

CHAPTER 40

Kevin treasured the time between patients. He liked to "clear his palate," to think about the patient who left and the patient who would be next.

Kevin knew that Kathleen would arrive exactly at seven o clock. He had ten minutes. Kevin saw in her the child who continued to be flooded with guilt and shame, but he also saw an incredibly strong woman who was determined to change. *It happens this way,* he mused. *A patient has been stuck in a place for years, acting out old messages and scripts, and suddenly makes a shift to go in a different direction.*

Kevin struggled with an issue common to all therapists. How much should he reveal about his own life, his own struggles? Will sharing personal information benefit the patient or only relieve his own angst? He was taken by how troubled Kathleen felt over having saved some lives. Was there a physician out there who was pained because they had to amputate Kevin's leg? How does one put a value on the quality of life?

Kevin thought about telling Kathleen about his journey: a journey he would have never taken if his right leg had not been amputated, a journey that had brought him here, to join Kathleen on her odyssey. He sensed it wasn't time.

The call light blinked. Kevin opened his office door. Kathleen smiled. It was the first time she had smiled directly at him.

Kathleen sat on the couch. "I had two dreams last night," she announced. "In the first dream I descended into hell. There were caves on either side of the path through hell. Inside the caves people were being tortured. It was horrible to see. I could hear their screams and saw people being whipped and hung up by hooks. I felt I had a choice. I had to walk through hell, but I didn't have to stay there. As I continued to walk, I became younger and younger. When I came to the end of the cave, I could see the sun shining. I was little, maybe three or four years old, and there was a tricycle waiting for me. I got on the trike and rode away into the sunlight.

"In the second dream, I was on a commercial flight. The pilot came out of the cockpit and asked if there was a doctor on board. I stood up. The pilot explained that there was an Army transport plane with a medical emergency and they needed a doctor to transfer onto their plane. They were going to position the plane under ours, and I would have to jump from one to the other. I wasn't afraid and thought what did I have to lose?

"I jumped and landed on the wing of the other plane. I began to lose my balance and nearly fell off. A man came out of the plane, grabbed hold of my arm, and helped me inside. I can't remember anything about the medical emergency, except that I took care of it. I remember feeling important and needed, the way I did when I was in the Army.

"The dream shifted and I was in Texas at Fort Bliss." When Kathleen said Fort Bliss, she looked directly at Kevin and laughed. "I guess I dreamed right into that one."

Kevin couldn't help but chuckle along with Kathleen.

Kathleen continued, "Well, I was in civvies and was being thanked by this female officer. I had the urge to salute, but I remembered I was a civilian and saluting wouldn't have been appropriate. I felt a longing to be back in the service, but I knew it was too late. There was no going back. The female officer smiled and I felt this really strong sexual attraction. I thought of the 'Don't ask, don't tell, policy,' and turned around and walked away. That's when I woke up."

Kevin sat quietly waiting for Kathleen's associations.

"I felt free, jumping from one plane to another, as if I had nothing to lose and I wanted to be of help. I've missed that part, the camaraderie that comes from being part of the Army. Mostly, the dream was about living, taking risks and not being afraid. I think, because of my fears, I've tried to control my life and everything around it. In the dream I gave up control."

"What about the woman? You walked away."

"I didn't want to hide anymore. I didn't want to pretend I was somebody I wasn't."

Kevin nodded and sat back in his chair. "You were on the wing of the plane, trying to balance. Do you know who the man was who pulled you inside?"

"It was just a man. But wait—" Her eyes closed as if she was reviewing the dream. She continued to speak with her eyes closed. "It was strange, because he was helping me to keep my balance, but he only had one leg. He had a below the knee amputation—" Kathleen opened her eyes. A look of awareness and a small smile played across her face. "It was you, Kevin."

Kevin nodded. "It sounds as if we were working as a team, balancing and supporting each other. It's about being able to accept help and be in a relationship."

He was quiet for a moment. "I'm wondering, perhaps it's time for you to call Claire. Any thoughts about that?"

PART SEVEN

Second Spring

CHAPTER 41

Kathleen parked outside of Claire's apartment. She was early. *A nasty habit,* she thought.

She rested her head against the headrest and closed her eyes. Her mind drifted to the day when she brought Oscar home from the vet's, and she and Claire spoke about San Francisco. She remembered the times she would sneak away from Los Angeles to meet Gary. Sitting in a bar, waiting to strike up a conversation with another woman, walking back to a hotel together, but always waking up in the morning to find she was alone.

How different it was to be with Claire. Falling asleep, bodies touching. Stirring at night to hear soft breathing, knowing she was there. Waking in the morning, to discover arms and legs tangled as if one started where the other left off. Sleeping late, waking to find Claire staring with love in her eyes, and words that told her how much she was loved.

Kathleen tried to remember when she realized she was in love with Claire. Was it when she placed her hand on Claire's forehead to see if she had a fever? Would that count? Was it when they went to the beach and Claire put sunscreen on her back? Or, when they went river rafting and Claire clung to her, crying? Kathleen realized that there wasn't a particular moment. She had opened her heart to this quirky, sometimes brassy woman from New York and her love crept in to fill the emptiness.

Kathleen looked at the clock on the dashboard. It was exactly six o'clock. She hoped Claire liked the wine she was bringing. Kathleen walked the short distance to the building. She was careful to avoid the cracks in the sidewalk. She didn't want to conjure up a bad omen.

❀ ❀ ❀

Claire's apartment building was covered in cedar siding, stained a dark red, creating a rustic appearance. A small waterfall, emptying into a serene pond stocked with koi and surrounded by ferns, decorated the front of the building, and softened the noise from the street. Kathleen's heart leaped when she rang the entry button and heard Claire's voice. She was torn in half between "I can't wait to see her" and "I can't do this."

Kathleen entered the elevator, pressed the third floor button, felt the elevator bounce twice and begin its ascent. The elevator lurched, and she thought how strange it would be if she got stuck and spent the evening in the elevator, alone. At least she had the wine, but realized she had no way to open the bottle. There were obstacles everywhere.

The elevator stopped with a jolt and brought her back to reality. She was on the third floor. She was in deep, with no way out unless lightning struck or aliens abducted her. She contemplated the odds. The sky was clear and there was no sign of a spaceship. Kathleen rang the doorbell.

There was an awkward moment as they hugged briefly. Kathleen handed Claire the wine. "I forgot to ask what you were serving. I hope this is all right."

Claire looked at the label. "Napa Valley, Sauvignon Blanc. It's one of my favorites. It will be perfect with dinner and even better before."

She touched Kathleen's arm and walked toward the kitchen. Claire, with her usual flair, had made novel use of the small space.

Potted flowers lined the window ledge and colorful potholders and dishtowels lent the room a homey cheer. Kathleen admired two small prints of Monet's timeless paintings of fruit and a whimsical sign with the motto *Sexy Women Have Messy Kitchens*. Claire was nothing if not eclectic.

Kathleen breathed in deeply. "Whatever you're cooking, it smells delicious."

Claire laughed. "Don't tell anyone, but dinner is compliments of an excellent chef just down the street—he says I'm culinary-challenged and takes pity on me. So, how is everyone? I really miss Sam and Helen—especially Helen's cooking—and, of course, Oscar."

Kathleen smiled. "Oscar Tilquist, the Third is fine. Everyone else is, too."

"Good!" said Claire. She handed Kathleen a glass of wine and guided her toward the living room. "Let's sit down and catch up."

Kathleen sat on the couch, Claire on a nearby chair. They talked for a while, keeping the conversation light and safe.

"How's your project going?" Kathleen asked.

"I'm really excited; you know how much storytelling means to me. It's something we all have inside. I believe it's the way we connect.

"The displays are going to be awesome and completely interactive—hands-on for all the kids. We're beginning with storytelling in the prehistoric era. One display is replicas of cave paintings, and we'll have an area for kids to create their own stories through art.

"The design part is finished, and I'll be wrapping up the first part of my job next week. I've started to work on the accompanying book. Would you like to see the sketches?"

Kathleen smiled. "I'd love to."

Like a kid, Claire bolted from her chair as if ejected from it. Kathleen heard the shuffling of papers from the other room and thought about Claire's uniquely haphazard filing system. Claire returned and handed a binder to Kathleen. She smiled embarrassedly, "I knew it was somewhere."

Kathleen held the binder as if she was holding Claire's dreams in her hands. She moved slowly through the sketches. When she finished she looked at Claire. "I'm really proud of you. I always knew you were talented, and it shows in your work. I hope you never feel like a failure again."

Kathleen closed the binder and placed it on the coffee table. "We need to talk."

Claire's lips quivered. "I may have had this conversation before. Is this where you tell me it's not going to work out between us?"

"No, not at all. Claire, come sit next to me and let me hold you."

Claire sighed as she moved into Kathleen's arms.

Kathleen said, "It feels so natural for me to hold you. I've always been afraid I couldn't comfort you, to give you what you needed. You've been the one to hold me—us—together. Do you remember that first time, when we hiked to Christmas River and we sat in the truck? I told you I was damaged goods, and wouldn't tell you why. I was ashamed and shut you out. I know now that a relationship can't be built on secrets.

"These last months have shaken my foundation and I don't know quite where to begin. Part of me has been this lonely, scared little girl, who has filled her life with make-believe. I rewrote my history for so many years, I'm not sure if I knew what was real.

"I told everyone my parents were both dead. My father died, but not in a car accident. He committed suicide. My mother didn't die in childbirth; she was mentally ill and homeless for years. I got a phone call from my brother Devon on Christmas Day and he took me to our mother. It all feels so unreal, to see Devon, not as I remembered him, but as a grown man. And my mother... I held her hand as she died."

It was getting harder for Kathleen to speak. Her mouth was dry and her words stuck in her throat. She took a sip of wine and fought the tears that were stinging her eyes. "I want to tell you the truth, about everything. I don't know if you'll still want me. I'm so ashamed about some of the things I've done."

Claire took her hand. "Whatever you're ashamed of can't be worse than keeping it a secret."

"I know you're right." Kathleen wiped the few tears from her eyes. "My... my..." she stammered and shook her head. "It's really hard to get it out."

Claire continued to hold her hand. "I'm not going anywhere."

Kathleen looked at Claire, gathering strength from the love she saw in her eyes. "It started when I was eight and a half. Things were bad with my family. My mother was pregnant, my father out of work." She shook her head. "Not enough food, no heat in the house. He started taking it out on me with his belt. Afterward, he would put alcohol on the wound and I wasn't allowed to cry. It's what I use after I hurt myself. I've used it for years. There are times when I feel dirty, and I can't feel clean, no matter what I do.

"That's when I use the scrub pad and alcohol. I used it the night of the fire, and I couldn't tell you. That night, you wouldn't let me run away and you kept loving me. I don't know if you can forgive me for pushing you, your love, away.

"Claire, I'm so sorry I couldn't hold your hand when you wanted me to. I know that hurt you. More than anything, I'm sorry I couldn't tell you how much I love you."

Claire gathered Kathleen close to her, rubbing her back, making soothing sounds.

Kathleen stayed in Claire's arms until she went limp. "I'm so tired of fighting it."

"You don't have to fight it, not anymore," Claire cooed. "Let me love you, just love you."

"Can you? Can you still love me?"

Claire abruptly seized Kathleen's chin in her hand, turned her face, and kissed her passionately. "Do I have to draw you a picture, too?" she said in mock exasperation.

Kathleen looked at her for a long moment, her eyes glistening. "There's more."

"I'm listening," Claire said. "So far, you haven't frightened me away."

"A mother came to see me, concerned about her daughter, whom she thought was gay, and thought I might be able to help," she said at last, her voice very soft. "It seems the whole town suspected you and I were a couple, and most of them didn't care."

"Told you so!" Claire crowed.

Kathleen smiled at Claire's remark. "I feel like such a fool. I couldn't see it then, but I can see it now."

Kathleen hesitated before speaking. "There is something I've wanted to tell you for a very long time. I love you, Claire, I've loved you for so long—please come home to me."

Claire reached up, as she did that day at Christmas River, and brushed away the hair that had fallen around Kathleen's face. "I don't know how you survived, but you have, and I love you for it." She drew Kathleen close, holding her tightly against her breasts. "I've missed you... I've missed *us*. I want our life back.

"I was in this as much as you. I should have told you I was getting angry. I shouldn't have waited until I erupted." Claire stopped. "You told me you loved me. I've wanted to hear those words since we first kissed. That's all I care about.

"Stay with me tonight? I don't want us to be separated, and I need to know you're safe."

"I'm not sure I could manage to walk back to my car let alone drive to the hotel. I can't remember ever being this exhausted."

"We'll have dinner and then I'm tucking you into bed."

"Will you be there with me?"

"Always."

❀ ❀ ❀

Kathleen snuggled next to Claire in bed. "Claire..."

"Hmm..."

"Tell me a story."

"Hmm... do you want a kinda funny, kinda sad one?"

"I want a Claire story."

"Do you know how I thought babies were born?"

"No."

"The stork. My bubba told me I was dropped down our chimney by a stork, wrapped tightly in a padded pink blanket, so I wouldn't get any bumps. When I was in fourth grade, they showed us The Film. You know the one I mean? About menstruation and how babies are born. I ran home crying. Sobbing. I knew it was true, because it suddenly occurred to me that we didn't have a chimney.

"That afternoon my bubba sat me on her lap and rocked me, back and forth, back and forth. 'What is it, darling?' she asked, 'Did someone tease you in school?' I couldn't stop crying. Finally, between sobs, I managed to tell her, 'Bubba, the stork doesn't bring babies.' She held me tightly and said, 'I know, I know... Claire, if you want, you can suck your thumb.'

"Well, I knew if I was going to be allowed to do that, there must be something big coming down the road. So, I started to suck my thumb. Bubba said, 'Sweetheart, there's no stork, no Santa, and no Passover Bunny. They're make-believe stories to make little boys and girls happy. Would you like to know what is real?'

"I had to take my thumb out of my mouth to ask, 'What, Bubba?' She said, 'True love, that is the one thing that is real.' Then I said, 'Does that mean I won't get any more bunnies for Passover?' I got Mr. Fluffy for the next Passover, and I've been searching for true love ever since."

"Did you find your true love?"

Claire traced Kathleen's face, gently moving from her forehead to her lips. Claire leaned over until their lips brushed. "Does that answer your question?"

A quiet whimper was Kathleen's response. "I've been so afraid."

"Are you crying?"

"Sort of. I leak all the time. I was doing a well baby check with a six-month-old little dumpling, and I started crying. Not sobbing but the tears were streaming down my face, like a flood. The mom got really scared, she thought something was wrong."

"What'd you say?"

"That I was touched by her daughter's perfection."

"I'll bet she liked that."

"Liked it? It was all over town. Now, all the moms want to see if I cry over their babies."

"Do you?"

Kathleen nodded. "All the time."

"I'm glad."

"Do you know how I thought babies were born?"

"I'd love to hear."

"I believed there was a zipper that grew when you became a woman. When I saw my mother's red stretch marks, I was sure she used a magic marker to let the doctors know where the zipper was hidden."

"That was very creative."

Kathleen chuckled. "I've never thought about it without feeling sad. Now, it seems sweet."

Claire said, "Do you know when I started to fall in love with you?"

"I want to know."

"Remember when I came upstairs for the first time and you found Mr. Fluffy for me? You couldn't stop laughing."

"I was worried I might have offended you."

"You have a wonderful laugh, and the way you examined Mr. Fluffy... Well, Dr. Moore, I've been head over heels for you from that moment on."

They talked quietly into the night, exchanging stories, sharing secrets until they fell asleep, two heads resting softly on one pillow.

❀ ❀ ❀

Claire woke up early, made coffee, and took a steaming cup into the bedroom. Kathleen was sleeping on her belly, with one arm beneath her and the other hanging over the side of the bed. Claire knelt down next to her and called her name. Kathleen turned over, groaned, and kept her eyes closed.

Claire kissed her eyelids. "Time to get up, honey."

Kathleen threw her left arm over her eyes and rubbed her right one gingerly. "Crap, my arm fell asleep." She squinted to keep the light out. "What time is it?"

"Six thirty."

Kathleen turned over. "Too early," she said, covering her head with the pillow.

Claire stood up and her voice was firmer. "Kathleen, smell the coffee and get your butt out of bed."

Kathleen grumbled, sat up, and looked confused. She patted the bed, beckoning Claire to sit next to her.

"Nah-ha," said Claire. "I'm not budging until you're out of bed and in the bathroom."

Kathleen cocked her head. "Did we make love last night?"

"Not in the way you're thinking. We both pooped out."

Kathleen looked disappointed.

"I want you to listen to me. I learned more about you last night than in the year we've known each other. And that, my dear, is a different way to make love. Thank you for that."

Kathleen murmured, "I love you."

Claire smiled, "I know."

Some part of Kathleen was stirring and she stood up, trembling. "Christ, I feel like I've been run over by a truck."

"You have in a way. You've had some hard times." She took Kathleen's arm. Come on, bathroom's this way." It was only a few feet from the bedroom to the bathroom, but Claire gave Kathleen a tour as she steered her in that direction. "Your clothes are in here," she pointed to the closet. "Towels, toothbrush, hair dryer—" she pointed in another direction. "I have to warn you, there is only enough hot water for a quick shower so you better hop to it. I'm going to fix breakfast; I have a feeling you're really hungry."

Kathleen dressed and followed the scent of waffles and eggs into the kitchen. "God, I'm starving."

Claire laughed. "For what?"

"Waffles first, then?"

"What's your schedule for today?"

"I'm presenting first and should be done around noon. I forgot Gayle and Robert are coming. There's a luncheon afterward, I'm thinking around two o'clock."

"Any plans for this evening?"

"I could think of all kinds of plans."

"Me too. When do you have to leave?"

"Tomorrow morning."

"Come out with me tonight?"

"You mean a date? It'll be my first," she said shyly.

"Then it will have to be special, in every way." Claire stared at Kathleen. "I think I should drive you to the hotel. You do look a little green around the gills."

"I don't know how I'll get through the day."

"What are you presenting?"

Kathleen groaned, "Don't laugh. The seminar is on PTSD in returning vets. The government is recruiting psychotherapists to treat veterans and it's a full house. I'm afraid something might get triggered and I'll start to unravel. What if I start crying in front of three hundred therapists?"

"I imagine all of them will run onto the stage with tissues in their hands." Claire held Kathleen's hand tightly. "These are professionals who will take back whatever you say and apply it to their patients. Level with them—talk from your heart, not your head. You have so much to share. You know what it's like to be at both ends. If you can get across half of what you've learned, you can help hundreds of struggling vets."

"Claire, come to the seminar?"

"Honey, I can't hold your hand."

"It's not about that, I want you to hear what I have to say. Afterward, I want you to have lunch with me... with us. I'd like to introduce you to everyone."

Attendees were standing in long lines, completing their registration. Kathleen found a chair for Claire toward the middle of the room. Before walking to the stage, Kathleen put her arms around Claire and whispered the words that had been held inside. They were simple words spoken everyday: "I love you."

After her introduction Kathleen walked to the podium. "Good morning, I'm Kathleen Moore, and I've been thinking about how I can best serve you and your patients. We can spend the next three hours looking at slides about the symptoms and treatment of PTSD, or we can try something else. How many of you are currently treating someone with PTSD, military related or not?" Almost every hand went up. "Is there anyone who is not sure about diagnosing PTSD?" A few hands remained raised. "I think I will be able to cover the diagnostic criteria, but not in the usual way."

Kathleen paused while an excited murmur flowed through the crowd.

"I'm going to begin again. My name is Kathleen Moore. You've heard that I am a physician, and you probably know that I served in a Combat Support Hospital in Iraq. What you haven't heard is that I was injured while serving and I also have PTSD."

Again, the crowd murmured, and there was a smattering of applause.

"I'd like to begin by telling you about my experience as a physician in a Combat Support Hospital and then continue with my experience as a patient. We'll take a short break around ten-thirty, and then follow with your questions or comments. Microphones have been placed in the center aisle. Okay? Let's get started."

Kathleen stood on stage for almost three hours, passionately relating her experiences in the CSH as a physician and then as a patient. She spoke about the emotional pain experienced by caregivers.

"There are heroes that don't get decorated. The families that care for the disabled veterans don't receive a medal. They are subject to crises, financial strain, and, oftentimes, a loss of intimacy. It's important, as therapists, for you to remember that your patient may extend beyond the injured vet you are treating. Keep in mind, not every veteran has a family to care for them and too many are homeless. Dr. Mark Epson will be speaking this afternoon on that subject."

She glanced up and saw Gayle and Robert sitting hand in hand next to Claire. "I was blessed to have people in my life to love me, so many people." She placed her hands together in a prayerful attitude and bowed toward the beaming couple. "When I wanted to give up, my mom and dad wouldn't let me." Her voice broke. "They never gave up on me, even when I threw a tantrum or two. Robert and Gayle, thank you. Thank you from the bottom of my heart."

The audience erupted in applause and rose to their feet. Robert and Gayle stood briefly in acknowledgment and sat back down.

"There are triggers that can still send me spiraling downwards, and I don't always know how to handle them," Kathleen continued. "I had a severe flashback while I was working part-time in an ER. Sounds of emergency helicopters, screams from burn patients transported me back in time to Iraq.

"The most difficult part about PTSD is that I couldn't let my girlfriend in, when she wanted to comfort me. I was afraid I would contaminate her, as if I had a contagious disease. The most amazing thing is that she still loves me and for that, I am so very grateful. Thank you, Claire... for being in my life."

At noon the seminar broke for lunch. Kathleen ran down to the three people who meant so much to her. She hugged Robert and Gayle. "I'm glad you were here. I hope it was okay to call you Mom and Dad."

Robert said, "I've been waiting for years to be called Dad."

Gayle hugged her. "Baby, I'm so proud of you."

Kathleen draped her arm over Claire's shoulder.

Gayle smiled. "You know, you really do make a cute couple. Robert, we should leave these two alone. They need time to reconnect, and I saw this very romantic restaurant on the corner that I've got my heart set on for lunch."

"Only if you're buying," Robert quipped. He winked at Kathleen and Claire as he and Gayle took their leave.

A table had been reserved in the hotel dining room for the presenters. A man sitting at the table leaned over toward Claire and said, "I don't think we've met."

Claire started to speak but Kathleen took her hand. "I'm sorry, I didn't properly introduce you. This is Claire Hollander. Claire is my partner in life."

❀ ❀ ❀

That night, Kathleen opened the hotel room door and moved confidently toward Claire. "I missed you," she said as she brought Claire closer until their lips gently touched. They lingered, not wanting to separate, pulled back for a moment to look at each other, and returned with the intensity and longings of lovers reunited after a separation.

"Hmm..." said Claire, "have you been practicing?"

"Every night, in my dreams, and you?"

"I was waiting for you."

Kathleen spoke softly. "I wasn't sure; I was afraid you wouldn't wait."

"I've only wanted you. That's why I took Mr. Fluffy with me. He's not much in the sack, but he's good company otherwise." Claire looked at the clock on the dresser. "You know—" she touched Kathleen's face. "I really hate to stop, but I don't want us to be late. Can we get back to our practicing later?"

Claire surprised Kathleen with tickets to a local production of *Young Frankenstein: The Musical.* They laughed hysterically throughout the show, mouthing immortal lines they already knew from the movie. Kathleen held Claire's hand wherever they went; she was afraid to let go.

Afterward, when Claire asked Kathleen what she might like for dinner, Kathleen said, "Do you know what I would really like?"

Claire laughed. "Shall I guess? Hamburger, fries, and a chocolate shake. Hey, have you ever eaten at Pete's Joint?"

Claire took Kathleen to the best-kept secret in LA: Pete's Joint, a humble hamburger stand, owned by—who else?—Pete. Pete hand ground the meat, used real ice cream in the shakes, and left the skin on the fried potatoes. It was simple fare with flair, as Claire called it.

They took their order back to the hotel. Pete's food was too special to be shared in the company of others.

❀ ❀ ❀

They made love in the hotel sitting room, found their way to the compact shower, and finally discovered the bed.

Claire rested in Kathleen's arms. "I really missed you. I was worried we might not find our way back."

"Me, too. The house seems so empty without you. You know I love you, don't you?"

Claire nodded and smiled. Since Kathleen had learned how to say those three simple words, she couldn't seem to stop saying them.

"I'm ready to leave the ER. Kevin thinks, and I agree, that I'm asking for trouble by working there. Besides, I want us to spend more time together." Kathleen spoke shyly. "I have a special surprise for you at home. It's your belated Christmas gift."

Claire snuggled up to Kathleen. "A special surprise? Hmm. Now you have my snoopy side all stirred up. I'm glad you're leaving the ER. Maybe you had to work there so you could unravel and finally exorcise your demons."

Kathleen nodded. "That's what Kevin thinks. Claire weren't you going to see a therapist. How did that go?"

"I guess it went. I saw the therapist one time. I told her I was feeling bad about my behavior, that I couldn't seem to settle down, and I had tantrums. We talked for a while and she said, 'Claire, you are a spoiled brat, but you have a good heart. My advice to you is, don't change!'"

"You've got to be kidding." Kathleen laughed. "What kind of therapist would tell you that after one session?"

Claire looked down and blushed. Her eyes widened as she looked up at Kathleen.

Kathleen was howling. "You're kidding, tell me you're kidding."

Claire shook her head. "I called Gayle to get a referral, and she invited me to lunch."

"Oh, sweetie, you were suckered by Gayle. Did she tell you anything else?"

Claire looked down. "This is totally embarrassing."

Kathleen was having the time of her life, but feigned a serious expression. "I can understand that you don't want to say too much, so let me guess." Kathleen did her best to imitate Gayle. 'Claire, perhaps you need to have children. You know, having children helps one to mature.'"

Claire hid her face behind her hands. "How did you know?"

"Don't you think I've heard it more than once? Gayle wants grandchildren. Did she call you Baby?"

"Oh, shit. Only once. I hope you're not mad."

Kathleen was laughing too hard to answer and could only manage to shake her head. Her expression changed and she became thoughtful. "The one luncheon date; that was the extent of your therapy?"

A strange look passed over Claire. "Not exactly."

"What happened?"

"A friend at work gave me a referral to a lesbian support group."

"So... what did you wear?"

"How did you know I would struggle with that? I thought about wearing my Levi's, flannel shirt, and hiking boots, but I didn't want to be too obvious."

"Of course not."

"So, I went incognito."

"Incognito?"

"Yeah, the way I dress for the museum. I walked in and everyone was welcoming. That was week one. Week two, I talked about your being in the war and having PTSD, and my being pissed because you weren't out. A couple of the women, vets with PTSD, took my head off. Ouch!"

"Oh, honey, I'm so sorry," said Kathleen.

"I almost left crying. Then the leader asked me about my background and the next thing I knew, I was telling them about my dad coming back from Vietnam, a drug addict, and the way my mother walked out when I was eighteen. Did I ever tell you she left a birthday card with eighteen crisp one-dollar bills? She wrote inside it,

'Paid In Fool.' Everyone got quiet, because they realized how their PTSD might affect their families, their kids."

"You're the bravest."

"Really? They're my new best friends, and I thought it'd be fun for us to do a women's weekend with them."

Kathleen held Claire. "God, I love you, and of course, we'll do a weekend. Devon and I have been talking about a family reunion. Claire, I have a family. I hope they'll be your family, too."

The hotel phone rang. Kathleen picked up the receiver. "Hello? Yes." She was silent for a moment, then her hand rose to her mouth to stifle her giggling. "I'm so sorry. I didn't realize it was so late. Yes. Goodbye." She hung up and turned to Claire. "We've had complaints against our laughing and talking. What time is it?"

"Almost three."

Kathleen whispered, "Do you think we should take Gayle's advice under consideration? Not right away, but down the road?"

Claire snuggled closer. "You would consider it?"

"Yes. I discovered that my heart does handsprings when I hold a baby. I do think I—we—have a way to go, though."

"That's all I ever wanted to hear, just a maybe."

Kathleen looked at the clock. "I don't think I'll be able to leave in the morning." She called the desk and changed her check out time. Kathleen reached over to Claire. "Let's practice."

They slept until noon. They woke up, bodies touching, arms and legs wrapped around each other.

Kathleen said, "I hate that we'll be separated again, but I have a full schedule tomorrow."

"I have to work in LA for another week. I can write the book anywhere. Can I come home?"

"Can you? It's your home, too."

CHAPTER 42

Helen and Kathleen sat at the kitchen table having their morning coffee. Helen had never seen Kathleen so happy and relaxed. "How was the seminar?"

Kathleen smiled broadly. "It was very successful."

Helen shot her a knowing look. "Did you have time for anything else?"

"Helen, are you asking if I saw Claire?"

"Only if you want to tell me, um... anything."

"We owe you. You are a fabulous Cupid. I owe you big time. If it wasn't for your magic, I still wouldn't be able to use my hand."

"You were one of my greater challenges."

"Let's face it; I was a major pain in the ass."

"That, too."

"I'm sorry, I hit a brick wall."

"I know. You needed some magic to get through it."

"Have you ever used that massage technique with anyone else?"

"Do you want to know if you're special?"

"Am I?"

"Of course you are. So, how was your weekend?"

"I saw Claire—as if you hadn't figured that out. She's coming home on Friday. We're in love, but I guess you knew that all along, too."

"Probably *way* before the two of you."

"Do you think Sam will be upset?"

"Sam adores you. He'll be all right. He'll mope for a while, but I'll comfort him."

"Ain't love grand?"

"Yes, it is." Helen looked at her watch. "Dr. Moore, it's almost nine o'clock and time for your first patient."

The look of pain on Sam's face told Kathleen he felt betrayed. It was one of the most difficult things she had ever done. He listened, stood up, and walked out without saying a word. She would never know what Helen said to him or what transpired, but Sam came looking for her later that evening. He found Kathleen sitting at her desk.

He knocked on the door. "Is this a good time?"

Kathleen motioned to the couch, and they sat next to each other.

Sam spoke slowly. "I guess you didn't know it, but I had a crush on you when we first met. I knew nothing would come of it, because I thought Gary was your boyfriend. After a while my feelings changed, and I came to see you as the sister I never had.

"You need to know, I was raised in a fundamentalist home. We went to church every Sunday, and preachers warned us about all the deadly sins. I didn't always agree with everything, but I believed they were right about homosexuality, that it's an abomination.

"What you told me about you and Claire... it was hard for me to hear. I don't know if I can change my belief in a few hours, but I love you like a sister and I really like Claire. She certainly has added spice to this recipe. I want you both to be happy. That's my truth."

Sam stood up and Kathleen took his hand.

"Sam, don't go," said Kathleen. "If I could become romantically involved with a man, I would have wanted him to be someone like you. You saved my life, and you stayed with me. I love you for that and for being here, right now. This isn't something I chose. God knows my life would have been easier if it was a matter of choice."

Sam nodded. "Helen thinks we should go to Los Angeles for the weekend so you and Claire can have the place to yourselves. I suspect Helen used her matchmaking skills to bring the two of you together. She tried to tell me when Claire first came, but I couldn't or didn't want to see it. You and Gary… it all makes sense now.

"I know Claire's good for you, she's the other piece of the puzzle that fits."

CHAPTER 43

Kathleen heard the VW chugging up the driveway and stood on the steps waiting for Claire. A familiar feeling of shyness came over her, until Claire hugged her and said, "I'm home." They stood for a moment, arms embracing, eyes gazing, lips touching.

Claire stepped back and looked at the front lawn now covered in a random pattern, as intended by nature, of bulbs in full bloom. Purple and white crocus peeked their heads between the yellow and white daffodils. Tulips in an array of red, yellow, and orange colors stood guard over the purple hyacinth.

"It's splendid," she said softly.

Kathleen spoke huskily, "I was hoping… I was praying, you'd be here."

Claire nodded. "Me too."

They carried bags, boxes, and luggage to Kathleen's room. Kathleen thought it was time to make Claire's bedroom into an office and make her bedroom their permanent nest.

Oscar came in, meowed loudly at Claire, and snuggled up to Kathleen. Claire was hurt but Kathleen knew exactly what he was doing.

"Oscar's like a child whose mom has gone away on an extended vacation," she said.

"He's letting you know he's angry. He's really trying to tell you how much he's missed you."

Kathleen was right. In a few minutes Oscar jumped on Claire's lap for his hugs and kisses.

Kathleen held Claire's hand. "Let's go downstairs to the solarium. I made some lemonade."

They sat on a wicker couch, close to each other, still searching for a new balance.

Kathleen said, "I got you something." She brought out two boxes. "I hope you like these."

Claire opened the first box and her face lit up. She held a sleeveless summer dress with a scooped neck. The dress had been embroidered with colorful flowers around the neckline. "It's a Gypsy dress. The embroidery is beautiful. I love it! Thank you." She snuggled up to Kathleen. The tension was melting.

"I'm glad you like it. I did the embroidery and didn't stick my fingers once."

"It's lovely, I'll treasure it."

"I can't wait to see you in it. It reminds me of your story about Deborah and Ferka. Are you ready for gift number two?"

"I'm always ready for presents."

Claire opened the second gift and started laughing. She threw her arms around Kathleen and spoke excitedly as she put on her gray Sherlock Holmes deerstalker cap, complete with bills in front and back and earflaps that tied on top, and held the magnifying glass up to her eye, enlarging it comically.

"I've always wanted these. I love them; it's the best gift ever! Now I'm ready to solve any crime." Claire was finally wearing the perfect outfit: her 501 Levi's, a flannel shirt, hiking boots, and an official Sherlock Holmes cap.

Claire said, "I have two things for you, too." She got up and came back with a beautifully wrapped gift and a bag filled with brightly colored tissue. "Open the bag first."

Kathleen reached into the bag and found a soft package wrapped in Christmas paper. She opened it and looked at the contents quizzically. "A fanny pack?"

"You have to see what's inside."

Kathleen opened the fanny pack and began to laugh.

"Put it on," ordered Claire.

Kathleen stood up, shook the gift out, and swung it around her back.

"Fabulous!" said Claire. "We're both ready for Halloween. You'll wear your red cape emblazoned with the words Super Doc, and I'll go as Sherlock Holmes. Now, it's time for gift number two."

Kathleen savored every moment, carefully and slowly removing the black-and-white paisley wrapping paper. She carefully lifted one end of the box and peeked in. She shook her head. "How did you know?"

"Well, I'm not a super-sleuth for nothing. I just followed the clues. A book on your shelf with well worn, dog-eared pages and a card inside with the name of an antique shop."

Kathleen held the Alice in Wonderland doll next to her heart. "I'll put Alice on the bed, but you have to promise not to play with her."

Claire chuckled. "I promise. Alice is for you and only you."

Kathleen put her arm around Claire. This time she didn't need any prompting. "I have one more gift for you."

"You're spoiling me, but I have to say I really like it."

"You're going to have to wait a bit for this gift. Would you mind wearing the Victorian dress you wore at the party and meeting me here at six?" Kathleen spoke sternly. "Not a minute before, Claire—and no snooping!"

"Is this another mystery, like the attic?"

"Everything is a mystery to you, but this is more of a surprise."

Kathleen had planned this gift for weeks, counting the days when Claire might be returning home. She hoped she wouldn't truly faint during the process.

❀ ❀ ❀

Kathleen walked into the solarium at five-thirty. She made certain that the room was perfectly arranged and turned on the music.

When she heard Claire walking downstairs, she stepped behind one of the big palms and, as Claire entered the solarium, told her to close her eyes. As one of Claire's favorite songs, "The Way You Look To-night," began, she walked over and put her arm around Claire's waist.

"Dance with me?"

Claire opened her eyes. Kathleen was wearing a tuxedo, complete with tails, top hat, and boutonniere. "You did this for *me*?"

Kathleen pulled Claire closer, kissing her passionately. "For you, for us, my darling," then broke out in a broad grin. "Outfit *and* dance lessons included."

She thought about what her dance instructor, Miss Margo, had said: "Take Claire in your arms and let the music enter your soul."

With Kathleen leading, they floated around the solarium like two feathers caught on a gentle breeze.

Claire looked at Kathleen with shining eyes. "You're exactly who I have always wanted," Claire murmured in Kathleen's ear, "and you are so much prettier than Fred Astaire."

ACKNOWLEDGMENTS

My deepest appreciation to my children for their support as I do the dance called, *My Life*.

To my grandchildren, you are my special blessings.

To my brother, Howard—you will always be Howie to me. Thank you for believing in me and giving me hope.

I feel fortunate to have *Proofed to Perfection, www.proofedtoperfection.com*, as my editors. Pamela Guerrieri and Kevin Cook gently nudged me toward a greater depth of writing and enriched *Flowers from Iraq*, in every way.

Marc "Sid" LaBarbera, Paramedic Intensivist, CC-EMTP, contributed invaluable technical research on the medical scenes for *Flowers from Iraq*. Marc, I am so grateful for your help and for having expressed your wish for all our troops to return home safely.

D.P. Lyle, MD, *www.dplylemd.com*, reviewed and edited the medical scenes in *Flowers from Iraq*, for content and accuracy. Doug, thank you for your feedback and for helping to make the medical scenes workable and realistic.

Donna Casey, *www.digitaldonna.com*, created the cover for Flowers from Iraq. She is amazing. A cover does speak more than a thousand words.

I would be remiss not to thank my characters that made my fingers hit the keyboard for hours and hours each and every day. You taught me never to give up.

May we meet again in the sequel to *Flowers from Iraq: God Laughs: The Storyteller and The Healer.*

ABOUT THE AUTHOR

Sunny Alexander is from Los Angeles, and was born into a time when men and women followed their proscribed social roles. In her own case, she married at an early age in the 1950s. Impacted by the social revolution of the 1960s and '70s, Sunny Alexander returned to school and became a Licensed Marriage and Family Therapist. Fascinated by the power of dreams, she continued her education and received her doctorate in psychoanalysis. In private practice since 1988 she often treats adults abused as children.

Flowers from Iraq was born from her own introspections at a time when the Iraq War was raging. As a gay woman herself, she sought to portray the suffering of those who feel compelled to hide their identity.

She is currently writing *The Girls*, a novel that follows a group of gay women from the 1970s to 2020, a hypothetical future when the United States Senate passes the Freedom to Marry Act.

Sunny Alexander can be contacted at:
www.sunnyalexander.com

Made in the USA
Charleston, SC
20 April 2012